Praise for John Francome's previous novels:

'Follows in the footsteps of Dick Francis – the story races along, with plot twist succeeding surprise revelation . . . descriptions of the races, from the jockey's saddle, are realistic enough to excite a confirmed non-racegoer' *Scotsman*

'Has all the right ingredients . . . offers a revealing insight into weighing room antics' *Sunday Express*

'Francome has produced his best thriller by far. An action-packed storyline that gallops to a thrilling end . . . Likely to get the thumbs-up from Dick Francis' *Racing Post*

'Thrills to the final furlong . . . Francome knows how to write a good racing thriller' *Daily Express*

'Francome brings authenticity to tales of the horse-racing circuit and, like Dick Francis, goes beyond the thunder of the turf to the skulduggery of the trading ring . . . the twists and turns of the last few hundred yards prove Francome to be a winner on the home stretch' *Mail on Sunday*

'The natural successor to Dick Francis' *Irish Times*

'Mr Francome adeptly teases to the very end and cleverly keeps a few twists up his sleeve until the closing chapters' *Country Life*

'Pacy racing and racy pacing . . . Francome has found his stride as a solo novelist' *Horse and Hound*

Stalking Horse

John Francome

headline

First published in 2003
by HEADLINE BOOK PUBLISHING

First published in paperback in 2004
by HEADLINE BOOK PUBLISHING

10 9 8 7 6 5 4 3

ISBN 0 7553 0680 5

Typeset in Times by Avon DataSet Ltd,
Bidford-on-Avon, Warwickshire

Printed and bound in Great Britain by
Clays Ltd, St Ives plc

Headline's policy is to use papers that are natural, renewable and
recyclable products and made from wood grown in sustainable
forests. The logging and manufacturing processes are expected to
conform to the environmental regulations of the country of origin.

HEADLINE BOOK PUBLISHING
A division of Hodder Headline
338 Euston Road
London NW1 3BH

www.headline.co.uk
www.hodderheadline.com

Thanks to Gary Nutting (www.harrythehorse.net) and Dr Miranda Wolpert.

Prologue

Mouse changed trains at Baker Street, catching the tube just before the doors closed – that was a good omen. There was a seat available too, another good sign. She wedged herself between a tall scruffy girl cradling a backpack on her lap and a middle-aged woman with an enormous black handbag. Mouse couldn't understand why other women burdened themselves in this way. She herself travelled light, with her essentials squirrelled away in the pockets of her coat. It was important to be able to move around without clutter.

The lad opposite her was a Prince William lookalike. He checked her out as she sat down, his eyes flicking over her without interest. She was used to that. She never raised much interest on first sight. But she could get a man's attention, all right – when she wanted to.

Prince William turned back to his paper, raising it to shield his handsome face from her view. Which was OK by her as she found herself staring at the best omen of all. There, on the raised page, was the smile that looked down on her at night and which welcomed her to each new day. The off-centre grin, firm jaw and blazing bright eyes – jade green when reproduced in colour, like in the photo on her bedroom wall – of the man who held the key to her heart. Just like she held the key to his. Not that he knew it yet but it was only a matter of time.

The train slowed as it approached Edgware Road and Prince William got to his feet, tossing his paper on to his seat as he moved to the door. A man in a suit reached for it but Mouse got there first, lunging across the carriage and snatching it almost out of the other's grasp.

The man flashed her a dirty look but before he could protest Mouse said, 'Thank you very much', with a tight little smile, which seemed to do the trick. He gave her a curt nod of the head, as if it had been his intention to pass the paper to her all along.

She knew his type – the teacher/doctor/magistrate sort. Professional big shots. Keen on the appearance of things, like being polite, while underneath they despised people like her.

But she knew how to get even with his kind. Pay a visit to his wife with a carving knife in her hand. He wouldn't be so full of himself after that.

Everyone around was looking at her, making her squirm inside, and it wouldn't have been so long ago that such scrutiny would have brought on one of her panic attacks. But things were different now; she could ignore all the nosy parkers around her because what they thought was not her problem. Mr Carter had taught her that. Even if he had turned out to be such a two-faced bastard. Not that he mattered one bit to her these days. She had someone much better.

Her fingers shaking with excitement, she quickly turned the paper over to the page she had seen across the aisle. There were two photographs side by side under the banner 'HEAD-TO-HEAD HOTS UP' but Mouse only had eyes for the one on the left. It was a disgrace horse racing didn't have more space in the newspapers. If Josh were a footballer, his lovely face would be on the back page every day, blown up big, just like it was on her wall. As it was, she had to make do with pictures like this, sharing coverage with the other rider, the one who was leading in the race for champion jockey.

That's what the article was all about. She read the words but they told her nothing new. Her eyes caressed Josh's image. He was wearing a riding helmet, which was a pity, because she liked him best bare-headed, with his fair hair flopping over his forehead. The truth was, she thought as she smiled mischievously to herself, she'd really like him best bare all over, his lean sinewy body hard against hers, his strong arms crushing her. Ooh, yes. It made her positively light-headed.

The train slowed and she looked up. The man in a suit was still staring at her, as if he knew just what she was thinking and didn't approve. Maybe she'd been giggling out loud. Well, too bad.

This was her stop. She stood up abruptly and thrust the newspaper at Mr Suit. 'You can have it now,' she said boldly, her Midlands accent cutting through the snotty London silence.

She didn't want it anyway, there was a coffee stain right across the page. She'd buy another copy later, a clean one.

Mouse emerged on to the streets of grey wintry London. On holiday trips as a kid, she'd never liked the big city – the traffic, the tall buildings, the way people looked through you as if you weren't there. Of course, in those days she didn't feel she was anywhere and didn't want to be anywhere either. Certainly not being herded around Madame Tussaud's or the Science Museum by her sort of stepfather, Mum's partner, Denis, and tagging on to a group of kids who treated her like dirt.

But now she was beginning to feel like she could handle the Big Smoke. The people didn't freak her out any more, even though they were just as creepy as they'd always been. Like the man on the tube trying to take her paper. But she'd not let him get away with it – these days she knew how to stand up for herself.

If she were still having sessions, Mr Carter – Gavin – would have claimed the credit for her becoming more assertive. He wouldn't have said so exactly but he'd have implied it. 'See how much better you feel once you express your feelings,' he'd say, running a hand through his thick mop of black hair. 'I think we're making genuine progress.'

Of course, he hadn't wanted her to express her real feelings. Not around him, at any rate, outside the hours of three to four on a Thursday afternoon. He might have sounded excited and enthusiastic about her 'progress' but that was just jargon, wasn't it? The kind of phoney baloney they teach at psychiatrist school. And Mr Gavin Carter was the biggest phoney of them all.

But she was done with him. There was a new man in her life. And she wasn't going to screw it up like last time. All those letters and phone calls had been a mistake. Take it slowly, she said to herself as she reached into her inside pocket to check that the keys were still in place. She'd be lost without them, they made everything possible.

When she'd first started helping out on reception at her cousin's garage, she'd been amazed at how carefree people were with their keys. They'd hand over a whole bunch just because they were too lazy to take off the car key. Or maybe too trusting. That's how it was with Josh. He must have thought that she was honest when he'd pressed them into her hand.

How sweet. It made her love him all the more.

She waited impatiently by the zebra crossing, looking across the road at her destination, the five-storey apartment building of weathered terracotta and cream brick. How many flats did it hold? She didn't know, but in her pocket was the key to number 48 and that was in the middle of the block. There were three separate entrances at the front and spaces for cars, most of them new or else well-maintained fancy models like Bentleys or BMWs – nothing like the crap motors parked in the narrow streets where she lived. This was a northwest London mansion block and the people who lived here didn't know how well off they were.

At last, the cars came to a halt and allowed her to cross. It was a wide road, six lanes of traffic, full of motorists heading in and out of town. She could sense their impatience as she sauntered across. She wasn't going to hurry for these southern bastards – let them wait.

She followed the pavement off the main thoroughfare into the access road that led to the front of the building and walked up the steps to the middle door. The dark wood and brass furnishings gleamed as if they had just been polished which, she supposed, they had been. Though she'd never come across a cleaner or a caretaker, from the pristine state of the building she knew they must be regularly at work. Her heart was pumping as she put the downstairs key into the lock. Once, on her second visit when she was still all of a quiver at the thought of being caught, she'd found the door propped open. When she'd reached the first landing she'd come face to face with an old lady carrying Marks and Spencer bags into her flat. 'I've left the downstairs door open,' she'd announced in plummy tones. 'Be a good girl and shut it for me, will you? You've got younger legs.'

Mouse had nearly run off there and then but she'd realised that would look odd so she'd shut the door as instructed and simply accepted the elderly resident's thanks as she'd passed her on the way upstairs. She'd worked out then what she would say if she were asked to identify herself: 'I'm Mr Swallow's sister. He's asked me to pop in and water the plants.' But no one had challenged her yet.

The staircase was laid with plush maroon carpet and the banisters were of dark mahogany, the same shade as the downstairs door. The heat was high, as ever, in contrast to the winter chill of the street. Mouse loved it in here. The posts of the stairwell were decorated with carved leaf shapes and topped with big glossy wooden balls the size of grapefruits that fitted snugly into the palm of your hand. It was like being in a hotel, a real ritzy one.

She liked the idea of being rich. The woman who married Josh would be rich. It would be better even than being the wife of a psychiatrist. All the papers said Josh was going to retire soon so they'd be able to travel the world together, staying at the swankiest places. He'd probably want to attend posh racing events; she wouldn't mind that, provided she got to do stuff she wanted. She could go on shopping sprees in places like Milan and Paris and New York. Get herself some smart clothes – there was a limit to the charm of man-made fabric.

Of course, they couldn't go swanning around all the time. Josh would have to find a new direction in life (apart from her, of course). She'd help him. She'd chuck in the rubbish job and be Josh's manager. Get him on telly with those other ex-jockeys, all banging on about horses. He'd be a sensation on the box with those sparkling eyes and that grin that sent shivers down your spine. Women would fancy the pants off him. Which would be too bad for them, because Josh would be all hers. God help any slutty bitch who gave her man the come-on. She knew how to defend her territory.

Mouse was on the fourth-floor landing now with Josh's door on the right. She stood – as she always did, it was sort of a ritual – quite still, facing the polished surface of his door, gathering herself. Her heart was pounding with excitement and the urge to rush inside was almost irresistible. But she resisted – she had to. She made herself follow the strategy she had devised. Just to be safe.

First she put on her gloves, the thin semi-transparent surgical sort. It was a bit of a nuisance keeping them on all the time but she was proud of her newfound attention to detail. After what had happened BJ – Before Josh – she wasn't taking any chances.

Next she placed her eye to the small brass spy hole in the centre of the door. Not that you could see much inside but it was possible to tell if a light was on in the hallway beyond.

There was no light.

As she stood there, she listened intently – for a radio, a television, anything that would indicate the flat was occupied. Though she knew Josh was riding at Huntingdon that afternoon, someone else might possibly be there. A cleaner, or a friend or – and this was the most likely – the Mistake. The blonde waste of space who was currently clinging to Josh's coat-tails.

Mouse pressed the bell. It was the last act in her list of precautions. If anyone was inside that should flush them out. And, if the door opened, she'd ask for Mrs Watson who, she'd discovered from studying the name tags at the next entrance along, lived at number 38. 'Oh, this is *forty*-eight,' she'd say – she had it all prepared – 'my mistake. So sorry.'

She hoped that wouldn't happen. Not least because if the door opened to reveal the Mistake standing there in all her perfect prettiness she might Do Something. Like stick her fingers in the cow's big saucer eyes. Or gouge her nails down the girl's peachy soft cheeks. Or – and she let the picture build in her mind – wrap her fist in her shiny blonde hair and smash her face into the door frame, wham, wham, wham! Mouse could almost taste it. The Mistake wouldn't be so perfect pretty by the time she'd finished with her.

But no one came to the door and Mouse forced herself to clear her head. Take a deep breath. Count to ten. That's what Denis used to say to her, not that she'd ever taken any advice off that wally. 'Control yourself, for heaven's sake', was how they put it at school – the first couple of times, anyway, before they'd decided to chuck her out. 'Banish the negative thoughts' or some other smartarse claptrap would be Gavin's way of putting it. All of which amounted to the same thing. Get a grip, girl.

She focused on the practical. First, turn the key in the bottom lock, the big chunky one that Josh thought kept his private world so safe. Then into the main lock and turn it twice. She heard the bolts shifting and then, with a satisfying click, the door swung open at her push. She stepped quickly inside and closed the solid barrier behind her. A lot of security had been invested in keeping intruders out, but it was all operated by a single key. And she had a copy – it was brilliant.

She leaned back against the door and savoured the moment, as she always did. The thickly carpeted hallway stretched before her, daylight falling in rectangles of light from the open doors on either side. Sitting room and bedroom on one side, kitchen, bathroom and dining room on the other. It wasn't big but it seemed so. Like the stairway it was luxurious, full of old-fashioned quality – Regency-striped wallpaper, a chandelier in the dining room, picture rails with real pictures in heavy gilt frames. She'd once worked as a maid in a country-house hotel – it reminded her of that place. There was a four-poster bed in the honeymoon suite and the guests took tea in a wood-panelled lounge serenaded by a real live harpist. She'd liked working there.

One day she'd get Josh to take her back to that hotel as a proper guest. She'd insist on the honeymoon suite.

In the meantime, she had his London apartment to herself. A corner of his private world to share for the afternoon.

One day it would be hers by right.

Chapter One

Another dark January morning, another draining day ahead. Josh Swallow flexed his left arm as he drove through the crush of ring-road traffic around Derby. At least his shoulder didn't feel so stiff, maybe he'd make it to the end of the jump-racing season after all. Only about twenty weeks to go – not that he was counting.

For two pins he'd have stayed at home. When he'd bent to kiss Susie goodbye, the urge to snuggle down beside her in bed had been overwhelming.

'Is it morning already?' she'd murmured, her arm circling his neck as she raised her sleep-smudged face to his.

It hadn't been easy to turn away but who said becoming champion jockey was easy? And that's what this was about. If you wanted to win horse races – lots of horse races – you made plans and stuck to them. You arrived early, walked the course to find the best ground, sweated in the sauna – and refrained from climbing back into bed with the woman in your life.

Susie had looked tiny in the big bed, her slender frame wrapped in the folds of his pyjama jacket. She pushed a spiky lock of honey-blonde hair out of her eyes and grinned up at him. The bow of her mulberry-pink lips was irresistible and he no longer had the will to resist. He recalled a friend's favourite saying: 'Behind every successful man is a woman he doesn't want to go home to.' In his case, it couldn't have been further from the truth.

He subsided on to the bed and wrapped his arms around her.

'Josh,' she murmured after a moment, 'haven't you got to go?'

'I suppose. I don't like leaving you.'

She sat up. 'I'll be fine. I don't want to make you late – my man with a mission.'

Now, as he drove, Josh tried to clear his mind and focus on the race meeting ahead. Susie would indeed be fine; her problems were behind her and, as she had said, he was a man with a mission.

He'd been a leading jump jockey for fifteen years. He'd won all of the major National Hunt races including the Cheltenham Gold Cup (twice) and the Grand National. He had well over a thousand victories on British courses and a couple of hundred more on overseas tracks, from Ireland to America and Australia.

But he'd never been the season's champion jockey, the rider with the most wins to his name, and at the age of thirty-four his time was running out; not many jump jockeys stay at the top once they pass their mid-thirties. Josh had never had a problem with motivation nor with making a racing weight, two of the factors that undermined ageing jockeys. Josh's bugbear was chronic injury. The older you got, the longer it took to recover from being hurt. Falls that Josh had once been able to walk away from now knocked the stuffing out of him. There was only so much routine wear and tear of the jumping game that a man could take.

This year, Josh had decided, would be his last. He didn't know how he'd adjust to such a complete revolution in his life but he knew retirement was coming closer, whether he welcomed it or not. The best thing would be to go out on his own terms – as champion jockey.

There was no reason he couldn't do it, he told himself. He'd come close in the past but there had always been an obstacle or two in his way. Specifically, Patrick Lane, an obsessed horseman who, in combination with the horses of top trainer Peter Stone, had been unbeatable over the last five seasons. But Patrick had retired to, as he told the racing press, 'lie on a tropical beach while Page Three girls feed me chips'. In less jocular style, he'd said to Josh, 'It's your turn now, mate. And the best of British.'

More to the point, with Patrick out of the way, Peter Stone had been quick to secure Josh's services for the year. Stone was only interested in winning races and turned out a stream of brilliantly prepared animals, competing at all levels. Josh knew that provided he could stay fit, he could rely on a supply of ammunition from Stone's yard to rack up the numbers he needed to help him towards the title. Of course, Stone's horses on their own wouldn't be enough. He had to be prepared to travel the country to ride for whoever had horses available. Fortunately, he had on his side Tony Wylie, the best agent in the business, and the task of booking those spare rides was down to him.

As he thought of Tony, Josh's eyes darted to the clock on the dashboard. Ten minutes past nine. His stomach fluttered, the familiar anxiety that came hand in hand with his self-imposed mission. Tony should have rung by now. Josh had four rides at Newbury that afternoon but only three for Wincanton the next day and he wanted more. He knew Tony would have been ringing round yards for the past hour, trying to hustle up business for his clients, and Josh was confident that his own name would have been the first on the agent's lips.

Tony was the only agent Josh had ever had. A former jockey, whose riding career had been finished by a life-threatening encounter with an open ditch at Chepstow, Tony did his business from a wheelchair in a customised bungalow in Sussex. Equipped as he was with phone lines, internet connections and a bank of televisions tuned to racing feeds, he had no need ever to leave his command post.

Josh's eyes flicked to the clock once more. Twenty past nine. *Come on, Tony*. There was no point in calling him, his line would be busy, as it was every morning of the racing week.

Josh's four rides that afternoon were all for Peter Stone. Two of them should win, but would that be good enough to keep in touch with Ben O'Brien?

Ben O'Brien was the factor Josh hadn't taken into account at the start of the season. Ben was just a lad, a 21-year-old in only his second year over from Ireland, but he rode with the cunning of a veteran and the confidence of youth. Everyone agreed he was special, a champion in waiting, but he was ambitious to the point of being ruthless. It was an unwritten code in racing that you didn't phone trainers for rides when you knew that they were earmarked for somebody else. But that never bothered Ben. He'd go out of his way to chat up owners if he thought he could get on a decent horse. Ben had currently ridden 103 winners and was ahead of Josh in the championship by fourteen – not an insurmountable lead at this stage of the season, but the gap preyed on Josh's mind. Every day he checked on their relative positions, on the horses Ben was riding, on the number of spares he was picking up. The lad never seemed short of a ride; the irony was that he too was represented by Tony Wylie.

The phone rang at last. Josh answered and spoke through the microphone round his neck.

'Tony? What kept you?'

The agent's voice, amplified by a speaker, filled the car. 'Calm down, Josh. I've been chasing on your behalf all morning.'

'And?' Josh realised he sounded stressed but he couldn't help it. That's how he was these days.

'And I think you're going to like this.'

Josh knew Tony was teasing him, stringing him along for a moment just to maximise the drama. He forced himself to keep quiet.

'Cherrypicker for Belinda Giles in the last at Wincanton. She says you rode him at Fontwell last April.'

Josh recalled the big bay horse – jumped well, plenty of petrol in his tank. To be reunited with him now was just the tonic he needed.

Suddenly he felt an enormous sense of relief. It was only one ride but picking up a spare he really fancied calmed his nerves somehow. Not that I'm obsessed or anything, he thought.

'Thanks, Tony. Good job.'

'Wait. I haven't finished. There's a ride in the fourth.'

'I know. Snowy Hills.'

'I'm not talking about tomorrow, Josh. I mean the fourth race today.'

Josh quickly reassessed. The runners and riders had been fixed yesterday for today's card at Newbury but last-minute changes were possible if a jockey had to pull out.

Instantly he brought to mind the entries in the fourth race, a C-class handicap chase. There were only seven runners. What magic had Tony been working on his behalf?

'How do you fancy King Archibald?' Tony asked.

The shock was such that Josh was slow to register the red flicker of brake lights on the van ahead in the middle lane of the motorway. He stamped his foot on the pedal and the car jerked.

'Are you serious?' King Archibald was Ben's ride. Trained, what's more, by Leo Lovall, a man who'd cut his own throat rather than do Josh any kind of favour.

'Ben can't make it and the ride's yours if you want it.'

'Of course I want it.' King Archibald was a decent horse, game for three and a bit miles of slogging through the mud and able to find something at the end to hold off his rivals, an attribute Josh had recently admired from amongst the chasing pack at Newton Abbot.

It was just as well Tony couldn't see him. He was grinning like a kid as he took in the implications of this windfall. He made an effort to keep the glee out of his voice as he said,

'What's up with Ben, then?' Nothing trivial, I hope. It was on the tip of his tongue but he didn't say it.

'He took a bit of a tumble riding out. He'll have to miss Newbury but it's nothing serious.'

Josh didn't believe it for a moment, it had to be serious for Ben to sit out a chance to notch up more winners. Nothing short of a couple of broken legs would keep that boy off a fancied horse.

'So what happened to him exactly? Is he OK?'

Tony chuckled, the laughter booming from the car speaker. 'You kill me, Josh. What you mean is how long is Ben going to be out.'

It was hard to deny. Had he always been so callous? Or was it this championship rivalry that was turning him into a completely heartless sod?

'He got buried at a practice ditch,' Tony continued, 'Lost consciousness for a minute or two apparently, though he denies it.'

Ouch. Josh knew what it felt like to end up beneath half a ton of racehorse. It was much like being run over by a truck, and sometimes just as damaging. Of course – the thought flashed through his mind – nobody knew that better than the man on the other end of the line.

'I'm sorry to hear it,' he said. 'I hope he's not badly hurt.'

'Sure you do,' Tony replied and signed off.

Josh couldn't blame him for the note of cynicism.

So Ben had been knocked out. The medical authorities had become particularly hot on concussion over the last couple of seasons and if Ben's accident had happened at a racecourse, the consequences could have been serious. The doctors would have insisted on a lay-off from racing based on the length of Ben's black-out – two days for dizziness, six days for unconsciousness of around a minute, and twenty-one days for anything over. He would also have been put through a series of mental agility tests before he could resume and the results compared with previous tests so that any progressive damage could be noted.

With a schooling accident like this, however, everything would be hushed up.

Still, maybe Ben would have to miss more than a day's racing. Maybe he wouldn't make Wincanton tomorrow. Better still, perhaps he'd be away for even longer. Josh didn't wish Ben any serious harm but a fortnight's convalescence for the lad could turn the championship right round in his favour.

Jesus, what was he thinking?

But he was only looking at the matter like any jockey in his situation. As Ben would were he in Josh's situation. They were head-to-head in a war being waged across the country, spread over a full twelve months and dependent on hundreds of highly strung and irrational beasts. According to the back pages of the newspapers it was one of the epic encounters in sport. To emerge as champion jockey, Josh would have to be as tough and bloody-minded as his opponent and he was entitled to take advantage of every piece of luck that came his way. And it couldn't be denied that Ben suffering a bad fall that morning was a piece of luck.

One day he'd go back to being a nice guy again – after this was all over. But not now.

*

It blew a gale all afternoon at Newbury, hurling rain into the faces of the small midweek crowd as they scurried between the stand and the parade ring, nursing hot drinks and scoffing bacon rolls. Josh reckoned they deserved better from the elements though he himself wasn't complaining.

So far, his mounts had enjoyed the heavy going and his first three rides for Peter Stone had all lived up to expectation. Whirlybird in the first had skipped home over the thirteen fences of the two-mile steeplechase with plenty in hand, as expected of a 6/4 favourite. After making all the running in the longer chase that followed, Velocipede had been caught in the back straight and finished a game second. This disappointment had been erased, however, by the performance of a novice hurdler who had revelled in the mud and bolted up to the surprise of all, leaving his fancied rivals ten lengths adrift.

That put Josh two winners up on the day, with two more favoured contenders to come. At this rate, maybe he could cut Ben's advantage to single figures within twenty-four hours; it was distinctly possible if Ben had to miss tomorrow's meeting at Wincanton as well.

Josh shut the thought out of his mind and forced himself to concentrate. The afternoon wasn't over yet and he had work to do. Next up was King Archibald, the ride Tony had miraculously stolen from under Ben's nose. Josh knew he had to make the most of him. Apart from the possibility of increasing his tally of winners, he didn't want anyone making unfavourable comparisons between himself and Ben. If he failed to win on King Archibald, some observers would be bound to say that Ben would have succeeded. The thought was not pleasant and he entered the parade ring pumped up for the business ahead.

But it wasn't just the race that had Josh on edge. The luck that had put his young rival on the sidelines had distracted him from the real issue of his unexpected engagement on King Archibald. He couldn't fathom why he had been offered the ride in the first place. On several occasions since his conversation with Tony he had been on the point of ringing him back and asking how the offer had come about. Had Tony called Leo Lovall? Or had the trainer called Tony? And what precisely had been said?

As far as Josh was aware, he was about the last jockey in the world that Leo would want on his horse. If duelling were still in fashion, Leo would have levelled a pistol at Josh's breast with relish – he'd said so two years ago, on the last occasion they'd exchanged words. So what had caused Leo to do him a favour now? Could it be – the idea beckoned seductively – that Leo had had a change of heart? If this was an olive branch Josh was determined to grab it with both hands. He'd give a lot to put his friendship with Leo back together.

Ten years ago he'd been Leo's stable jockey. In a sense, they'd started out together. On the death of his father, Leo had resigned his army commission and invested his inheritance in a small training operation. Josh, without an agent in those days, had blagged a few rides at the new yard, ridden Leo's first winner and the relationship had developed successfully from there. The pair were opposites – patrician army officer brought up on a Gloucestershire estate and council-house electrician's son from Derby – but their partnership worked. It continued to blossom during Leo's courtship and marriage to Annabelle, a raven-haired, well-spoken county girl with a shy smile. The two seemed ideally suited and, along with everyone else, Josh waited for them to produce a family.

But as the years went by no children appeared. Leo's yard was growing fast but his domestic life was shrinking. He and Annabelle seemed stiff and distant with one another. Leo enjoyed life less and became obsessed with his horses; Annabelle spent less time in the yard and never smiled when her husband was around. Josh, stuck in the middle, tried to put Annabelle's grin back in place and discovered with a jolt that she wasn't so shy after all. Believing that the marriage was as good as over, Josh fell for her hard.

The repercussions were explosive. Josh lost his job and Leo lost his wife – for a while. After a stormy nine months Annabelle returned to her husband and Josh was left to pick up the pieces. Though he'd never consciously set out to betray his friend and employer, he knew he was the guilty party. He'd tried to mend fences with Leo but some things, it was made painfully clear, could not be mended.

So why had he been granted a ride on one of Leo's horses?

He looked around the ring for the familiar figure, tall and broad, belted into a cashmere overcoat, as a rule bare-headed and disdainful of the rain – Leo would be hard to miss. Josh scrutinised the groups of owners and trainers, overcoats flapping and hats jammed tight, but saw no sign of his former friend.

A bearded fellow in an anorak appeared by Josh's side. Tim Daniels, Leo's assistant. 'Come and meet the owners,' he said as they shook hands. Despite Josh's problems with his boss, Tim was always polite enough.

'Where's Leo?' Josh asked as they squelched over the grass to two women sheltering under a large golfing umbrella held by a middle-aged gent in a Barbour and wellies.

'In the States. Won't be back till the weekend.'

It was a reply that raised as many questions as it answered and there was no time to take the conversation further.

'We're so pleased you could step in for poor Ben,' said the elder of the two women stiffly.

'It was the most ghastly rotten luck,' cried the other, a generation younger, Josh realised.

'Best laid plans, eh?' said the man as he gripped Josh's hand with unnecessary force. 'Still, give it your best shot.'

Had these people – mother, daughter and father, no doubt – requested he ride the horse in Ben's absence? If so, they didn't seem particularly confident in his abilities. Well, that was their problem. It made Josh even more determined to get the best out of King Archibald. He had his own agenda.

'What's he like?' he asked Tim as he was legged up.

'Bags of class, can run through a brick wall on his day. Takes a bit of handling, though.'

And that was all there was time to say before Josh had to follow the other runners out of the ring. It confirmed what he had learned from the form book when he'd looked the horse up. He'd considered ringing Ben to see if he had anything to add – and to check on his condition, of course – but had thought better of it. Any inquiries of that nature might be misconstrued.

In any case, he and Ben had limited conversation; the lad was the only person in the weighing room Josh couldn't get on with. And he wasn't alone. Since Ben had arrived from Ireland, just about every other jockey had found reason to argue with him. And anyway, Josh was damned if he'd phone a surly 21-year-old for advice.

He made his way down to the start on the other side of the course, opposite the stands. The wind was stronger out here, cutting through his thin riding silks. His vision through his goggles was already obscured and he dragged his sleeve across the lenses to clear them – a futile gesture. Beneath him his mount tripped gingerly over the muddy turf, shaking his big burnt-sugar head as if in disgust at the elements.

The race began and the seven runners bunched together as they headed away towards the far corner of the course. Unusually for Newbury, the wind was blowing from the east, directly into their faces, making the five obstacles down the back straight even stiffer than usual. King Archibald was plainly unhappy though Josh could tell that the powerful, long-striding animal beneath him had the equipment to overcome the wind and rain. 'Bags of class,' Tim had said. Josh hoped so. It was up to him to make sure the King ran like one.

He decided to tuck in at the rear of the group for the first circuit. Three miles plus on a day like this would take for ever – around seven minutes – and he'd win nothing by leading the field in the early stages. He tried to let the other runners protect him from the wind as much as he could. It seemed an age before they reached the end of the back straight and he had to fight the horse every inch of the way, forcing him off the gluey ground to jump into the wind. At last they rounded the curve at the top end of the course and turned back towards the stands. Once they were into the home straight, with the gale at his back, King Archibald began to find a proper rhythm.

This is more like it, Josh thought, as they flew the open ditch and took the next two fences in style. He could feel the power flowing through the broad frame beneath him as King Archibald cruised to the head of the pack. Josh tried to hold him back but the horse was putting on a show for the brave spectators, devouring the water jump and flashing past the winning post – or what would be the winning post on the next circuit.

As Josh pushed him round the bend that led out into the country again, it seemed the horse realised the race was far from over, and he didn't like it. Suddenly all the urgency vanished from his limbs. He stuck his toes into the sodden ground, hung out obstinately to the right and almost came to a standstill.

Josh knew instantly what the matter was – the horse had had enough and intended to run off the course back to the stables. They were losing ground fast and, for a moment, Josh wondered whether it might not be best to let him go. The other runners were far ahead now and he'd look a bit of a Charlie pushing the horse around in a hopeless cause. On the other hand, he was damned if would let the lazy brute put one over on him. What else was it Tim had said? 'Takes a bit of handling.' If a lad like Ben could handle the animal, he was sure he could too.

The path that led back to the stables was coming up on the right but, before they reached it, Josh yanked the horse's head to the left with venom, straightening the animal up and kicking him on. King Archibald resisted. Josh worked hard with legs and arms, putting in as much effort as if he were riding a finish to the line – which was a bit of a joke, considering they still had a circuit to go. The horse appeared to dither. There was nothing Josh could have done had the big animal decided to run off the track but some ingrained instinct to obey his rider was holding him back.

'Come on, you lazy bugger!' Josh roared into his ear, pulling hard to the left. 'Get out there and earn your keep.'

Then they were past the turn-off to the stables, cantering into the full force of the wind, well adrift of the pack. Josh could see the leading horses taking the first fence in the back straight. Maybe he would have been better off letting King Archibald have his way after all. Cajoling the reluctant beast round almost an entire circuit was not going to be much fun.

Fortunately his mount appeared to have decided there was no longer any point in fighting his jockey and had slipped back into a racing rhythm. He certainly knew how to clear a fence and set about jumping the obstacles down the back straight as if they were dandy brushes. The rain, thank the Lord, had eased off for the moment and it was exhilarating to cut through the wind on the big strong beast. If only they hadn't lost so much ground.

It wasn't until they'd rounded the bend at the end of the back straight and were leaping the cross fence that Josh realised the other runners were coming back to him. At the turn into the home straight he passed two stragglers who looked dead on their feet. He wouldn't be last home, at any rate. He was glad he'd forced King Archibald to keep going. At least he'd given the horse's connections a run for their money – though he had no doubt they'd consider it scant consolation for the winning ride Ben would have provided.

Or would he? Ben was young and fit, it was true, but Josh had made his name through his authority in the saddle. Despite all his injuries, his strength had never deserted him and his lungs were as sound as ever – which was just as well as the lazy sod beneath him was taking a fair bit of stoking.

With the wind at their backs and the finishing line in the distance the horse seemed to find fresh appetite. He flew the fences, just as he had done on the first circuit. They passed more exhausted horses, danced round a faller at the open ditch and cleared the next obstacle with just two contenders ahead of them.

Josh had ridden plenty of cunning old horses like this before. King Archibald was competing as if that was what he'd wanted to do all along. He had the last two runners in his sights now and was catching up fast, racing like a world-beater. Above the whistling wind and creaking tack, Josh heard the yells of the crowd, urging them on to the finish. He had no doubt the horse heard them too for he kicked on harder, clearing the last jump with feet to spare and leaving his two remaining rivals struggling in the rear.

King Archibald charged regally past the roaring crowd in the stands and over the line in first place as if his superiority had never been in doubt.

Josh pulled him up and turned him towards the unsaddling enclosure. A beaming Tim was rushing towards them, closely followed by the three ecstatic owners.

He now had three winners for the afternoon and Ben's lead was cut to eleven. Josh was already thinking ahead to his next race. This one was history.

The hotel was excellent – tastefully furnished bedrooms, gift-wrapped chocolates on the pillow and, so Josh had been told, a five-star restaurant worthy of special occasions. All of which was pretty much wasted on him in his present isolation, though he appreciated the scalding heat of the water in the king-sized bath as he soaked away the aches and pains of a hard afternoon in the saddle. Later he'd dine on a small, grilled steak accompanied by an (undressed) salad, courtesy of room service. Perhaps there'd be a movie to help pass the time. Then there was his homework for tomorrow – a review of his next day's rides at Wincanton as announced in the evening paper, followed by a study of their form in the bulky guide that was his ever-present – and only – bedside reading.

How he wished Susie were with him. He'd have happily watched her tackle the dinner menu in the restaurant and persuaded her to join him in the bath, not to mention the bed. There was little pleasure in a luxurious hotel room for one.

He could, of course, have driven home but, with the next day's meeting just down the road in Somerset, it made no sense to drive to Derbyshire and back. And he'd arranged to ride out at a nearby yard first thing in the morning, a favour which should pay off in terms of a few good rides. He'd have been unable to do that if he'd gone home. Still, it was hard not to be in his own bed with Susie.

His mobile lay on a chair by the side of the bath. He'd been putting off calling her, saving it up really – it was the high point of his evening.

The phone rang for a long time, long enough for him to wonder if she had gone out. When she finally answered she sounded distracted and, as he cheerfully filled her in on the afternoon's four wins – his mount had romped home in the last – he could tell her thoughts were elsewhere.

Josh knew what that meant: she was working and his phone call had come at an awkward time.

He'd first met Susie in the stables at Towcester on a cold, crystal-clear winter day. There was no woman in his life and he was happy to keep it that way – his Annabelle wounds still hurt. The last thing he needed was a girl who looked barely out of school. But he couldn't help noticing the wide-eyed, tufty-haired blonde intently studying the horse he was due to ride. Her breath fogged around her face which was flushed pink with the cold, and she shivered beneath a thin denim jacket. She ignored the bustle of grooms around her as she sketched in a small, spiral-bound pad, from time to time blowing on her fingers for warmth before returning to her task.

It turned out she was a local artist who had been commissioned to paint the horse. She was making preliminary drawings which, together with photographs, would enable her to complete the picture at home. She explained this shyly to a variety of passers-by as she continued to work.

Her eyes, Josh noticed, were a milky grey rimmed with black.

'What you need,' he said to her as she blew on her fingers for the umpteenth time, 'is a pair of gloves with the fingers cut out.'

Her gaze rested on him for a moment and he realised she was not the overgrown schoolkid she first appeared.

She nodded hesitantly and returned to her task. He felt like a fool and tried to put her out of his mind.

Her small form kept appearing at racecourses throughout the Midlands. Obviously her paintings must be good. On a foul and chilly Saturday at Uttoxeter in March, he bought a pair of thin calfskin gloves from a stall selling tweedy country paraphernalia and carefully cut the fingers off the left hand – her drawing hand, he had observed. She was reluctant to take them from him but when she realised he wasn't making fun of her, she'd smiled at him for the first time.

Later, after he'd returned from winning the four-and-a-quarter-mile slog of the Midlands Grand National, splattered from head to toe in mud, she'd made a fast sketch of him as a thank you. In the drawing, he gazed out of the page like a warrior returning from battle, covered in the scars of war, victory gleaming in his eye. Within a few weeks, as he laid siege to her in earnest, he found she'd chased all the Annabelle blues from his soul.

The artist girl had turned out to be shy and mysterious – getting her to reveal her past was like pulling teeth. She'd owned up to a tortured adolescence, brought up by an aunt following the death of her mother. There'd been drugs and pilfering but, finally, salvation when she'd turned herself around at art college.

Josh didn't want to pry further, in case he scared her off. She seemed nervous. He guessed that along with the adolescent rebellion had come tough retribution. There was something vulnerable about her, and that was probably what he found attractive. Even now, with Susie living and working in his home, he was not sure that one day he wouldn't return to find her gone.

But the future was what counted, not the past.

He'd tempted her to move in with him by offering the long attic room in his house as a studio. She'd loved it from the first, using it almost as a sanctuary. That was where she would have been when he called, either working on one of her horse commissions or on the large abstracts that she couldn't sell but which were her real passion. Josh didn't really understand them. A picture of a horse, precisely painted in a realistic style, was one thing – Susie was brilliant at them, it was obvious. But the canvases that didn't feature animals or concrete things but expressed mood and emotion through subtle use of colour and texture – as she had tried to explain to him – left him in the dark. He was as ignorant of her work as she was of his – reading a horse race, timing a stride into a fence, getting the most out of the animal beneath him. In their separate spheres of expertise, they were both a mystery to each other.

Now, as they spoke, he realised she wanted to get back to whatever she was doing. In her way she was as focused on her occupation as he was on his. She'd disappear into the attic for eight hours at a stretch or work all night when the mood took her, not eating, ignoring the phone, lost in her own world. 'Painting's not about what you do with your hands,' she'd said to him. 'It's about what's in your head.' When she was working hard she spent a lot of time locked in her head. That he could understand, it was the same for him. They were both obsessed.

'You should see the size of my bed,' he said. 'I wish you were here.'

She laughed. 'You always get horny when you've ridden a few winners.'

Was that true? Not that it mattered. 'I only get horny for you.'

'Me too.' Her voice was faint, almost a whisper. 'Josh?' She sounded anxious.

'What is it?'

There was a long pause. He could hear the sound of her breathing, ragged and fast.

'Nothing,' she said. 'I must get back to work.' And she put the phone down.

He grinned to himself. She was funny like that.

Susie sat in the unlit hall by the phone, unable to move. Josh had sounded so warm and loving. As if there was nothing about her he didn't want to embrace. But there were some things she couldn't share.

Like the letter and all that it implied.

It was hardly a letter, just a few printed lines.

Dear Susie Sausage,

Does Josh know the truth about you? The real truth.

Why don't you get out of his life before you muck that up too?

It was unsigned, of course. A cowardly, spiteful note that she should throw away. Then get back to what she was doing before she'd found it on the mat. Get back to work as she had promised Josh.

Or she could simply ring Josh and tell him. That would solve everything.

She did neither, just sat and shivered with fear.

Somebody knew.

Chapter Two

Josh lay in bed reading, the small print of *Chaseform* beginning to blur before his eyes. As he reached for the light switch the room filled with a shrill buzz, jerking him into full wakefulness. The bedside phone was ringing. Susie.

He snatched up the receiver and spoke into it warmly. 'Hello, darling.'

There was a pause, then a smoky chuckle which immediately wiped Susie from his thoughts.

'How sweet,' said a familiar voice. 'It's nice to know you still think of me with affection.'

'Annabelle?' The question was redundant. He'd not spoken to her for two years but every intake of breath on the other end of the line was as familiar as an old song.

'Aren't you pleased to hear from me?'

'Why are you calling?'

'I'm downstairs in the bar. I thought you might want to join me.'

He was fully awake now, suspicious thoughts racing through his mind. 'I don't think that would be a good idea.'

'Why on earth not? You've obviously not got anyone else to entertain you. Besides, I thought you'd like the opportunity to thank me in person.'

He knew he ought to put the phone down. A curt goodbye would do, then leave the receiver off the hook. But what on earth was she talking about?

'I don't owe you thanks for anything, Annabelle.'

'Really? How about King Archibald this afternoon?'

Five minutes later he was walking into the downstairs bar. He spotted her at once. The tumbling fall of blue-black hair was unmistakable. So, too, the long, slender legs that she insisted were her best feature – they were certainly eye-catching as she perched on a stool by the counter.

'Hi, Josh,' she murmured, lifting her face to his. It seemed natural to kiss her, putting his lips to her cheek and breathing in her perfume once again – a subtle musk that instantly brought to mind past intimacies.

He hurriedly stepped away from her and turned to the waiting barman. He could feel her eyes boring into him as he ordered. Be careful, he said to himself, she's after something. So what's new?

They took their drinks – Diet Coke for him, white wine for her – to a seat in an alcove so small their knees rubbed against each other beneath the table. The light was dim and flattering but, even so, beneath the surface glamour Annabelle looked drawn, with hollows in her cheeks. Josh was struck forcibly by how very different she was in looks and style to Susie. Annabelle's face was long – like a horse, she used to say – with a strong nose and high, sharp bones. In this light her almond-shaped eyes were almost black, the deep shadows beneath them making them seem bigger than ever. She reached for her wine and he noticed the thinness of her wrist. She'd lost weight since he'd last seen her. Nonetheless, her appearance remained as striking as ever.

'You're looking good,' he said, telling himself he'd only spoken out of politeness.

She pulled a face, turning her lips down in denial. 'Hardly.' She reached into her bag and pulled out a packet of cigarettes. He watched as her slender fingers placed the white tube to her lips and fumbled with a book of matches.

'Let me,' he said, taking the matches from her. He was not a smoker and disliked the habit in others. He'd never minded it in Annabelle, however.

'What's this about King Archibald then?'

She lifted her face and blew smoke upwards, away from him. Her lips curled into a feline grin. 'Well done to you,' she said. 'He's not the easiest to ride, I'm told.'

'Get on with it, Annabelle. What about him?'

She sipped her wine. She was going to spin this out, it was clear. 'Didn't you wonder how come you got the ride?'

'I hoped it might be Leo.'

She shot him a look of rank disbelief. 'Get real, Josh. He'd rather get on the horse himself and put up five stone overweight.'

He shrugged. He'd feared as much. There was obviously no prospect of making peace.

'Leo's out of the country at the moment,' she continued. 'He was conveniently lost between time zones when the jockey pulled out. Polly Kirby decided she wanted the best man for the job, and that was you.'

'Who on earth is Polly Kirby?'

'The owner – technically. Her mum and dad put the horse in her name. You must have seen them at the racecourse.'

Of course he had. The unenthusiastic threesome in the parade ring. At least he'd reversed their opinion of his abilities – they were all over him after the race.

'Polly happens to be an old friend of mine,' Annabelle continued. 'Took my word for everything when we were at school. Things haven't changed.'

So Annabelle had procured him the ride. But why? He asked her as much.

'Look, Josh.' She reached across the table and clasped his hand. 'We might not see each other any more but you still matter to me. Can't I do an old friend a favour?'

He pulled his hand away from hers. 'We don't see each other because you dumped me. I'm not an old friend, I'm a rejected lover. As a rule, friendship goes out of the window.'

She flinched. 'I only wanted to help out. I know you're in this head-to-head with Ben.'

'Thank you for the interest in my affairs, Annabelle, but I can manage without your assistance.'

She tilted her head back, looking down her nose at him. 'Don't be such a pompous prick. I know you. You don't care where the good rides come from.'

'This is different.' He knew he didn't sound convincing.

'How far behind are you now? Ten?'

He nodded. So she'd been keeping score.

'Winning on King Archibald could make all the difference. Just suppose you end up champion jockey by one.'

There was an awkward silence. She stared at him with a superior smile, having made her point. He felt uncomfortable, torn between his desire to confide in her as he used to and a conviction that her sudden interest in him spelt danger. He couldn't allow himself to trust her.

Her smile evaporated. 'I stuck my neck out for you, Josh. The least you can say is thanks.'

'What do you mean?'

'Leo will go mad when he gets back.'

'But that's down to the owners, surely. Polly what's-her-name.'

She laughed without humour. 'He knows about me and Polly. He'll realise it was my idea. Not that I care.' She lifted her glass, only seeming to notice it was empty when it was halfway to her lips. 'How about another drink?'

Josh took his time fetching her a large Scotch. He ought to hand it over and leave her to it. When it's finished with a woman, walk away and don't look back, that had always been his motto. But he'd never been able to walk away from Annabelle. She was different.

'So, how's it going with the artist?' she asked as he resumed his seat. She'd lit another cigarette and was surveying him mischievously through the smoke. 'I'm sorry, I've forgotten her name.'

'Susie, and it's going brilliantly, since you ask. She's living with me now.'

'How sweet.' Annabelle drew out the long vowel sound, an affectation Josh remembered well. She sipped her fresh drink greedily. 'I must give her a call. Give her a few tips on how to handle you.'

Josh didn't like this turn in the conversation. Discussing Susie with Annabelle was off limits.

'I'd better go. I've got an early start.'

She rolled her eyes in disgust. 'You could at least stay while I finish my drink. Then you can see me safely to my car.' She swallowed half the amber liquid in the glass and set it down unsteadily on the table. Josh recognised the signs.

'How much have you had?' he asked.

'Just this. Though I did have a couple of gins earlier. I had to get up my nerve to call you.'

'You can't drive, Annabelle. I'll call you a taxi.'

She shook her head. 'I'm not getting into a car with some man I don't know, even if he does drive a taxi.'

'Stay the night here then. Drive home in the morning.'

She smiled at him slyly, lights dancing in the pools of her eyes. 'Is that an invitation?'

He ignored the implication. 'They might have a spare room. Let's ask.'

Her hand stole across the table once more and found his. 'I bet there's lots of room in your bed.'

'Don't even joke about it,' he said primly.

She giggled. 'Why not? After all, we don't have to do anything.'

Her face was close to his, her lips curling suggestively, her scent whispering a familiar summons. A picture of Annabelle in his bed upstairs took shape in his mind. Her dark hair on the pillow, her slender legs entwined with his, the hot breath of her excitement on his face as they made love. Despite the pain of his rejection, despite his distrust – despite Susie – he still wanted her.

And who would ever know?

He would, for one.

He stood up. 'Come on, Annabelle, I'm driving you home.'

If she was disappointed, she didn't show it. She obediently finished her drink and followed him to his car, her face an unreadable mask.

Even though he'd not made the journey recently, Josh knew the way to Leo's yard without need of prompting. He'd travelled these roads hundreds of times in the past.

There was little conversation as they drove, Josh concentrating on the twists and turns of the unlit carriageway, resenting the fact that the day had ended as it had begun, with another stint behind the wheel.

After almost half an hour he pulled up outside the white gates of Leo Lovall's yard. Even though Leo was away, Josh had no intention of going any further. The main house, a sprawling redbrick mansion, was plainly visible from the road and he could watch Annabelle reach her front door safely without getting out of the car.

He turned towards her, eager to bring this unexpected interlude to an end. She sat staring straight ahead. In the half-light spilling from the yard he could see tears on her cheeks. His heart sank. It was evident this wasn't going to be easy.

'This was a mistake,' she said, her voice thick. 'I shouldn't have bothered you.'

'It's OK.' It wasn't, but he said it anyway.

'It was stupid of me to think I could buy my way back into your life.'

He supposed she meant the business with King Archibald but he didn't say anything.

'The thing is, Josh,' she turned to look at him, her face, hatched by shadow, crumpled in misery, 'I made a terrible mistake going back to Leo.'

This was his cue to put his arm round her and comfort her. He resisted the impulse.

'It was your choice,' was all he said.

'I know.' Her voice was barely a whisper.

Josh waited for her to get out of the car but she put her hands to her face and began to weep in earnest. The silence in the small space was broken only by the sound of her sobs. It was excruciating.

'Bella . . .' he murmured at last, speaking his pet name for her without thinking. 'Enough now. Please.'

'I'm sorry.' She took her hands from her face and began to scrabble in her handbag. He pulled a packet of paper tissues from the glove compartment and watched as she dried her face. 'I shouldn't dump on you, Josh. You don't want to know about me and Leo.'

He said nothing. He couldn't bring himself to ask but he willed her to carry on.

'He's changed, Josh. He doesn't like me any more. He's never forgiven me for going away with you.'

'But you went back. You chose him over me.'

'Yes, well . . .' She blew her nose and spoke more firmly, with resentment in her tone. 'He doesn't believe a wife of his should have a choice. I'm something he owns, like a dog or a horse.'

'I'm surprised you put up with that.' He grinned. 'As far

as I remember, you were pretty good at standing up for your rights.'

She didn't smile back. 'He frightens me.'

She flicked on the overhead light and pushed her coat off her shoulders. Then she took the hem of her high-necked skinny-ribbed sweater and began to tug it upwards.

'Annabelle!' cried Josh in alarm. If anyone should be looking out of a window or driving along the road, the scene in the car would take some explaining.

But she ignored him and pulled the garment over her head. Her flesh glowed whitely in the small dull light. He was right, he thought irrelevantly, she had indeed lost weight. Beneath the oyster-pink satin of her bra he could count the bones of her ribcage.

But his gaze was fixed elsewhere, as she had obviously intended. A livid bruise enveloped the shoulder nearest to him and spread downwards across her chest and upper arm in a mosaic of purple and yellow.

'He did it,' she said. 'He put his hands in my hair and forced me to kneel in front of him. Then he kicked me.'

'My God.' The sight was obscene yet mesmerising. Josh wanted to look away but he couldn't. Thankfully she shut off the light and slipped the sweater back over her head.

'Why do you stay with him?' he asked.

'Because I've nowhere to go. He knows all my friends and family. He'd come after me and kill me.'

Despite the bruising, Josh found this hard to believe. 'But he didn't come after you before. When you were with me.'

'I told you, he's changed. He says he won't let me make a fool of him again. It's like he doesn't want me any more but he won't let anyone else have me. I don't know what to do.'

'You've got to talk to the police and a solicitor. And you've got to leave.'

'That's easy to say.' Her tone was full of resignation.

They sat in silence. Josh was torn. He resented being drawn into this – Annabelle's problems were no longer his. Their relationship was over, killed off by her, and he owed her nothing. Nothing, that is, except the loyalty that comes from a shared history. The memory of good times as well as bad. Tender, loving moments that still played on in his head, sentimental fool that he was.

'Why can't you just go and stay with Jenny?' he asked. Jenny was Annabelle's sister, married to a Frenchman and living near Bordeaux. 'Surely you could lie low there for a bit until Leo has calmed down.'

'I can't.'

'Why not? She'd love to have you.' This was true; in Josh's experience Jenny had always been Annabelle's staunchest ally.

'I can't leave Suky.'

'Who?'

'Suky, my dog. She's a springer spaniel, not much more than a puppy. She's simply adorable. I couldn't leave her with Leo but if I took her out of the country she'd have to go into quarantine.'

'I see.' Josh contained a laugh. The woman was saying she was in fear of her life but she couldn't do anything about it because of her pet dog. It was typical Annabelle.

'Josh?'

Warning bells rang – he knew that tone of voice. She wanted something.

'Do you still have that flat in London? The one that used to belong to your mother?'

'Yes,' he said.

'We had some good times there, didn't we?'

He nodded. In the early days of their affair they had sneaked a couple of nights in London. This had been after his mother had died and her flat had been up for sale. It had been Annabelle who persuaded him a London base would have its uses and he'd taken it off the market. He still used it two or three times a month, when there were meetings in the south.

He knew what was coming. Was this the reason Annabelle had turned up at the hotel? The reason she'd wangled him the ride on King Archibald? She was a cunning witch but he'd never been able to say no to her.

'Do you still lend it out sometimes?' she said.

Suddenly he felt very weary. He badly wanted to get back to the hotel and a good night's sleep – or what remained of it.

'Yes,' he said and pulled the keys from the ignition. Working quickly he disengaged two of them from the bunch and held them out to her. 'Only use it if you're desperate. Just so you've got somewhere to go if Leo turns violent.'

She looked at him. 'I don't know what to say, Josh.'

'Thank you is fine. Just let me know if you're going to be there.'

She put her arms round his neck and hugged him hard, pressing her thin perfumed body against his and holding on as if she'd never let go.

At last she relaxed her grip and took the keys from him. 'I was a bloody fool to let you go,' she said as she opened the car door.

Josh watched her walk up the drive to the house and unlock the front door. She turned and raised a hand in his direction, then closed the door behind her. Josh remained where he was for a few moments more, replaying their conversation in his head. Annabelle had always had a taste for the dramatic and no one could ever accuse her of pulling her punches. Things couldn't be that bad with Leo, surely? But however much she had exaggerated, the bruises on her body were real.

It was nearly one by the time he reached the hotel. The night porter handed over a message with his room key – Susie had called at twelve fifteen.

As he climbed the stairs to his room he forced himself to think how best to handle matters. Susie would be wondering where he was, especially since he'd told her he had no plans for the evening beyond watching the TV and going to bed. On the other hand, he was reluctant to recount his adventure with Annabelle.

Susie knew about Annabelle, not all the gory details of their doomed affair and its aftermath, but more than enough for her to be suspicious about late-night rendezvous in hotels. Much as he hated lying to her, it would not be wise to tell her the truth.

She answered the phone on the first ring.

'Where were you, Josh?' she said as she heard his voice.

'I've been over at Casper's.' The lie came out fluently. Susie knew he was due to ride out for trainer Jack Casper in the morning. 'I got so bored I invited myself round. I've only just got back.'

'It's a bit late, isn't it? I thought you wanted an early night.'

'I know. We just got talking.' He was aware how feeble that sounded. 'You know, rehashing this champion jockey business and how I'm going. I'm afraid I bent his ear a bit.'

She laughed, a soft musical chuckle that meant she'd swallowed his explanation. That was a relief. 'The poor man.'

'Yes, well, think what a lucky escape you had – it could have been you.'

'I wish it had been, Josh.'

So he'd got away with it. He put the phone down guiltily, his mind on the golden girl lying in his bed a hundred miles away. This time tomorrow night he'd be lying in bed beside her – he couldn't wait.

Just as his head hit the pillow an uncomfortable thought wormed into his mind. He'd have to tell Susie about Annabelle after all. Though Susie rarely used his London flat, she ought to know he'd lent Annabelle the key. There must be ways of explaining the situation that wouldn't upset her.

He'd think of one tomorrow.

Leo Lovall strode into the arrivals hall at Heathrow airport, still picturing the trim legs of the stewardess with the silky black hair. She'd certainly added some glamour to the overnight journey. He'd always admired brunettes with pins stretching up to the armpit. Hell, he'd even married one.

His mood soured at the thought of Annabelle. The bloody trouble-and-strife. She'd never done a day's work since he'd married her, and yet she'd claimed to be too busy to drive him to the airport when he'd left. So now he would have to extract his car from the car park and, knackered as he was, drive himself home. She probably wouldn't even be there when he got back to give him the kind of welcome a husband deserved. Even if she just lay there like a waxwork he wouldn't mind – Stewardess Sarah had him all fired up. Not that that would last.

He grabbed a newspaper from a stall and grumbled to the assistant as he sorted some English change from the assorted shrapnel in his pocket. They didn't have a copy of the racing paper. Bloody disgrace.

He sat in the car for a few minutes to get himself up to date with the news. Wars, pestilence and scandal might make up the bulk of the paper but he couldn't give a fig about any of that. He honed in on what really mattered – the racing results.

His eye picked out the small print of 'Yesterday's Results' and his heart leapt at the sight of 'King Archibald'. That warmed the old cockles. The horse was a bastard to train and he'd pulled it off yet again! Fantastic!

Then he took in the notation in parenthesis after the horse's name: 'J Swallow'.

He blinked then read it over again. He could feel the pressure pumping dangerously through his veins and took a deep breath. Stay calm. There had to be an explanation for this. It must be a misprint.

He anxiously scanned the page. There was never much commentary on the previous day's events but there had to be something. Had to be.

'Following the indisposition of leading jockey Ben O'Brien, Josh Swallow coaxed home King Archibald in magnificent style at Newbury yesterday . . .'

Leo hurled the paper across the passenger seat and fired up the engine. He could feel the heat burning in his face and his heart beating like a drum but he didn't care. He was going to kill someone for letting that little shit ride one of his horses.

Chapter Three

'So what do you think I should do, Josh?' Susie's liquid grey eyes scanned his face.

They were standing in the converted attic up a steep narrow staircase at the top of the house. The previous owner had spent money on it, putting in a balcony window and a big sink which made it ideal for Susie's work. She'd stuffed it full of all sorts of clutter which, Josh supposed, must have some significance for her, though what anyone would want with an old sewing machine and an iron, or a collection of empty bottles, he couldn't imagine.

Susie was in her painting clothes: stained jeans and a once-white decorator's coat. Her hair was tied haphazardly off her face and she still held a loaded brush, her hand raised as if it wanted to carry on painting independent of the rest of her. He'd been in the house all of five minutes.

'Sorry,' he said. 'What were you saying?'

It was funny, Josh thought, how anticipation was often so much better than the thing you anticipated. It was one of life's little tricks. As a kid, the thought of Christmas or a birthday or a day off school seemed like heaven. But when it happened, it was usually a let-down – being bored at some aunt's house, not getting the one present you really wanted, being forced to catch up on homework instead of going down to the stables.

Or maybe it was him. So screwed up by the pressure of chasing Ben O'Brien that he couldn't leave his troubles outside the door and devote himself to Susie.

She put the brush down and shrugged off her coat. 'Let's go downstairs,' she said.

Was there a note of reluctance in her voice? He knew he'd interrupted her; perhaps she'd prefer to carry on with her work. But he wasn't noble enough to let her. He'd had a crap day and he was going to dump it on her. They both knew it.

That morning he'd arrived at Wincanton in good spirits and, with four likely prospects lined up, hopeful of keeping his Newbury fortune going. But from the moment he'd stepped out of his car, things had gone wrong. Peter Stone was parking next to him and, true to form, the trainer didn't bother with the social niceties as they walked briskly towards the racecourse entrance.

'You might have to look after Blue Bay,' Stone muttered. 'He didn't work well yesterday but I can't put my finger on anything.'

Blue Bay was Josh's first ride of the afternoon, a reliable ten-year-old chaser who'd served him well in the past, so this wasn't welcome news. He'd entered the weighing room brooding on the information and immediately caught sight of a familiar figure, changing in his customary spot.

'Hi, Ben. Good to see you in one piece.' Josh forced warmth into his tone. Even though he had reservations about the lad, he hadn't actually given up on him. Sometimes it took Irish jockeys as long to settle in England as it did their horses.

Ben O'Brien nodded, as if measuring the sincerity of Josh's words. 'I hear King Archibald made you earn your fee.'

Josh laughed. 'He tried to run out on me on the second circuit. Nobody warned me.'

Ben shrugged. 'I've never had any problems with him.'

There was something about the lad that got up Josh's nose. Maybe it was his fish-eyed stare – unblinking blue eyes in a long pale face that scarcely moved a muscle. Or was it the know-it-all arrogance that went with his undeniable talent? Or just the fact that Ben stood between him and the only achievement in his career that had so far eluded him?

Being champion jockey meant much more to Josh than just the title. It would give him the chance to stand up at the annual jockeys' dinner at Cheltenham and pay tribute to his parents. It preyed on his mind that he'd never really thanked them enough for what they'd done for him. Even though they were both dead now, he wanted everyone to know the sacrifices they'd made for him when he was a boy. They'd had no money in those days – it was before his father had gone into business with his uncle. Back then his dad had worked all hours so that Josh could have riding lessons. His mother had taken in washing and all sorts, cutting hair and making curtains to make ends meet.

Josh turned away and began to unpack his holdall. It had been a blow to hear about Blue Bay but Ben's presence was a kick in the guts. Subconsciously, he realised, he'd been banking on his rival sitting on his hands once again. His optimism, always fragile, withered away completely.

As predicted, Blue Bay underperformed and finished fifth out of a field of eight. A couple of punters had a go at him for not pushing the horse hard at the end of the race but they didn't know the background. In the circumstances, racing three miles over twenty-one fences was a pretty good performance for an animal that was under the weather.

There were seventeen runners in the next, a two-mile claiming hurdle, and his mount was unable to get into a rhythm round the tight bends. As a result they'd never got into the race. Josh wasn't so far back, though, that he couldn't see Ben riding a finish for his second winner of the afternoon.

By the end of the meeting their relative positions were the same as they had been before Newbury: Ben was back to fourteen in front, winning the last two events on the card. Josh won nothing. His big hope in the fourth, Snowy Hills, had been going like a train approaching the second-to-last fence, three lengths clear, when he'd broken a blood vessel. The strength had drained out of the horse as if someone had yanked the plug from a bath and Josh had ended up with crimson britches as he dismounted and led the animal back in.

But the worst was reserved for the last race, his spare ride on Cherrypicker. As he lined up for the two-mile hurdle Josh was determined to salvage something from the afternoon. At that point, Ben had ridden three winners and Josh was desperate. He thought that if he could get Cherrypicker to come good, the afternoon wouldn't be a total washout. Then he'd have clawed two back on Ben over the two days at Newbury and Wincanton – and he'd have settled for that before he'd left home.

But it hadn't worked out. Cherrypicker was a game performer, the best in the race, bar one. Heading into the back straight, Ben's horse, High Tide, was a length up. Josh went to work and Cherrypicker flew the penultimate hurdle and lengthened his stride. High Tide answered him, finding more to protect his lead. A length still separated them as they approached the last. With the post in sight Josh pulled out all the stops – too many, as it happened, in the opinion of the stewards. High Tide won the race and Josh picked up a three-day ban for misuse of the whip.

He poured it all out to Susie as she busied herself around the stove, producing supper.

'Poor you,' she said as she placed a messy-looking omelette in front of him. 'It just wasn't your day.'

'Tell me something I don't know,' he muttered. 'Sorry,' he added hastily as he registered the blink of distress on her face, as if he'd slapped her. It wasn't her fault. 'It was meant to be a joke – it just came out wrong.' The words sounded pretty lame.

She sat opposite him and reached for his hand. 'It's OK. You might be an old grump but I'm still pleased to have you back. Anyhow,' she removed her hand and picked up her fork, 'look on the bright side.'

Bright side? He'd be twiddling his thumbs for three days

while Ben notched up more winners. He could easily increase his lead to twenty or more in that time. Then the championship race would be just about over with nearly a third of the season still to go. Josh's thoughts were black but he kept his tone neutral as he said, 'How's that?'

'You get three days' rest. No driving, no falling off horses, no sweating in saunas. You can stay here with me.'

She shot him a seductive smile but he wasn't in the mood. He pushed his plate away. The eggs tasted a damn sight better than they looked but he didn't dare finish them – too much butter.

'I know it's not your fault, Susie, but you haven't got a clue. How the hell can I relax when Ben's out there winning races and I'm not? I'm going to go sodding spare for three days, that's all I know.'

The smile froze on her face then faded. She stood up and carried the plates to the sink. She hadn't finished her food either, he noticed.

She returned to the table with a new light in her eye, as if she'd made a conscious effort to have another try. She was a game girl. She deserved better than him in this mood.

'I had a job offer today,' she said, resuming her seat. 'I was trying to tell you upstairs but I don't think it penetrated.'

He forced a smile. 'Sorry.'

'That's all right.' She reached for his hand again. 'Some South African woman wants me to go out to Cape Town and paint one of her horses. Carmen Cook.'

Josh perked up. 'She runs a lot of horses in Dubai and Hong Kong. And the occasional Flat horse over here as well. What's the money like?'

'It's more than I usually get. She says she'll pay my air fare and I can stay in their house.'

'Fantastic. When are you going?'

'Well.' She looked sheepish. 'I don't know if I'm going to do it. I'm not sure I'm up to it.'

He laughed. 'You can't be serious. You're the best painter of horses I've ever seen. You've got to go – you'll have a great time.'

'You're not just saying that?' She eyed him suspiciously. 'You don't mind me going off to Cape Town?'

'Of course not – provided you come back.' He squeezed her hand, more cheered by her news than she appeared to be. She'd have a darn sight more fun in Cape Town than kicking around here, putting up with him.

Mouse was tired too. Big Rose had lumbered her with some really tedious cross-checking of customer lists at the holiday rentals business where she worked. Then she'd done an after-hours stint at her cousin's garage, working on the computers. Baz was not really a proper cousin but she didn't know what she'd do without him. The IT people at the office were grudging about their computers and sneered at her half-assed evening class qualifications but Baz was happy to let her loose on his brand-new system.

Though he drove her up the wall sometimes, Baz had always looked after her, more than Denis, more than her own mother. Mum and Denis were big on advice, telling her what to do, giving her lectures about how to live her life. But when it came down to it, what use were they? She'd asked them to come to the special hearing of psychiatric people and social workers and they'd said how they would provide a caring, supportive family environment to enable her to put her youthful aberrations behind her. At least, that's what Denis had said, being as he was a schoolmaster and always had a mouth full of bullshitty jargon. Mum had just nodded her head like she was mounted in the rear window of a Sierra. Three months later they were telling her to sling her hook and get her own place to live. How caring and supportive was that? Denis's concern ran as far as offering to heave her things into the back of a minicab.

In the event, Baz had helped her move, and he hadn't banged on in public about all he was doing for her. He'd found her the flat, which was OK, a bit cold and cramped but still a pretty good deal. And he'd fixed her up with her own motor, a ten-year-old Fiesta with barely forty thousand on the clock, one previous careful owner et cetera, which was the best present anyone had ever given her.

So she supposed she loved Baz. He'd been the one who'd cared and supported. Thanks to him, with her own flat and the car, she had a new life. She could do stuff that busybody Denis would never let her do if she'd still been living under the same roof.

It was dead chilly parked off the road, just under the brow of the hill. Every so often Mouse ran the engine with the heater full on to try and keep the cold out of her bones. She'd warmed up at Baz's garage, where they kept the temperature up so high you could grow tropical plants. 'The punters expect it,' Baz said. She just wished she could bottle some of it and take it back to her place.

It had taken a few hours to make headway with the garage computers but the pair of them had finally sorted the problem out, though Mouse had no doubt that something else would go wrong in a day or two.

As Baz had paid her off he'd said, as he always did, 'You're really good with this stuff. Why don't you get yourself to college and get some proper qualifications?'

But she'd just pocketed the notes and left him to clear up the pizza packages from their takeaway.

He was right, of course, she was good with computers. Machines, technical stuff, boy's toys had always appealed to her. But she couldn't face the thought of all that back-to-school crap. It wouldn't work. She'd been kicked out of a few educational establishments in her time and she wasn't going back down that road again.

Besides, as Mrs Josh Swallow, she wouldn't have to earn a bean if she didn't want to.

Right now though she was grateful for the extra quid Baz regularly put her way. Apart from the everyday necessities, there were costs she couldn't help incurring, such as her away-days in London. She couldn't live without them. Then there was other stuff. She'd forked out around a hundred and thirty quid for the little black box in her hand, its earpiece quietly hissing into her left ear.

She adjusted the tuning dial gently, just to make sure she hadn't drifted off the correct waveband (which might explain why she wasn't getting anything) and ended up where she started – listening to silence. Maybe that was good news. She couldn't be sure.

Strictly speaking the receiver, which at first glance looked just like a pocket-sized radio, had only set her back thirty or so. The more expensive component was the transmitter, currently broadcasting from Ridge House, the sprawling building some fifty yards down the hill from where Mouse now sat. Josh Swallow's house which, for the moment, he shared with the Mistake.

Mouse had thought long and hard about how best to bug Josh's home. She knew you could get cool spy stuff from the internet: transmitters that looked like pens or briefcases or credit cards – not that they would suit her purpose. Not to mention that they cost way out of her league. Fortunately, the kind of thing that did suit her – permanent, low maintenance and innocent looking – was also affordable. At a pinch.

She'd chosen a transmitter that looked just like an ordinary three-pin adapter. According to the online catalogue the device could be inserted into any electrical socket, where it would function like a proper adapter but would also transmit whatever took place in the room to an outside receiver. It ran off the mains, so Mouse wouldn't have to bother with replacing batteries, and it looked just like any old household plug. With luck, she'd be able to replace one already in use and no one would notice.

For preference, Mouse would have liked to bug the sitting room. Surely that's where Josh would relax of an evening and she'd be able to listen in to his conversations. But, when she looked, the room was well supplied with electrical sockets. There were no adapters and no places where they were called for. She could just plant the device anyway and hope it wouldn't be noticed but she wasn't happy with that.

There was a risk a spare adapter could be consigned to the back of a drawer or, worse still, chucked out. She thought again.

In the end it was a pretty easy decision.

The first floor was not so well provided with wall sockets and Mouse noticed a couple of adapters in use. And in the bedroom, beneath the bedside table, was just what she was looking for: a light and a radio were doubled up on the same outlet.

In some ways a bedroom was the best place of all. This was where she would hear exactly what went on between Josh and the Mistake. There'd be late-night conversations, private phone calls and all sorts of other secret stuff. Like the sound of them screwing. Mouse thought about this. She didn't like it but she had to face facts. The picture of Josh in bed, naked, making love was daily in her thoughts. But in those thoughts he made love to her.

Of course he'd screw the blonde, why else was she there? Josh was a real man and he'd be like a bull in the bedroom. So, naturally, he'd cover the cow in his bed. She was pretty enough, in a conventional, icky-pink, princessy sort of fashion.

Face it, she thought, as she knelt by the bed and swapped over the adapter, he doesn't know any better. He'll poke the princess till he finds the woman he can really love.

And we know who that is, don't we?

But, no matter how she rationalised it, the thought lodged in her mind like grit under a contact lens. It hurt and she couldn't wash it away. So she'd done something silly, just to balance things up and make her feel better. It was hard to be sensible all the time and, anyway, she'd bet he'd never miss just one sweater, he had so many. She'd made sure to take the oldest and tattiest. Now she wore it to bed at night and dreaded the day when she'd have to wash it – it still smelt of him.

She'd only been into Josh's home three times since she'd acquired a set of his keys. It was much more of a risk up here than down in London. Here everybody knew everyone else's business, so she couldn't just gaily march up his drive and open his front door without the risk of being spotted. Josh was well-known and his affairs were of interest. Who could say who might not be keeping an eye on his place in his absence? Down in those fancy London apartments, Mouse had concluded, nobody cared a hoot about what happened next door – if her experience was anything to go by.

Of course, what really made visiting Josh's house risky was the Mistake. It was easy to find out when Josh would be away from home, she only had to check the racecards in the morning paper, but knowing the movements of the useless blonde was not so simple. At least, that's what she'd first thought. In the end, she'd cracked it simply by investing time in watching the house.

The Mistake had a routine, Mouse discovered, based on regular visits to a health club. Two or three mornings a week, usually after Josh had made an early-morning start or when he was away overnight, the blonde girl would make the twenty-minute drive to the Acorn Fitness Centre and disappear inside for a good hour. She'd follow this up with a trip to a nearby supermarket or a journey into other shops in

Derby itself. After tailing her three times over a fortnight, waiting patiently while she worked out and shopped, Mouse reckoned that she was away from the house for two to three hours on each excursion. That was enough.

The first time Mouse had entered Ridge House, she wasn't sure exactly what she was going to do. She just knew that the keys had been heaven-sent, a sign that she and Josh were destined to mean something to each other. She'd stood in the porch, her hands shaking as she tried one of the keys in the little bunch. She'd expected problems. Maybe her copies wouldn't work the lock. Or perhaps there'd be some burglar alarm inside which she wouldn't know how to disable – in which case, she'd just have to disappear fast.

But there'd been no problem at all. The door had swung open after a double turn of the first key she tried. Simple.

Mouse reckoned she had a clear hour and a half – probably more but she couldn't risk it. She'd watched Susie's cherry-red Golf turn into the Acorn car park at ten and had driven back as quickly as she could. Unless the girl completely abandoned her routine, Mouse was safe till eleven thirty at least.

On reflection, she had wasted her first half-hour alone in the house. She just wandered around nervously, afraid to touch things, but opening every door and looking into every room, imagining what it would be like to live here. With him.

She lingered for a long while in the bedroom, trying to ignore the female things that littered every surface – the tubes and jars of make-up on the dressing table, the hairbrush with the golden strands on the bedside table, the discarded camisole crumpled on the bed. She had the urge to chuck all the girl's stuff in one of the black bin liners she'd seen in a kitchen drawer. Then she'd dump it all in a dustbin when she left. That would be a right laugh. Let Blondie work that out.

But it would also be stupid, the kind of thing she'd have done before Gavin Carter. She was smarter than that now. If she wanted to return, no one must know she'd been here.

So she'd just put the Mistake's things out of her mind. They were superficial – rubbish waiting to be collected. Instead, she'd focused on Josh.

She spent a long time with his clothes. Fingering his shirts and ties, imagining how he would look in some of the outfits she found hanging in his wardrobe. She wrapped his dressing gown round her and sprinkled drops of his after-shave on her wrist. These garments had been next to his skin, they smelt of him. And she smelt of him. It was wonderful. The next best thing to being wrapped in his arms.

Then she'd looked at her watch and panicked. Over an hour had gone by. Maybe the Mistake would come back early. If she were caught there would be trouble. She didn't know how she'd react if she came face to face with the blonde bitch here in this house. And, however it turned out, it would mean she'd never be able to return.

So she'd fled, with time still left on the clock, and regretted it bitterly later. But when she'd calmed down she realised it had been for the best. Then she started planning what she would do the next time.

She played it cool the following week. She only allowed herself half an hour with Josh's clothes. Then she went through all the drawers of his desk.

She'd noticed the study on her first visit but she only thought about its significance afterwards. The desk must be where he'd keep important papers – letters, business documents, bank statements. She didn't want to steal money from him or anything like that but she wanted to know everything. Surely his desk would yield all sorts of interesting information.

At first, she was disappointed. True, there were bank statements and credit card papers – he seemed to spend a lot on hotels and petrol – but their appeal was limited. Then she discovered a file of papers from a solicitor in London. She nearly shoved the folder back in the drawer but there wasn't much else to look at. The file was labelled 'Mum' and turned out to be all about Josh's mother's estate. It seemed the old girl had popped off three years ago and left Josh a flat in London. There were reams of letters about managing agents and service charges and possible lease extensions. From what Mouse could make out, it seemed Josh had first of all instructed the solicitor to sell the flat and then changed his mind. All of which was pretty boring, except for one thing.

Beneath the file was an envelope containing two keys and on the flap were the words 'Arlington Mansions'. Mouse reached into the pocket of her jeans and pulled out the keys – her copies. There were four on the ring. One fitted the Ridge House front door, another small one looked like the key to a padlock or a garden shed, which left two she hadn't identified.

She compared them to the keys in the envelope. You didn't have to be a genius to work it out. She turned back to the letters in the file, the ones about managing agents. By the time she left the house she had the address of Josh's London flat and was already planning her first trip to the city. If she chose her time carefully she reckoned she could spend a lot longer than an hour or so in Josh's world. A place where, with luck, there wouldn't be so much girlfriend crap around and she could have Josh all to herself. And so it had proved.

Mouse shivered in the cold car. She didn't fancy sitting here much longer listening to nothing.

Josh tried hard to concentrate on the television screen but his thoughts kept wandering and his head lolled heavily on his neck. The urge to lie back on the sofa and drift off was strong. It was probably the painkillers he'd taken to ease his sore back. Or the late night the day before. Or maybe just the sheer bloody stress of riding and driving and worrying and kicking himself on through this never-ending season. It was, he sometimes thought, like an endless Grand National – there was always another obstacle, another crowded road ahead, another mad-eyed temperamental horse eager to dump him on his arse. He'd always loved the jockey's life – till this season, stuck in a neck-and-neck struggle with that cocky kid, O'Brien.

He became aware that some chat-show host was gabbling at him from the television in the corner; he felt heavy-limbed and disorientated. He must have dropped off. He remembered he'd been watching a video of Meter Maid, a six-year-old hurdler he was due to ride the next day.

She looked an awkward ride but he knew he could get a tune out of her. It was his job and what he excelled at:

getting horses to relax. If they didn't settle, you were wasting your time with racehorses – or any horse, come to that. Josh was adamant that the most important race in a horse's life was his first. The animal had to settle and get into a rhythm, learn to breathe and finish faster than he had begun. In other words, a horse had to enjoy himself. Many horses never recovered from the trauma of their debuts.

Josh reflected that there wouldn't be too many more Meter Maids. Would he miss the hurly-burly of race-riding? Right now, he didn't think so.

He reached for the remote control. He'd better watch Meter Maid once again; he couldn't afford to go to bed just yet.

Susie folded her clothes carefully – just like she'd cleaned her brushes and the tray she used as a palette, scouring with a rag and white spirit until she was satisfied. It was important to her to get everything as spotless as possible so she could begin the next day without her colours being muddied by what had gone before. If only it were as easy to do that with feelings.

So she was going to South Africa. She didn't want to go without Josh. For all the irritations of living with an obsessive, blinded by the demands of his profession, she needed him to lean on. She felt safe in his world.

At least, she had done until the postman had called.

She took her nightdress from under her pillow and pulled it on hastily, as if someone was watching. It was silly of her.

She burrowed beneath the covers and turned off the light. Josh would be up when he'd finished watching his video. Until then she'd wait in the dark.

She shivered though she wasn't cold. No matter how dark it was, somebody knew where Susie Sausage was hiding.

The kind of transmitter Mouse could afford only had a range of a hundred metres, which meant she'd had to find a spot nearby where she could listen, the kind of place where she could park for an hour or two at a time without attracting attention. Fortunately, the lane just up the road from Ridge House did the trick. It led to a car park provided for walkers who took the tracks up the hill to explore the southern fringes of the Peak District. In the summer months it was packed with the rambling fraternity and, in all kinds of weather, climbers and dog-walkers would park on the wide verge along the lane. A person could sit in a car along there for hours without attracting a second glance.

A click sounded in her earpiece, the sound of a door opening. Then closing again with a thud. She heard movement in the bedroom, the opening of drawers and cupboards, the slither of bedsheets. It had to be just one person, there was no conversation.

Then the phone rang.

Mouse stuffed her finger in her other ear to shut out the noise of a car climbing the hill on the main road and concentrated.

Susie snatched up the bedside phone. It was probably for Josh but she tried to filter his calls when he was working.

'Susan?' Oh dear. Only one person called her by her full name.

'Hello, Brenda.'

Her aunt's voice, so familiar, insinuated itself into her ear. 'So you're in the land of the living after all. Sometimes I think you're too posh these days to remember your own flesh and blood.'

If only she were that lucky. Some things weren't easy to forget.

'I'm sorry. I've been a bit—'

'Busy.' Brenda cut her off. 'Yes, I can imagine. Well, I won't take up your time but I wanted you to know that I'm going to see him this weekend.'

Susie gritted her teeth. She couldn't believe Brenda was about to ask her again.

'I've told you,' she said, 'I won't go with you. I never will.'

There was a silence, broken only by the sound of her aunt breathing heavily. 'If that's how you feel.'

'I do.' Stated firmly to end the matter.

'Oh well.' Brenda sighed, then injected some unconvincing cheer into her voice. 'And how's John?'

'Josh,' Susie corrected. Brenda didn't approve of Susie living with a man ten years her senior. 'He's great. It's all great here, really it is.'

'I see.' Brenda didn't sound convinced. 'Well, if it all goes wrong, you can have your room here back. It would be just like old times.'

And what a terrible thought that was.

'Brenda, that's sweet of you but I'm OK. I've never been happier in my life.'

She put the phone down and burst into tears.

*

How fascinating, Mouse thought. And how gratifying. It looked like the wheels were coming off for the Mistake. She sounded as if she was about to slit her wrists (not a bad idea, girl) even when she was proclaiming her life was so great.

And now she was boo-hooing in her bedroom all on her ownsome. Poor cow. Where exactly was Josh – especially if their life was so great?

Mouse was grinning fit to bust as she listened to the sobs from the house down below.

Get the message, you silly bitch. He doesn't want you around.

Josh jerked awake suddenly. For a few seconds he was still locked in the world of his dreams, dislocated from his surroundings. Then he took in the soft support of the living-room sofa at his back, the television remote control in his hand, the blank screen in front of him. And Susie.

She turned from the TV to face him. She must just have turned it off.

'You were asleep,' she said. 'It's gone midnight.' Her hair was loose and she wore a turquoise and green kimono that he'd bought her for Christmas.

He reached for her hand and pulled her into his lap, her body soft and scented beneath the silk. 'I'm sorry,' he murmured into her neck.

'No, you're not.'

She sounded stern but they'd played this game before. His fingers found the knot in her kimono as his mouth sought hers.

'No, Josh,' she said as the robe parted and his hands slipped inside. 'Please.'

He stopped. She wasn't playing after all. In the shaft of light from the side lamp he saw her eyes were red, her cheeks puffy.

His heart plummeted. 'What is it, Susie? I'm sorry I've been such a bore. I'm so thoughtless sometimes.'

'No, you're not,' she whispered.

'Is it this South Africa thing? If you don't want to do it, just say no.'

She shook her head. 'It's nothing.'

He didn't believe her. 'I'll pack the riding in at the end of the season and everything will be different.'

'I've heard that before.'

'It's true. Then I'll devote myself to your career. I'll be your easel-carrier and paint-mixer.'

At last, a tiny smile began to tug at the corners of her mouth.

She took his hand and placed it back beneath her kimono.

Mouse could barely read her watch by the dim moonlight filtering into the cramped and cold interior of the car. It was nearly midnight and she was due back at the grind at Hilltop Holidays first thing in the morning. Time to get moving.

Reluctantly she pulled the plug from her ear and turned off the receiver. She'd heard nothing for ages but her excitement had barely faded. Josh had not come into the bedroom, that was certain. Maybe he slept in a separate room these days. What a laugh that would be.

She could believe it, though. She wouldn't be surprised if, for all her well-toned figure, the Mistake was hopeless at pleasing a man. It was often the case, magazines were full of it. Girls with dolly faces and perky tits thought that all they had to do was lie in bed and look gorgeous. But men soon got bored with that. They wanted real women with heart and passion.

Mouse knew about passion. Her whole life was a struggle to control the feelings that boiled within her. Josh would understand that and she'd give him passion in full measure when her turn came. He wouldn't be leaving her alone in bed to cry herself to sleep at night.

The sound of the Mistake's sobbing echoed in Mouse's mind as she started the engine. She was weary and stiff but she had a warm glow inside as she drove home to her icy cold flat.

Leo poured himself another thimble of Scotch. He knew he shouldn't but there were many things a person shouldn't do. Many things worse than sitting up past midnight and getting pissed. He'd have to live with the consequences tomorrow at sparrow fart up on the gallops. It wouldn't be the first time.

When it came down to it he'd not actually killed anyone today, much as he'd felt like it as he barrelled down the motorway from the airport. He'd barked at the stable staff and he'd given Tim Daniels the kind of bollocking he wouldn't forget in a hurry. He'd even had a go at young Ben O'Brien.

'Huh, I see you're fit enough to ride today,' he'd said as Ben showed up at the yard shortly after he himself had arrived. 'If you'd been doing your job yesterday I wouldn't have had to put up with outsiders on my horses.'

Ben knew well enough who Leo meant by outsiders and for his own reasons Ben had no time for Josh Swallow. 'I can't afford to like the bastard if I've got to beat him, can I?' he'd said to Leo recently. It wasn't how most jockeys viewed their rivals but it suited Leo well enough. Ben was a fantastic young rider and a sound fellow all round. Leo knew how lucky he was to have him.

In response to Leo's jibe this morning, the lad had simply said, 'Sorry, guv'nor. If I could have seen straight yesterday afternoon I'd never have let Swallow take the ride off me.'

That was fair enough. Ben wasn't to blame. Unfortunately, the person who was, the one Leo really wanted to throttle, had appeared quite unconcerned by his fury.

'Don't get in too much of a paddy, darling,' Annabelle had said. 'You know it's not good for you.'

They'd had a row about Josh riding King Archibald. Sort of a row, because he was the only one shouting while she simply played the tune of sweet reason.

'Ben wasn't available and Josh was the best alternative. As it happened, he did a fine job so I don't see what you're complaining about.'

'You know I've banned him from my yard and my horses. You did it deliberately.'

She'd rolled her eyes and lit a cigarette. 'Don't be such a baby. The horse won, didn't it? The owner was jolly happy.'

He hadn't wanted to let it rest there but she'd blown smoke in his face and announced she was off to bed. 'See you in the morning, darling.'

She was the only woman he knew who used the word 'darling' like an insult. See you in the morning, you useless prick. After you've spent the night in the spare room on your own.

Then he'd had the phone call from the hotel, which hadn't exactly improved his mood. Had in fact sent him spiralling into this black cloud of impotence and self-pity.

'Mr Lovall? It's Eamon, the barman at the Grange.'

Eamon had been apologetic about calling so late but there was something Mr Lovall ought to know.

Eamon often called with something Leo ought to know, as did one or two other purveyors of alcohol in the vicinity. It was remarkable what mischief young stable staff could get up to when they'd had a jar or two. Leo had greased a few palms behind various bars. As a result, he'd often nipped trouble in the bud as well as coming by useful information.

Eamon's information, however, was not so much useful as bloody depressing.

'It's Mrs Lovall, sir. She was here late last night in the bar. She'd had a few so she left the car behind. Seeing as she'd told me you were away in America, I thought you'd like to know.'

It wasn't the first time he'd had reports of Annabelle sucking up the booze. In fact, it was the kind of thing he'd specifically asked to be told about.

Eamon was warming to his theme. 'She had a hotel guest with her, sir. I believe he drove her home, though I don't know whether he came back because I'd closed up and gone by then.'

'She had a man with her?'

71

'A jockey, sir. A Mr Swallow.'

It hadn't really come as much of a surprise. If he was away and Josh was staying over, what better opportunity would she have of seeing her old lover?

So he sat in the dark, brooding. It was starting all over again, he could feel it in his bones. She'd come back to him swearing everlasting fidelity, promising to put everything into their marriage, but somehow they were back at the point of breakdown. And it wasn't his fault!

He wanted to go upstairs and barge into the bedroom she'd annexed for her own. He'd rip the covers from the bed and the nightdress from her back and reclaim her for himself. She was his! He'd married her, paid for her, even taken her back after her last betrayal. Every fibre of him ached for her.

He could do it. He'd done it before – forced himself on her in a storm of desire that had blown itself out in a twinkling. And she'd not moved a muscle, not even to protest. 'Satisfied?' she'd said when he'd finished, the word loaded with contempt.

Well, he hadn't been satisfied, not one bit, and he'd not laid a finger on her since.

What he should do now was go upstairs and extract justice. Snap the slender stem of her neck and put her beyond the risk of temptation. He'd have to kill himself afterwards, of course, but that would be easy. He'd eat his service revolver. Put himself out of his misery like setting a wounded animal to rest. That wouldn't be a problem.

He drained his glass and climbed unsteadily to his feet. Who was he kidding? He could never hurt Annabelle. For all her faults, he loved his wife. Loved her with a fervour that, he knew, would never be reciprocated. Josh Swallow had seen to that.

Now there was someone he'd have no qualms about hurting.

Chapter Four

Josh didn't recognise the number that flashed up on his phone. Whoever it was had been trying to reach him for the past hour while he'd been sweating it out in the sauna. No message had been left, just four failed attempts listed under Missed Calls.

He tried the number and hung on as it rang half a dozen times. If there was no reply he'd try later. It might be a trainer offering him a spare ride.

'Hello?' It was a woman's voice, instantly recognisable.

'Annabelle, it's me.'

There was a slight pause then the voice cried effusively, 'Lizzie, hi! Thanks so much for calling me back.'

So Annabelle wasn't on her own and didn't want whoever she was with to know his identity. He'd been on the end of her antics many times.

A scuffling sounded on the line and he heard her voice from far off, addressing someone else. 'I must take this call, do you mind?'

He hung on patiently, imagining Annabelle's retreat from the unknown person's presence. He had a fair idea who it was, however, and Annabelle confirmed it when she came back on the line.

'Sorry, darling,' she whispered. 'Leo would go spare if he knew I was talking to you.'

The image of her cruelly bruised shoulder exposed in the dim light of his car took shape in his mind. He had no doubt Leo would indeed 'go spare'. But why *was* she talking to him? It was almost a fortnight since she'd turned up at the hotel in Newbury and their meeting had taken a back seat in his mind.

'Josh,' she continued, 'you know you said I could stay at your flat?'

'Yes.' So that was it.

'Is it still OK?'

On reflection, it wasn't. He'd handed over the keys on impulse, his urge to protect his former lover overriding common sense. Thinking about it in the cold light of day, he knew he shouldn't give Annabelle any excuse to regain a foothold in his life. More to the point, he'd not been able to tell Susie about his noble gesture, or even that he'd seen Annabelle once again. He had the feeling she wouldn't be entirely understanding.

'Only I can't stand it any longer,' Annabelle continued. 'I've got to get away from Leo now or I never will.'

Josh knew he ought to retract the offer but he couldn't disregard the past. And he'd given his word. 'It's OK,' he said.

'Thank you, darling. I promise it won't be for long. Just a day or two while I sort myself out. A week at the most.'

Susie would be away in South Africa for the next week, working on her commission for Carmen Cook. Not that that was of any relevance. However, it made Josh feel better about the whole business.

'If you could keep it under a week I'd be grateful.'

'No problem. I'll get to town and make a few calls. It'll be easier to fix things when I'm off Leo's radar, if you know what I mean.'

'He hasn't hurt you again, has he?'

'No – well, not exactly. But he's convinced I'm cheating on him. I swear he's got murder in his eyes every time he looks at me. I should never have left you, Josh. Going back to Leo was the biggest mistake of my life.'

She'd said it, not him. But Josh didn't want to get into any of this. The sooner he could shake the mud of his old love life off his boots the better. He just hoped the loan of the flat wouldn't have any repercussions. It had better not.

'You'll come and see me, won't you, Josh?'

What?

'I'm leaving today. I'm just waiting for Leo to clear off then Suky and I are getting out of here for good. We could celebrate my escape.'

He stalled. 'I'm at Leicester this afternoon.'

'Well, couldn't you pop in this evening?'

He supposed he could. With Susie going off to Cape Town there was no particular reason for him to go home. The next day's meeting was at Fontwell Park and he could break the journey by staying overnight en route. He could go to London and make sure Annabelle had everything she needed.

'Fantastic,' she cried as he agreed to her suggestion. 'I'll cook you a special dinner, just to show you how grateful I am.'

'No, Annabelle.'

'Just joking, darling. You can have a lettuce sandwich. I swear Suky eats more than you jockeys.'

Her soft laughter rolled merrily down the line. Was this really a woman on the brink of walking out of her marriage? Josh wondered if she was on medication of some sort, or maybe it was the hysterical reaction of someone on the edge. Or was she hitting the bottle too hard? He'd better pay her a visit this evening, just to make sure she was all right.

'Drive safely,' he said. 'I'll see you later.'

'OK.' Her tone changed in an instant. 'Josh, I won't forget this. You're a true friend – a rock.'

He ended the call with a wry smile on his face. No one had ever called him a rock before. He wasn't sure he deserved it.

Susie, for example, would be less than impressed by him staying overnight in London, with Annabelle tucked up in the spare bedroom. But Susie, he told himself, had no need to be jealous. He was just tidying up the loose ends from his past.

In any case, Susie would soon be out of the country. He glanced at his watch and wondered whether she'd left home yet. Her flight wasn't till this evening but she was catching the train down and wanted to avoid the London rush hour. Knowing Susie, she'd get to the airport early.

It was less than two days since he'd been at an airport with her himself, when they'd flown in to Birmingham after four days of snatched holiday. At least his time out from riding had been put to good use as they'd enjoyed a short but sweet interlude prowling the bars, shops and fantastical buildings of Barcelona. Josh had even allowed Susie to drag him round an art gallery or two. He'd threatened revenge in extracting a promise to visit the football stadium but, in the end, they'd simply spent the afternoon in bed. And he'd not thought about Ben O'Brien once.

He'd made up for the omission in spades since his return to the saddle at Wetherby the previous day. Before beginning his ban, Josh had reduced his rival's lead to twelve but in his absence Ben had booted home another four winners – a bit of a blow but it could have been worse. With both of them drawing a blank at Wetherby, Josh was now sixteen victories behind. Ben's lead was healthy but not decisive. To have ridden 111 winners by this time of the season was Josh's best effort to date. The third in the table was over thirty winners adrift of him. Josh could break an arm and still hang on to second spot but that wasn't what he wanted – he'd been runner-up five times already. This year it was all or nothing. There was a long time to go before the end of the season. It was essential to hang on in the championship race and hope that something caused the young Irishman to slip up.

The door to the flat swung open sweetly as always, closing behind Mouse with a familiar, satisfying clunk. But this time something was different.

Mouse pressed her back against the big solid barrier like she always did, savouring the magic moment when she stepped into Josh's world. But now, even though everything seemed just the same – the hallway shadowed by winter sunlight, the steady ticking of the grandfather clock, the glimpsed corner of a roll-top desk in the doorway of the small bedroom at the end – she knew in an instant it was spoiled.

It was the smell. Perfume thick like honey, earthy and expensive – and tobacco. Josh didn't smoke, she knew that well enough. She'd seen no ashtrays, cigarette packets or butts in either of his homes. There was even a small magnetic No Smoking symbol attached to the fridge in the kitchen in the house in Derbyshire. So it wasn't him.

And it wasn't the Mistake's scent, either. She'd had a good sniff of Blondie's perfume when she'd had the chance. She'd toyed for a few entertaining moments with the thought of somehow adulterating it – adding a dash of gin or, maybe, curry powder. She'd bet Josh wouldn't fancy snogging a woman who stank like a Sunday morning hangover.

She took a cautious pace forward. The place felt empty but maybe someone was still here – in the bathroom, perhaps, unable to get to the door when, as usual, she had taken the precaution of ringing the bell. But from here she could see the bathroom door standing ajar. There was no one in the flat, she was sure of it.

Mouse relaxed, breathing out a whoosh of breath that she'd been holding unaware. So Josh had entertained visitors recently and their pong still stank up the place. She could live with that. Maybe things weren't spoiled after all.

She made for the master bedroom, always her first port of call, where she could stretch out on the wide soft bed and luxuriate in the knowledge that she was in command of Josh's domain.

As she pushed open the door the sight of an open suitcase on the bed stopped her in her tracks. For a few seconds she could make no sense of this unfamiliar sight. It was a small square case made of a patterned fabric she recognised, beige with black and red stripes like a tartan – a posh case made by a fancy London shop in its distinctive own-brand style. She'd seen articles like it in catalogues which offered expensive designer gear and she'd sneered at the thought of paying over the odds for the privilege of advertising some brand name.

She stepped up to the bed, staring in disbelief. There was a matching case like the first, only much bigger, on the floor behind the door. She prodded it with her foot and it fell on its side with a small weightless *crump* – empty. The contents of the case on the bed spilled carelessly across the covers, as if someone had rooted through them in a hurry. Shoes, a hairdryer and women's clothes lay in disarray. Mouse picked up an item and found she was holding a flimsy, apricot-gold slip with shoulder straps barely more substantial than dental floss. The musky perfume that had first assailed her seemed to wrap her in a suffocating cloud. A knot of nausea formed in her stomach and her heart began to thump.

Angrily she yanked open the wardrobe door. Josh's things – two suits in zipped-up covers and some neatly pressed shirts – had been shoved along the rail to make space for a collection of women's clothes. Skirts, jackets, blouses and several slinky almost-nothing dresses hung there in open defiance. What the frigging hell was going on?

But the answer to that was obvious and the import of her discovery was sending her into freak-out mode. She turned her face to the window and looked over the treetops to the building on the other side of the street, forcing herself to breathe deeply and slowly, just like Gavin had shown her. She had to be strong and keep herself under control. There was no need to panic but she must think this through.

Once she had regained her grip she made a quick tour of the flat, looking for further evidence of this unwelcome invasion. In the bathroom she found a hairbrush and a washbag bulging with female toiletries. The kettle was warm on the kitchen worktop and a lipstick-stained mug sat on the table, next to a small sideplate bearing three cigarette stubs. They too were marked with lipstick and had been smoked, Mouse noted, right down to the filters. And that was it, apart from a bowl of water on the floor by the fridge which Mouse almost stepped in.

She took a seat on the sofa in the living room, out of sight of the invader's possessions. She had to face the facts: a woman had taken up residence and it wasn't the Mistake, she was sure of that. Mouse didn't recognise any of the clothes in the wardrobe and there were dark hairs, not blonde, snagged in the bristles of the hairbrush. Not to mention that musty sickening perfume, and the cigarettes.

A female visitor. She didn't like that.

Maybe the woman was a relative. An old aunt up in London for the January sales.

An old aunt with a case full of cashmere and silk. Who wore gauzy openwork brassieres and thongs that wouldn't look out of place on a Brazilian beach. Whose skinny pampered body was splashed with perfume that screamed 'Rich bitch on heat'.

Aunt, my arse. He's got a new woman.

So she'd been right about the Mistake. The relationship with the blonde had been going off the rails big time, just as she'd suspected. She might have guessed something funny was up from what she'd been hearing these past few nights up the lane from Ridge House. Or, rather, what she *hadn't* been hearing. There'd been no noise from within at the end of last week and over the weekend. Then she'd remembered about the racing ban Josh had been landed with and reasoned that he'd gone away – with Her, of course. Mouse had not gone up there on Sunday night – a fourth night on the trot listening to nothing wasn't on, even for one as devoted as she was. But she'd tried last night, Monday, after she'd seen Josh's name in the papers listed as riding at Wetherby. And he'd been on his own in the house. She'd not thought it significant.

She did now. Maybe he'd booted Blondie out. It was what she'd been praying for. It was what she'd expected.

But she'd not expected a replacement for the Mistake already. It wasn't meant to happen this way.

I'm the replacement.

Or maybe, she reflected as she bit into a nail on her left hand – bit, actually, into the flesh around the cuticle as there wasn't enough nail to provide a satisfying crunch – maybe this intruder was just a tart. A short-term stopgap for a virile man who had to answer his needs. He'd just spent a year with that sickly sweet Susie after all, he'd need to sink his teeth into something more savoury.

All the same, Mouse didn't like it. A man could be excused perhaps, especially since he didn't realise that a new, passionate, devoted admirer was waiting in the wings. The tart was trash though, not fit for Josh to wipe his feet on.

Perhaps she'd take those smelly, filmy, disgusting clothes and set fire to them. Chuck them out of the window. Stuff them down the toilet and pull the chain.

No. She couldn't. But how she wanted to. Sometimes she wished she'd never met Gavin and 'made progress'. It was satisfying to let yourself go sometimes.

A sudden rattle from down the hall interrupted her train of thought. Then came a click and a sticky sound, as of one layer of varnished wood being separated from another. The front door was opening.

Mouse lurched to her feet.

She heard the rustle of plastic – shopping bags – the thud of the door being closed and the noise of footsteps coming down the hall. Towards her.

Mouse knew she must hide but she was frozen in indecision.

The sitting-room door was half closed, enough to prevent her catching sight of the newcomer – and vice versa. The footsteps, thank God, did not stop but carried on to the kitchen, a few feet further on and across the hall. Mouse heard the scrape of a chair, then the thump of bags being set down.

A scratchy, rattling sound was mixed in with the other noises – Mouse couldn't place it. Then came a voice, 'Are you thirsty, darling?'

It was the smoky, up-itself drawl of a southerner. The kind of voice that expected instant attention, that was accustomed to getting its own way. Mouse would have hated the sound of it anyway even if it hadn't belonged to the tart.

There came the sound of running water, the clink of china against metal and more rattling, as of claws on linoleum. The picture fell into place as a greedy lapping filled the air and Mouse remembered the bowl on the floor. The bloody woman must have a dog.

Jesus Christ, what am I going to do?

If she went right now she could slip down the hall and be out of the door unseen.

So let's go!

As Mouse took her first step, a small brown and cream speckled head appeared at knee height round the door and stared up at her with eyes gleaming like just-picked chestnuts.

The frigging dog.

The animal gave a small grunt of good cheer and padded towards her companionably.

What now?

Over the sound of shuffling plastic the tart's voice called, 'Suky, what are you up to?'

For a second the dog hesitated, then cocked its head winsomely at Mouse, expectation writ large on its furry face. But Mouse was immune to canine charm at the best of times and this could not be said to be that. Any moment now the tart would finish unpacking the shopping, then she'd come hunting her precious pooch.

'Wuff!' went the dog and pawed at Mouse's knee. She shoved it away with her foot but it came straight back at her, happy now that it had a response. Dogs never gave up – that was one of the things she hated about them. And this sort, frisky and eager, was the worst. Any second now the repulsive beast would stick its nose in her crotch.

'Just coming, darling,' called the voice from the kitchen. 'I've nearly finished.'

Mouse cast her eyes wildly around the room which, though a reasonable size, was hardly fashioned to provide hiding places. She could conceivably have hidden behind the full-length curtains or squeezed between the back of the sofa and the wall, waited there till the woman disappeared into the toilet and then slipped out. But not with a dog in the flat. She'd be discovered in seconds.

Then Mouse spotted her escape route – the balcony. She'd been out there once or twice on her visits and she knew it ran the full width of the room, with some six or seven feet out of view from inside. She could hide there and the dog wouldn't be able to get at her.

She stepped quickly to the french windows and turned the door handle. It wasn't kept locked apparently, there was no point, it being forty feet above the ground and quite unreachable. She slipped quickly through the gap into the chill of the outdoor air. The dog tried to follow her but she was alert to that, closing the door with her left hand and bending to flick out a finger with her right, smack on to the animal's inquisitive black nose. That stopped the stupid mutt in its tracks and she shut the door in its face with a small but comforting *click*.

Stepping smartly to her right, she eased her body into the recess that flanked the balcony doorway and leaned back against the wall of the building. She'd be completely invisible from the inside in this position. Thank God for that. She'd thought she'd been caught for certain.

She stood completely still, aware of her heart decelerating as her panic began to fade. She breathed in deeply, appreciating the cold clean winter atmosphere in her lungs. Was the air purer up here? It couldn't be, not with the London traffic belching up and down the street below. But it felt like it all the same.

After a few minutes she was less appreciative of the fresh air. A wind was gusting into her face and she could feel the chill of the brickwork behind her seeping through her thin sweater into her body. Where's my coat? she asked herself stupidly even though she knew the answer full well. It was lying on a chair in the corner of the sitting room behind her, while she was shivering out here. *What a prat!*

It didn't matter, she rationalised. The tart woman probably wouldn't notice and, even if she did, she'd just think it had always been there.

Oh yeah? A man-made hippy sheepskin coat with purple patterned pockets looks like it belongs in that flat?

Even so, why should the woman care? It was only a coat.

A coat with my keys in the pocket. And Josh's keys too. And my purse – with my bus pass.

Mouse shivered, as much with dismay as cold. Though, come to think of it, it was turning bitter. It dawned on her she might be stuck out here for hours, though the woman would surely have to walk the dog at some point.

Her ratty woollen scarf still hung round her neck and she wrapped it over her head to cover her ears.

Then she waited. What else could she do?

There wasn't much room in the weighing area at Leicester, not in the half-hour between races. Trainers, owners and officials hovered outside the jockeys' changing room, all with their own urgent business to conduct. Certainly there wasn't much space to manoeuvre round someone you'd rather avoid.

As he pushed through the doors into the glass-roofed anteroom, Josh was still worrying over the race he'd just finished, which he'd lost by two lengths after he'd thought the win was in his pocket. It always hurt to be caught on the run-in, especially when you had already passed the winner in the last couple of furlongs. When you allowed a horse to get back to you, it usually meant that you had hit the front too soon. On this occasion, Josh put it down to the fact that the winner had made an awful mistake at the last and Josh had had no choice but to go on. Fortunately it wasn't Ben who'd beaten him. He'd already pulled one back on the Irish jockey in the first race and this had looked like another. Was there anything he could have done? In all honesty, there hadn't been but it didn't stop Josh gnawing on the thought.

So his mind was elsewhere when he stepped into the room, straight into the path of a big man with crumpled, good-natured features. As their eyes met, the man's soft spaniel face changed in an instant to reveal an expression that was more like an angry bulldog. The chin jutted, the full lips pulled back in a snarl and the liquid brown eyes contracted to dots of red-rimmed black.

'Hi, Leo,' said Josh, though the words caught in his throat and the sound was lost in the hubbub of the busy room.

The trainer was holding a saddle and he thrust it between them, as if he'd like to jab its hard plastic edge into Josh's face. His head jerked in an involuntary nod of recognition and then he swirled past. The two men didn't touch but it was a near thing and, if they had, Josh would have been flattened against the plate-glass doors.

As he changed for the next race Josh pondered on this display of aggression from his former friend. It was in the nature of things that he and Leo should frequently be in the same place, on racecourses and at social functions and, once or twice, in TV studios. Leo's method of dealing with it was simply to look through Josh as if he didn't exist.

This aggressive display was something new. The mask of his public indifference had slipped, affording Josh a glimpse of the rage that seethed beneath. He wondered whether Leo had discovered that Annabelle was leaving him again. If so, he hoped Leo wasn't aware that she had moved into Josh's London flat. But, even if he had, so what? A husband who beat up his wife deserved to lose her.

Out of the corner of his eye he saw Ben O'Brien pulling on his silks for the next race. The Irishman had been more taciturn than ever since Josh had returned from his ban. Maybe their on-course competition was the reason. Ben was young, after all, and maybe he needed the psychological edge of disliking his chief rival. Or was he simply taking his cue from Leo, his boss and chief supplier of quality horses?

Whatever it was, in Josh's opinion Ben and Leo deserved one another. They were a right pair of tossers.

He lined up for the third race, a two-mile novice hurdle, on a pretty chestnut of Peter Stone's, Wide Water, so-called because the owner had once sailed the Atlantic single-handed. Peter had another runner in the race, Black Bull; the pair of them had run on the Flat and were here making their debuts over jumps. There wasn't anything between them on Flat form. Josh, with the choice of mounts, had opted for the smaller horse, Wide Water, on the basis of his schooling form. He'd seemed eager to jump, whereas Black Bull had rattled a few hurdles and seemed scared. Josh hoped he'd made the right choice, particularly since the ride on Black Bull had been given to Ben.

This wasn't the first time one of Peter's spares had been offered to Josh's rival and he knew there was no use in protesting. Peter had made it clear from the start of their association that he was in the business of saddling winners. Much as he might like to see Josh become champion, there was no room for sentiment when it came to finding the best available rider for a horse. And there was no doubt Ben was the best – or soon would be, Josh thought, when he himself retired.

Lining up for the start of the race in a freezing wind, it occurred to Josh that retirement couldn't come quickly enough if it meant missing days like this. The weather had turned bitter overnight and he was so cold he could scarcely feel his fingers. The scything gale seemed to breathe life into all his old injuries – the ankle infected after a kick from a bad-tempered novice chaser, the ribs broken when a horse had stood on his chest after a fall at Bangor and, worst of all, his left shoulder, the area on which he always seemed to land when thrown, which now throbbed with a bone-deep ache.

The tapes flew up and the twelve-strong field headed off into the gloom of the winter afternoon, past the stands on the outward journey. Josh tucked into the pack and tried to focus on the task of the moment. Forget pain and retirement, just concentrate on getting home ahead of the rest.

But it wasn't easy to blot out the thought of Ben O'Brien when he could see his lean and wiry figure a couple of lengths ahead, nudging his barrel-chested mount around in the bunch at the head of the pack. As was often the case, it seemed the excitement of the race had given Black Bull the courage he'd lacked in training. Or maybe it was Ben, giving the horse confidence.

Josh concentrated on his own mount, squeezing his knees into the horse's sides and feeling him respond immediately. There was nothing like the feel of a horse quickening into an obstacle, knowing the animal was on a perfect stride and enjoying himself.

It was one of the peculiarities of racing at Leicester that the ground on the hurdle course was heavier than on the steeplechase track. Today it was verging on the bottomless, the accumulation of three days' rain, now cut short by the sudden cold snap. The race promised to be a true test of stamina.

Down the long slope of the back straight the field began to string out, some animals already finding the conditions a struggle. Josh hugged the rail in third, pleased now to be out of the pack. Things could get quite hairy at the bottom of the back stretch where the course narrowed; sometimes just one stumble could bring down a group of horses, all flying downhill in a bunch.

As they turned for home, Josh cursed at the sight of Black Bull stretching ahead in front. From ten lengths back, it looked as though Ben would take an awful lot of catching. Nevertheless, Josh had no intention of giving up. The finishing line was four furlongs and four hurdles off, anything could happen.

Wide Water was coping well, as yet showing no signs of flagging – unlike the horse lying second who suddenly lost impetus, clipped the first hurdle in the back straight and subsided slowly to the ground. Josh wished fervently that something similar would happen to Black Bull but he had no expectations.

They were heading downhill into the dip that preceded the energy-sapping slope up to the stands and the finishing post. Josh had been on horses who had simply run out of steam at this point too many times to count. As Wide Water missed his footing in the mud and made a mess of the next hurdle Josh expected a similar result.

To his surprise the horse plugged on. There was steel as well as style in his delicate appearance – a good sign for the future. But it was this race that concerned Josh right now. The gap between himself and Black Bull was closing, but not fast enough. Then halfway up the long run-in, as they squelched through the puddles, he sensed Black Bull beginning to falter. Ben was giving the horse every assistance but it seemed emptied of all strength.

We can do this! The thought burst into Josh's head and he gave his mount a slap of encouragement with his stick. Remarkably, Wide Water lengthened his stride, finding something extra just when it was most needed.

The pair of them caught Ben and Black Bull just before the line and won by half a length.

All Josh's aches and pains vanished in an instant. It didn't even seem cold any more. Now his score was 113.

The bright winter afternoon was fading into evening as Mouse stood shivering on the balcony. This was not how she had imagined spending her day in London. She'd give anything to be on the train heading back home. She couldn't stay here much longer.

She'd been outside for ages – about three-quarters of an hour by her watch. In that time she'd been aware of sounds from within as the tart's voice carried through the windows. The woman seemed to keep up a steady stream of conversation. Mouse guessed she was talking on the phone, punctuated by commands issued at the dog.

Sometimes the voice seemed louder, as if the woman were walking around, talking into a mobile phone.

'Jenny, guess what? I've done it. I've buggered off and this time I swear I'm not going back. I can't tell you what a relief it is to get a life again.'

The tart was doing her smoky chuckle, driving nails of irritation into Mouse's skull.

'No, darling, I don't just mean a sex life. Though that does loom large, I admit.'

It was bad enough knowing this monster was screwing Josh without it being rubbed in her face like this.

Mercifully, the dog started up again, drowning out the woman's conversation. It had been fractious throughout the time Mouse had been out on the balcony, given to short but intense bouts of barking, just on the other side of the glass.

She heard the tart finally wrap up her conversation then address the animal in irritated tones. 'For heaven's sake, Suky, what's got into you?'

Mouse could have provided the answer to that. The dog was still chuntering on about the woman he'd met who wouldn't play with him and had flicked him on the nose when she'd gone through the window and wouldn't let him follow. Thank God dogs couldn't make themselves understood in any but the most general fashion. Mouse was praying that the tart would misinterpret the racket and take the animal for a walk to foul the pavement. That would be her chance.

The barking opened up with renewed intensity and the glass door rattled as something banged against it from the other side. Claws skittered against the panes.

'You don't give up, do you?' came the woman's voice loud and clear. 'I'll let you have one little peek but there's nothing out there, I promise you.'

Oh no!

Mouse was paralysed with fear. She had nowhere to hide. The recess behind the door was no more than nine inches deep. The moment the woman looked to the side of the doorway she would see her.

Nevertheless Mouse pressed her body hard against the wall behind her, knowing it was futile. Much as she wished it, she knew the unyielding brick would not magically open and swallow her up.

The glass in the windows rattled as someone tugged the door from the inside. The dog's barking had stopped, replaced by an excited keening as the animal's impatience rose to a new pitch. Peering round the edge of the recess, Mouse saw the shaft of the door handle dip like a railway signal as it was turned from the inside.

What am I going to do?

A scrape of wood on wood and Mouse jerked her head back.

The tart's voice rang out loudly. 'Out you go, you daft dog. Just for a moment – it's absolutely perishing.'

There was the skitter of paws on the stone of the balcony as the animal emerged. To Mouse's surprise it did not immediately appear in front of her, leaping and barking. It must have begun its exploration of this new territory in the other direction. It was only a matter of time, of course – a thirty-second reprieve.

Then she saw the tart, the back of her anyway, as a woman of above average height with dark shoulder-length hair stepped up to the balustrade and looked down into the street. In a thick cream cable-knit sweater and black slacks, she didn't look like Mouse's mental image of a siren in see-through lingerie. Carelessly draped around her shoulders was one of those scarf-cum-shawl things in pastel blue – a pashmina, Mouse knew.

'How simply marvellous,' the woman drawled, dragging

out the vowel sounds in her posh southern voice that acted on Mouse like fingernails on a blackboard.

Maybe that was what made her do it. That and the way the tart had spoken on the phone, like having Josh was her right.

Anyway, the stupid bitch was asking for it, standing there.

Somewhere, from far off, sounded a yelp of doggy delight, but being spotted by the dog was an irrelevance now.

The tart might be tall but she was stick-thin with no flesh on her at all. Mouse took hold of her round her skinny thighs and straightened up, flipping her over the parapet and out into the clean winter air.

The carriage wasn't crowded and there was no one sitting near Susie in the London-bound train. After all the fuss she'd made about not wanting to go to South Africa, she was pleased to be on her way. Josh had been right. Things had been getting to her.

One thing in particular.

She took the envelope from her bag and considered it. Maybe she'd got it wrong and it wasn't one of those.

On the other hand . . . bog-standard brown office stationery, a second-class stamp, her name printed just like the other one: Ms Susan Merrivale. Her birth name but not the one she went by now. She'd changed it to Brown, Brenda's married name, when she'd gone to live with her. It was nice and anonymous. There were many more Browns in the world than Merrivales.

She ripped it open, tearing the envelope, surprising herself.

Dear Susie Sausage

Have you told Josh yet?

Does he know all the gory details about Mummy Sausage and little Sharon Sausage, too?

Why don't you spare him and get out of his life?

Oh God. The sight of Sharon's name on the slip of paper turned her stomach over. Whoever was doing this was evil.

The sensible thing, the only safe thing to do was to tell Josh everything. But would it be safe? He would look at her differently afterwards, that was certain.

If she and Josh were really going to be together for ever then, of course, he had to know. But not now. She wasn't strong enough. And, anyway, were they going to be together for ever? She didn't know.

Maybe she'd tell him next week when she got back.

It was cruel tormenting her like this. Who was writing these letters? How had they found out about her? And how did they know where she lived?

She sat deep in thought for a long time as the train rattled south.

Mouse stayed low, ducking her head below the stone barrier, frozen in fearful expectation. She waited for screams, the smack of flesh on concrete, cries of alarm – something. But the only sound that floated up to her from below was the regular pulse of the traffic.

A wetness on her cheek roused her. The bloody dog was licking her, cheerful and eager to play. Stupid animal.

She shut it out on the balcony, grabbed her coat and fled.

Ten minutes later she was sitting on a tube train amidst the usual assortment of mind-your-own-business types.

She'd met no one on the staircase, nor on the steps outside. She'd glanced to her left as she left the building – at a brisk walk, not running, trying to look purposeful but innocent, for the benefit of witnesses. But there had been no witnesses. No group of horrified spectators, gawping over a broken corpse. Nothing and no one. Just the usual row of parked cars and, though she'd not broken stride, a scarf of pale blue snagged on the basement railing, flapping in the stiff breeze.

It was hard to believe anything unusual had happened back at the flat. Maybe she'd imagined it; in the past sometimes she had got muddled over what was real and what had just gone on in her head.

She looked at her watch. Unbelievably, she was going to make her regular train.

It was a hard slog at the end of a day's racing, with heavy traffic all the way from Leicester to London, but for once Josh wasn't grumbling. He'd finished the afternoon with three victories; the magic of Wide Water's run seemed to have rubbed off on his ride in the last, and Ben for once had not scored any. The lad had looked sick after Josh had caught Black Bull on the line – he'd probably not even seen Wide Water coming – and he'd not looked like winning for the rest of the afternoon. To be frank, the Irishman had been pretty lacklustre, and long may it last.

Only thirteen behind. Josh longed to tell Susie about it but she was on her way by now. To be honest, given that he was spending the evening with Annabelle, it was probably just as well that they were out of touch.

Eventually the sluggish river of vehicles flowed through the familiar bottleneck of the high street just north of Arlington Mansions. At least he wasn't travelling in the opposite direction, he thought, as he turned right through the logjam of cars making their way out of town. Parking spaces were reserved for residents in front of the building and, maybe due to the warning notices threatening to clamp the unauthorised, it was usually possible to find a space. Josh located a spot at the far end and walked towards the middle entrance to the block.

He wasn't particularly looking forward to seeing Annabelle. Not so long ago it would have been the height of his ambition to be serenaded for an evening by her husky chuckle, topping up her glass, lighting her cigarettes and waiting for the moment when she'd finally open her arms to him. But not any more. It was almost disloyal to think it but, now the lovelight had faded, he wondered how she had ever had a hold on him. He hoped to God he'd never feel this way about Susie.

An empty police car was parked on the yellow road hatching that marked the emergency entrance and, as he climbed the steps to the front door, he noticed an area just in front of the basement railings that had been cordoned off with emergency-services masking tape. He didn't take much notice, his mind on the evening ahead.

Almost as soon as he turned the key in the lock – the spare he'd retrieved from home after giving Annabelle the one he usually carried – he was aware of movement in the hall in front of him. He stepped inside, to be confronted by the caretaker, Archie, and Nigel Johnson, a middle-aged civil servant who lived on the ground floor with his mother.

The pair of them gazed at him with what appeared to be excitement and relief.

'Here he is – I told you he'd turn up,' shouted Archie.

'We've been trying to get hold of you,' Nigel Johnson announced accusingly.

'What's going on?' asked Josh.

The pair of them fell silent as, from the open door of the ground floor flat behind them, stepped a uniformed police officer.

He was a young man with a nasty pimple flush on the point of his nose. The expression on his face, however, was far from comic.

Josh listened in increasing disbelief as the policeman broke the terrible news.

In the hotel the next morning – there'd been no question of his staying at the flat after what had happened – Josh devoured the newspapers. The headline of the leading tabloid set the tone: TRAINER'S WIFE IN SUICIDE PLUNGE. The story that followed recounted the discovery of Annabelle's body beneath the balcony of his flat, and went on to describe her relationship with Josh. Though Susie was out of the country, there was no way he could shield her from news like this.

He called her at once.

'Sweetheart, something awful's happened. Annabelle's dead.'

A beat. 'Annabelle? Oh Josh, I'm sorry.' Her voice was rich with sympathy.

'She was staying at the flat and fell off the balcony.'

'The flat?'

'My flat. Arlington Mansions. She wanted to get away from Leo so I said she could stay there.'

Then he blurted out the whole story. How he'd met Annabelle at Newbury and she'd shown him her bruises and he'd given her the key so she'd be safe from Leo.

'I was going to tell you all about it but I didn't want to upset you. She said she had nowhere else to go.'

'I see,' she said but she didn't sound certain. Her voice was small and distant.

'I should have told you, Susie.'

'No, it's OK, Josh. I mean, it's not OK, it's terrible. How could it have happened?'

That, of course, was the question, one that had kept him awake all night.

What the hell had Annabelle been doing? The question endlessly chased its tail around his head. The fall must have been an accident – he couldn't imagine Annabelle killing herself intentionally. At least, he didn't think he could. She hadn't sounded depressed. On the contrary, when he'd spoken to her yesterday morning she'd sounded positively light-hearted. Almost too light-hearted for a woman who was leaving her husband.

You went to London to check up on her. Remember?

He still didn't believe it could be suicide. She was too squeamish, for a start. Even though she called herself a countrywoman, Annabelle would blanch at the sight of blood.

But she didn't cut her wrists, did she? She took a flyer off your balcony.

Maybe it was something to do with the dog. The animal had been discovered out on the balcony, yapping its head off. Perhaps it had jumped up onto the parapet ledge and Annabelle had slipped trying to get it down. Was that likely?

He didn't have a clue.

Chapter Five

Leo sleepwalked through the days. He'd been up to London to identify Annabelle's body and talk to the police – and to see the place where she had died. It had all seemed unreal. Particularly viewing the corpse. That pale-faced doll was not the Annabelle he knew.

He'd rushed back to the yard as soon as he could. It was the only thing that made sense, marching to the rhythm of the racing day and the demands of the fixture list. Horses knew eff-all and cared less about the troubles of men and women, and that was how it should be.

His staff were a different matter. Some wouldn't meet his eye. One or two girls hugged him and cried, so he'd ended up comforting them instead. Tim Daniels kept urging him to take days off, which was the last thing he wanted to do. And, wherever he went, conversation dwindled into embarrassed silence.

Only Ben's reaction seemed genuine to Leo. He'd grasped Leo's hand and said nothing but Leo could feel the intensity of emotion in his grip and see it in the liquid depth of his gaze. But the boy didn't blub, even though Leo could see he was close to breaking down. Leo wasn't surprised. Ben had lived in their house when he'd first come over from Ireland and Annabelle had looked after him like a mother. No wonder the lad was cut up.

The funeral kept Leo busy, what with relatives and friends unseen for years turning up to see her buried. They all had questions and by the time he'd repeated some answers he almost believed them himself.

'She'd just taken a few days off in London,' he said, and why not? No one could contradict him since he'd destroyed her farewell note telling him she was buggering off for good. Besides, he'd only found it after he knew she was dead and that made it seem somehow irrelevant.

'Josh Swallow's an old friend of hers.' There was no point in denying that, they'd all read the papers.

'It must have been some kind of freak accident.' Well, what else could it have been?

She could have been blind drunk, for a start.

Or she could have jumped. But why? In remorse for treating him like dirt? No chance.

Or –? He just didn't know.

All he knew was that just a few days ago he was wishing her dead and now she was. The guilt was like a stone in his guts.

Susie was aware she was hiding by extending her stay in South Africa. She ought to return and give Josh what support she could. After all, he'd simply loaned Arlington Mansions to an old friend and there'd been a terrible accident.

But the old friend was the former love of his life. And

he'd not told her about the arrangement. What's more, he'd installed Annabelle on the very day she herself was flying out of the country. She couldn't help feeling suspicious. If the accident hadn't occurred, Josh would have had a whole week to make merry with his former love and she would have been none the wiser.

Furthermore, Josh was not the kind of man for a one-week fling. If his romance with Annabelle had been rekindled then Susie knew it would have been over for her. She'd often compared herself to Annabelle and she knew she didn't measure up. In looks, sophistication and knowledge of Josh's world, she was sure the other woman had the edge. And, of course, the pair of them shared the kind of fraught romantic past that binds people together for the long run.

While she was having these thoughts, Carmen Cook had told her she ought to stay on after her painting was finished. Susie liked Carmen. She was a big ball of energy with an enthusiasm for any number of things, chief among them British racing. She had taken Susie under her wing.

'Stick around and get some sun. We'll have a few days at the beach.' Carmen owned several houses. One was a cottage in a fishing village on the Eastern Cape. It was tempting but she'd told Josh she'd only be away for a week.

'It's OK, sweetheart,' he'd said when she told him of the offer. 'Things aren't great here. You stay there and enjoy yourself.'

She felt bad for him but he'd insisted.

There was another thing – she was sure no one in the Eastern Cape knew anything about Susie Sausage.

*

Josh stared up into the darkness. It was pitch black in this room, except on rare cloudless nights when a full moon crept beneath the hem of the thick curtain. Right now he couldn't even make out the white lampshade which hung from the middle of the ceiling. What was the time? Two, maybe, or half past.

Outside he could hear the wind stirring the branches of the winter-bare trees at the bottom of the paddock and, from the hill at the front of the house, came the occasional rumble of a passing vehicle. Inside, the old timbers creaked in response to the prompting of the central heating pipes. Close up, there was the tick of the clock and the drip of a bathroom tap whose washer he never seemed to have the energy to fix.

What he couldn't hear, however, was the soft breath of another human being, the regular inhale-exhale of the woman he loved lying by his side. Was it because Susie no longer lay beside him that the night seemed so black?

He missed her, missed her in the way he'd missed Annabelle when she'd returned to Leo. He didn't like making the comparison, it seemed inappropriate in the circumstances, but it told him how important Susie had become to him. He'd had plenty of female companions in his life but only two of them had become part of him.

But Susie was still in South Africa. She'd completed her first commission and had been staying by the sea. Now she had embarked on another painting. He could hardly complain, as he'd urged her to make the most of the opportunity, but he was beginning to wonder when she would return. There was something elusive about her he couldn't pin down, a part of her she was holding back. He hoped he hadn't lost his chance to discover it.

With these thoughts in mind he'd spent time amongst the clutter in her attic studio, looking afresh at her collections of bottles and old household appliances and musty, filmy silk scarves from charity shops. 'I'm planning some big still-life paintings,' she'd told him when he'd asked her about them. 'You'll see.' He wondered if he ever would.

He'd discovered a stash of her paintings, half a dozen large completed canvases stacked against one wall. They were the big formless abstracts whose appeal had always eluded him. Not now though. He thought of the grades of tone gliding over one another, building from below, like blocks of pain sliding together as numbed tissue came to life and nerve ends shrieked. If he were a painter, that's what he would try to paint, the degrees of pain he'd felt after falling from horses and having his bones reset.

Surely she'd come back for these paintings – but when?

As he looked into the blackness he considered the disagreeable nature of the next few weeks. Like the forthcoming inquest into Annabelle's death. Who could blame Susie for staying away?

Josh was not looking forward to the proceedings due to take place at the Westminster Coroner's Court. His affair with Annabelle, though common knowledge in racing circles, had not been of interest to a wider public. Her death, however, had changed all that. Now the tabloids had dragged it into the open and dressed it up as only they knew how. And though things had died down in the weeks since the accident, the inquest was bound to start it up again. Even one of the broadsheets had trailed the court date under the headline THE JOCKEY, THE TRAINER AND THE FALLEN FILLY – which had provoked a protest from Annabelle's family and thus added further fuel to the flames.

Colin Smart, his solicitor, had said it might be possible for Josh to avoid appearing in court. He could ask if the coroner would accept a written statement which could be read out in his absence, thus minimising his exposure. But Josh had declined to try. It looked like the coward's way out.

Whatever conclusions were drawn at the inquest – and Colin had pointed out that it was not a trial – Josh had every expectation of being found guilty in the eyes of the world. After all, he was the man who had broken the Lovalls' marriage not once but twice. Why else, people would ask, had Annabelle taken refuge in his flat? Their affair must still have been going on. This was the conclusion the general public would be bound to draw.

But pining for his reputation was not what was keeping him awake at night. What did that matter compared to the death of a woman he'd once loved? He had offered Annabelle a place of sanctuary and her blood – by inference or association or some past crime – was now on his hands. In some strange, inexplicable way he knew himself to be guilty. If it hadn't been for him, Annabelle would never have left Leo. She'd still be happily married. Certainly, if it hadn't been for him she wouldn't have been in a flat with a balcony and forty-foot drop on to iron railings.

I'm sorry, Annabelle. I was only trying to help – to be your rock.

Some rock.

He was fully awake now, with no hope of getting back to sleep. He could get up, make a cup of tea, watch videos of the horses he was due to ride later. Instead he picked up the phone.

It had barely rung before it was answered. 'Wylie,' said a voice in a soft west of England burr. Tony Wylie's phone was a physical extension of himself, answered in a reflex at all hours of the day or night. Josh had no idea when the agent slept but the wee hours of the morning had always been a good time to talk to him, before the bustle of the day ahead. These days he talked to him almost every night.

They never discussed Annabelle's death, however, or Susie's absence or Ben O'Brien's lead in the jockey's championship, except when such matters were relevant to Josh's riding programme. Like the timing of the inquest, for example. Colin had said the proceedings were liable to last for the morning, which meant Josh could get to Chepstow in time for the last couple of races on the card and Tony had booked him rides accordingly. Then Josh had had second thoughts. Suppose the inquest took all day? He wouldn't want to leave until things had been brought to a proper conclusion. Accordingly, Tony had pulled him off a couple of horses. He'd leave Chepstow to Ben – it couldn't be helped.

But though Josh's conversations with his agent were confined to racing matters, that still left a multitude of things to discuss. Often their early-hours chats lasted for an hour or more. And when he finally put down the phone Josh found he could sleep for the remainder of the night. Somehow the discussions of prospective rides, the form of a trainer, the mistakes of the handicapper – the business trivia of his professional life – seemed to blot out the regrets and fears that kept him awake. It was as if Tony offered a weird kind of therapy and Josh was grateful.

'I'm glad you rang,' said Tony without preamble. 'I've got some Cheltenham news. I reckon I've found you one for the Champion Bumper.'

'Yes?' Josh was suddenly cheered. The Cheltenham Festival was less than three weeks off and the scramble for the right rides was in full swing. He had good prospects lined up for most of the major races but there were still some gaps. 'What is it?'

'Vendange, a French name. It means grape harvest.'

Josh couldn't give tuppence what the name meant, as Tony well knew, but the agent liked to spin things out when he had good news. So this was a promising sign.

'He's a five-year-old at Billy Christie's yard,' Tony continued. 'Billy says he's raw but full of promise. You can go and ride him work if you like but he's yours anyway. Apparently the owner asked for you.'

'Who's that?'

Tony paused but his answer came off a straight bat. 'Carmen Cook.'

Susie's South African patron. She must have put in a word for him.

'I thought she only raced Flat horses over here.'

'So did I. This is her first potential jumper. She's got high hopes for it and so has Billy.'

It was easy to get back to sleep after that.

*

It was Brenda, surprisingly, who made up Susie's mind to return, which probably wasn't her aunt's intention. During the phone call Brenda had rabbited on about the scandal of Annabelle's death, which had jumped back into the news following the announcement of the inquest date.

'Thank God you've left that jockey,' she'd said. 'All those jockeys cheat on women, just like they fix their races.' Brenda had a low opinion of a man's ability to remain faithful, fuelled by her own short-lived marriage.

As Susie listened to that hectoring voice, familiar to her from daily exposure throughout her adolescence, a thought occurred.

'You've not been writing me letters, have you, Aunt?'

'Eh?' Brenda sounded genuinely surprised.

'Letters addressed to Susan Merrivale.'

There was a shocked silence. 'What do you mean, girl? Nobody knows about that.'

'Somebody does. Or knows enough to make mischief.'

'Oh dear, Susan. That's horrible.'

Susie hadn't really thought it was her aunt, much as Brenda might want to separate her from Josh. Now, listening to her, it was plain she'd had nothing to do with the vicious little notes. The thing was, there were only three people in the world who knew enough to write them and she and Brenda were two of the trio. It couldn't, surely, be the third. The letters he'd written to her were entirely different.

Josh seemed overwhelmed when Susie rang to say she'd be back in time to accompany him to the inquest.

'That's fantastic, Susie. Just get yourself back here. You

don't have to come to the inquest, though. There'll be press there and all Leo's lot. You'd be better off out of it.'

'Sounds like you'll be outnumbered.'

'It's OK. My solicitor will keep me company.'

But that was hardly the same thing. She couldn't let Josh face the music alone. Besides, the inquest was designed to get to the truth of Annabelle's death and she was curious – much more than curious – about what had really happened.

Only one area of Josh's life had given him any pleasure during the misery of the last few weeks. He'd noticed in the past that when times were tough – when his mother died, when Annabelle left him – race riding helped him get through. Though his mind might be flooded with dismal thoughts, by the time he had stepped into the changing room and begun the familiar routine of preparation, his troubles could be put to one side, if only for the afternoon. And that's the way it had been since Annabelle's death and Susie's departure.

Today at Warwick was no different, except that, with the promise of Susie's support at the inquest, the burden he had to unload was that bit lighter. Even Peter Stone picked up on it as he legged Josh into the saddle.

'Let me guess,' he said. 'Your bird's bleedin' well come back.'

Peter was the son of a London taxi driver who'd sent him to work in a stables at the age of fifteen – because he was knee high to a flea, as Peter put it. He'd been phenomenally successful, first as a rider and now as a trainer. And though he'd performed both functions for some of the most refined people in the land, he expressed himself in forthright Cockney at all times.

'I'm right, aren't?' Stone continued. 'You're looking perky all of a sudden.'

'You obviously know more than I do.'

Stone laughed. 'You bet. I know that little blonde bird's better than you deserve. And I know you're sitting on the best jumper in this ring.' He patted his runner with a big square hand. 'So you'd better not cock up, had you?'

It wasn't clear whether he was referring to Josh's love life or the race ahead. Both probably. In either case, Josh didn't need telling. If he got another chance with Susie he swore to himself he wouldn't blow it.

As for the race, that was much easier to deal with. His mount, Mr Macready, was an ideal horse for this course, nimble and sure-footed, with plenty of stamina. He had a tendency to jump to the left which, though a drawback on many tracks, was a positive advantage on the anti-clockwise course at Warwick. What counted here was the ability to jump the five big fences set close together on the far side. Josh had had some nasty moments on less talented animals but he had every confidence in his mount today.

He was further buoyed by events at the meeting so far. He'd had a winner in the first, a smooth ride round the hurdle course on Little Ashley, a horse who'd been transformed by wearing blinkers. That had put him on 132, just ten behind Ben, the closest it had been since the start of the season. And if that wasn't enough cause for celebration, he'd sat out the next and watched the Irishman fail to bring home the hot favourite in a novice chase. Though leading the field at the last, Ben's horse had pecked at the fence and he'd been unseated, like a seven-pound claimer. The incident had brought a loud cheer from the jockeys watching on the closed-circuit TV in the changing room. It struck Josh that Ben had rather gone off the boil lately. It wasn't really surprising; it was impossible to perform at your peak the whole year round.

Ben's fortuitous dip in form was all the more reason for Josh to keep up the pressure. The race ahead was a case in point. This time it was Ben who was without a ride. Whatever happened, Josh swore he wouldn't give his rival the pleasure of seeing Mr Macready caught on the run-in. He'd carry the ruddy animal over the line himself if he had to.

But Mr Macready had no need of such unlikely heroics. He made light work of the heavy ground and Josh was able to drop him in behind the leaders for the first circuit, where he cruised comfortably, eating the fences. Going down the hill on the far side for the second time, he moved up on his rivals, taking the five fast-arriving obstacles clinically, to round the final bend in the lead.

There were two fences remaining in the home straight and Josh was aware of a horse arriving fast on his outside. Clearing the penultimate obstacle, Josh risked a quick glance to his right. The fancied grey, Snowball's Chance, was just a few yards adrift, looking strong. For a split second Josh thought he was about to be caught. And Ben would be back in the weighing room watching. Even the taciturn Irishman might manage a smile if that's how things turned out.

But both Josh and Mr Macready relished a challenge. It was this kind of competition Josh would miss most when he retired. He set to work as he always did, crouching low in the saddle, squeezing tight with his legs and making sure his weight was behind Mr Macready's shoulders. They flew the last in style and had the upper hand twenty yards before the line.

As Josh trotted his admirable companion to the winner's enclosure, his off-the-course troubles could not have been further from his mind. Just one thought dominated as he contemplated Ben's reduced lead.

I'm down to single figures.

The phone rang in Leo's study. Rang and rang. Three feet away, Leo stared at it. Waited hazily for it to stop. Poured himself another drink while it droned on.

Only one person would have the patience to hang on so long. He supposed he should answer the call – he couldn't hide for ever.

'Leo.' The familiar voice was full of warmth and intimacy. 'You're not drinking yourself into a stupor, are you, you silly bugger?'

Was he a silly bugger? If his half-brother said so, then he supposed he must be. No one else he knew was so clever. No one else could read him like a book.

'I'm just ringing in case you want to talk.'

'Why should I want to talk?'

He didn't believe in all that bleeding-heart therapy. Soppy stuff. An invitation to bawl like a baby in front of someone else. And when you'd done, poured out all your anger and self-pity and guilt, did you feel any better? And did the person you'd bled all over think any better of you?

No to both questions. He knew because he'd been there last time Annabelle had left him. And this time there was no chance she'd be coming back, so he'd have to get used to how he felt all on his own.

'Leo, did you hear me?'

'No, I don't want to talk.'

'OK. That's fine. But if you change your mind, I'll drop everything. You know that, don't you?'

'Thanks,' Leo mumbled. He put down the receiver. He hoped he would be strong enough never to make that call.

Chapter Six

Though a substantial late-Victorian building, Westminster Coroner's Court was dwarfed by nearby modern edifices of red brick. It reminded Susie of an old-fashioned town hall, with its carpeted staircase and large oils of council worthies. It was like stepping into another world, where civic duty and time-honoured social values called men to account.

That was fine by her. She was accompanying Josh to give him support, of course, but also to satisfy her own curiosity.

A middle-aged woman approached them but was beaten to it by a young man with ginger sideburns and a patterned waistcoat beneath his jacket – Colin Smart, Josh's solicitor.

'It's all right,' he said to the court official, 'I'll take them up.'

'You're cutting it a bit fine,' Colin muttered as they mounted the stairs. 'I think he's about to start.'

He ushered them through solid double doors into a room somewhat smaller than a tennis court which seemed full to bursting. Susie and Josh were guided to the back and spaces found for them on wooden benches like church pews. A sea of faces turned towards them, Annabelle's family out in force, Susie assumed. She found herself looking into a face that seemed familiar and realised it must belong to Annabelle's younger sister, Jenny, who lived in France. Though the sister was considerably plumper, there was no denying the resemblance. Susie was pleased to see Jenny return Josh's nervous nod of acknowledgement – he'd said she was by far the nicest of Annabelle's relatives.

Susie registered white and duck-egg blue panelling curving up to a high ceiling. A large rectangular skylight augmented the lights which hung in clusters above the crowded tables and benches, much needed in the dim late-February morning. Three muffled knocks sounded and, at an officer's bidding, the spectators shuffled to their feet, like a church congregation.

A short man in a charcoal grey suit entered from a door in the far corner of the room. This, Susie assumed, was the coroner, Dr Jamieson. His hair was greying but he was boyish of face and he moved with vigour as he took his seat at a raised desk. He peered through rimless spectacles at the table immediately in front of him and appeared to register surprise at the number of bodies sitting around it, notebooks open. This was the press table, according to Colin, who was sitting at the next table where there were still empty spaces reserved, according to a notice, for legal representatives.

Susie was conscious of Josh's leg trembling slightly as it pressed into hers in the cramped pew. She sought his hand and squeezed it reassuringly. The poor guy was scared stiff.

She, on the other hand, found herself looking forward to events with keen anticipation.

As proceedings got underway and the coroner's cultured tones were broadcast around the room, Josh began to feel less nervous. It was apparent that Jamieson was keen to make things as painless as possible for the dead woman's family and friends. Calling Jenny to the witness stand, he took her through a statement obviously intended to provide a picture of the kind of person her sister had been. He described her as 'a woman of thirty-five, lively and sociable, an animal lover who enjoyed horse riding and was devoted to her dog, Suky', inviting Jenny to agree with him, which she did, muttering 'Yes' into the microphone.

'She had been happily married for the past seven years?'

Jenny hesitated. 'Yes,' she said finally. 'She'd been married for seven years.'

'Happily married?'

'That's not really for me to say.' Her voice dropped almost to a whisper. 'There was a period when she lived apart from Leo.' She looked away from the coroner to the front row of spectators, to the unmistakable dome of Leo Lovall's large head, then spoke louder. 'She went back two years ago and as far as I know she was perfectly happy.'

Jamieson next called Leo, who declared in ringing tones, 'Annabelle and I went through a rocky patch but we got over all that. Our marriage was stronger than ever.'

Josh couldn't tell if Jamieson was convinced. The coroner referred to the pile of papers by his elbow and asked when Leo had last seen his wife.

'The morning of the day she died. I went up to the house after first lot. Annabelle was in the kitchen and we had breakfast together. Like we usually do.'

'Were you aware that she was going up to London that day?'

'No. But she didn't always tell me what she was up to. It didn't bother me.'

'It didn't bother you that she packed two cases of clothes and took her dog with her?'

'No. She must have decided to take off for a couple of days on the spur of the moment. She wouldn't necessarily have told me till later.'

So that was how Leo was going to play it. That he and Annabelle were a devoted couple with their own lives to lead. Josh could see the reporters busily making notes.

Proceedings moved on to the grisly details of Annabelle's death. A court official read statements from the resident who had discovered the body in the forecourt of Arlington Mansions and the ambulance officer who had attended the emergency call.

A hospital pathologist took the stand next. He looked like a TV presenter, with luxuriant blond hair and an unlikely tan, but he spoke precisely of a broken pelvis, injuries to the skull and the deep puncture wounds caused by the spiked iron railings on to which she had fallen. Alcohol was present in the bloodstream, he said, consistent in his opinion with the consumption of four or five glasses of wine.

So Annabelle had been drinking – it didn't surprise Josh

in the least. But Annabelle was accustomed to alcohol; would four or five glasses of wine have been enough to cause her to fall over the balcony?

'Was there anything else about Mrs Lovall's condition that struck you as significant?' prompted the Coroner.

'She had extensive bruising on her right shoulder and down her ribcage which was completely unrelated to her recent injuries.'

'So these bruises had been sustained before the fall?'

'Considerably before. From the nature of the marks I'd estimate some two or three weeks.'

Yes. Josh knew all too well that such bruising existed – it was the reason, after all, why he was sitting here – but hearing it officially entered into the record somehow confirmed his actions in offering Annabelle a bolt hole from her abusive marriage.

His thoughts were so focused on this track that he almost missed the next exchange.

'Anything else?' the coroner asked.

'Indeed.' The pathologist paused. 'The lady was approximately four weeks pregnant.'

The small courtroom was not the kind of forum in which people might be expected to show their emotions. But this statement had an effect on the closely packed benches of spectators. First came a profound silence, like a collective suspension of breath, then throats were cleared and heads turned as the information was digested. Josh, like many, looked instinctively towards Leo but the rear view of his head gave no clue as to his reaction. Though sentiment had no place in their present relationship, Josh felt for his former friend. To lose not only his wife but also his unborn child. Poor sod.

He became conscious that Susie's grey eyes were examining him intently, searching his face like a lost traveller scrutinising a map. He was taken aback. Surely she didn't think that Annabelle's pregnancy was anything to do with him? But suddenly it was obvious – that's exactly what she was thinking. She's wondering whether I'm the child's father – along with half the people in this courtroom.

That's ridiculous. I wasn't interested in Annabelle like that – not any more.

You thought about it though. At that hotel in Newbury you considered inviting her upstairs for an encore of All Our Yesterdays.

But I didn't. I took the damned woman home and never laid a finger on her.

Susie's expression had changed; now she was nudging his arm and indicating with a nod of her head that he should look towards the coroner's bench. In the turmoil following the revelations of the last witness he had not heard them call his name.

All eyes followed Josh's progress to the witness box, many of them hostile, others simply curious. He was used to being the focus of attention on the racecourse, striding into the parade ring with whip in hand or standing up in the stirrups in triumph after booting a winner home. Here, in his funeral suit in the claustrophobic atmosphere of the crowded courtroom, he felt more trepidation than before any big race. As he took the oath he fought the impulse to gabble the words. This was his chance to put his side of the story. He mustn't blow it.

From this standpoint, with the gold seal of office gleaming on the wall above the coroner's bench, Dr Jamieson seemed bigger and more imposing. Behind his rimless spectacles his eyes examined Josh dispassionately. He didn't look like a man who missed much.

In response to the coroner's opening questions Josh gave an account of his meeting with Annabelle in the hotel at Newbury, saying that he'd driven her home at the end of the evening because she'd been drinking.

'And what happened when you drove her home?'

'When we stopped outside her place she told me her marriage was in trouble. That Leo was being violent towards her.'

Josh was aware of movement on the benches to his left where Leo and the family were sitting. This was the first time he'd told his story in public and it was bound to cause a stir. He kept his eyes on Jamieson as he continued.

'She pulled up her sweater and showed me a nasty bruise. It was all over her chest and shoulder on her right side. She said Leo had done it to her.'

'Did she say how he had done it?'

'She told me he had kicked her.'

'That's a lie!' Leo's voice wasn't loud but the vehemence with which he spoke echoed round the room.

The coroner looked towards the table in the centre of the court. 'I believe Mr Lovall is represented here, is he not?'

A woman with short-cropped hair responded. 'By me, sir.'

Jamieson spoke directly to Leo. 'I can understand that

you might find this distressing, Mr Lovall, but Miss Duncan will be able to question Mr Swallow shortly on your behalf. In the meantime you must allow the witness to answer without interruption.'

Leo nodded slowly, and it occurred to Josh that he was struggling to control his emotions. Josh looked away quickly. He could not allow himself to be sidetracked by Leo. The coroner was waiting for him to continue.

'I told Annabelle that if Leo was being violent towards her she ought to go to the police. And that if things were as bad as she made out, she should leave him. She said she didn't have anywhere to go, that Leo knew all her friends and he'd come after her. The upshot was that I gave her the keys to my mother's old flat in London, in Arlington Mansions. I said she could stay there if she was desperate.'

'And she took you up on the offer.'

'She got in touch with me about a fortnight later and asked if it was still OK. I said yes.'

'That was Tuesday, the twenty-second of January?'

'Yes. I was riding at Leicester. I said I'd drop in that evening to see if she was all right. When I got there, the police told me a woman had fallen from the building and they thought she might have come from my flat. The caretaker had let them in and they'd found a dog on my balcony on its own. I was able to confirm that a friend of mine had come to stay and that she owned a dog. I went up with them and I could see that Annabelle had arrived. She'd unpacked her clothes and put food in the fridge but there was no sign of her. I realised then that it must have been her who had fallen.'

Realisation, in fact, had come later. The presence of Annabelle's things – the familiar suitcase, the tumble of underwear on the bed, the smell of her perfume – had only emphasised her presence. At that stage he'd not known the woman they'd retrieved from the forecourt was dead; the police had talked euphemistically of a casualty and of her removal to St Mary's in Paddington. 'I'll go there at once,' he'd announced but the uniformed officer who'd first approached him downstairs said, 'I don't think there's much you'll be able to do, sir,' and so he'd stayed to answer their questions.

Only out on the balcony, looking down to the basement railings and the space taped off in the parking area below, did the enormity of the situation begin to sink in. He fancied he could see a stain on the ground and his imagination at once stepped in to conjure up the awful damage to Annabelle's slender frame as it smashed into the metal. He well knew how fragile the human body was when tumbling from the back of a horse on to rough turf. The thought of falling forty feet on to spiked iron railings did not bear contemplating.

'She's dead, isn't she?' he'd said and the policeman had nodded.

Miss Duncan was now on her feet eyeing Josh in an unfriendly fashion. The coroner had finished with him for the moment and Josh realised that Leo's bloodhound was out for his blood. To his surprise, however – and evidently to Miss Duncan's – the coroner intervened, asking for another statement to be read out 'to prevent us heading in an unprofitable direction'.

Josh stepped gratefully from the witness box, aware that he had been granted a temporary reprieve. In his place, a court officer read from the account given by Annabelle's GP, which said that he had seen her on 2 January this year, when she had presented herself at the surgery with an injured right shoulder, following an accident with a horse. He had sent her for an X-ray which revealed that she had no broken bones; the bruising, however, was severe.

For a moment Josh was stunned. That's not what Annabelle had told him. On the other hand, she had been reluctant to go on record with Leo's treatment of her. She must have spun the doctor a line about the horse to keep the matter quiet.

Then a stable girl was called to the box and a statement read on behalf of Tim Daniels. Both confirmed that Annabelle had indeed been kicked by a horse. Josh felt a complete fool.

What on earth had Annabelle been playing at? Had she been out to gain his sympathy with this ridiculous story of Leo beating her up? And why? Was she simply looking for an escape route from an unhappy marriage and chose him? He'd been compliant enough in the past. Whatever her reasons, she had paid a heavy price.

He returned to the witness box in a daze to face Leo's legal representative, Miss Duncan, who seemed in an altogether better humour.

'It's true, is it not, Mr Swallow, that you used to be more than just a friend to Mrs Lovall?'

'Yes.' Josh held his head up. He wasn't ashamed of it.

'And that having tried to steal Mr Lovall's wife once, you were trying to do so again by placing your London home at her disposal?'

'Certainly not. She approached me at Newbury. I hadn't seen her for about two years.'

'So you weren't still in love with her?'

'No. But when she told me that story about Leo hurting her I wanted to help. She appealed to me as an old friend and that's how I responded – as a friend.'

'Some friend,' remarked Duncan drily. 'It's thanks to you she's dead, isn't it?'

To Josh's relief, the coroner interrupted. 'Can we leave out the point-scoring, Miss Duncan? You don't have a jury to impress on this occasion.'

'Yes, sir,' she said without contrition and turned back to Josh. 'Can you just tell us whether you were currently having an affair with Annabelle Lovall?'

'No, I wasn't.' Josh was indignant and the words came out more forcefully than intended.

Duncan raised her eyebrows but suppressed whatever sarcastic retort was on her lips.

'Finally, then, would you like to revise any of your testimony in the light of what we have heard of Mrs Lovall's accident at the stables?' she said.

Josh took a deep breath. 'I don't see why I should. Annabelle told me Leo had assaulted her and I believed her. That's why I gave her the key to the flat, so she'd have somewhere to go if she needed to.' He looked across at Leo. Maybe this was his chance to make some amends. 'It was only when she showed me that terrible bruise that I believed Mr Lovall had hurt her. Obviously I was mistaken. I'm sorry.'

'It's a bit late for apologies, if you ask me,' muttered Duncan as she resumed her seat.

'Well done,' said Susie, leaning across the cafe table to squeeze Josh's arm.

The coroner had ordered a short break in proceedings following Josh's testimony and Colin Smart had rushed them round the corner for a quick cup of coffee. 'I'd use the loo here, too,' he said. 'You don't want to find yourself in the queue back there next to Leo Lovall.'

Susie was grateful for the respite from the intense courtroom atmosphere. Apart from anything else it was a relief to get off that hard wooden bench, and watching Josh's discomfort had not been pretty.

'No, it wasn't well done,' Josh said. 'I came over like a complete idiot.'

'An honest idiot anyway,' said Colin, slurping heartily at his coffee.

Josh raised a half-hearted grin and covered Susie's hand with his. She liked the feel of his flesh on hers once more. She'd only returned the day before and they'd spent the night in an airport hotel. Tonight they'd be going back to Derby. She was looking forward to it.

'So, whose baby was it?' she asked, studying every flicker of Josh's expression, just as she had done in court. She'd come to the conclusion that he was as surprised at the revelation as anyone but she wanted to be sure.

Colin chuckled. 'I bet there's a few in the frame.'

'It must be Leo's,' Josh said. 'Poor sod. He's always wanted kids.'

Susie wasn't so sure. 'Will the coroner ask Leo if they were still sleeping together?'

Colin shook his head. 'Only if he thinks it's relevant to the case. And in this instance I'd say it was highly unlikely.'

The inquest resumed with a lengthy discussion of the balcony parapet over which Annabelle had fallen to her death. A uniformed police officer was called to the witness stand and photographs of the site were distributed around the court.

Susie found it strange to be examining police pictures of a building with which she was familiar. During a hot spell the previous summer she'd spent two blissful days sunbathing on that same balcony, even making sketches of the trees and street below, but she felt she'd never scrutinised the place as closely as she did now.

The balcony wall was just over three feet high, a height at which the inspector and other witnesses judged it improbable for Annabelle to have toppled over simply by, for example, losing her balance and stumbling against the parapet.

Leo was recalled and quizzed about the dog, Suky. He characterised the animal as young and frisky, in need of lots of exercise.

'Would you say that Suky was ill-disciplined?' asked the coroner.

'I'd say she could be a ruddy nuisance. I asked Annabelle to keep her out of the yard.'

'Had the dog had previous experience of being on the balcony of a building such as Arlington Mansions?'

'Not as far as I know.' Leo didn't sound sure of himself. It struck Susie that he must be questioning quite a few things he had taken for granted. Colin had told them that the family would only have had prior knowledge of written evidence submitted to the court. As the pathologist had appeared in person to present the post mortem results, it was quite possible Leo had not been aware of Annabelle's pregnancy until now. No wonder he sounded less certain of himself.

'Would she have jumped up on to the parapet?'

Leo shrugged. 'I've never seen her do anything like that but who knows? She liked drawing attention to herself.'

The coroner then recalled Jenny, and began a line of inquiry obviously intended to shed light on the dead woman's state of mind. Susie was gripped. Was suicide the answer to the mystery?

It transpired that the two sisters had talked on the phone just before Annabelle had fallen to her death.

'It's terrible but I can't really remember what we talked about. I rattled on about my kids because she didn't see them as often as she wanted to, since I live in France.'

'Did you discuss her pregnancy?'

'I wasn't aware she was pregnant.'

'But,' the coroner leaned forward, 'you would expect your sister to discuss such a significant event with you, surely?'

'Of course, but I don't think she knew either. Annabelle longed to have children but she didn't think she was capable.'

'So how would you characterise your sister's state of mind on the afternoon she died? It would seem that you were the last person to talk to her.'

'I know.' Her voice shook and Susie felt for her. 'Annabelle was fine – better than fine. In great spirits. We only stopped talking because Suky was making a fuss in the background. Annabelle said she was probably dying for a pee and she had to take her out for a walk. That was the last thing she said to me.'

'One last question, Mrs Claudel. Do you think it is possible your sister took her own life?'

'No.' Jenny took a deep breath, obviously trying to control her feelings. 'That's a ridiculous suggestion. She'd never talked to me about killing herself even when she was feeling down, and she wasn't feeling down on that afternoon. I should know. If you want to know what I think, she was a bit tipsy. She was out on the balcony playing with the dog and she just somehow fell off, silly thing. I'm sorry.' And she burst into tears.

The little woman stepped into the witness box, fumbling inside her handbag. The court officer stood impassively by her side, holding a Bible, while the new witness located her spectacles. As she rummaged she spoke in the clear-cut tones of a bygone era.

'I do apologise, I meant to get them out before.'

'Take your time, Mrs Glazier,' said the coroner kindly. 'I'm always losing my glasses, too.'

'Oh, they're not lost,' she corrected him. 'Here they are,' and she hoisted a pair of round tortoiseshell spectacles on to her nose and read the oath. Then she proceeded to replace them carefully in their case, which she tucked away into her bag.

Jamieson waited patiently until she had finished and then asked, without discernible irony, if she was happy for him to proceed.

'Of course. That's what we're all here for, isn't it?'

It transpired that Mrs Glazier, a 76-year-old widow, lived opposite Josh's London flat, in the corresponding block on the other side of the road. On the afternoon of 22 January she had been at home, preparing to host an evening bridge party. In the course of performing her afternoon chores in anticipation of her card-playing friends, it seemed that Mrs Glazier had had occasion to venture out on to her balcony.

'I wouldn't have gone out there if I hadn't run out of tuna,' she said brightly.

Dr Jamieson blinked. It was the first time Susie had observed him looking anything less than in total control of proceedings. 'Would you like to expand upon that statement, Mrs Glazier?'

'Well, I often do tuna-and-pasta bake but I'd run out of tuna so I used bacon instead. I always put the rinds out on the balcony for the birds. That was when I saw the woman on the opposite balcony.'

The casual statement brought the collective fidgeting in the courtroom to a halt. Mrs Glazier cocked her grey head to one side and glanced quickly round the crowded room, her small black eyes gleaming with triumph. She was a bit like a bird herself, thought Susie, and by no means as foolish as she appeared. She was well aware of the attention now focused upon her words.

'What time would this be, Mrs Glazier?'

'It would be at two thirty-three or thirty-four.'

The coroner nodded, apparently unsurprised at the precision of the answer. But of course, Susie realised, he had prior knowledge of Mrs Glazier's testimony.

'Would you care to explain how you can be so sure?'

'Because it was just before *Murder She Wrote* began on BBC1. It's a bit American for my taste but I always watch Angela Lansbury. We're the same age, you know.'

'And what time does the programme begin?'

'Two thirty-five, and I went to put the bacon rinds out just a minute or two before it started. That's when I saw someone on the balcony of Mrs Swallow's flat across the road. Well, I know it's not her flat any more, she's dead. But I know where she lived because I played cards with her once or twice.'

The coroner stopped Mrs Glazier at that point to confirm the timing of the sighting. Earlier, the court had heard statements from drivers leaving the Arlington Mansions forecourt and from the resident who had discovered Annabelle's body; as a result, the time of her fall had been calculated at approximately 3:20. And now a witness was claiming to have seen a woman on the balcony some three-quarters of an hour earlier.

'Would you care to describe the person you saw on the balcony, Mrs Glazier?'

'It was a young woman – well, young to me, that is. In her twenties, I would imagine. I'd say she was three or four inches taller than I am, so that makes her about five foot five. She had a light blue scarf over her head and wore a dark jumper. Navy blue, I'd say. Of course, I could only see her top half.'

'And what was this woman doing?'

'She was just standing there, to one side of the door into the flat. She had her hands down by her sides and she was leaning back against the wall. I thought it was most odd.'

'Why did you think that?'

'Because it was very cold. And she was standing quite still, staring straight ahead. I must say I wasn't entirely surprised when I heard that she'd jumped off.'

The coroner paused, waiting for her to elaborate but for once she remained silent. 'Would you like to tell us why you weren't surprised, Mrs Glazier?'

'Because she was obviously getting up her nerve, poor thing. It must take an awful lot of courage to throw yourself to your death. Like Tosca.'

'I'd rather we avoided the operatic allusions, Mrs Glazier, and stuck to precisely what you saw. I would be grateful if you'd look at some photographs for me.'

More photocopies were distributed round the courtroom. Susie glanced quickly at the sheets she was handed: Annabelle Lovall in close-up, high cheekbones, big black pools for eyes, a superior smile on her wide curling mouth; Annabelle full length, standing beside a horse in riding clothes; photographs of clothes laid out on a white table – a cream-coloured sweater, a pair of black slacks, a long pale blue scarf.

The coroner waited for Mrs Glazier to relocate her spectacles before indicating the photograph of Annabelle. 'Was this the woman you saw on the balcony?'

The grey head canted first to one side, then the other. 'It's hard to be sure,' she announced finally. 'She looks taller than the girl I saw but I really find it very difficult to judge.'

'And what about the clothes?'

'She was wearing a dark top, as I said. Not like this one at all. But she could. have been wearing the blue scarf. It's really very difficult to say.'

The coroner smiled at her in conciliatory fashion. 'I'm sure it is. We all appreciate how difficult this must be.' It occurred to Susie that he must have had long experience of difficult witnesses, from grief-stricken relatives to incoherent bystanders, young and old. At least Mrs Glazier was trying to be helpful.

'The problem, Mrs Glazier, as I'm sure you're aware, is that if it wasn't the deceased you saw, then who was it? I believe there are two possibilities. First of all, was there someone else in the flat with Mrs Lovall? Someone who chose to spend time outside on the balcony in the cold.' He looked across the courtroom to Jenny. 'Mrs Claudel – you are still under oath – was there any suggestion during your conversation with your sister that there was anybody else with her?'

Jenny shook her head and the surprise was evident in her voice. 'Not at all. She said she was spending the afternoon on her own. Apart from Suky, of course.'

'And would you call Suky an effective guard dog?'

'Rather. Annabelle said she'd feel perfectly safe anywhere if Suky was by her side.'

'In that case,' said Jamieson, 'I'd prefer to discount the theory that some unknown personage appeared miraculously on a balcony four storeys above the street undetected by Mrs Lovall and her vigilant hound. So let us move on to the second possibility. Are you certain, Mrs Glazier, that you were looking at the balcony of number forty-eight Arlington Mansions.'

Mrs Glazier blinked at him. 'I don't know the numbers of the flats.'

'I mean, are you positive that the balcony on which you saw this figure was the one which your friend Mrs Swallow used?'

'I wouldn't call her a friend, exactly. But, yes. I am.'

The coroner shuffled some of the papers in front of him. 'How far away would you say that this balcony is from your own?'

'It's just across the street. Of course, it's quite a wide street and the buildings are set back from the pavement.' Mrs Glazier appeared to be playing for time.

The coroner had located the piece of paper he was looking for and he looked up. 'How far, in your estimation, Mrs Glazier?'

'I'm not very good on distances these days. Fifty feet?'

'According to the police report it is thirty-three metres which is, I think, about a hundred feet. Twice your estimate.'

Mrs Glazier took umbrage. 'I'm only telling you what I saw. I'm not a surveyor.'

'Of course not.' Jamieson's voice was conciliation itself though his next question was not calculated to smooth the woman's ruffled feathers. 'I notice that you sometimes wear spectacles. May I ask when you last had your eyesight tested?'

'If you are implying that I can't see across the street I can assure you that my sight has always been thoroughly reliable.'

'I'm sure it has but can you tell us roughly when your eyes were last tested?'

'I can't remember. I only wear glasses for reading, you know.' She looked around defiantly, as if waiting for Jamieson to contradict her. When he continued to look at her encouragingly she added, 'It must have been after my last pair broke. My grandson put them in the toaster.'

'And that would be . . .?'

'He was a toddler then and, since he's just had his eighth birthday, it must be about four or five years ago.'

'Five years since your eyes were last tested?'

'What's wrong with that? I can still see perfectly well, better than many people half my age. And I know what I saw that afternoon.'

The coroner nodded, as if he'd come to the conclusion that he wasn't going to get any change out of this redoubtable old bird. He looked over to the table of legal representatives. Only Colin Smart and Miss Duncan sat there, making it the least populated location in the whole room.

Miss Duncan was on her feet in a flash. 'If I may—'

'Miss Duncan is speaking for Mr Lovall,' Jamieson said

to Mrs Glazier. He would doubtless have said more but Mrs Glazier stopped him.

'I know who she is, thank you,' she snapped.

'I only have one question,' the lawyer said. 'Could you tell me, Mrs Glazier, how many balconies there are on the front of Arlington Mansions?'

'How many balconies?'

'Yes. How many could you see from your own balcony? Assuming of course that it's not high summer and there are no leaves on the trees? Which there aren't, of course, in January.'

'Oh.' For the first time, the old lady looked flustered. She reached for her bag and began to pull out the sheaves of photocopies that had been distributed throughout the hearing.

'Could you tell us please,' said Duncan, 'without referring to any documents.'

Mrs Glazier stopped rummaging. 'I'll have to think.'

'Please do,' Duncan said sweetly.

'Twelve.'

'You are sure about that? Well, you would be, wouldn't you, as you've seen them every day for – how long have you lived there, Mrs Glazier?'

'Thirteen years. No, no, I'm sorry, it's fourteen.' She sounded less sure of herself than at any time in the proceedings, thought Susie.

'So, for fourteen years you've been looking at these balconies and so you can say with confidence, and with the benefit of your thoroughly reliable eyesight, that there are twelve of them on the front of Arlington Mansions.'

'Yes!' Mrs Glazier spat out the word with venom. Susie wouldn't fancy being her partner across the card table if things weren't going well.

Duncan smiled greasily. She was enjoying herself. 'In that case, you might be interested to know that there are in fact sixteen balconies.'

'No!' cried Mrs Glazier. She couldn't help herself.

'Oh yes, there are. And I would suggest that your mystery woman was playing guardsman on one of the four you failed to count. Five years really is too long between eye tests, Mrs Glazier.'

A flash of irritation crossed the coroner's face. 'Thank you for that glimpse of High Court cut-and-thrust, Miss Duncan. I'm not sure it's appropriate here. Have you any other questions?'

But she hadn't. Susie, along with everyone else, knew that one had been quite enough.

'So, Colin, what happens next?' Susie asked. They were sitting in the same cafe as before, this time crammed with the lunchtime clientele from nearby offices – and the court, too, no doubt.

The solicitor swallowed his last chip and wiped his fingers on a paper serviette. 'We've had all the evidence. The coroner's just got to sum up the facts and deliver his verdict.'

'What's it going to be, do you think? I'm confused.'

'Join the club,' murmured Josh. He'd not said much during lunch and Susie was concerned about him. On the other hand, knowing him, it was possible he was simply worried about slipping behind in his duel with Ben O'Brien. He'd not mentioned it but she knew that missing out on the Chepstow meeting must be preying on his mind.

'There're three conclusions the coroner could come to,' Colin replied in answer to Susie's question. 'Suicide, accident or an open verdict. And he won't go for suicide because a higher standard of proof is required.'

'What do you mean?' Susie asked.

'It's got to be established beyond reasonable doubt that Annabelle intended to kill herself and then did so.'

'You mean, if she'd left a suicide note?'

'Even that might not be good enough on its own. She'd been drinking so it could be argued she wasn't aware of what she was doing.'

'But what *was* she doing?' blurted Josh. 'I still don't see how she managed to fall off the balcony even if she had had a drink. It doesn't make sense.'

'Doesn't it?' The lawyer grinned. He was a bit smug for Susie's taste but nevertheless she was keen to hear his interpretation of events. 'I reckon it's pretty obvious. The woman's got an alcohol problem. And, whatever the husband says, the marriage is on the rocks. I bet they've not slept together for months.'

'You're presuming a lot, aren't you?' said Susie.

Colin shrugged. 'This is just my theory, right? Anyhow, she's looking for another guy to latch on to – obviously she found at least one, that's how she ends up pregnant. But the new guy doesn't want to know and she's so desperate to find a way out she even digs up an old flame like Josh. But he's not interested either. So, she's all alone and miserable in

Josh's flat, not to mention a bit pissed, and decides to end it all.'

'But Jenny said she was in good spirits, she spoke to her just before it happened.' Susie held no brief for Annabelle but Colin was hardly being fair.

'The sister's lying. They probably spent half an hour rehashing the pregnancy, the boyfriend, the whole mess. Maybe Jenny tried to talk her out of it and failed. I don't blame her for not spilling the beans in court.'

'Well, what about Mrs Glazier?'

Colin laughed. 'Complete red herring. She probably saw Angela Lansbury on the balcony too.'

'Come off it. She's a bit cranky but perfectly rational. That was just a cheap trick that Duncan woman pulled on her.' Susie really didn't like Leo's lawyer.

Colin obviously did not share her antipathy. 'Actually, Fiona Duncan's a pretty good brief – we use her a lot. She was only acting under instructions.'

'Yes, but why?'

'Because Leo and the family don't like the suggestion that the person Mrs Glazier saw was Annabelle getting ready to jump – which it must have been. She could easily have gone out there to chuck herself off at two thirty and funked it. Then she came back in, put on a warmer sweater and got on the phone to her sister. Three-quarters of an hour later she's back out there, she's had another drink or two, and this time she goes through with it.'

'Oh,' said Susie. Put like that, it did make some kind of sense.

'Jamieson's a smart fellow. He'll have worked all this out

but he'd lean over backwards anyway to avoid a verdict of suicide because he won't want to upset the family. And whatever anyone might say about tripping over the dog, as Josh says it doesn't make sense. That balcony is perfectly safe and everyone knows it. So that's accident out of the window. Got to be an open verdict. I'd put money on it. Any takers?'

Depressingly, to Susie's mind, Jamieson appeared to follow Colin's script. He took them back through the morning's evidence, painting a picture of the happily married Mrs Lovall borrowing an old friend's London flat for a few days. He gave weight to her sister's evidence that she sounded upbeat and positive during their phone conversation, then reminded the court of the post mortem finding of alcohol in the blood, the presence of the frisky dog and the height of the balcony parapet.

When he came to Mrs Glazier's evidence he didn't exactly dismiss it but Susie could tell that he was going to discount the inconvenient sighting of a figure on the balcony three-quarters of an hour before Annabelle's fall. Referring to Mrs Glazier as 'admirably forthright' he briefly summarised her testimony, before adding some remarks of his own.

'Our purpose here is to inquire into the circumstances of Mrs Lovall's death. Each witness brings a piece of the jigsaw to the table and it is my job to assemble as complete a picture as possible. However, in my experience, there is often an inconvenient piece that does not fit; sometimes, in fact, it appears to come from a completely separate puzzle.

I would be inclined to put Mrs Glazier's sighting of a woman in a navy blue sweater in this category.'

Susie was keeping an eye on the old lady on the other side of the room and she noted the defiant jut of her chin at these words. She half expected her to speak up in disagreement as the coroner continued.

'I cast no aspersions on Mrs Glazier's character or intellect when I say that our powers of observation do not improve as we get older. By her own admission, this seventy-six-year-old lady has not had her eyesight tested for four, maybe five years. Though she requires spectacles for reading she tells us she does not need them to see over distances. I'm sure that, for general purposes, that is the case. But her evidence here is of a specific observation, a woman in different-coloured clothing from Mrs Lovall, standing in a posture which suggested she was going to throw herself from the balcony. With the best will in the world, I do not think we can credibly infer such a thing from body language read at such a distance. And this sighting is, by Mrs Glazier's own, admirably precise, testimony, some forty-five minutes before the unfortunate event itself.

'It may well be, as Miss Duncan has maintained, that Mrs Glazier was simply looking at a different balcony. I have no doubt she did see the figure she said she did but I am not convinced it has relevance to these proceedings. The police, as we have heard, conducted inquiries amongst the other residents of the block who are unable to throw any light on the matter. No one can remember stepping out on to any of the nearby balconies at the time in question. Consequently, I fear Mrs Glazier's sighting must remain a mystery. With reference to my earlier remarks, I would judge this evidence to be a piece from a different jigsaw puzzle.'

Mrs Glazier's mouth, Susie noted, was clamped in a tight thin line, as if she were fighting the impulse to tell the coroner he was talking rot.

Having removed the awkward piece of the picture from the table, Jamieson moved on swiftly.

'We have to consider that Mrs Lovall might have taken her own life deliberately. However, there is no direct evidence that this was her intention. She did not leave a suicide note, for example, nor did she suggest that such a thing was on her mind during her conversation with her sister. Indeed Mrs Claudel says that Mrs Lovall was in excellent spirits just a few minutes before her death. And then there is the matter of her pregnancy which, the pathologist has told us, was four weeks advanced. Though it is possible she was unaware of it, it is also possible that she was. As she was a woman who, we are told, longed to have a family, this is surely strong evidence to suggest that she would not have intentionally taken her life.'

The coroner paused for a moment to allow his words to sink in. He was ruling out suicide. Susie looked towards the pews in front of her but could read no significance in the postures of Leo or Jenny. They must surely be relieved.

'Similarly,' the coroner continued, 'I can find no convincing evidence to suggest that the death was due to accidental causes. It is possible that in playing with her exuberant dog, Mrs Lovall might have lost her balance and fallen over the balcony wall, especially since she had consumed approximately two-thirds of a bottle of wine. On the other hand, the wall was of a safe height and it is hard to conceive of the precise circumstances which would have resulted in such a freakish outcome.

'In the circumstances, therefore, I pronounce an open verdict on the death of Annabelle Lovall of Hoar Frost Farm, Newbury, on the twenty-second of January two thousand and two.'

Susie was aware that Colin Smart was smirking at her from the table in the centre of the court.

'So what exactly is an open verdict?' Susie asked Colin.

The three of them had walked back to the car park, avoiding the huddle of Annabelle's family members who had congregated outside the court.

'It's used where there's not enough evidence to bring in any other verdict,' the solicitor replied.

'A cop-out, you mean.' To Susie's way of thinking, Josh sounded bitter.

Colin shrugged. 'What else could he do? Like I said, she probably killed herself but it can't be proved beyond reasonable doubt.'

Josh sighed. Susie knew what he was thinking: to end up with no proper conclusion made the dramas of the whole day seem pointless.

After the inquest Leo extricated himself from Jenny and the rest of Annabelle's relatives as swiftly as he could. They all meant well but, God, how they got on his tits, especially her cousin bleating on about what a tragedy it was that two lives had been lost and how she hoped that one day he'd be a father. Talking to Jenny had been worse, though. She and Annabelle had been thick as thieves. She'd know for sure the child couldn't have been his.

So whose was it? What swine had not only been stuffing his wife but had put a bun in her oven? Something which, to his shame, he'd never been able to do. If only he had, how different their lives might have been. Annabelle might still be alive.

There was only one candidate in his book: Josh Swallow. He wouldn't put it past the jockey to have got her pregnant. In fact he wouldn't put anything past Josh Swallow. Annabelle had died at his flat, hadn't she?

An open verdict didn't satisfy Leo. Someone must be responsible.

Chapter Seven

Mouse curbed her impatience throughout the morning rush at the service reception. By ten, after the customers had dropped off their cars, it was relatively quiet and she nicked a couple of newspapers from the waiting area and fled to the toilet. When Baz had expanded the business a couple of years back he'd put in a separate ladies' loo and since Maureen was off skiving again, Mouse reckoned there was a good chance she wouldn't be disturbed for ten minutes. She wouldn't dare risk longer.

Baz was very much Mr Fordyce during office hours. He wore a suit and tie and ran a mental stopwatch over his employees' comings and goings. Mouse knew he wouldn't show her any favours, even though she was his cousin. And though she'd helped him out before, on reception and after hours on the computers, this was different; now she was almost a permanent member of staff. It was a vote of confidence after all the trouble she'd been in. She couldn't afford to let Baz down, though he could be such a prat.

He'd made her the offer in a funny way, like he couldn't

come right out and say, 'Come and work for me.' What he'd said was, 'I'm going to murder that Mat Cover.'

'You what?' They were sharing a curry after an evening fiddling with his computers.

'Mat Cover. First he nicks Gabby off me, then Teresa, and I've not seen a whisker of them since. Now it's Louise.'

These were all girls who'd worked on reception for Fordyce Motors. Mouse finally got the joke. Gabby and Teresa were now proud young mums and it must be Louise's turn to leave Baz in the lurch, looking for maternity cover. That's what he always put in the job advert though the girls never seemed to return to work. Mouse supposed Baz lived in hope.

So here she was, a proper employee, and though she knew it wasn't the brightest thing to have her cousin as her boss, the offer had come as a bit of a life-saver. And he'd seemed dead keen to have her, presenting her with her own name tag to pin on her blouse 'to make it official'. Only, typical Baz, he'd printed it up with her real name which she hated. 'You don't put nicknames on your lapel badge,' he'd said to her when she'd objected. 'I mean, I'm Barry on my badge, not Baz, aren't I?' She supposed there was no arguing with that.

It was a small thing anyway, considering.

On the train journey back from London, after *it* had happened, she'd thought she'd be OK. What she'd felt was mostly relief. Standing on that balcony, getting colder and colder, she'd not known how she was ever going to get away without being discovered. But a path had opened up for her, like a miraculous parting of the waves, and she'd escaped unseen and unscathed. It had been bloody Biblical. Like it was meant to be.

But that night when she got home she made the mistake of turning on the TV. The death of the tart was the lead item on *News At Ten* and the papers the next day were packed with photos of the dead woman looking like some soulful movie star. It had freaked her out. It was like this one woman's death was the worst thing since Princess Di's car crash, with pages devoted to her doomed love affair with Josh and all that crap. Mouse was convinced it was only a matter of time before there'd be a knock at the door and it would be her on the news and in the dock. And then in prison for the rest of her life.

She didn't go in to work at Hilltop Holidays and she didn't answer the phone. And when Big Rose came round and shouted through the door, she'd pretended not to hear. She'd only gone out for basics and lost herself in the online chatroom.

By the time Baz turned up, the tart wasn't on the news at all. There'd been a rail crash and a politician's wife had been caught screwing her personal trainer – the media spotlight was trained elsewhere.

Mouse had burnt her boats at Hilltop Holidays, though she didn't mention it to Baz as she accepted his offer of a job.

'Thank God for that,' he'd said. 'I can't stand all that interviewing and checking out references. At least with you I know the bad news already, don't I?'

She'd laughed even harder than he did; in fact it was hard to stop.

'Leave it out,' he'd protested. 'It wasn't that funny.'

Oh no?

Since then she no longer lay awake in the early hours, expecting the police to turn up at her door. In fact, she'd come to terms with the whole thing. It wasn't as if she had planned to dispose of the tart that way – it had just happened. Anyway, she'd had no choice. It would have been too terrible to have been caught, not after what had gone on before, with Gavin Carter's wife, and not now everyone was saying she was doing so well to turn her life around. And, let's face it, she said to herself at nights when making her positive statements – affirmations, Gavin had called them – that woman deserved it. She deserved to die.

She'd read all about the tart and Josh. Annabelle Lovall had been a cancer in his life. She'd gone away and then come back to destroy him all over again. But she, Mouse, had cut the cancer out.

Really, Josh ought to be grateful.

Right now, she had a few minutes to read what had happened at the inquest. They'd hardly said a word about it on the news. After all that fuss the first time round, talk about a five-minute wonder. However, the papers would cover it.

She locked the bog door and settled down in the stall. The headline on page 5 read OPEN VERDICT ON DEATH OF PREGNANT WIFE. That shook her. The woman was pregnant? She hadn't looked it. How could she have known the stupid cow was pregnant?

Mouse couldn't afford to worry about that. A subheading caught her eye: 'Appearance of mystery woman on balcony discounted by coroner.' What the hell was that about?

She found the relevant paragraph: 'Mrs Emily Glazier, 76, told the court that 45 minutes before the fatal event she had seen a woman in a navy blue top on the balcony from which Mrs Lovall fell. She failed to identify the woman as Mrs Lovall, who was wearing a cream sweater at the time of her death.'

Mouse's heart thumped. So some curtain-twitching old busybody from across the street had spotted her on the balcony. She read on anxiously.

'Mrs Glazier admitted that her eyesight had not been tested for five years and Miss Duncan, appearing for the Lovall family, opened the possibility that Mrs Glazier had been looking at the wrong balcony. The coroner concluded that this was likely to be the case and that Mrs Glazier's evidence had been "a piece of the jigsaw that belonged to a different puzzle".'

So the old bat was half-blind and they'd ignored her – thank God for that.

She picked up the other paper. This one was easy to read, full of pictures and big print, though it didn't mention the batty old lady at all. Good.

But on the inside back page, in the Clive Cooper racing round-up, was a picture that jumped out of the page and caused Mouse more anguish than anything she'd read so far. The head shot was of the Mistake, making her shy doe-eyed face. The text that accompanied it read: 'The only good thing to have emerged at yesterday's inquest into the tragic death of Annabelle Lovall was the re-emergence of racing artist Susie Brown who has returned to these shores to support beleaguered jockey Josh Swallow. We hope to see much more of this talented and delightful young woman in happier circumstances very soon.'

Mouse felt like she'd been thumped in the stomach. Susie was meant to have gone off for good. According to the tabloid gossip columns she'd disappeared abroad and left Josh to stew in the aftermath of his ex-lover's probable suicide. And now she was back. Jesus Christ.

She'd thought the Susie Sausage letters might have done the trick. Obviously Blondie was tougher than she looked.

Mouse would have to think of something else. The bitch was asking for it.

Susie thought she'd be thrilled to return to the house in Derbyshire. Her South African trip had turned out far better than she could have hoped and all her worries had been put in perspective, especially since she'd come to terms with the Annabelle business.

But, stepping back inside Ridge House on the night of the inquest, she'd felt a niggle of anxiety as she spotted the small pile of post that was waiting for her. Josh offered to fix her a drink and, while he did so, she rifled through the stack. It contained no threatening brown envelope, though that didn't necessarily mean one hadn't arrived. Josh wouldn't have kept a letter addressed to Susan Merrivale, would he? She certainly wasn't going to ask him.

At first, the place seemed just the same, only messier – nothing that a few fresh flowers and some elbow grease wouldn't put right. Then she walked into the living room to find one of her paintings on the wall – a big abstract canvas that spoke to her of their early days together. And there were more hanging throughout the house.

It knocked her for six that Josh had put these paintings where he could see them every day. She herself wasn't sure she liked them – at least, she'd been unsure of their worth, though keen to pursue a line of artistic inquiry far removed from the kind of work that earned her money. But Josh had loathed them. Not that he'd said so, but his failure to come up with any convincing appreciation and his extravagant praise for her naturalistic pieces had told her all she needed to know. Josh was not a good liar – a comforting thought – and he'd not been able to hide his feelings.

So why were these paintings on the wall? And not hidden away, but hanging where they couldn't be avoided. The first thing Josh would have looked at in the morning and the last thing he'd have seen at night would have been the big blue abstract that hung on the bedroom wall, overwhelming every other object in the room.

'Will this do?' The voice by her side interrupted her thoughts. Josh was holding a bottle of champagne and two glasses. 'It's not very cold but I can rig up an ice bucket.'

'Why,' she said, 'have you hung my paintings all over the house?'

'I can easily take them down.'

'That's not what I asked.'

He was pulling the foil off the top of the bottle. Finally he looked up at her. 'You weren't here.' He popped the cork and poured. 'And,' he added, 'I've decided I really like them.' He handed her a glass.

How could she ever have doubted him?

*

Unusually for him, Clive Cooper was at his desk with the clock reading five to one. His lunch date had cancelled and so he was banging out a puff piece on one of the Cheltenham favourites. Who said racing correspondents had an easy time of it? Mind you, his fellow journos had all been in the pub for the past half-hour. So the room was empty when the phone rang, which was just as well given the nature of the call.

'Clive, what the effing hell are you playing at?'

Clive was used to Leo Lovall's abrasive style. Apart from being an old pal and a useful source of information, Leo trained Clive's horse, the injury-prone Miss Misty. In consequence he could be as rude to Clive as he liked.

'Hi, Leo. I assume you're not ringing to tell me some good news about my horse.' Fat chance of that. She'd pulled a tendon three days ago.

Leo didn't take the bait but continued in the same gruff tone. 'I've got a bone to pick with you.'

Clive abandoned his one-handed hunt-and-peck across the keyboard and gave the phone call his full attention. This must be serious.

'I've just read your column. Why are you polishing Josh Swallow's arse?'

'Sorry, Leo. I don't get you.'

'This stuff about his girlfriend, Susie whatsit. It's an insult.'

Clive was puzzled.

'It's just a filler, mate. An excuse to run a picture of a pretty girl. All sporting chaps should be happy to see crumpet like that back on the scene.'

There was a pause before Leo spoke again. 'She's shacked up with Josh Swallow. In my book, that's tantamount to living with a murderer. After what he did to Annabelle the man should be thrown out of racing, at the very least. And anything that makes him seem acceptable to decent people, like froth about his girlfriend, should be stopped.'

'Leo,' the journalist began, determined to deal with him gently, 'I hope you are not trying to censure what I write. I'm afraid our friendship cannot come between me and my duty to the readers of this paper.'

To Clive's surprise, the trainer gave an insulting burst of laughter. 'Spare me the noble speech about the principles of the fourth estate. Just you remember that we go back a bloody long way and I've shown a damn sight more loyalty to you than any of your Fleet Street employers.'

This was true. It was Leo's inside tips that had got Clive back into a job when the *Racing Beacon* had given him the heave-ho.

'And another thing,' Leo continued. 'I shall shortly be presenting you with a hefty bill for the upkeep of that horse of yours. If you play ball with me, I might send the bill to the dustbin instead.'

It was embarrassing how quickly the words tumbled out of Clive's mouth.

'Tell me again what's bothering you, Leo.'

Josh could have got down on himself about the inquest. The more he thought about it, the more he realised Colin was right: Annabelle must have killed herself. In which case, given his suspicions about her state of mind and his knowledge of her moods, why hadn't he seen it coming?

'And done what?' Susie said as they debated the point. 'She'd long ago ceased to be your responsibility and you'd done more than enough to help her by lending her the flat. If you ask me, she used you shamefully.'

'What do you mean?'

'If she was going to kill herself she should have jumped off a cliff, not your balcony. She landed you right in it.' This was true, the papers had been predictably snide about him after the inquest. 'So don't go beating yourself up. There's nothing more you could have done. In fact,' she added, 'I think you were very brave and generous to help her in the first place.'

He looked at her quizzically. 'Brave?'

'You risked all sorts of exposure by helping Annabelle leave her husband again. And you never expected Annabelle to lie to you because you wouldn't lie to her,' she said. 'It was brave of you to help her. Naive, maybe, but it took courage.'

'Oh.' He hadn't allowed himself to think of it like that. 'So you don't think I've been a fool?'

She shook her head. 'You always look for the best in people, Josh. I'd rather you were that way than the opposite.'

He'd had conversations like this with women before, in which they'd made judgements on his emotional outlook. They'd always made him feel uncomfortable, as if he were treading on boggy ground that might give way beneath him. Things weren't like that with Susie though, with her he felt he was walking on solid earth.

Since she'd come back he'd made an effort not to talk about racing – his usual escape.

'How did Ben get on at Chepstow?' Susie had asked him on Wednesday night, the day they'd returned to Derbyshire.

'I don't know,' he'd said.

They were lying in bed, naked and entwined, the champagne going flat on the bedside table as they became thoroughly reacquainted.

'Really?' she'd murmured, her eyes huge with surprise. 'Aren't you dying to find out?'

'I suppose so.' He could truthfully say that the thought of Ben O'Brien and the jockeys' championship had not entered his head for the last hour.

So they'd pulled on a few clothes and cuddled up together on the sofa downstairs in front of the television. Josh flicked through the Teletext screens to the racing results. He'd been just seven wins behind Ben going into the day but his rival had been due to ride some good horses that afternoon. He prepared himself for the lead to have stretched to double figures once more.

At first, he couldn't make sense of the results. Was he even looking at the right meeting? He couldn't see Ben's horses at all. Then he spotted one, Wireless Willy, the odds-on favourite in the fifth race – it had come in second. And that was it.

'I don't believe it,' he'd muttered. 'He's drawn a blank.'

Even more perplexing, Ben had not ridden on the Thursday at Ludlow or on Friday, during the first day of the Doncaster meeting. The racing press said he was suffering from 'a heavy cold', which made no sense to Josh. Only double pneumonia would keep a jockey like Ben out of the saddle, particularly in the current circumstances when he was being chased so hard for the championship.

Josh tried to get the truth out of Tony, who knew pretty well everything relating to his clients' fitness, but, if he knew what was the matter with Ben, he wasn't telling.

'If I were you,' he said to Josh, 'I'd make the most of it.'

Josh had needed no urging and he'd capitalised on Ben's absence with four winning rides. That put Ben just three ahead going into Saturday's Doncaster meeting. It was an almost nonexistent advantage, the kind that could be wiped out in one afternoon. Josh wondered if this was to be that afternoon. Why not? Far stranger things had happened.

The day almost began brilliantly. Josh was in spitting distance of the winning post in the opening novice hurdle when he became aware of a blur of movement to his left – someone was coming up his inside at a terrific lick. He'd caught a glimpse of blue and white – Ben's colours – and his first thought was that he was going to lose to his rival.

As the other horse surged past him to win on the line, Josh felt relief as much as frustration. Though it was irritating to be touched off in such a tight finish, it wasn't Ben who had beaten him but a lad with a similar cap. In the circumstances, he didn't mind losing half as much.

Ben won the next while Josh watched from a bench in the weighing room. He swore to himself he wouldn't let the gap grow larger, not this afternoon at any rate.

But it did. Ben won the fourth race, a novice chase, on an unfancied runner from Leo's yard, hunting down the firm favourite and riding a furious finish to leave him for dead after the last fence. Josh had to concede that the Irish lad's two-day absence seemed to have revitalised him. He was now riding with all his old flair and a newfound intensity. Be that as it may, Josh was determined not to let all his recent gains in the championship race be snatched away. He was due a winner himself and the next race, a two-mile three-furlong hurdle, represented his best chance.

Little Vixen, his mount, was a favourite at Peter Stone's yard and a favourite in the betting too. A nimble, coal-black eight-year-old, she possessed a turn of speed and more guts than seemed possible given her slight build. Josh had won three times on her in the past couple of seasons and been placed just as often. She was calm at the start and furious at the finish, which was how it should be – though the reverse was often the case.

Walking round the parade ring, Josh had his eyes on Ben's mount, Revolutionary. Josh knew him to be a big raw-boned sod, who needed stoking along the whole way, just the kind of animal the Irish lad excelled on. The thought made Josh even more determined that his rival shouldn't finish in front of him.

Peter saw where he was looking. 'Don't worry about him,' he said. 'That's the one you need to keep tabs on.' He waved his racecard in the direction of a dark chestnut who looked as if it was in need of a good wash. 'Betty Murphy hasn't brought him over from Ireland for nothing.'

Josh nodded. Peter probably had a point – he usually did.

The trainer continued. 'I saw him at Punchestown last

year. He looks all over the shop but he's got a bit of oomph when he gets going.'

'Did he win?'

'He should have done. Jockey cocked it up at the last flight. Coyle won't make that mistake so don't let him get away from you.'

Charlie Coyle was a bit of a journeyman, in Josh's opinion, but when he put his mind to it, he was as good as anyone.

'Got it, boss,' he said. It was always best to let Peter know you'd taken in his instructions – even if you then had to ignore them. In any case, as far as Josh was concerned, if Little Vixen was in any kind of shape, all the other horses would be left scrapping for the minor placings.

The ten runners set off in a bunch from the starting point at the beginning of the home straight, past the stands, only beginning to string out as they rounded the turn beyond the winning post. Josh had been on one or two horses, juvenile hurdlers, who'd had trouble handling the sharp bend and by the time they'd completed it had lost enough ground to put them out of meaningful contention. But Little Vixen negotiated the curve in style, like a quality 200-metre runner, and tucked up against the inside rail with just a couple of horses ahead, one of them Betty Murphy's Irish horse, Twilight, which Peter had pointed out to him.

From this position, Josh had a good view of Twilight's eccentric running style. 'All over the shop' Peter had said – that just about summed it up. But when it came to the actual jumping, the horse was good.

Little Vixen was going easily as they headed out into the

country and the first of three hurdles before the turn for home. On this part of the course there was no running rail dividing the chase and hurdle tracks, just a thirty-foot lead-in of white plastic up to the hurdles, to stop horses from running out. The unwritten code in racing is that you only overtake on the inside when the rider in front lets you, which is rare, or else when you are travelling so much better that he can't stop you. If you're not certain, you must stay where you are or travel round the outside. Sometimes, inevitably, you chanced your luck on the inner and risked getting forced through the wing of the fence – a painful experience, though not as bad as when the wings were made of solid timber and a nudge was enough to break a leg.

As Josh approached the railing in front of the first hurdle in the straight he could sense a horse just on his inside. He moved Little Vixen tighter to the wing as they flew the stiff brush with its tangerine-painted boards and raced towards the next. She was travelling easily. He had the Irish horse covered in front but Josh knew the animal on his inner still hadn't gone away, even though he'd given the rider fair warning. The jockey was trying the sort of move that you'd expect from a brash conditional jockey, but when Josh turned to his left to tell whoever it was to sod off, he saw it was Ben.

Josh reacted instinctively, pulling Little Vixen further to his left, away from the direct line to the next flight. If Ben was going to pass him on his inside, then he'd need to be on a bloody fast horse – and he wasn't. But Ben kept coming, and the more he moved up the inside, the further over Josh went. They were now closer to the chase course than the hurdle track. Ben was trying hard to get far enough ahead so that he could use his horse's strength to force Josh back but neither he nor Little Vixen were having any of it. Eventually one of them had to give in and it was Ben. Josh yanked Little Vixen violently back to her right and skimmed the edge of the rail at almost ninety degrees. Ben screamed abuse at him as he attempted a similar manoeuvre.

Serve you right, you cocky bastard, thought Josh as he re-focused his thoughts on winning the race. But it was too late. Bravely though he and Little Vixen fought, they couldn't quite make up the ground they'd given away by fighting with Ben. The Irish horse beat them a length.

Josh knew he was in trouble by the glare he received from Peter Stone as he walked Little Vixen into the unsaddling enclosure. And, as his pulse slowed and the excitement of the race faded, he had a feeling that it wouldn't just be the trainer who'd be gunning for him.

Mouse wasn't officially expected to work on Saturday afternoons. The garage wasn't open for service or repair work but the sales boys next door worked all weekend and Baz was always present. He used the time to sort paperwork, clear his backlog of calls and snoop around. He'd get into all the computers in the place and make sure there weren't any inappropriate files. All employees had to log their passwords with him and he used the knowledge shamelessly. Mouse didn't blame him – it was his business. Sometimes she helped him, though she'd not found anything particularly incriminating beyond a few downloaded porno photos and

Baz wasn't bothered by those. All he cared about was people being rude about him in emails.

The fact of the matter was that Baz preferred being at work, where he was king of the castle, to being at home with his wife and toddlers, where he definitely wasn't. Since she'd had children, sweet simpering Denise had turned into a household tyrant and at home Barry Fordyce, self-made businessman, was treated like a supernumerary domestic. At any rate, that was his side of the story and it was good enough for Mouse.

The upshot was that the pair of them drifted into the empty service office on Saturday morning. The understanding was that she'd help him out for a couple of hours, then watch the racing on his portable television in the afternoon.

She had Gavin to thank for getting into horse racing. He knew lots about it himself – family connections and things. A couple of years ago he'd fixed for her to spend time helping out at a stables, as part of her therapy. Apparently it was good for people like her – people with 'psychological issues' – to spend time with animals. She'd thought so too and she'd even enjoyed shovelling horseshit. Unfortunately some of the others on the course preferred to chuck the shit around and they'd all got bounced out as a result. It hadn't been fair.

Still, it had given her another interest, as wallies like Denis would say, something else to do with her time apart from stare at a computer screen. Baz thought it was great, the gambling side of it appealed to him. He was always looking for a good tip and sometimes she'd been able to oblige.

Mouse got a particular thrill out of watching Josh this afternoon. Nine months ago, when she'd first developed an interest in him, it had been simple adoration. The way he slapped his boot with his whip as he strode into the parade ring, the tightness of his britches across his backside as he rode a finish, the chuckle in his voice as he was interviewed after a race – well, well, basically she'd just fancied the pants off him. But things had developed, of course. Now her pleasure was much more complex.

In those early days, she'd worshipped from afar – apart from one occasion. The meeting that changed her life, when she'd come in to help Baz one morning after his first receptionist had gone AWOL and Josh Swallow had turned up.

She'd not known who he was till later but she'd clocked him the moment he'd stepped in the door. He reminded her of someone. Perhaps it was the gloss about him, the kind of film-star glow that ordinary people didn't have, as if he'd never had a zit in his life, as if he didn't even have to wipe his arse. And when he'd walked up to the desk she'd noticed his clothes. At first glance, they seemed nothing special. You could buy a simple cotton jacket like that in any high street in the country. Only it wouldn't hang just so on the shoulders like it was made to measure. It occurred to her it probably had been made to measure. Certainly, it was expensive, like his checked shirt and smart-but-casual blue jeans and shiny brown loafers.

Her first thought was that she resented this man who appeared to have stepped straight out of an advert for country casual clothing. Perhaps that's who he was – a male model. Some softie gay boy from down south. He could frigging well go back to where he came from.

It turned out that where he came from was just up the road and he was dropping his car off for a service like any other customer. Unlike other customers, though, he had shimmering green pools for eyes which looked directly into hers without a trace of disdain or patronage or boredom. And when he wished her good morning and asked how she was, it was as if he actually wanted to know.

'I'm fine, thank you, sir,' she said automatically but he frowned and, to her astonishment, took hold of her wrist.

'No, you're not, you're bleeding.'

And she'd looked down in alarm to see the streak of blood across the desktop from where she'd bitten into her thumb. She'd tried to yank her hand free but he held on to it with a grip that was soft but unbreakable. She felt her face blazing as he peered at her skinny red fingers with their chewed-up nails, leaking shamefully on to his hand.

'Here.' He had a handkerchief in his other hand. A big pale blue one of crisp cotton. Who on earth carried a handkerchief these days? Mouse only knew people whose pockets were stuffed with grubby Kleenex.

'No,' she protested. 'It'll get ruined.' But he'd taken no notice, wrapping it neatly round her fingers.

'Don't you worry about it,' he said. Then he'd added, after she'd completed his paperwork with her good hand, 'I used to bite my nails worse than that.'

She didn't believe him but it was kind of him to say it. And then she'd realised who it was he reminded her of – Gavin. Gavin in the days when she'd first known him. He'd been so unlike the educational psychologists and social workers she'd come across before. His clothes were casual but smart and cared for, and he'd carried himself as if he could sort out the world's problems. He had green eyes too, and a way of talking to you that made you feel as if he really cared.

She'd found out later that Gavin Carter cared for her like a scientist cares for a microbe.

Josh Swallow turned out to be a jockey, which was another connection. She liked horses, from her time at the stable, though she'd never seriously followed racing until Josh walked into the garage. His visit intensified her interest.

That afternoon, she'd gone home and thrown out all her mementos of Gavin Carter. And she'd done one other thing that, in retrospect, she regretted, one of those impulsive, not-thinking things that her new in-control self would not approve of. Leaving a final up-yours message on Gavin's answerphone had not been bright, she knew that now.

Anyhow, she'd felt better for it and afterwards she'd washed and ironed the blue handkerchief. She still had it. It had been her first souvenir of the man who'd become her new obsession.

Today, as she watched the ritual of horse racing unfold on the television, she was conscious of how far she had come since she'd first set eyes on the man of her dreams. Then she had been a tongue-tied acolyte, grateful for the crumbs of compassion that had come her way. He had been up there, on a pedestal, while she grovelled at his feet. Now things were different. She'd stepped into his world, tasted for a few hours here and there what it was like to live in his home, lie on his bed, drink from his cup. More than that, in her brief encounter with the tart, she had rattled the cage of his life. He'd been pilloried in the press, compelled to give evidence at an inquest, had missed a race meeting. He would have suffered the woman's loss, been forced to explain himself to those in authority and those closest to him. And much more, she had no doubt, though she could only guess at the details. Not that they mattered. The fact that she'd yanked on a string and he'd danced, that's what mattered.

On the television Josh was the subject of speculation among the commentators. His resilience in the face of his 'off-the-course troubles' and his tenacious pursuit of the young genius Ben O'Brien in the jockeys' championship were remarked on frequently. This afternoon, they said, could mark a turning point in the championship race. By the end of the day, it was even possible Josh Swallow could be in the lead.

Mouse was nervous. Apart from the fact that it was only fair Josh became champion jockey – it was his turn, everyone said so – it was the kind of thing that mattered on a future media pundit's CV. She was ambitious for Josh and if he was to become the marketable sporting icon he ought to be, then it was important for him to win the championship. They all said it was his retirement season and what better way to bow out?

The afternoon was not going as planned, however. Far from getting on terms with 'the young genius' – oh, do me a favour – Josh was falling behind again.

Mouse called Baz in to watch the fifth race because he had money on it. He'd nagged her for a tip and she'd given him Little Vixen, even though it was a short price. Now, as the race unfolded and Josh careered left to block off Revolutionary, Baz became excited.

'What's he doing? He's going the wrong ruddy way!'

'He doesn't want the other jockey to get past him.'

'I can see that. Is it legal?'

Mouse didn't reply, she was too wrapped up in the contest, elated that Revolutionary had missed the hurdle and was out of the race, but concerned that Josh was too far behind.

'Go on, Josh!' she yelled. 'You can do it!'

But he couldn't. Baz wasn't impressed. 'If he hadn't spent his time shoving the other one out of the race he might have won. Stupid berk.' And he'd stamped out of the room, mourning his lost tenner.

Mouse tried to make the best of it. At least the young genius hadn't extended his lead.

Josh had hardly climbed off the scales before he spotted David Evans, the stipendiary steward, heading in his direction. The inquiry had been announced and he knew that his riding of Little Vixen would be at the centre of it.

He'd already had a slanging match with Ben. 'You're a brainless knacker,' were his first words to the Irishman as they'd pulled up after the race. Ben had retaliated in similar vein and temperatures were running high. Now, as they stepped into the stewards' room, Josh was certain that it was Ben who would be in trouble. Then he spotted the squat ruddy-faced figure of Harcourt Davis, sitting between two other stewards, and his confidence drained away. The Old Etonian was a crony of Leo's father and he couldn't expect any favours from him. In fact, if the old toad had half a chance he'd throw the book at Josh.

The stipendiary steward cleared his throat and addressed the two jockeys, though it seemed to Josh that he had his eyes fixed squarely in his direction.

'I think it's obvious why you're in here. The owner of Revolutionary is alleging obstruction on the part of Little Vixen. Have either of you got anything to say before we take a look at the video?'

'He was trying to poke up my inside,' Josh said loudly. In his experience it did no harm to show these tweedy old farts how you felt.

'You cut me off,' protested Ben with surprising heat, 'and you weren't on the inside either. You were a good horse-width away.'

'Bollocks.'

'All right, gentlemen.' Evans spoke softly but his authority was plain. 'Why don't we take a look at the tape?'

Josh watched the re-run on the television screen, convinced it would show Revolutionary trying to steal his own horse's ground. But with a sinking heart he saw Ben was right. There was indeed just enough room for him to go, when Josh had tried to shut him off. Five years ago, he would have got away with it. These days, it was a different matter.

The sequence was played again, then again from a different angle, this time showing Josh's glance over his shoulder which preceded his move to shut Ben out. With each successive re-run, Josh's anger evaporated, to be replaced by anxiety. He was looking at a ban, he had no doubt. The only question was, how long for?

It seemed Evans was able to read his mind. 'Have you anything you'd like to add, Mr Swallow?'

'Yes.' He had to come up with something by way of damage limitation, but what? 'I didn't realise I'd gone so far over. Without the rail it's not easy to judge.'

Josh and Ben stood awkwardly in the corridor while the stewards deliberated. Josh knew it wouldn't take long.

He turned to the Irishman. 'I'm going to get stuffed, aren't I?'

No emotion registered in Ben's pale blue eyes, though his mouth might have tightened in a small self-satisfied grin. Before he could reply – if indeed he was going to – the stewards' door opened and Evans summoned them back in for the verdict.

It could have been worse, a longer ban than a week. But no other week in the racing calendar mattered so much to a jockey. Josh's stomach turned over as he realised he was going to miss the Cheltenham Festival.

'If you're expecting sympathy, you'll get sod all from me.' Peter Stone was not a happy man. 'I told you to stay in touch with the Irish horse but you go buggering off on some private war and lose the effing race. I mean, Josh, you're not wet behind the ears any more. Where were your brains?'

Josh listened to the lecture without complaint. To be honest, he couldn't explain himself. He'd allowed his personal preoccupations to get the better of him and blown a great opportunity.

'I'm sorry, boss,' he said when Peter had run out of steam. 'I'll apologise to the owner.'

The trainer shrugged. 'As you like. You realise I've now got half a dozen Cheltenham horses without a rider?'

Josh realised all too well. There would be no shortage of jockeys after them, however – including Ben. Even in his current mood of remorse, the thought of Ben enjoying a couple of Festival winners at his expense made him want to spit.

Peter confirmed his suspicions. 'I've already had Tony Wylie on the phone checking out the angles.'

They were standing in the corner of the weighing room after the last race which, predictably, Ben had won. On reflection – and Josh had hardly started the process – it had been a disastrous day.

Mouse knew a bit about the Cheltenham Festival. That it was a big deal, bigger than the Grand National meeting, which was basically a one-race occasion. And this year she'd been devouring the build-up in the papers, much of it focused on the duel between Josh and Ben O'Brien – which now, so she'd just learned, wouldn't be happening. The TV types were making much of the cruel timing of Josh's ban. It cropped up in every interview as they wound up their coverage of the Doncaster meeting.

The pale lugubrious face of Ben O'Brien was now on the screen, a microphone held under his nose. He looked far from happy, as if answering questions on the television was the last thing he wanted to be doing.

'You and Josh Swallow must have had a right old tussle out there in the last hurdle.'

'Yeah.'

'Do you want to tell us exactly what happened?'

Obviously he didn't but nevertheless he said, 'Little Vixen came across me and I missed out the hurdle.'

'So, do you think Josh Swallow's ban is fair?'

'It wouldn't have happened if he hadn't blocked me off.'

'Yes, but he's going to miss Cheltenham, possibly the last Cheltenham of his career.'

O'Brien shrugged. 'I suppose so.'

'Don't you feel sorry for him?'

'Not if I'm honest.' Ben's milky blue eyes gazed steadily into the camera. 'There's no room for sentiment in this business, you know.'

Mouse blinked in surprise. Weren't these jockeys all meant to be fair-minded sportsmen, bonded by the common dangers of their profession?

Not Ben O'Brien obviously.

Chapter Eight

Clive Cooper ripped open the A4 envelope hastily, already preparing to chuck the contents on to the pile of things to do when he got round to it. He'd only nipped into the office en route to Sandown in case there was anything urgent – he was running late.

If it hadn't been for his recent conversation with Leo, he'd certainly have chucked this communication. But attached to two photocopied sides of handwriting was a newspaper clipping he instantly recognised – his own column featuring the photo of Susie Brown, the piece that had so infuriated Leo.

Scrawled in ballpoint across the top of the cutting were the words: 'The truth about SB would make a much better story – why don't you print it?'

He turned to the first photocopied sheet. It was page one of a letter written on stationery headed 'HM Prison Wakely Moor'. Below the printed address was written Merrivale, Stephen G., and a date, 12 June 1998. The letter began 'Dear Susie Sausage'.

There was no covering note of explanation, or

identification of the sender. Of course not. It didn't take a genius to see that someone was out to make mischief.

One thing was certain, if there was any dirt to be dished in the direction of Josh Swallow's lady friend it was an opportunity not to be missed.

His old pal Leo would be so pleased.

They met in a pub for dinner, which was something of a disappointment in Clive's book. He would have preferred more than two rounds of beef sandwiches for sustenance but Leo was calling the tune and he liked his food in a glass.

'So, what have you got?' the trainer demanded after they'd found a table in the corner of the snug. It was a tight fit for two such substantial men but at least they weren't likely to be overheard.

Clive handed over the morning's postal surprise. 'I remember this case and I've been checking out the details on my laptop. In nineteen ninety a doctor in Cumbria called Merrivale killed his wife and youngest daughter, dumped them in Coniston Water, and told everyone they'd gone to Scotland to visit relatives. Then he invited his mistress into the family home to play mum to his other daughter and carried on as normal. It was two weeks before the body of the little girl surfaced. He came clean about the murders as soon as the police showed up. When they arrested him, apparently he said, "This has been the best two weeks of my life. Pity it had to end." '

'Why,' Leo asked, 'did he kill only one child? You'd think he'd murder the whole brood and bugger off to some far corner of the earth with his floozy.'

Clive shook his head. 'Not exactly the type. The floozy was a thirty-five-year-old district nurse who honestly thought Merrivale's wife had walked out on him. He claimed the daughter's death was unfortunate. She turned up just as he was strangling the wife and started to make a fuss. So he strangled her too.'

Leo looked down at the letter in his hand with some disgust. 'Good God. Worst thing we ever did, getting rid of hanging.'

Clive nodded sagely without committing himself. Leo was not the most liberal of fellows but in this case he had a point.

'I take it that Susie Brown is the surviving child,' Leo said.

'That's the implication. She'd be about the right age. Susan Merrivale was ten when the murders took place.'

Leo pointed to the letter. 'Susie Sausage.'

'Her father's pet name for her. I'm not surprised she dumped Merrivale. It might have made sense to change Susie too.'

Leo grunted and studied the ice in his glass as he ruminated.

Clive waited for a moment or two, then plunged on. 'I could easily flush her out into the open. Pay a surprise visit and get her to confirm her identity. She was kept under wraps at the trial, of course, but she's an adult now. If she wanted to spill the beans on her killer dad she could make a bit of money. If she won't play ball, we could splash the story anyway. And some of the dirt would rub off on Josh Swallow. That's what you want, isn't it?'

*

Was it what he wanted?

Leo thought about his conversation with Clive over a nightcap.

Yes and no. He wanted any available mud to be thrown in Josh Swallow's direction and, he supposed, a link to the ghoulish Merrivale case was a start. But it wasn't enough. It might elicit sympathy for the girl and that wouldn't help at all.

And anyway, what he really wanted was evidence that Swallow had killed Annabelle, directly or indirectly, through negligence or design.

Because he had killed her; if she'd not been in his flat she wouldn't have died, would she?

He'd said this to Clive. Suggested he work on the Merrivale story but also ferret around for something more. Clive was a pretty good ferret, who knew what he might unearth? He had the incentive, after all.

Susie realised, as Josh appeared in the kitchen with the morning post, that she'd let things slip. She'd made a point, each day when Josh did not have an early start, of listening out for the crunch of the postman's boot on the gravel of the drive. It was important to get to the mail first, just in case.

But today she hadn't and she could see, amongst the bundle in Josh's hand, one of those dreaded brown envelopes. How could she have been so stupid? She'd allowed herself to get slack and now she was going to be punished.

Josh glanced at the name on the envelope and for a moment her heart skipped a beat. Surely he didn't know her real name?

'Looks like they've got the wrong Susan,' he said, handing it to her. 'Doesn't mean anything to you, does it?'

'No,' she said, barely getting the word out. She was a hopeless liar.

If she'd been a better liar maybe her entire life would have been different. And two people she loved would still be alive.

But Josh didn't notice her burning cheeks, he was grinning ruefully at a credit card bill. 'Give it here,' he said. 'I'll write "not known at this address" on it and shove it in the box when I go out.'

'I'll do it,' she said hastily. 'You haven't got time. Shouldn't you have left by now?'

Thankfully he took the hint without appearing to notice her anxiety. She'd never felt like this about Josh before, desperate to see the back of him. Desperate to find out what her tormentor had in store for her next.

So you've come back. Naughty Susie Sausage. You've had your chance to keep your secret and you've just blown it.

Susie crumpled the note in her fist and wept.

Clive took a piece of cake by reflex – it was not the sort of thing he refused – and only noticed the stray cat hairs after he'd taken a substantial bite and there was nothing for it but to swallow. At least the tea was strong.

Nevertheless, sitting in this shabby Midlands terrace house, he was full of good cheer. This little assignment made a change from flogging the racing beat. It was almost like being an investigative reporter, a role he rather fancied.

As for the cats, he should have been alerted by the smell of the house and, now he looked, the balls of cat fluff on the orange rug in front of the imitation coal fire. There were slinky felines everywhere in the home of Mrs Brenda Brown.

He'd been lucky to track her down so easily but, being Stephen Merrivale's only sister, she had appeared as a witness at his trial. The defence had called her to testify that the late Mrs Merrivale had been a shrew of the first water whose frequent and violent displays of temper had driven her mild-mannered husband to the borders of insanity. Not that her testimony had cut a great deal of ice with the jury.

The surname had tipped Clive off – was her aunt the reason why Susie had changed her name to Brown? He'd been lucky in that a colleague who'd covered the case was in the habit of keeping his notes – useful for his sideline as an author of lurid true crime – and had turned up Brenda's old address, where she still lived.

'I'm convinced your niece is about to be discovered in a big way,' Clive said as the rancid lump of cake sank like a stone to his stomach. He'd been banging on about Susie the artist ever since the aunt had opened the door. First he'd handed over his press pass and shown her a copy of his column – headed by a small and flattering head shot of his good self – and her initial stony-faced indifference had melted to the point of offering him refreshment.

Brenda, it was obvious, was happy to talk about her talented niece – in her present incarnation anyway – and Clive had given her the impression he was simply researching an article on equine artists.

'I believe Susie has just come back from foreign parts,' he said, nudging the conversation into the relevant area.

'She was in South Africa.' The aunt, a gaunt, be-cardiganed figure with a lantern jaw, glowed with family pride. 'On commission for a very wealthy woman. She got Susan to paint one of her horses.'

'You can't recall this lady's name, can you?'

'Why?' Suspicion flickered across the woman's face.

'Maybe I could talk to the owner about her appreciation of Susie's work. You never know, it might get her a few more commissions.'

Brenda softened. 'Oh, I see. Susan just called her Carmen.'

'Carmen Cook?' The rich South African rumoured to be on the brink of launching herself at British jump racing. Clive had heard of her.

'When did Susie go out to South Africa?' he asked innocently, pretending to nibble at the cake.

The woman shrugged. 'I can't remember exactly. Some time around the back end of January.'

'Was that before the terrible accident at Josh Swallow's flat?'

Brenda looked at him in surprise. 'What's that got to do with it? All I know is she was away for a sight longer than she said. She was only meant to be going for a week.'

'Do you know if she flew out from Heathrow?'

Now she really was glaring at him suspiciously. 'You'd have to ask her that. Must be a bit of a funny article you're writing.'

'It's all good background, Mrs Brown. I say,' and he jumped to his feet, 'is that a picture of the young Susie?'

He'd spotted the photograph when he'd first entered the little sitting room and now was a good moment for a diversion. He had the framed print in his hand in an instant and examined it closely. A sullen-looking adolescent posed dutifully in a school blazer and skirt, obviously hating every moment. Clive's last doubts about her identity evaporated. The wide-spaced eyes and downturned lips were unmistakable. This was Susie all right – Susie Sausage, whose father had killed her mother and sister three or four years before this photo was taken. Poor kid.

'That's her in her last year at school,' said Brenda. 'I wanted her to stay on but she wouldn't. I brought her up, you know.'

'What happened to her parents?' More innocence – he had the measure of old birds like this one. Keep the smile going and the tone intimate.

There was no hesitation in the reply. 'Killed in a car crash when she was ten. And her sister too.'

'Tragic,' he said.

He wasn't going to get any more out of her, he knew. But he didn't need to.

Josh had spent the week before his ban came into effect going flat out in search of winners, hoping to get something in the bank before his lay-off. He'd ridden anything and everything, and travelled by helicopter between meetings to get on the scoreboard. But by the end of the week, though he had ridden six winners, Ben's lead was still the same – seven. In the context of a season it wasn't that much. But when he'd been so close to wiping it out altogether, and with Cheltenham now denied him, it was a sickener.

In the past, faced with a ban like this, he'd have flown off for a holiday and tried to forget about racing. But that didn't seem the right thing to do now. It was about time he faced up to a few things. Like how to earn a living at the end of the season when he retired from riding.

What was he going to do? He wasn't going to quit the racing business, that was self-evident to him, though possibly not to everyone else. Ever since he'd climbed on a horse – in fact, a donkey, on Broadstairs beach when he was six – he'd known that he had a special connection with these animals. When, shortly afterwards, he'd discovered that people rode them in races, his mind was made up. It hadn't really changed since.

Susie had looked perplexed when he told her this. 'What you're saying is that you don't want to retire.'

No, he wasn't. It was time to change direction, that's all. 'If I can't ride, I'll train,' he said, articulating a thought that he'd never expressed out loud before.

Since he'd been with Peter Stone he'd always been more than just a stable jockey. He helped Peter with the entries, spent time with the head lad dealing with the never-ending list of health problems and got involved with the administration, making sure the horse passports were in order and so on.

The moment he'd said it, he knew it felt right. It was a big decision though. A jockey didn't just become a trainer. It required a level of energy and commitment and specialised skill that he didn't yet know whether he possessed. Just because you could ride didn't mean you could train. Most of the best trainers he knew were either moderate jockeys, or had never sat on a horse at all. Training required a sixth sense. Being able to tell when a horse was ready to do more work. Possessing the nous to judge an animal's potential and, most importantly, having the courage to get rid of a horse if you thought it was no good. You also needed a big slice of luck.

There was only one way to find out if he had what it took to make a go of it.

'Suppose,' he said to Susie, 'we get rid of the flat and the house and sink all the money in proper training premises somewhere. And, I promise, wherever it is, there'll be a big studio for you to work in. If there isn't space, I'll build one specially. What do you say?'

'OK.'

'Only OK?' he said. 'If you don't like the idea, tell me. We'll think of something else.'

'No, Josh. That's wonderful.'

She had a funny way of showing her enthusiasm, he

thought. But she'd gripped his hand and said she knew he'd be a marvellous trainer.

He felt sure she was sincere but he couldn't work her out sometimes. She'd been fantastic support at the time of the inquest but since then her confidence seemed to have drained away. And whenever he tried to get to the bottom of it she shied away from him and returned even less sure of herself.

One thing did appear to cheer her up though – the thought of moving somewhere else. So they were spending Cheltenham week at Arlington Mansions, putting the place in shape.

Josh had only been back once since Annabelle's death, a fleeting visit the week after the tragedy. Though the dead woman's clothes and belongings had been removed, her presence had been palpable. And clearing the fridge of food intended for the dinner they'd never eaten had given him the creeps.

But returning with Susie by his side was bearable, and there were jobs which soon took his mind off Annabelle – like tackling the boxes that he'd shoved out of sight after his mother's death.

He waded through files of family memorabilia: birth and death certificates, his grandfather's war medals, piles of pension correspondence, his old school reports, boxes of photos taken over the past century – many of people in tiny black-and-white, scalloped-edged prints whom he didn't recognise. How shameful that he didn't know what connection he had with these smiling ghosts from his family past.

One thing puzzled him though. He couldn't find the photos taken of him with Blackie, his first pony. His dad had finally succumbed to his daily nagging and bought the pony from a milkman when Josh was eight. Without Blackie, Josh had often thought, he'd never have turned out a rider at all. His dad had been going through a rough patch at the time and hadn't been able to afford a saddle as well as a pony. As a consequence, Josh had had to learn to ride bareback, gripping with his legs to maintain a proper balance – on reflection, an invaluable lesson. But now he couldn't find those photos. He could have sworn his mum had kept them.

'Perhaps they'll turn up at Ridge Hill,' Susie said. But he knew they wouldn't. It just showed you should take care of your memories, he reflected as he packed away the boxes.

He contacted Brownlows, the estate agency that had brokered the deal on the sale to his mother, years previously. He recalled a gentle middle-aged man who had flirted in a courtly manner with his mum. These days Brownlows were represented by a smart Asian woman in leather trousers touting the smallest mobile phone Josh had ever seen, whose irritating peeps constantly interrupted her brief tour of the premises.

Before she'd arrived, Josh and Susie had discussed at length what to say about Annabelle's fall. Presumably it was relevant to the sale of the property. Josh broached the subject as Mira completed her tour of inspection.

'Really?' she'd said, squinting through the window at the balcony. 'Looks quite safe to me.'

'Don't you think a buyer should be told?' Josh said.

The estate agent gave the matter the benefit of her expertise. 'Let's just keep it between ourselves.'

'But they'll be bound to find out.' Probably the moment they ran into Archie the caretaker, now he thought about it.

Mira smiled, white teeth flashing. 'With luck that won't be until after they've exchanged contracts.'

It was five to two and Josh's mind was at Cheltenham. They'd be going down to the start for the Supreme Novices' Hurdle, the Festival opener. He'd been due to partner Nanny Knows Best, a five-year-old trained by Peter Stone who had been grooming her for this race. If she jumped a bit quicker than she had in the past, she would have a chance.

Josh was missing the Festival atmosphere but he'd enjoyed seventeen years of that already. To be honest, Cheltenham could be a complete scrum. All crowd and *craic* and no air to breathe but a pent-up excitement that could turn legs to jelly and brave riders into lunatics as they strove for victories harder to come by here than anywhere else. He'd had the worst lows of his career at Cheltenham. Five times he'd come away without a single winner despite being on some of the most fancied horses. He'd had a horse die under him, attempting an impossible leap, and he'd been in tears in the weighing room. Once, he'd been in the clear on the favourite in the Champion Hurdle and turned a somersault at the last, breaking a leg and handing a few million pounds to the bookmakers. The fall had been his fault – as a critical world showed no reluctance in telling him for weeks afterwards. That had been an unhappy experience.

But he'd also been first past the post in some tight finishes, sucked home by the enthusiasm of fans determined to make this the day of their sporting lives. His first Gold Cup victory had come at the age of nineteen, when he'd been just another name on the racecard to most race-goers. He'd been on an unfancied outsider, Eden Rock, trained in Yorkshire by Don Jarvis, a horse-mad farmer with a gift for publicity. After Eden Rock had won, Don told the press he'd played the horse a video of the 1965 Gold Cup by way of inspiration. 'When he went out there he thought he were Arkle – no wonder he bloomin' well walked it!' It made a great story and the victory had turned Josh into a star. There was no place like Cheltenham.

He reached for the TV remote control. As he did so, the doorbell rang. Thank God for that – he didn't really want to watch it anyway.

In their discussions with Mira, she had tut-tutted over the absence of a lift. 'The stairs are a big downside,' she'd stated. Josh had objected, pointing out that climbing six short flights of stairs was a reasonable price to pay for being high up above the traffic-filled street. His mother had never found them a problem. However, he had conceded that some people might be put off.

So he was surprised that the first interested party Mira ushered through the door was a puce-faced woman who must have weighed over sixteen stone. She subsided into a chair in the hall and left her bantamweight husband to enjoy a cursory look around. They were out of the door within five minutes – after she'd got her breath back.

As soon as they had disappeared, Josh turned on the television. A jockey standing in his stirrups was waving his stick in triumph as his horse, a familiar-looking animal, was being led past a cheering crowd packed in front of the stand.

'I don't believe it,' Josh muttered, flicking to the Teletext. But the result was there in black and white.

'What's happened?' Susie was eyeing him anxiously.

'Nanny Knows Best just won the first.'

She said nothing but slipped an arm round his waist. Together they watched the re-run of the closing stages of the race.

Nanny Knows Best was lying fourth or fifth coming into the second hurdle from home, out of touch with the leading group. It looked like that was where he'd finish. Some distance ahead, the favourite clipped the hurdle and dived into the turf, causing chaos. The horse behind tried to change direction in mid-air to avoid the faller and pitched his jockey on to the floor. The horse on the inside veered into the rail and lost his momentum. Nanny Knows Best, five lengths behind and out of trouble on the outside, went round the pile-up, calmly took the last hurdle and strode up the hill to win.

'That's brilliant for Jason,' said Josh, thinking of Peter Stone's second jockey, who'd stepped in to take the ride when he had been banned. The owners had wanted a star name from outside but there hadn't been one available so Jason had got the nod. 'Really well done.'

Susie was less impressed. 'Just lucky, if you ask me. He only won because he stayed on his feet.'

Josh thought of telling her how Jason deserved the chance because, in his opinion, there wasn't a nicer lad around. But he kept his mouth shut and, for a moment, allowed himself to wallow in the feeling that it should have been him on Nanny Knows Best, watching the favourites fall like ninepins and picking up an easy win.

'At least it wasn't Ben,' said Susie, voicing a crumb of comfort.

But by four thirty, after Ben O'Brien had won the Champion Hurdle and the National Hunt Chase, that consolation had gone.

On Wednesday Susie volunteered to get another key cut so they could leave it with the estate agent and get out of London. She'd thought that a few days out of the reach of the letter-writer – who couldn't surely know the Arlington Mansions address – would be good for her nerves. But it hadn't worked out like that. She hated the flat with its heavy dark-wood décor and the balcony gave her the creeps. At least, back in Derbyshire, she could paint.

Josh said, 'It means a trip to Logan Brothers in Hammersmith. I'll have to do it.'

'Why?'

'Mum got the most secure lock she could find. They only issue new keys to the signature holder and that's me.'

She supposed it made sense. It sounded reassuring, at any rate.

In the event, Josh had got on the phone to the locksmith

and, after clearing a few security hurdles, had arranged for Susie to pick up a new key. His task for the afternoon was to open the door to Mira and another possible buyer. Neither of them mentioned the second day's racing from Cheltenham but she had no doubt he would be watching.

Walking the streets was a relief. She felt anonymous in the big city, which was how she liked it. But she could hardly expect Josh to set up a training business in London, could she? Up in Ridge House, as part of a small community, she felt exposed. As far as she knew the letter-writer hadn't yet spread the word about her. Or maybe he had. Maybe the neighbours were already discussing the girl whose father was a killer.

At least Josh had promised they would move. Her tormentor was local, she knew that from the franking on the envelopes which had all been posted in Derby. When they moved, surely the letters would cease.

But she knew the hope was hollow. Josh would be easily traced and if she stayed with him she'd be a sitting duck.

In the reassuringly old-fashioned showroom of Logan Bros., where historic locks were displayed alongside the newest inventions, a leathery-faced assistant in a brown apron scrutinised the paperwork that Josh had given her as bona fides of her errand. He took his time, before asking her to wait and disappearing into a back room.

When he reappeared five minutes later he had a grin on his face. He presented her with the shiny new key with a satirical flourish.

'So that's the precious key,' she said. 'I suppose all this cross-checking makes sense.'

'As a matter of fact, madam, you could have had a copy made of this key anywhere you liked.'

This was news to her. 'But I was told I could only get one here. For security.'

'With one of our recent keys that would have been correct, madam. But this one must be getting on for ten years old – it's out of copyright. Any shop can knock out a duplicate. Of course, it might not be as good a copy as this.'

'But it would still open the door?'

'Unless they completely botched the job.'

Susie couldn't imagine Logan Bros. ever botching anything.

When she got back to the flat Josh was looking gloomy in front of the television.

'Ben won the first,' he said, 'so he's ten ahead of me now. And Carmen Cook's horse is in the next. The one I was going to ride.'

Susie took her place by Josh's side on the sofa, scanning the screen for a sight of her South African patron as the camera focused on the horses in the parade ring.

'There she is.' A statuesque woman in a short skirt and scarlet jacket, her flag of deep auburn hair blowing in the stiff breeze, was enthusiastically pumping a jockey's hand. She looked about twice his size.

'She'll catch her death,' said Josh.

Susie thought that Carmen probably hadn't even noticed the weather. She was something of a force of nature herself.

The camera had switched to Vendange, Carmen's entry. As his elegant caramel frame strode across the screen, a pundit informed them the horse's chances were reasonable. Only five years old, Vendange was a typical French type, athletic, wiry and strong. He had won his first bumper at Bangor. However, he was up against some strong contenders here, including ten from Ireland, all with big reputations.

For all his inexperience, Vendange put on a good show. His jockey kept him up with the leading group throughout the race and he seemed to have plenty in reserve.

Susie kept a surreptitious eye on Josh as the race progressed. His concentration was total, as if he were riding the horse after all, urging him round the course he knew so well.

Vendange was continuing to show as the leaders raced downhill from the far side of the course.

'Not yet,' instructed Josh as the young lad on Vendange pressed to the front. 'Damn!' He leaned back in his seat and turned to Susie. 'He's gone too early.'

'No, it's OK!' Susie was caught up in the excitement now. 'Look, he's in the lead!' Though she knew Josh would be disappointed to miss out on another winner, it would be marvellous for Carmen – how could she not want her friend's horse to win? 'Come on, Vendange!' she shouted.

But Vendange was undone, as so many before him, by the switchback nature of the course which now led up a sapping gradient to the line. Suddenly the horse was labouring, as if he were wading through treacle, while others streamed past him.

'Oh well,' she said. 'I suppose fifth's not bad for your first Cheltenham run.'

Josh said nothing. She could only guess at his mixed feelings. She knew one thing though; he'd been right about the jockey mistiming his bid for glory.

She put her arm round his shoulder. 'He'd have won if you'd been riding.' And she wasn't just saying it to make him feel better.

Clive Cooper was of the opinion that Carmen Cook was destined to make an impact on British racing in more ways than one. The flame-red hair, no-nonsense manner and gravel-filled chuckle marked her out as a character, not to mention her exceptional curves. Clive was a fan of the paintings of Peter Paul Rubens.

He'd worked hard to get ten minutes of her time. In the jam-packed bars and watering holes of Cheltenham it was impossible to get any privacy but he'd managed to manoeuvre her behind a large group of tipsy Irishmen. He hoped that she would remain out of sight of the many trainers who were sniffing around such an attractive new owner.

So far things had gone swimmingly. He had enough information on Carmen's plans for her horses to contribute a piece in his daily Cheltenham Diary. Now it was time to move on to Leo's agenda.

'I understand you're a patron of the arts, Carmen. A little bird tells me you've been sponsoring Susie Brown.'

Carmen's grin widened. 'You bet. I invited her over for a week to do me a painting and she stayed for six and did three. And there's more to come.'

'It was a good time to be enjoying some African sun,'

Clive ventured. 'I don't know if you heard but there was a terrible tragedy at her boyfriend's flat in London.'

Carmen nodded. 'Yeah, I know. The poor thing was in a bit of a state.'

'Was she staying with you at the time of the accident?'

Fortunately Carmen wasn't as suspicious as the aunt. 'She left on the day it happened and flew in overnight. Bloody awful business.'

'A terrible shame. What flight did she catch?'

This time Carmen did look at him strangely. 'Hell, you British journalists want to know everything, don't you?'

Clive smiled at her expectantly, his pencil poised.

'She came in direct from Heathrow on South African Airways. Are you sure your readers are going to be interested?'

His readers couldn't care less, Clive thought. But he knew someone who would be very interested indeed.

By Thursday, the number of prospective buyers Mira had brought round had reached double figures. One interested party, a middle-aged woman with stylishly cropped fair hair, returned for a second look, accompanied by her brother. Mira was not present.

Susie left them poking around the kitchen and found Josh fretting in the living room. She knew the Gold Cup was due off in ten minutes but that couldn't be helped.

'Her brother likes it,' she said. 'I think she's going to make an offer.'

There wasn't time to say any more but she hoped Josh

would take the hint. It wasn't her place to tell the buyers about Annabelle.

'Can we go out on the balcony?' said the woman. 'I'm dying to show Giles the view from up here.'

'Of course.' Josh opened the door and ushered the pair of them ahead of him into the open air. Then he followed them out to tell them the balcony's history.

Five minutes later the couple had gone.

'Perfect timing,' said Josh as he switched on the television.

'How did they take it?' Susie asked.

'I don't think he was bothered but she went a bit quiet.'

'Oh.' Susie felt bad about it. 'You had to tell her, Josh. It wouldn't have been fair otherwise.'

The phone rang just as the race reached its climax. Susie took the call, keeping one eye on the screen. Last year's winner, the favourite, was caught on the line by a big raw-boned powerhouse that she couldn't identify.

She listened to Mira with her hand over the mouthpiece, preventing the noise of the television from travelling back down the line.

Josh turned his head towards her but he didn't have to ask.

'It's Mira,' she said. 'They're not going to offer.'

'There's a surprise.'

She put down the phone. 'Who won the race?'

'Loose Connection.'

At least it wasn't the horse Josh had been due to ride. He didn't look too pleased about it, however.

'Who was the jockey?'

As she spoke she realised it was a silly question. That made Ben eleven ahead in the jockeys' championship.

'Josh,' she said, deliberately planting herself in front of the television, 'we don't need to stay in London now Mira has a key, do we? Let's go home.'

'When?'

'How about this evening?'

Josh didn't need much persuading. He accepted her offer to clear up and disappeared to warn Archie about Mira, in case he met her ferrying people in and out.

Susie was interrupted by the doorbell and buzzed the visitor up. A minute later she was opening the door to a small, grey-haired figure with bright beady eyes.

'Mrs Glazier,' she blurted in surprise.

The older woman cocked her head on one side. 'Have we met?'

'I saw you in the Coroner's Court. When you gave evidence at the inquest.'

The eyes narrowed for a moment. 'Of course. You were sitting next to Mr Swallow.' Mrs Glazier moved closer. 'I heard that he was putting this flat up for sale.'

'That's right.'

'I wonder if I might have a look around. Or would you prefer that I make an appointment through the estate agent?'

'Gosh, no. Come in.' But the visitor was already in the door, her eyes darting everywhere.

'I've been here before, you know,' she said as she set off down the hall, 'so I know my way around.'

'You used to play bridge with Mrs Swallow, didn't you?'

Mrs Glazier shot her a look of exasperation before

adjusting a picture frame which, now Susie looked at it, was slightly askew. 'No head for cards, that woman. What she liked was a few gins and a chinwag. If you ask me, she was a bit lonely.' And she ducked into the bedroom.

Susie followed her. Mrs Glazier had made a beeline for the roll-top desk that stood in the corner.

'I used to be in antiques,' Mrs Glazier said as if confiding a great secret. 'You'd be surprised how many nice pieces I've acquired from people who are selling up. Like this desk.' She rolled back the top and peered into the drawers. 'I don't suppose Mr Swallow is thinking of parting with it?'

'Old habits die hard then.'

The little woman shrugged and abruptly pulled the top back down. 'You're right, it's just a habit. Forget I mentioned it.' She looked unsure of herself and, for once, all of her seventy-six years.

'Why don't I make us a cup of tea?' suggested Susie.

They drank it in the kitchen and, with Susie prompting, Mrs Glazier talked about her acquaintance with Josh's mother, her other friends in the area and her days spent running an antiques shop with her husband Lionel, now sadly departed for almost seventeen years. It was plain to Susie that Josh's mother had not been the only lonely senior citizen on the street.

One thing they did not talk about was the inquest.

Finally the older woman stood up and Susie accompanied her to the door.

On the threshold, Mrs Glazier hesitated. 'I'm sorry,' she said. 'I really don't want to do it but this is my last chance.'

Susie looked at her blankly. Her mind was on Josh and

how much longer he was likely to be. It was time they were on their way.

But Mrs Glazier had turned round and was heading back inside. 'I hope you don't mind, my dear, but I must, I really must go out there.'

Go where? For a moment Susie was puzzled, but as the small figure in her brown woollen coat turned into the living room it soon became clear what she wanted.

Susie opened the door and the pair of them stepped on to the balcony. The late afternoon chill cut into them and the rumble of traffic filled their ears.

Mrs Glazier stepped up to the parapet and pointed directly ahead. 'That's my flat directly opposite. You can see straight into my front room, can't you?'

Susie agreed. She could see a balcony not dissimilar to the one they now stood on and, behind, a set of french windows. Through the glass she could make out some shadowy furniture, with what looked like the dark wood of a sideboard next to an internal door which stood ajar.

'On the day Mrs Lovall died I was at home, looking over here, as you know because you heard me say so at the inquest. And I wasn't confused about which balcony I was looking at despite what that Duncan woman said.'

'She's a hotshot barrister. They know some sneaky tricks.'

Mrs Glazier's head bobbed in eager agreement. 'Indeed they do and she made me look a silly old fool. But I know very well what I saw. I was over there and *she* was standing here.' Mrs Glazier pointed to the left of the balcony door.

'She?' Susie knew who the little woman meant but she wanted to hear the details again.

Mrs Glazier did better than that. She took up a position to the side of the door.

'The woman I saw was standing here, just like this. As if she was on sentry duty.'

The diminutive figure leaned back against the wall, ramrod straight, her arms by her side. Susie was tempted to smile at the spectacle of the little grey-haired lady playing soldier if it hadn't been for the expression on Mrs Glazier's face. She was in deadly earnest.

Instead she said, 'Are you certain this person wasn't Annabelle?'

'If you remember, I said in court that I couldn't be sure.'

'You're not in court now, Mrs Glazier. What's your gut feeling? Do you think it was?'

'No. At first I assumed it was the same woman but, on reflection, the person I saw wasn't tall and thin like Mrs Lovall, she had a bigger build. And I didn't recognise any of the clothes in the photographs at the inquest. The person I saw wasn't wearing anything like that.'

'But,' Susie objected, the words of Colin Smart springing to mind, 'suppose she was outside at the time you saw her, intending to jump, but couldn't go through with it. Then she went indoors and put on warmer clothes. And forty-five minutes later, when she'd got fresh courage, she came back out here and threw herself off the balcony.' This was still the explanation that made the most sense to Susie.

Mrs Glazier didn't seem impressed. 'It's very ingenious

of you, my dear, but the more I think about it the more I'm convinced that I saw someone completely different.'

The old lady's conviction was hard to ignore. Suppose she was right and there had been someone else out here on the balcony before Annabelle fell? Susie shivered and not just because of the chill air.

But what Mrs Glazier said next surprised her even more. 'There's a reporter interested in my story, you know. He believes me. He came to see me last week and showed me a picture of the young woman he thought I might have seen.'

'Who was it?'

The older woman fixed her beady eyes on Susie and smiled. It wasn't a nice smile.

'He didn't give me her name but I tell you one thing. She looked remarkably like you.'

It had not been a good Cheltenham for Leo Lovall. In fact, it had been the worst for years. If you discounted a second in the Arkle, it had been a complete wash-out, with all his fancied runners under-achieving. Perhaps, like him, they'd had their minds on other things.

He couldn't think of anything but Annabelle and the circumstances of her death. Of her, pregnant by Josh Swallow, turning up at the man's flat in London. And dying while he was riding at Leicester.

It had to be Swallow's fault.

Suppose, just for a moment, Josh didn't want Annabelle – pregnant Annabelle – barging back into his life now he was shacked up with his new lady love, the artist. How convenient that she went over the balcony while he was riding in front of hundreds of people a three-hour drive away.

So he couldn't have pushed her.

But he could have got someone else to do it, couldn't he?

At the inquest Leo had been happy to see his brief, Miss Duncan, pour scorn on the evidence of the woman who'd claimed to see Annabelle on the balcony preparing to jump. But now he thought about it, the old lady had not been certain it *was* Annabelle.

Suppose it was the killer – put there by Josh Swallow?

That was his hypothesis but he needed some facts to go with it. He couldn't wait for his next meeting with Clive Cooper.

*

Now the dust has settled on the Cheltenham Festival for another year and the equine gods who have thrilled our days have been tucked away in their horseboxes with an extra carrot or two, it's time to reflect on the emergence of a new, two-footed hero. Step forward, Ben O'Brien, the latest in a long line of legendary jockeys. It may seem premature to crown a 21-year-old who is barely wet behind the ears but every generation throws up a rider head and shoulders above the rest.

Mouse irritably shuffled the pages of the Saturday edition of the *Racing Beacon*. Ben O'Brien had cleaned up at Cheltenham – most unfairly, in her opinion, since two of his winning rides came from the Peter Stone stable and would obviously have been partnered by Josh. Even such a one-sided article as this would surely acknowledge Josh's contribution but so far he had not even merited a name check.

Morbid fascination compelled her to read on.

A star of the Irish point-to-point circuit at the precocious age of sixteen, Ben learned his business in an uncompromising school. 'My dad was keener on horses than cows and he had a reputation for turning round bad-tempered animals. He used to train all sorts on the farm and he used me. He says it was to give me an education in horses but I reckon it's because he never had to pay me.'

In his comparatively short time in England under the wing of Leo Lovall, Ben has established himself as the number one jockey in the country. Though his rise from relative obscurity has been meteoric, nothing on or off the racecourse appears to faze him. 'The strangest thing,' he says, 'is living on my own. I've got two brothers and three sisters back in Ireland and our house is fairly lively. Plus, of course, I miss my mum's cooking – though all us jockeys have got to watch our weight, of course,' he adds with a twinkle in his periwinkle-blue eye.

On the rails, in the bars and in bookmakers' shops throughout the land the public have taken to this young Irishman. Already the tag of 'young genius' that dogged the first half of this season has lost its tinge of irony. Those of us who follow the turf are fast learning that Ben O'Brien does everything he can 'in the best possible way'.

What a load of piffle, thought Mouse. The hack who'd churned it out was a complete tosser. As for the periwinkle-eyed genius . . .

Surely Ben O'Brien couldn't just turn up out of the bogs of Ireland and walk off with the jockeys' championship in only his second proper season? How fair was that? You were supposed to pay your dues in sport. Like Josh had done.

Finally there was a mention of Josh. Along with other racing names he'd been asked to pass judgement on Ben's performance at Cheltenham. 'The lad's too darn good,' he'd said. 'He rides horses the way they should be ridden.'

That was pretty magnanimous of him, given the circumstances.

Mouse peered closely at the photograph of Ben in his fancy new Lambourn home. There was no call for her to feel magnanimous towards the Irishman. She didn't have to think or say the right thing, no journalist was going to ask her for a quote. So she could own up to her real feelings about Josh's rival for the jockeys' championship. She didn't like him.

Wouldn't it be nice if something happened to him so he couldn't ride for a bit? If only Ben were banned for a week, as had happened to Josh. It would give Josh a chance to get back into the championship race.

Or suppose he got injured. It happened to jockeys all the time. Suppose some horse trod on his foot or he broke a bone or – this would be great – he fell off while in the lead and the rest of the runners just rode over him, kicking him like a football, smacking his head with their great pistoning hooves, stamping him flat into the ground so they'd have to lever him off the turf like some piece of squished road kill.

Mouse caught herself giggling out loud and choked off the sound, embarrassed at herself. She didn't do stuff like that any more.

At least she wasn't in public.

Leo pushed the whisky bottle in Clive's direction across the desk top but the journalist refused a refill. He had to drive back to London, so it made sense. They were sitting in the office at Hoar Frost. They could have gone up to the house but Leo preferred it here. He still wasn't used to the house without Annabelle.

Clive was running through the results of his ferreting.

'I've checked out the aunt and there's no doubt Josh Swallow's little friend is Susan Merrivale, now known as Brown. The aunt told me the girl was in South Africa, working on commission for Carmen Cook, just after Annabelle died. Then I paid a visit to the Glazier woman who lives opposite Arlington Mansions. She's still quite determined she saw someone on the balcony who wasn't Annabelle, despite the inquest finding.'

'Excellent.'

The reporter inclined his head modestly. 'I've also been talking to Carmen Cook.'

So it hadn't been all hard work. It seemed to Leo that the over-sized Carmen had had most men of a certain age in a spin all Cheltenham. She wasn't his type – though he wouldn't mind taking on some of her horses.

'It turns out,' Clive continued, 'that Susie flew South African Airways from Heathrow to Cape Town on the day Annabelle was killed. There was only one direct flight and it was scheduled to take off at a quarter past eight in the evening.'

'Ah,' said Leo with satisfaction. Clive eyed him shrewdly.

In previous discussions they'd talked of the likelihood of Susie being the mystery woman on the balcony. Leo had pointed out that she would have had access to the flat. Might she not have been Annabelle's executioner, acting on behalf of her lover?

Until now, however, they had not been sure whether Susie had actually been in the country at the time of the murder. But Clive's latest snippet of information made it clear that she'd have had plenty of time to push Annabelle off the balcony at half past three and get to the airport in time for her flight.

After Clive had left, Leo made a phone call. One of the advantages of being a successful racehorse trainer was that you met powerful men and women from all walks of life, many of whom were only too pleased to help you should you need a favour. In this instance, Leo was grateful to be able to talk directly to a man who spent his working hours in the looming edifice of New Scotland Yard while dreaming of the gallops above Hoar Frost Farm where the promising steeplechaser he had a leg in was put through his paces.

Leo was careful not to overstate his case. But he registered his dissatisfaction with the police investigation into his wife's death, especially in light of the fact that another woman had been placed at the scene by a witness. He pointed out that Josh Swallow's current girlfriend had access to the flat and was not, as had been thought, out of the country at the time.

What's more, he added – though only a man of the turf would really understand – it was in her blood.

Chapter Nine

Susie knew that the sky was about to fall on her but she was not prepared for the manner in which it fell.

Mrs Glazier's comment had sent a chill up her spine. The idea of a reporter talking to people behind her back, showing her photograph around, was frightening and perplexing. She told Josh, who tried to make a joke of it.

'Why would anyone want to do that? I thought the old lady was a bit potty at the inquest.'

'She's not potty at all, Josh.'

'Mistaken then.'

'How can she be mistaken about a reporter showing my picture?'

'Mistaken about it being you, I mean. Maybe she didn't have her reading glasses on.' And he laughed.

She let it drop. They were driving back to Derby and she was at the wheel, to give him a break. The mid-March evening was bathed in unseasonal sunshine and the world looked a cheerful place. She felt she was travelling in a personal capsule of gloom.

Before they'd left London she'd rung Brenda – a duty

call. 'I've been trying to get hold of you,' her aunt said. 'I had a visit from the man who's giving you a write-up in the papers.'

'What man?'

'Clive someone. A real gentleman. He said he was doing a story on horse painters. Has he talked to you yet?'

She'd not told Josh about this second report of a journalist on her tail. It could be harmless, couldn't it? Someone writing an article puffing her art. But if so, why hadn't he been in touch with her? That was the logical way to go about it. It was more likely – much more likely – that the letter-writer had tipped off the papers about her past. She wondered which one of the red-tops was about to dig up all those old headlines about Doctor Death and tie it all in with her new life. If they did that, it wouldn't just be her who suffered.

Now, as they drove north, would be a good time to tell Josh the truth. She mustn't put it off any longer.

'Josh,' she said softly.

There was no reply. She shot a glance to her left and saw his head lolling forward on his chest.

It gave her an excuse and, coward that she was, she took it. She'd tell him when they got home. Definitely.

But she never got the chance. As she pulled into the drive of Ridge House, the car headlights swept across an unfamiliar parked vehicle. At once, the doors opened and a man and a woman got out. Both wore suits.

Josh, who'd woken up five minutes ago, muttered, 'That's a policeman from London. I spoke to him after Annabelle died.'

The policeman introduced himself, Detective Inspector Picard, and his colleague too but Susie didn't catch her name. She was filled with dread. Something terrible had happened – that was the only reason the police turned up at your door.

Josh was talking to Picard in his usual friendly fashion but the other one, the female whose name she had not caught, was staring at her.

She soon discovered why. They wanted her to go with them to answer some questions about the death of Annabelle Lovall. Now.

'What? All the way back to London?' Susie blurted. Somehow the thought of retracing the journey she'd just made seemed the worst thing of all.

Picard smiled. He looked a genial sort. 'Oh no. The Derbyshire Constabulary have been kind enough to provide us with an interview room.'

Josh was objecting fiercely. 'This is ridiculous. She knows nothing about Annabelle and she's not going anywhere.' But it was plain to Susie that she had no choice.

They took her to a police station in town where she used the loo but refused refreshment. Then they put her in a bleak little room and left her. To soften me up, she thought.

Eventually, the door opened and a cadaverous balding man entered, carrying a briefcase.

'Paul Beale,' he said, holding out his hand. 'Colin Smart asked me to represent you.'

So Josh had been busy. He must have been on the phone

to his solicitor before the police car had cleared the drive at Ridge Hill.

Logically, Susie couldn't believe the occasion warranted such a fuss. Surely this was just a silly misunderstanding which could be cleared up in ten minutes.

But logic was of little comfort to her. She'd ignored those letters. She should have confessed all to Josh and she hadn't. And now something bad had happened. It was her fault, whatever logic said.

Their first question had her on the ropes.

'Would you like to tell me your name?'

'Susan Brown.'

'Is that your real name?'

'Er, yes.' Her cheeks were beginning to flush already. It was impossible for her to lie. 'Well, it has been since I was ten. I changed it.'

'And before that it was . . .?'

They knew already, they must do or they wouldn't have pressed the point.

'Susan Merrivale.'

The female – DC Potts, she'd discovered – smiled thinly. Picard looked faintly embarrassed.

What nasty game were they playing? Was this just to throw her off balance? To demonstrate that there was no point in her concealing anything from them as they knew her secrets already?

She clasped her hands tightly in her lap to stop them shaking. Paul Beale shot her an encouraging grin but he couldn't help her. He must be wondering what he'd been dragged into.

They switched their questions. Where had she been at two thirty on 22 January this year, the day of Annabelle's death?

'I was on my way to Heathrow to catch a plane to Cape Town.' She gave them the details, as well as she could remember them. The flight was due off at eight fifteen. She'd travelled down to St Pancras by train and caught the tube across London to the airport as she only had one bag. She'd reached Heathrow at about five – she liked to arrive early.

Perhaps she had caught an earlier train and stopped off at Arlington Mansions on the way.

'No, I didn't. Anyway, why would I drag all my stuff up to the flat?'

You just said you only had one bag.

'OK, but I had no reason to go to the flat. I don't even have a key.'

Really?

'I never have had. Honestly.'

Then they'd started asking her about what she was wearing that day.

'A shirt and jeans, I think. And a thick pullover because it was cold.'

What colour pullover?

Then she realised where this was heading. They were trying to place her on the balcony before Annabelle's death. A woman in a navy blue sweater. They thought she was Mrs Glazier's mystery woman.

It wasn't time they were accusing her of killing at the flat.

It was Annabelle.

*

Josh shook with anger as he sat in his car at Exeter racecourse. At the moment he didn't trust himself to the scrutiny of the weighing room – not after the conversation he'd just had with a reporter.

It had been a fraught few days. More than fraught. He felt like he'd been run over by a truck. But what doesn't destroy you makes you stronger; his mum used to say that. And it hadn't destroyed him yet – or his bond with Susie. That was the important thing.

Paul Beale, the solicitor, had brought Susie back to Ridge House at 8.30 a.m. They'd kept her all night, questioning her in sessions of two hours or more, coming back to the same allegations over and over. They thought she'd run into Annabelle at the flat and chucked her over the balcony, which was preposterous. And all, as far as Josh could see, because of that daft old bat who lived over the road.

'But there's been an inquest,' Josh protested to Paul. 'The coroner didn't think Mrs Glazier's testimony was relevant. The matter's closed.'

'It was an open verdict, as I understand it,' the solicitor replied. 'The police are quite at liberty to pursue fresh evidence.'

The only fresh evidence that Josh could see was some self-serving police officer out to make a name for himself. And he hadn't thought Picard was the type – unless he'd been put up to it.

These reflections hadn't occurred till later in the morning after the phone had started to ring and journalists laid siege to the front door. Susie's arrest was the day's big news and one of the tabloids was ahead of the pack. Nothing excited the papers so much as the thought that they were missing out on a hot story.

Josh spread the offending paper out on the kitchen table and stared at the headline in disbelief. DOCTOR DEATH'S DAUGHTER HELD IN MURDER SWOOP. On one side of the page was a recent picture of Susie in a cocktail dress, and facing it was a middle-aged man he did not recognise, wearing an open-necked shirt and a timid smile. He didn't look as if he'd say boo to a goose.

Susie, slumped on a chair, clinging tightly to a cooling mug of tea, watched him with hollow eyes as he read.

There were lots of pages, with more pictures of Susie, one of her as a smiling ten-year-old. The piece included photographs of Josh, too, and Annabelle. And also a handsome blonde woman and another small girl. Bells began to ring in Josh's head. He'd been in the first flush of his career when these events had taken place. He'd rarely read more than the racing pages back then, though some things could not be avoided.

He read it all in silence, aware of Susie just a few feet away, studying his every move.

Finally he looked up. Tears filmed her cheeks. She looked so lovely and so desperate.

'Why on earth didn't you tell me?' he said as he folded her in his arms.

That had been three days ago and things had calmed down a bit, though they'd never be the same. Susie was traumatised. She refused to talk about what had happened when she was a child and he had not wanted to press her.

'If you ever want to discuss it,' he said, 'then I'm ready to listen. But as far as I'm concerned it makes no difference to how I feel about you.'

It did, of course. It explained her inner secrecy. It was the reason why she always seemed to be holding something back from him. But after what her father had done, it was remarkable she was able to trust any man at all.

The police hadn't charged her, which was a comfort, but they made it clear they were 'pursuing their inquiries'. So there was a threat still hanging over her head.

What appeared to affect Susie even more was the loss of her new identity. The press had seen to that, with every paper running angles. She'd been offered money for her story from several quarters. A TV company had made a proposal for a documentary on her life and she'd been offered a couple of painting commissions at ludicrously inflated prices. She'd turned them all down. She loathed the spotlight that had been turned on her.

So today, when he'd resumed riding at Exeter, Josh had given short shrift to Bob Jarrett who covered racing for one of the broadsheet newspapers. Josh had always had him down as an OK fellow – until now.

Bob had approached him after the third race.

'Josh, would you like to comment on the latest rumours?'

That stopped Josh in his tracks. 'What rumours?' he said.

To his credit, Bob was looking sheepish but his notebook was in his hand.

'That Annabelle was pregnant with your child. And that you put Susie up to getting rid of her while you were racing at Leicester.'

The journalist obviously thought Josh was going to hit him because he moved sharply backwards. Maybe his suspicions were correct, because Josh found his fists were bunched and that he'd moved in close.

'You're a right little bastard, Bob. Don't come to me in the future when you want the inside track on anything.'

The reporter looked affronted, as if it were Josh who had stepped out of line. 'Sorry, mate, but I was told to ask.'

Josh had turned away. He'd kept going till he reached his car, his stomach twisting in his guts like a coiled rubber band.

Mouse would have liked more sugar in her cappuccino but she didn't want to show herself up among all the stylish office girls around her. She would never have come into one of these trendy coffee places if it had been up to her.

Sitting opposite, Rose from Hilltop Holidays sipped something called a tall skinny latte, looking reassuringly uncool and frumpish, not to mention large. It would take more than laying off full fat milk to bring her down to fashionable proportions.

'Basil says you're doing really well at the garage,' said Rose.

Basil? Oh, Baz. Her cousin.

'Yeah, Baz has been great. He's very supportive.'

Supportive was a good word, she'd learned. Along with

'positive' and 'special' and a host of other phrases that people like Gavin Carter dropped into their conversation like currants in a cake.

'Baz has always been there for me,' she added. These sort of sentiments got a big tick from the Gavins of this world. And the Roses, too.

Mouse didn't kid herself that Rose was simply offering the hand of friendship. The woman knew too much about her past. Rose was a 'family friend'.

If it had been left to Mouse, she wouldn't be sitting here sipping tasteless froth with some overweight busybody. Like most things in her life it was down to Baz. He was always on at her to go out, make friends – 'get a life' as he put it. That was another little phrase that was guaranteed to get up her nose.

He'd come in the other morning announcing he'd just bumped into Rose, who was keen to keep in touch. And, because she was on a high after the stuff in the paper about Blondie – what a result! – she'd called her up. So here they were.

'Your cousin tells me,' Rose was saying –

How I wish my frigging cousin would keep his mouth shut.

– 'that you're keen on horse racing.'

'Yeah. I follow it a bit. Just over the sticks.'

'Over the sticks?'

'Fences – jump-racing. I'm not that keen on the Flat.'

Mouse could see she'd lost Rose – not that she appeared bothered.

'Whatever,' she said. 'The thing is, my Uncle Jimmy is a

Red Cross volunteer at Uttoxeter racecourse. How would you like to go one day?'

Mouse was surprised. She'd never actually been to a racecourse, just followed the racing on the TV.

'You could come along with Geoff and me,' Rose continued. 'Uncle Jimmy says he can get you out on the course.'

Why the hell not?

'Yeah, OK, Rose,' she said, allowing herself a thin little grin. 'That'd be great.'

The other woman leaned over and patted her cheek. 'There, that wasn't so hard, was it?'

The patronising cow.

Resolving to put the exchange with the journalist out of his mind, Josh dialled Tony's number. With the end of the season only a month away, Ben's lead – now fourteen – was beginning to look unassailable. Josh needed every spare ride he could get to give himself a chance.

He reached Tony's answerphone and left a message, asking the agent to call him back urgently. Josh could afford to wait twenty minutes as he didn't have a ride in the next, which rankled.

This was Josh's first day back after his ban and, apart from rides for Peter, the week ahead didn't look much good. Spare rides were thin on the ground. Next week, however, things should improve – they'd have to.

His mobile chirped into life and he answered eagerly.

'How's it going, Josh?' Tony had been doing his best to help Josh cope over the last few days.

Josh didn't bother with the preliminaries. 'Any news on Street Smart?' he asked. He was banking on the ride for Belinda Giles at Aintree the following Friday. He'd ridden him successfully in his last two outings and considered the ride to be his. Belinda did not have a large yard and was loyal to her stable jockey but, for horses with ambitious owners, she sometimes went outside – usually to Josh.

'Sorry, Josh, he's spoken for.'

'Is Alan riding him?' Alan was the yard's regular jockey.

Tony hesitated. 'No. She asked for Ben.'

'For crying out loud, why?' To Josh's knowledge, Ben had never ridden for Belinda before. 'She as good as promised me.'

'I think the owner was the problem. She insisted Belinda went elsewhere.'

Josh cursed. He'd got on like a house on fire with Mrs Maxwell in the past – at least he'd always thought he had. When he'd brought Street Smart home first in a gruelling three-mile chase at Haydock last December he'd thought the woman was going to suffocate him with her gratitude.

'Is it these rubbish stories in the papers, Tony?'

'That and the internet. It's full of unsubstantiated rumours.'

'You mean, like I got Susie to kill Annabelle because I'd made her pregnant.'

'It's nonsense, I know, but there's not much you can do about it.'

Josh was plunged into gloom. 'This is my last season,

Tony. It's not meant to end like this.' Either on the track or off it.

To his surprise, Tony chuckled. 'I've got one piece of good news. Carmen Cook wants you to ride one of hers at Uttoxeter.'

Thank God for Susie's South African connection. At least one person hadn't been put off by the rumours. She probably hadn't heard them yet.

Mouse would have preferred it if Rose hadn't picked her up from her flat. But since Rose knew where she lived anyway it couldn't really make much difference. She just made sure the woman didn't get a peek inside.

A big old Mercedes saloon sat purring at the kerb and Rose opened the rear door for her with a flourish.

Mouse froze for a second. She knew that Geoff, Rose's other half, was accompanying them but there was someone else in the car.

'In you get,' Rose urged and Mouse sank into the scuffed but welcoming leather upholstery, next to a thin youth with long black hair curling over the collar of his leather jacket.

Rose made the introduction. 'This is Geoff's mate, Terry.'

Geoff, a barrel-chested figure in the driver's seat, put the car in gear and they glided to the end of the road. Mouse was in shock. She'd kill that frigging Rose.

Rose must have known what she was thinking. 'When Terry heard we were going racing,' she offered uncon-vincingly, 'he insisted on coming along. Didn't you, Terry?'

Terry ignored the remark; he was studying Mouse closely. She could feel her cheeks burn under his gaze.

'Terry's keen on the gee-gees, aren't you, Terry?' continued Rose.

Mouse thought he was going to ignore her again but he waited just on the borderline of rudeness before saying, 'Yeah, Rosie. I love 'em.' He spoke in a soft Cockney. Inclining his head towards Mouse, he murmured, 'I hope you don't mind me joining your little excursion.'

Excursion? Get him.

'Of course not.' What else could she say?

'So what do you think of him?' Carmen Cook's voice rang unnecessarily loudly round the confined space of the stable. She was not a woman, as far as Josh could tell on their short acquaintance, who was less than wholehearted about anything.

Mountain Range, the horse under scrutiny, looked well enough but a pit pony would have been welcome under the circumstances. Josh was desperate to get on anything with a chance.

'He's been living the life of Reilly over in France,' the owner continued, 'so it would be great if he could turn it on over here.'

They'd hit it off well over a lunchtime sandwich when she had given him a brisk rundown of her activities as an owner. She confirmed that she had big plans. 'I really want to get stuck into your National Hunt next season. Cheltenham was just a road test. So's this.'

She'd sympathised with him over his Cheltenham ban

before quizzing him about the run of Vendange, the ride he'd missed out on. Josh resisted the temptation to say that the jockey had wrongly timed his run for home, tempting though it was. It would be a pretty cheap shot at a fellow professional's expense and he hadn't even ridden a race for Carmen yet. He kept his mouth firmly shut.

At the racecourse Geoff announced that he was starving. Mouse thought to herself that he looked anything but, though she'd never have said so. She didn't particularly want to be steered into a smoky bar to fill her face with sausages and chips, however she could see that was what Geoff and Rose had in mind.

Fortunately, Terry had other ideas. 'It's getting a bit close to the first so I'm going to shoot off and have a dekko at the runners.' He looked at Mouse. 'What about you?'

'Can I come too?' said Mouse.

He nodded. 'Stick with me, babe,' he said, steering her away from the stand, through a knot of people. He appeared to know where he was going.

The crowd parted and Mouse found herself standing in front of a railing. Beyond it was a patch of green surrounded by a non-slip track.

'What time's the first race?' she said.

'Not for ages. I just don't want to hang around inside.' He was grinning at her, his pale face suddenly alive. She noticed he had a gold tooth. 'You don't either, do you?'

She shook her head and looked away from him. His gaze was too insistent.

'Why do they call you Mouse?' he asked.

She shrugged. 'Just a nickname.'

'I don't like it. I don't think it suits you.'

It had once, when she was at school. A long nose that twitched, and ran with snot on cold winter days in the playground. Dull brown hair, lifeless except when it was infested with nits. Little beady eyes magnified by those bottle-thick glasses with transparent National Health frames. And the squeak – that's what had done it for her, earned her the name – the noise she made when they yanked her lousy hair and slapped her pink cheeks and kicked her skinny legs. *Eek, eek!*

Things were different now, though. She wasn't a squeaky rodent any more. She was Mouse the computer wizard.

Terry grinned at her, his eyes twinkling, so sure of himself. 'I'm going to call you Foxy.'

She kept a straight face. 'Suit yourself,' she said in as bored a tone as she could muster.

Foxy. Well, why not? She might even get to like Terry.

The ring was filling up now as the runners were led over from the saddling boxes. The lawn in the middle was spotted with groups of people, owners and trainers. Mouse waited impatiently for the last arrivals, the ones who really counted – the jockeys.

It was like the entry of the gladiators, she thought as the riders began to emerge. Warriors in brightly coloured silks off to do battle. *Where is Josh?*

'Who do you fancy then?' Terry was interrupting her train of thought.

She giggled. *Josh, of course.*

But Terry hadn't meant that. 'Come on,' he said. 'Which of these nags do you reckon?'

Mouse's stable experience hadn't amounted to much but she had learned enough to tell when a horse was fit to run.

'The black one,' she said. It was passing in front of them now, its sable coat glistening in the spring sunlight.

Terry consulted the racing paper he'd bought on the way in.

There he is – she'd spotted Josh amongst a group in the middle of the ring. He was grinning at a red-faced man in a porkpie hat, just like he did on the TV.

Terry chuckled. 'No chance, Foxy.'

Mouse had not seen Josh in the flesh since that day at the garage. She'd been waiting ever since for him to come back.

'If it runs to form it'll be lucky to come last.'

She watched the red-faced man give Josh a leg-up into the saddle. She wouldn't mind having that job, making a step with her hands for his black shiny boot, taking his weight and then boosting him up till he sat above her, beaming down with gratitude. A knight on his steed.

'I like the look of Swallow's horse.' Terry was still ruminating on the runners' prospects.

The horse in question walked slowly in front of them, a compact muscular chestnut. Josh swayed above Mouse as he passed and, for a moment, she caught his eye. She could feel her heart pounding. He'd know her, wouldn't he? He'd stood as close to her as Terry did now, holding her hand, bandaging her wounded finger. Then he was gone, eye contact broken. Had he recognised her? She stared after him as he made his way out of the ring.

'Come on, Foxy,' said Terry, taking her by the arm and steering her through the crowd.

Mouse was unused to this kind of attention from a man. In the past, when boys had got saucy or tried anything she'd told them to piss off. She took no prisoners. Well, there had been a couple of exceptions when she was much younger. When she'd thought a boy really liked her and she'd granted him a favour or two – and regretted it soon after when she discovered he didn't really like her at all. Now she was much more mature. It was the feelings that counted, not the physical stuff – that could come later. She'd never got to the physical with Gavin, though she wouldn't half have minded. Luckily she'd found out what a bastard he was before things got that far. But Josh – Josh was a different story. With him she was going to do things right.

'OK, Foxy, here's where we do the business.' She found herself standing in the betting ring, alive with people, scurrying around looking for the best prices. Terry had taken a wallet from his pocket and was pulling out banknotes.

She stared at him in astonishment. He must have been holding over a thousand pounds.

'Come on, or we won't get on.' Terry was surveying the boards displayed on each pitch, where numbers had been scribbled in magic marker. 'We want the best odds for Mountain Range.' That was Josh's horse.

He took hold of her hand and dived into the crowd. She followed blindly as he made for a man in a trilby and a scarlet waistcoat. There was a quick interchange of conversation and Terry passed over some notes in exchange for two small printed slips.

'There you are, Foxy,' he said, flashing her a gold-toothed smile and handing her one of the small pieces of paper. 'I put a little something on Last Detective. The one you fancied.'

She stared at the slip in her hand. She hadn't fancied the horse at all – what was he playing at?

'You've got a funny way of saying thanks,' he said.

'Thanks,' she mumbled.

'How about a kiss?'

So that was his game. She was out of practice with men, that was for sure.

Josh had never sat on Mountain Range before. The horse was going off at a short price on the basis of his recent record in France where he'd been a regular winner. Sometimes, however, a horse's performance in one country was no indicator of how he would go in another. They were just like humans. Some travelled well and others didn't.

From the moment the lad let him go on to the course, Josh knew there was something wrong with the animal's teeth. He was hanging hard to the right, fidgeting with his head, and fussing about where the bit was sitting in his mouth. Josh tried to take the pressure off the bit by holding on to the horse's mane – which would have worked if Mountain Range had settled but he wouldn't. The result was a compromise for the early part of the race until the resistance went out of the horse. Once Mountain Range relaxed, Josh rode him with virtually no contact on the mouth at all and they settled into a good strong rhythm.

Josh didn't want to press the accelerator too early, but he had a feeling that when he did the horse would take off. As they raced downhill to the second last, Josh let out a reef of rein and, despite carrying top weight, Mountain Range changed into another gear, leaving everything around him for dead. It was a fantastic feeling as they cruised over the winning line.

Carmen was thrilled.

'He'll be even better when you get his teeth sorted.'

'His teeth?'

Josh told her what he thought was wrong. 'It must be affecting his eating. And, even if it doesn't improve him, you've still got a very good horse.'

After the race was over Mouse felt elated. She'd been shouting for Josh's horse all down the back straight as the animal suddenly came alight and overtook the field. Now she was aware she'd been drawing attention to herself.

Terry was giving her his sardonic look, as if he was amused by everything about her. In which case, he'd better watch it. Just because he'd been paying her attention didn't mean she'd allow herself to be laughed at.

'You're a funny one, you are,' he said. 'Why were you wetting yourself over Mountain Range? You fancied the other one.'

Because Josh was riding. But she couldn't say that. 'It was your horse, wasn't it?'

'Yeah. But yours was Last Detective and that finished second.'

Did it?

'I backed it each way for you at one hundred to one. Congratulations.'

Oh my God.

Mouse didn't know when she'd ever held so much cash, as she accepted the sheaf of notes from the man with the scarlet waistcoat.

'Here,' she said, thrusting the bundle into Terry's hand. 'It's yours really.'

But he wouldn't take the money, pulling his hands away.

'Terry, please,' she said. It wasn't right him giving her all this. She hadn't meant him to back the horse. If she'd thought about it she'd have put money on Mountain Range like he did.

'But I don't deserve it,' she cried.

'What did you say?'

'I don't deserve it.'

He manoeuvred her away from the crowd and stood close to her, his voice low and urgent. 'Don't say that, Foxy. I can tell you're special.'

What?

His trademark grin was back, together with narrowed eyes, a glint of gold and a swift pounce that had her pinned, his hands under her coat around her waist, his mouth on hers. She froze rigid.

'Get off,' she spluttered, jerking her head away.

'What, no thank-you snog?'

'I'm not like that,' she said, conscious of the money he'd given her in her hands.

'No, of course not.' That bloody grin was starting to annoy her. 'Let's just say that drinks are on you tonight, OK?'

'The drinks will be all over your big fat head if you try that again.'

There was venom in her voice and Terry looked at her warily.

'OK, Foxy. Just as you say.'

After his win Josh took a couple of minutes to go through his stretching routine, nothing too energetic but enough to keep himself loose for the next race. He'd been nursing chronic aches and pains for years now and he found the bends and flexes a physio had taught him as good a means as any of keeping his battered body on the road.

The jockeys in the weighing room were used to his antics and would chuck a few jibes his way, usually of a coarse but friendly nature. Today, however, nobody said anything. Though the lads were quick to poke fun at another fellow's misfortunes, it was difficult to find too many laughs in the newspaper revelations about Susie.

Josh tried to put his troubles to one side and focus on the professional challenges ahead. He had a couple of reasonable rides for Peter, and Belinda Giles had come up with another – to compensate for the Aintree ride he'd lost, according to Tony. Josh knew things didn't work like that but at least it demonstrated that Belinda was happy to use him, which was a relief.

From the talk in the weighing room he knew many of the lads had their minds on the Grand National later in the week. No one was immune to the press coverage as the papers whipped up the excitement of the once-a-year punters. As far as Josh was concerned, it was something of a lottery. He'd won it once and had no expectation of hitting the jackpot again. Recently he'd come to resent the hoopla that went with it, the assumption that this race mattered almost more than any other, that one victory at Aintree could make up for a season of disappointments.

In his current situation, locked in this head-to-head with Ben, the National was a distraction that he was determined to minimise. He was booked to ride Moondance, a seasoned chaser he'd won on at Chepstow and Uttoxeter. The horse was trained by a local man who'd secured his services for the occasion months ago. Ever since, people had been coming up to him, keen to point out how great it would be if he landed the race once more in his last season. Josh had refused to entertain the thought. When it came down to it, a victory here at Uttoxeter counted as much against Ben as winning the National.

He doubted that Ben felt the same. He'd noticed the Irish lad had been careful which horses he was getting on of late. He probably thought he was far enough ahead of Josh to allow himself the luxury of a little caution. Perhaps he was trying to reduce the likelihood of injury before the big day. Josh knew that it didn't always work like that. Sometimes it was the best jumpers who gave you the nastiest falls.

Josh turned these matters over in his mind as he gently stretched his hamstrings. Who could say what went on in

Ben O'Brien's head? Not him. But maybe he had a chance to make inroads on Ben's lead. He'd clawed one winner back already.

Thirteen to go. He still had time to catch up.

Uncle Jimmy was as thin as a rake, quite unlike any of Rose's other relatives that Mouse had caught sight of over the years. She'd been a bit worried what Rose might have said to him about her but Jim – that's what he told her to call him – was affable, if businesslike.

'Very well then,' he said in a tone that suggested he was telling her what was what, 'I can take you out on the course with me, if you like. I've got to keep an eye on the first jump away from the stands so you'll get a view of the action from up close.'

'Great,' she said, as was required, and Rose beamed and thanked Uncle Jimmy for the third or fourth time.

So Mouse took up her station beside the Red Cross volunteer for the fifth race of the afternoon, not displeased to get away from Terry for a bit.

The race began on a spur into the home straight. She watched the runners take the first four fences almost as one. 'It won't be long now,' said Jim. 'They're just coming up to the grandstand.'

Despite herself, Mouse was getting excited. She'd see Josh doing what he did best, striving with every muscle and sinew for victory. It would be like going back in time and having a ringside seat at some heroic cavalry action, with her man leading the charge.

The runners had left the stand behind now and were

rounding the bend to the first fence in the back straight. It was still and quiet out here away from the spectators so she could make out the drumming of the horses' hooves as the charge came closer. Mixed in with the thump of feet on turf was the jingle of tack and, to her surprise, the shouts of the jockeys.

Suddenly the bunch were rounding the bend and galloping towards them. Mouse frantically looked for Josh among the pack but she was confused. Which was his horse?

Then they were pouring over the obstacle in front of her. The first horse over the fence stumbled on landing. The jockey was pitched over the animal's head and rolled over and over in a ball, causing chaos among the following runners. The three horses directly behind veered towards Mouse as they tried to avoid the faller. There were oaths and cries and then another rider was down. The sound of hoof hitting helmet hung in the air as the rest of the field thundered on.

Just like in a battle charge, there were casualties – two jockeys stretched out on the turf in front of them.

Jim had told her that in the unlikely event of anything happening she must keep out of the way and leave it to him. He was the first line of assistance and, in any case, the ambulance with the paramedics would soon be on hand.

But he'd not told her what to do if more than one man was injured and one of them – the thought suddenly hit her – might be Josh.

Jim was already halfway across the course heading towards the first faller who had rolled to the far side. The second rider was closer to Mouse, stretched out on the grass about fifteen yards ahead. She ran towards him.

As she knelt by the prostrate figure and peered into his long pale face, she realised it was Ben O'Brien, out for the count.

She began to panic and fumbled stupidly at his wrist, thinking that she should see if he had a pulse. But she couldn't feel a thing.

Suppose he was dead? He looked dead. What was she meant to do?

She looked over to Jim and yelled. He was helping the other jockey to his feet. Beyond him she could see a white van with a red cross on its side bumping across the track towards them.

'Jim! Over here!'

She stared at the unconscious man, completely at a loss. What did you do for people who'd been knocked out? Weren't you supposed to open their mouths and pull their tongues out so they wouldn't choke? Why hadn't she ever done any first aid?

She bent down close to Ben's face. His lips were shut. Was he breathing all right? Shouldn't she try and open his mouth? She pushed down on his chin.

His eyes flicked opened suddenly. He was staring at her.

'What the hell are you doing?' he said with surprising vehemence for a man who'd appeared lifeless just an instant ago. 'Get your stupid hands off me,' he shouted and pulled himself into a sitting position.

Mouse was indignant. She wanted to protest that she was only trying to help but there were people all around now,

Jim and two men in green overalls who had leapt from the ambulance.

'Take it slowly,' said one of the paramedics to the fallen jockey.

Jim had hold of Mouse by the arm and she allowed herself to be manoeuvred backwards to give the medics room.

Ben was now on his feet, swinging his arms and stamping his feet – for the doctor's benefit, Mouse imagined.

'Are you feeling all right?' asked the first medic.

'Yeah, I'm fine,' said Ben cheerfully. 'It was just a bit of a bump.'

'You were unconscious when I got to you,' Mouse blurted out.

All heads swivelled in her direction. She couldn't believe she had said it but it seemed important.

'Who are you?' asked the second medic.

'She's with me,' said Jim, for which Mouse was grateful.

'Well, she's talking bollocks.' Ben glared at her. He turned back to the first medic. 'Honestly, doc, I was just winded.'

'You were out cold for at least a minute,' cried Mouse indignantly. He was calling her a liar!

Jim's hand on her arm now pulled her away insistently and she followed; she had no choice.

'It's true,' she said to him. 'He had his eyes shut and he was completely still. I thought he was seriously hurt.'

'That's as may be, lass, but you'd better keep your mouth shut now. Leave it to the doctors.'

A few yards away she watched the medics continuing to quiz the jockey. One of them was holding a finger in front of Ben's face and moving it slowly from left to right, observing his reactions. Ben was talking to them in an animated fashion, though she couldn't hear what he was saying. Finally, all parties seemed to relax and Ben clapped the doctor on the back and grinned.

'They're happy now,' muttered Jim. 'He's talked his way out of it.'

'What do you mean?' asked Mouse but Ben was striding towards them and Jim didn't reply.

The jockey's smile had been replaced by a look of pure venom and it was directed at Mouse.

'What's the matter with you, you boss-eyed cow? Next time keep your big nose out of other people's business.'

'I was only trying to help,' Mouse cried.

'Come on, then,' said Jim. 'It's Shanks's pony for us.'

Mouse stood where she was even as he nudged her arm to get going.

'That's so unfair,' she cried.

'He didn't mean it really. Jockeys get a bit fired up sometimes.'

'But he was so rude!'

'I've had worse than that, don't worry. What you've got to realise is you might have got him stood down. That's what got him so worked up – it wasn't personal.'

It had seemed personal to Mouse. Very personal.

Grudgingly she allowed Jim to steer her towards the far-off stands.

'What does that mean, "stood down"?' she asked.

'If a jockey gets concussed the doctor won't let him ride for a few days, so he'll try not to let on.' He chuckled.

'Especially if that means he's going to miss out on the Grand National meeting.'

'Oh.' That explained it to some extent but it didn't make Mouse feel any better. She hadn't thought much of Ben O'Brien before but her animosity had suddenly taken on a different colour.

'I wouldn't worry about it, if I were you,' added Jim. 'He were just letting off steam.'

But Mouse hardly heard him. She was thinking of Ben O'Brien lying unconscious at her feet. For a whole minute.

She'd had her chance to take him out of the race with Josh for champion jockey and she hadn't even realised it.

She didn't say another word on the long trudge back.

Chapter Ten

Mouse had too much alcohol swirling round her body to even contemplate going to bed – though that's the excuse she made to Terry.

'You sure you want to go on your own?' he murmured in her ear as she sent him away from her front door. 'To bed, I mean,' he added, just in case she hadn't got his meaning. No chance of that. He'd been making himself clear all evening. 'Where you're concerned, Foxy,' he'd said, lining her up another vodka in the Black Grape, 'my intentions are thoroughly dishonourable.'

She wondered what he saw in her. He was good-looking in a disreputable fashion, she saw girls looking at him in the pizza place and then in the pub. In comparison with Geoff, that great slab of beef, he was Leonardo Di Caprio so she could see why he caught some women's eyes. Of course, she was more of a George Clooney type, herself. Or Josh Swallow, that went without saying. Since she was pledged to Josh, she could be quite detached about Terry's attentions.

Rose and Geoff had not accompanied them to the pub

after the pizza – which Mouse had paid for out of her afternoon's winnings. She'd enjoyed playing Miss Flash. But Terry wouldn't let her pay in the pub and he'd continued to buy her drinks despite her refusals. 'Don't think I don't know what you're up to,' she'd said. 'You've got no chance of getting into my knickers, no matter how pissed I am.'

He'd looked affronted. All wide-eyed innocence and hurt, like a puppy who'd been kicked. Mouse had to hand it to him, he was some performer.

She cut the evening short at half past nine but she let him walk her home. And she allowed him a snog on the doorstep, just for her own amusement. And because she was a bit drunk.

But she never stopped wanting Josh as Terry kissed her. In fact, to get through it, she closed her eyes and imagined it was Josh with his breath hot and eager on her lips and his inquisitive fingers under her coat.

And when things had gone far enough, when she felt herself in danger of losing the upper hand, she dismissed him abruptly.

'Time for you to bugger off,' she murmured into his ear, the one with the little stud that matched his gold tooth. 'I'm going to bed.' Which was when he'd offered to accompany her.

Fat chance of that.

She did not go to bed. She drank some water to dilute the booze and drove to the lane just past Josh's house. She noticed the Mistake's car in the drive as she drove past. Damn.

She'd read that they'd let her out. 'We have not charged Ms Brown at this time,' a police spokesman said, 'and we are continuing to investigate the circumstances of Mrs Lovall's death.'

After the success of sending Doctor Death's letter to that journalist, Blondie's release was a bit of a blow. Especially if it caused the police to reopen the investigation into Annabelle's death. But then she hadn't foreseen the arrest, all she'd envisaged was the paper digging up the old scandal and flushing Miss Susie Brown aka Merrivale into the open.

It showed what a difficult game she was playing. But she was safe, she was sure of it. Nobody had a clue she even existed.

She switched on the wireless receiver. It was strange listening in after all this time, hearing the faint hiss on the line, waiting for the thump of footsteps, the bang of a door or, with luck, the sound of voices. But the hiss continued, unbroken by sounds of life from the house below.

After a few moments, growing impatient, Mouse re-tuned the device. Still nothing. Maybe the batteries were spent but, if so, why the hiss? More likely, Josh and the Mistake were still downstairs.

She looked at her watch. Eleven twenty. She could spare an hour or two. She'd spent much more than that in some of her past vigils.

As she sat, listening intently to nothing, she could feel herself coming down from the highs of the day. The edge of excitement, of being geared up to fight, was dulling. Part of it was the alcohol. It made you feel great then, just a couple of hours later, you felt crap – worse crap than if you hadn't had a drink in the first place. And the things you'd been drinking to avoid came back to roll over you just when your resistance was at its weakest.

She'd been avoiding the thought of Ben O'Brien. The way his mean little eyes had bored into hers and seen right through her Good Samaritan act even as she knelt by his side to help him. He'd known at once she was pleased he, not Josh, was lying there. That she didn't have a clue what she was doing as she tried to open his mouth.

He'd called her boss-eyed. Even Baz said her eyes were much better these days and, anyway, some of the most beautiful women in the world didn't look at you quite straight – it was what gave them their allure.

All her schooldays had been spent behind thick ugly glasses – the corrective operation hadn't spared her from those. Now, thank God, she wore contacts and she'd convinced herself that no one would ever notice her squint. But Ben O'Brien had.

It was a pity, she thought, that only one horse had clouted the jockey as he lay on the ground. It would have been better if the whole lot had run over him, pounding him into the turf, kicking his stupid head like a football till it came right off his body. He'd have missed the Grand National then for sure.

By rights he shouldn't be riding for the next week, that's what Jim had said. He should be sitting on the sidelines, giving Josh a chance to catch up in this champion jockey thing.

What on earth's gone wrong with this bloody radio?

There was still no sign of life on the airway. Stuff this.

It occurred to her that, since there was only the Mistake's Golf parked in the driveway, they might both be out in Josh's car. In which case why shouldn't she go inside? Maybe it was the booze but the urge was irresistible.

She had her essentials in the car – the keys and the latex gloves. She pulled them on as she stalked back along the lane to the road. After all, she'd not come all the way out here just to listen to the sound of nothing.

There was another way down to the back of Josh's house through the woods, she'd explored it last autumn. But she was damned if she was going to go blundering about in the dark. Instead she walked down the road, with the high hedge looming over her, obscuring her view of the house. She'd not been along here before in the dark. Everything seemed different. She felt invisible.

Then the wall of hedge abruptly fell away and she had a clear view of the house over the low-railed fence that ran across the front of Josh's property. There was Blondie's Golf parked in the driveway but no sign of the low sporty shape of Josh's Celica.

She slipped through the gateway and walked carefully over the grass verge, avoiding the gravel of the drive. There were no lights visible downstairs but a bright square of yellow beamed from above the front door. She was sure they were out.

She slipped the key into the lock and inched it open just enough to peep into the half-lit hallway. Empty. Brilliant.

She was in.

*

Susie turned over in bed, her back to the pale wedge of light spilling in from the corridor. She had to have some light while she slept.

She'd been in bed for an hour, craving sleep. It seemed she spent longer and longer in bed each day and less and less time enjoying the rest she sought. In any case, sleep was not restful but alive with faces and voices she was desperate to forget. It seemed disloyal to her mum and Sharon to wish them out of her head but they wouldn't want her shackled by the horrors of the past, would they? In any event, they didn't visit her often, not like her father. Her lovely, smiling, kind father, bringing her breakfast in bed, piggy-backing her down the lane, standing up for her with her mother when she got mad—

She jerked herself awake. She didn't want to think about any of that. It was as if recent events – the poisonous letters, the arrest, the newspaper stories – had disturbed the bottom of a particularly nasty pond and all the silt and scum of the past had floated to the top.

But who had stirred up the pond in the first place?

She'd not had the strength to get into an argument with Brenda but she called her to try and get the facts. Did her aunt have any idea why this journalist had turned up to see her out of the blue? What had he asked her? And what exactly had Brenda said?

The answers had not been satisfactory. He'd said he was writing an article about artists and he was a fan of her work. Brenda had told him her parents had died in a car crash. And her sister.

She wished they had done; it would have been better than this.

She hadn't had a Susie Sausage letter recently. What had the last one said?

You've had your chance to keep your secret and you've just blown it.

It was after that that she'd been arrested and she'd been exposed in the press. It looked like the letter-writer had tried to drive her away and, when she hadn't gone, had tipped off the newspaper.

Ever since the letters had arrived Susie had been wracking her brains, trying to work out who would want her out of Josh's house. She'd even wondered if Josh had had a cheap fling on the side and the other woman was trying to oust her by sending the letters. But she'd rejected the thought as unworthy.

Maybe it was a small-minded local who had somehow found out about her and was being malicious for the fun of it?

But found out how?

She was driving herself mad.

She tried to think about something good and clean. Josh. He'd been so good. Strong, supportive, sensitive to her delicate state. But she still hadn't been able to talk to him about her past. Not properly. Not so she was absolved.

And she was aware she'd become a millstone round his neck, sapping energy from him just when he needed it for the crucial climax to his career. He made light of it but surely, right now, he needed to be selfish and not think of her.

She was a liability to his future too, she knew that.

Newspaper exposés about child-killing and having a partner suspected of murder – these wouldn't help him attract owners to his proposed training venture.

It wasn't surprising she just wanted to hide away in bed.

Even though she thought the house was empty, Mouse tiptoed quietly up the staircase. At the top of the landing she turned left along the hall until she came to the bedroom. She peeped through the half-open door, letting her eyes adjust to the dimness within. There had been some changes since she'd last been here. A television had been introduced into the room and she could just make out an extension lead winding round the skirting board. That would explain why her bug had stopped working.

Another thing, and one that took her by surprise, was the sight of one of the Mistake's moody abstract pictures hanging above the bed. She'd looked at them up in the studio in the attic months back and hated them. Now the woman had hung one in the bedroom. How on earth had she managed to talk Josh into that?

Mouse's plan was to take something for her Josh collection, like cufflinks or a tie. Or would another letter from the secret collection Susie kept in a shoebox at the back of the wardrobe be more useful?

But then Mouse peered through the door and realised there was someone lying asleep on the bed. That gave her a different idea entirely. A mad, crazy, wicked idea which she ought to reject out of hand. After getting away with murder once, however, there was no reason to think she couldn't do it again.

*

Josh put the phone down softly, resisting the urge to smash it back into its cradle. He was getting used to hearing bad news from Tony but this hit home. Despite all he'd told himself about the Grand National being just another race, it was a bitter blow to lose his best chance of winning it for some years.

He turned out the lights in the living room and set off up the stairs. Susie had gone to bed about an hour ago but he doubted if she'd be asleep. In comparison with her nightly anguish his troubles were nothing. It was as well to remember that.

Mouse actually had the pillow in her hand when she heard a noise. Not the shallow, dragging breaths of the blonde woman lying at her mercy but a sound from beyond the room. Downstairs.

She was poised to drop the pillow on the Mistake's face and hold it down with all her weight, mash it hard into those sugar-pink features and hold it there while Blondie's limbs jerked and threshed and flailed until, like some toy with a failing battery, she came to a stop. That's how it would be, wouldn't it? Mouse bet it wouldn't take long. Two minutes? Maybe less.

But she didn't have that time. She heard the sound of tired footsteps plodding their way up the stairs. Josh was here after all. She had to escape.

She replaced the pillow on the bed and stepped behind the door. There was nowhere else to go.

The footsteps reached the top of the stairs. She crouched

down, frozen in fear as the footsteps came towards the room.

And stopped. She heard the sound of a door opening and the click of a light switch. The bathroom was just along the corridor.

She fled the room, ghosted downstairs and left the house. But she did think, as she ran up the hill, that she should have checked through the garage window for Josh's car.

Susie watched Josh unbuttoning his shirt in the dim light. She could tell from the tension in his shoulders and the stillness in his eyes when he thought he was unobserved that something was preying on his mind.

'What is it, Josh?'

He turned his head. 'So you're awake.'

'Only just. Tell me what's up.'

He slipped into bed next to her. 'I've just been talking to Tony. I've been jocked off Moondance for the National.'

'Oh no,' she said. She knew how highly Josh rated the horse. And she didn't have to ask why he'd lost the ride, she could guess. 'Does that mean you don't have a Grand National ride?'

She half hoped this was true. The epic steeplechase was the most dangerous race of the season and she wouldn't be sorry if her man sat it out.

He rolled his eyes. 'Oh, I've got one all right,' he said, in a tone which made her fear the worst. 'Tony's got me on some old stager of Billy Christie's. Wet Spring. He's run in the last four Nationals, a good jumper, but slow as a hearse. He wouldn't win if he set off now.'

Billy Christie was the trainer Carmen Cook had been using.

'Is this anything to do with Carmen?' she asked.

Josh shot her a wry grin. 'Not this time. The lad Billy booked got a better offer and took it. Wet Spring beat one home last time out – it could be my slowest National ever.'

Typically, he'd turned the whole fiasco into a bit of a joke but she knew it was no laughing matter.

Leo took careful aim at the beer can on the straw bale in the far paddock and gently squeezed the trigger of his revolver.

Smack! The empty receptacle somersaulted through the air and joined two of its punctured fellows in the grass.

Strictly speaking he didn't drink beer, whisky was his tipple. But beer cans made good targets so today he was drinking beer.

Of course he'd rather not be shooting at targets at all. In his mind's eye, certain faces were superimposed on those tin cans. Josh Swallow, of course. His principal object of loathing.

Bang! How satisfying it would be to put a bullet between those laughing green eyes. They'd been laughing at him for years, it seemed.

But there was another whose head would have been vulnerable had it appeared in his sights: Detective Inspector Harry Picard, with whom he had just terminated a most unsatisfactory conversation. Funny to think that just a few days ago Picard would have been top of his Christmas card list. The way Leo felt now he'd step over his body in the street and whistle as he went on his way.

'I'm sorry, Mr Lovall, you will have to let us handle this investigation our own way.'

'Of course, but I've handed it to you on a plate. You had my wife's killer in custody – what's the point of letting her go? Charge her with murder – and Swallow, the man who put her up to it.'

The policeman had sighed heavily, as if this was not the first time he'd had this conversation – which, true enough, it wasn't.

'I cannot charge people with any offence, let alone one as grave as this, without evidence that will stand up in court. As yet, I am of the opinion that we do not have a strong enough case to take to the Crown Prosecution Service. Rest assured, however, that we are continuing to investigate the circumstances of your wife's death.'

In other words, bog off and don't bother me any more, mush.

So – *Pow! Pow!* – after all the excitement of the arrest and the press hoopla, he was pretty much back to square one. It drove him mad.

Mira the estate agent had been hounding Josh for days and Susie had ended up fielding the calls. She didn't want to know anything about that horrible flat in London but she was involved, whether she liked it or not.

'Mira wants me to say which bits of furniture we want to keep,' she told Josh. 'Some Canadian is interested but he'd prefer to buy it furnished. He's in a hurry.'

Of course he was, people always were when they wanted you to do something. It was the eve of the big Aintree meeting and, to Josh's obvious relief, Susie had volunteered to go down to London. She was making a conscious effort to shake herself out of her lethargy. Her only proviso was that she'd stay in a hotel – she couldn't face spending the night in the flat. With luck, she'd be able to get up to Liverpool in time for the National on Saturday.

Josh had given her a list of items he wished to keep – two pictures and a table. 'The rest is up to you,' he said.

But what was concerning her at the moment was a dress.

She'd found it hanging in the wardrobe between two of Josh's suits, obscured by their zip-up bags – that's why she'd not noticed it before. Not that she'd ever paid much attention to the clothes hanging on his side. It was a lightweight summer print of gold and black, virtually backless, cut on the bias, and obviously brand new, with the price tag still attached. Even before she read the figure, Susie knew it was not a cheap garment. She could tell by the cut and also by the label – Dragon, a designer boutique she'd passed on nearby St John's Wood High Street. All the same, she gulped as she took in the price. She'd never in her life paid almost a thousand pounds for a dress.

Her first thought was that maybe Josh had bought it for her and was waiting for the right moment to surprise her with it. But, on reflection, that didn't seem likely. If that was so, why hadn't he given it to her? More to the point, it wasn't exactly her size. She held the dress against herself as she looked in the mirror. This was an item designed for a beanpole with endless legs.

So that solved one mystery – it must belong to Annabelle. She had had the opportunity to buy the dress on the day she died. According to her sister, Jenny's, evidence at the inquest, Annabelle had been out shopping before returning to the flat and opening a bottle of wine. It had not been established what she had bought but there was a good chance Susie was holding it in her hand right now.

She called Josh and left a message, asking him to phone when convenient, but she was already thinking ahead.

If the dress had been some cheap, off-the-peg item, Susie would have donated it to the Oxfam shop round the corner, but this was different. She laid the garment on the bed and stared out of the window, determined to think the matter through. The trees were now thick with leaves and blossom and birds sang over the hum of traffic from below. The rain clouds had blown away for the moment and suddenly it was a sumptuous spring afternoon. The dress on the bed gave her the creeps. Damn bloody Annabelle, would the ghastly woman never leave them alone?

Shortly after Annabelle's death, so Josh had told her, the police had brought Leo and Jenny to the flat so they could see for themselves where she had died. When they left they took Annabelle's possessions with them – though obviously not the dress which presumably had been overlooked in the wardrobe.

The phone rang. Josh sounded cheerful. 'Haven't you got the TV on?' he demanded. 'I've won two out of the first three.'

She asked if he knew anything about a gold dress in his wardrobe.

'Gold's not my colour, sweetheart.'

'It was Annabelle's though, wasn't it?'

He knew nothing about it.

She could hear the good spirits leaking out of his voice. His mind would be on the complications of returning the dress to Leo, and all that that entailed. To his obvious relief she told him she'd sort it out.

She decided Annabelle's sister, Jenny, ought to have first refusal.

Colin Smart, the solicitor, tracked down the number for her and she dialled it quickly, aware she was seizing on this business as an escape from her own preoccupations. Well, was that such a bad thing?

She was quite relishing an excuse to talk to Jenny, who had looked like a friendly sort even in the sombre setting of the Coroner's Court.

The phone was answered by a female voice and a burst of French.

Susie started to explain who she was and the voice switched to English. 'I know who you are. I saw you at the inquest.'

Susie broached the matter of the dress.

There was an intake of breath on the other end of the line. 'Gosh, you've just reminded me – Annabelle told me about that dress. I should have looked for it when we came to collect her things.'

'That's OK. I can send it to you.'

'Don't go to the trouble, it won't fit me anyway.'

'But it cost a lot of money. I suppose I could send it to Leo.'

'No.' Jenny's voice hardened. 'Whatever you do, don't have anything to do with him.'

'But shouldn't it be included in her estate?'

Jenny paused. 'You do know Leo blames Josh for everything, don't you? And you're part of it. Why else do you think you got arrested?'

'How do you know about that?'

'Because he rang me up and told me. And he sent me the cuttings from the paper all about what happened to you as a child. Leo's on some wild vengeance hunt. I don't approve but he doesn't care what I think.'

Susie was stunned. She knew about the bad blood between the trainer and Josh but she'd never imagined it had gone this far.

'Are you saying Leo is the reason I was arrested?'

'He got someone to dig up your family history and your movements on the day Annabelle died, then he went to the police. He's out of control. I'm surprised Annabelle stuck him for so long.'

'So Annabelle really had left him when she came to London?' Susie was determined to make the most of this conversation.

'Oh yes. That's why she bought the dress, to celebrate her freedom. She told me she'd bolted but it went against the party line to say so at the inquest.'

'What about the baby?'

'She never mentioned it – she couldn't have known. It definitely wouldn't have been Leo's though.'

'Whose then?'

There was a chuckle. 'You'll think I'm fibbing but I don't know. She stopped telling me about her men because I asked her not to. It made it a lot easier dealing with Leo. I knew about Josh though. I really wish she'd stayed with him – oops, I shouldn't have said that, should I?'

Susie didn't care. She'd decided she liked Jenny a lot.

'Look,' Jenny continued, 'about the dress, why don't you change it for something you like. You deserve it after what Leo's done to you.'

That was true enough.

'And don't make the mistake my sister made – you hang on tight to Josh.'

That was another matter, and the more she thought about it the more sense it made.

Dragon was a small boutique, sandwiched between a patisserie and an upmarket greengrocer's where Susie had once been offered a punnet of out-of-season blackberries for a fiver. It was no surprise to her that, in this neck of the woods, a simple little cocktail dress rang the till at close to four figures.

Inside, the shop seemed larger than at first glance and the bustle of the street was replaced by a reverential hush. For once, no background music played. This was a place for seriously minded connoisseurs of clothes.

A slim, suntanned woman of middle years smiled professionally as Susie approached. She wore a black trouser suit, extensively accessorised with gold jewellery and a silk scarf the colour of freshly sliced melon. She made Susie wish she'd changed out of her jeans before she'd left the flat.

She placed the bag containing the dress on the glass counter. She'd retrieved it from the kitchen cupboard where all the might-come-in-useful carrier bags were stuffed.

'I'd like to return something,' she said, indicating the bag. 'If that's possible.'

The woman in the suit extracted the dress and held it up.

'It's not been worn,' Susie added.

'Did you receive this as a gift?'

'Me? No.'

The woman appraised her shrewdly. 'But you didn't buy it, did you?'

'A friend of mine bought it a couple of months ago.' Susie wasn't happy describing Annabelle as a friend but she wanted to keep it simple. 'I haven't got the receipt, I'm afraid.'

The woman shrugged. 'That's not a problem. I remember selling it to your friend. She had her dog in a car just outside and it barked all the time she was in here. Mind you, she still took her time.'

'That sounds like Annabelle.'

The shop lady finished examining the dress. 'Do you want to exchange it for another item?'

Susie shook her head. It hadn't been her intention to walk out with something for herself. On the other hand, Jenny had offered it to her.

'I can't give you a refund, I'm afraid,' the woman continued. 'But I'll write you a credit note.'

'That would be fine.'

The woman slipped the dress on to a hanger and placed it on a rail beside her. Then she extracted a pad from the drawer of a desk and began to write.

Susie noticed a display of children's clothes on the other

side of the shop. Hadn't Josh told her Jenny had two small daughters? If she sent Jenny the credit note maybe the girls could benefit from their late aunt's extravagance. She was pleased with the thought.

The shop lady was rummaging in the back of the desk drawer. Then she straightened up. 'As a matter of fact, I was expecting your friend to come back ages ago. She left this behind. Perhaps you'd like to return it to her.'

The woman was holding out the note she'd written and a mobile phone with a cheap plastic cover of sugar pink decorated with scarlet hearts.

Susie was astonished. 'Are you sure?' The trashy object didn't look like anything the sophisticated Annabelle might own. Besides, hadn't Annabelle's mobile been found? They'd discussed the calls she'd made on it at the inquest.

But the shop lady was in no doubt. 'She turned her bag out to find her chequebook and this was among her things. After she'd gone I found it on the floor and put it to one side. Customers often leave their phones but they always come back to look for them. Except your friend, of course. I'm afraid I forgot all about it.'

That was Susie's cue to explain the real reason for Annabelle's absence but if the woman hadn't worked it out for herself, she wasn't going to tell her. Instead she thanked her for her assistance and headed back to the flat, her thoughts buzzing.

Why would Annabelle have a second phone? A phone that no one appeared to be aware of? It hadn't been mentioned at the inquest.

Who would a married woman, fleeing from her husband, talk to on a secret line?

Her lover, of course.

Susie was ashamed of herself but she was burning with curiosity.

For a horse whom few fancied to make any impression in the world's most famous steeplechase, Wet Spring was as luxurious a ride as any Josh had enjoyed all season. Perched on the broad back of the veteran grey, he surveyed the scenes of excitement preceding the Grand National with some detachment, determined to savour every moment of his last appearance in the legendary race.

The weather had performed its usual seasonal flip-flop and three days of solid rain had been followed by an afternoon of blistering sunshine, which was good news for the spectators. The going was still heavy, however, and around him Josh could see runners and riders sweating up as they circled in front of the stands waiting to be called to the start. This stage of proceedings was something of an ordeal for all forty contestants. They'd already cantered down for a look at the first fence and now they had to keep a lid on their excitement, while the band pumped out the national anthem and the vast crowd hummed with expectation. As if the race itself wasn't enough – all four and a half miles, ten minutes and thirty monumental fences of it – there were at least another five minutes before they could get going. For the inexperienced and the nervously inclined this was torture.

While jockeys and stable staff struggled to keep their

charges under control, Wet Spring moved serenely in the turning circle of horses.

'Is he always this switched off?' Josh asked the girl who was leading them round.

'You bet,' she said. 'He's the most laid-back horse in the yard.'

Laid-back wasn't exactly what was required of a racehorse, but Josh reminded himself he was lucky to have a ride at all, given that he'd been bumped off Moondance, now installed as joint favourite for the race. Josh wasn't surprised. After his wins on Moondance he knew precisely what formidable reserves of power and stamina the horse possessed. And he was like a cat at his fences; no matter what trouble he got into, he always managed to find a leg and get out of it.

He put the thought of Moondance out of his head. He was determined not to spoil the occasion by thinking of what might have been.

Wet Spring's owners had fully briefed him on the horse's past performances in the National. According to Mrs Murray-Watson, he'd been dreadfully unlucky on all four occasions, falling foul of loose horses, unsuitable going and incompetent riding. Mr Murray-Watson, a less garrulous conversationalist, had simply said that if Josh got the horse to complete the course he'd have exceeded his personal expectations. The bookmakers appeared to share this view. With the announcement that Josh would be taking the reins they had slashed the odds from 66/1 to 33/1. Personally, Josh wouldn't have risked a penny even if he'd been allowed to do so.

The starter called them into line and Josh edged to the outside of the field, holding back as the tapes sprang up and the runners lurched forward. The other thirty-nine horses thundered ahead of them, a river of multi-coloured shapes flowing at speed to the first of the great hedges that passed for fences on the famous course. Each year a steward came into the weighing room before the race and told the jockeys not to go too fast down to the first. And each year they took no notice whatsoever. The long run to the first fence meant that most of the runners were going too fast to jump by the time they took off and, with the unexpected drop on the landing side, invariably half a dozen toppled over as their hooves hit the turf.

The problem with being at the rear was that you had to clear fallen horses and jockeys as often as the fences themselves. Just ahead and to his inside a big chestnut hit the top of the obstacle and Josh instinctively tugged Wet Spring to the right as the horse took off. West Spring wobbled and took the top eighteen inches of loose fir with him as he gave the fence a belt. To Josh's immense relief he scraped clear and hit the ground on the other side still upright, veering away to the outside. As they flashed by, Josh saw a crumpled chestnut shape and a tumbling ball of scarlet and green that was the horse's rider. They missed him by a whisker.

Wet Spring was last down the long opening straight of the first circuit but Josh was exhilarated. In previous years he would have fretted about his position, even at this early stage. Now he was thrilled still to be in the race, as horses tumbled ahead of him and they picked their way through the mayhem. It was a miracle they hadn't fallen at the first, but it had taught Wet Spring a lesson. He was now giving every fence the respect it deserved.

His much-maligned mount was plugging on steadily and jumping with a reassuring rhythm. According to Billy Christie, his reputation was a little unfair. 'On his day,' he'd told Josh, 'Wet Spring can jump a barn and gallop with the best of them but he's easily put off. And he's always liable to make a ricket. Still, with a canny lad like you on board, who knows? Anything might happen.'

That was true enough. Every year jockeys set off in the National with those words echoing in their ears. Something unexpected always took place. The first of these, to Josh's mind, was the sight of Brief Encounter, the co-favourite with Moondance, standing on his nose, having misjudged the unexpected drop on the landing side of Becher's Brook. Wet Spring took the fence beautifully and carried Josh away from the faller as if he were the fancied horse.

They successfully rounded the sharp bend after the Canal Turn and Wet Spring proceeded to devour the succession of fences on the inward circuit with some style. Josh could hardly believe it, though he was far from inclined to trust the horse beneath him. His only concern was keeping the horse happy. 'Make him think he's the dog's whatsits,' had been Billy's words.

The course narrowed in front of the stands as the field, reduced in number and strung out over fifty yards, approached The Chair's yawning ditch and five-foot-plus fence. From the rear, Josh watched the obstacle take its toll. There were at least three fallers as far as he could tell, maybe more. He was prepared for any outcome, from refusal to a nose dive, but was amazed to be powered into the air as if jet-propelled. Even when he'd been on the winner, Josh had never leapt the course's biggest fence so comfortably. 'On his day, he can jump a barn,' Billy had said. It felt like he just had.

At the start of the second circuit, the heavy going was taking its toll. Though a long way behind the leaders, Josh was no longer last. Wet Spring was steadily overtaking fast-tiring horses though he seemed little fatigued himself. A loose horse had joined them and was happily flying along-side, jumping the fences for fun, unencumbered by a rider. Wet Spring seemed to enjoy the company though Josh kept a suspicious eye on the animal, hoping it would soon tire of the game and run out. Instead it picked up speed and shot off up the field.

They negotiated Becher's for the second time and rounded the turn at the far end of the course. As they took the next, some thirty yards to the rear of the leading group, Josh had a good view of their friend, the riderless horse. Now at the head of the field on the outside of the course he veered inside to leap the Canal Turn in a diagonal jump that took off the corner of the course. It was the equivalent of a car in the fast lane of the motorway turning sharp left across the inside lanes of traffic. A pile-up was inevitable.

Some horses and riders took evasive action, others were too committed to their chosen path, some just didn't notice the unguided missile careering across the track until too late. Horses crashed into one another even as they jumped. The loose horse brought down the three leaders in one sideswipe. The rest piled into the fallers as they landed on the other side of the fence. It was carnage.

Far enough in the rear to pick a path to the outside, away from the trouble, Josh steered Wet Spring over the fence and around the fallen. He leapt over one tumbling jockey and dragged the horse sharply round another, standing like a lone survivor on a battlefield. As they whipped by, Josh caught a clear glimpse of a long pale face over mud-streaked silks, his teeth bared in frustration. It was Ben.

Josh forgot about him in an instant as he swung Wet Spring into the long straight that led back to the stands and winning post. Ahead of him, nothing stood but the fences themselves. Wet Spring was finally leading the Grand National.

'I don't believe it.' Terry was on his feet. 'They've all ruddy well fallen over!'

'Apart from Josh,' said Mouse, no less amazed by events on the television screen in front of them. 'Wet Spring's still going.'

'I don't believe it,' Terry repeated, resuming his seat by Mouse's side on the white leather sofa, which squeaked as he pressed his thigh against hers. Personally, she didn't think a leather sofa was all that suitable for a so-called Casanova like Terry. His every move was accompanied by a sound effect that was distinctly un-erotic. Not that it made any odds to her.

The television commentator was getting excited. 'Wet Spring, a complete outsider, is approaching Valentine's and there's not another horse in sight. It could be Foinavon all over again.'

His co-commentator seized on this and began rabbiting on about some no-hoper winning back in the sixties. Mouse couldn't give a stuff about the ancient history. All she could think of was Josh winning the Grand National today. It would be fantastic. All he had to do was keep going.

'Some of the others are getting back on,' said Terry.

The camera had switched away from the leader back to the scene of the pile-up where a couple of jockeys had grabbed their horses and were attempting to remount.

The picture then shifted again to show a horse and rider already in full flow. The first commentator said, 'Ben O'Brien's got hold of Moondance and he's going after Wet Spring.'

'Fat chance he's got of catching him,' said Terry.

Mouse wasn't so sure.

'Come on, Josh,' she screamed. 'Come on!'

In all his years as a jockey, Josh had never experienced a ride like this one. He'd spent half the race on his own at the back of the field and now, just a few seconds later, he was heading them all, still alone but now in the lead.

They'd jumped the plain fence after Valentine's, which meant there were just four to go before the long stretch of almost 500 yards to the winning post. They might be miles in front but the race was far from won. Apart from anything else, there was no guarantee Wet Spring would reach the finish line at all. He'd never been this far ahead in a race in his life.

Josh glanced over his shoulder and caught a flash of colour, two fences back. At least one other horse was still in the race. But at the moment Josh wasn't worried about the competition so much. Wet Spring was plugging on gamely but his stride was shortening and he was struggling to keep his rhythm across the heavily churned-up turf.

The next was an open ditch, a severe enough test on its own, let alone coming as the twenty-seventh obstacle after almost four miles of heavy going.

Wet Spring jumped it perfectly which gave Josh the chance to shorten up the reins for a moment and get his mount back on the bridle. He leapt the next in similar style and was now getting a second wind. How could you doubt me? he appeared to be saying.

'He's going to do it, Foxy.'

'No, he's not. That other horse is going to catch him.'

'Never, he's miles behind.'

Mouse tuned Terry out, concentrating on the screen and Josh's progress. To her, it seemed agonisingly slow. Further back, but eating into his lead, came Ben O'Brien's horse. Ben O'Brien, who shouldn't even have been riding in the race. The camera cut backwards and forwards and the commentators' voices rose in a pitch of excitement. Could Wet Spring hang on? Could Moondance, the younger, stronger, better-fancied horse make up the ground in time?

She didn't think she could bear it.

Wet Spring saved his ricket for the last, taking off too early and smacking into the untidy hill of foliage on top of the fence. His nose kissed the ground on the far side and Josh thought he was about to be somersaulted helplessly into the air. But he gripped tight with his thighs and somehow remained glued to the saddle as the horse staggered forward, fighting to stay on his feet.

This was the race right here, he knew it. How ignominious to fall at the last when leading the world's greatest steeple-chase. He hauled back on the reins, fighting to keep the horse's head up and help him retain his balance.

Wet Spring did not fall but, as Josh steered him to the right to pick up the long run-in in front of the cheering crowd, he knew the horse had nothing left to give. All the strength had drained from him and he was treading water as they reached the rail on the left that led to the winning post.

There was pandemonium in the crowd – there always was at this stage of the National – and the noise seemed to disorientate Wet Spring even more. He'd never encountered such tumult before. He began to wobble, veering from side to side like a drunk trailing home from the pub.

The crowd noise ratcheted up a further notch, as if some new drama was at hand. Josh looked over his shoulder and saw the cause of their renewed excitement. Ben O'Brien on Moondance was eating up the ground between them as if this were the beginning of the race, not the end.

They weren't going to make it after all.

Mouse was in tears, burying her head in Terry's chest and soaking his shirt. He held her close and rocked her as the television continued to analyse and replay the drama of the race.

'Never mind, Foxy,' he said for the umpteenth time as he stroked her hair. 'You'll still get money for a place at those odds. And I've got the winner too.'

Stupid idiot. It wasn't about money. It wasn't even about Josh not winning. But losing to that mean milky-faced bastard Ben O'Brien *who shouldn't even have been riding anyway* – that hurt.

She smacked her fist into Terry's chest in frustration, trying to punch right through him.

'Steady on, Foxy,' he protested.

She hit him again but he didn't seem to mind at all.

The changing room was quiet after the excitement of earlier in the afternoon. Most of the jockeys had slipped off to exchange war stories of the great race in other, more glamorous, places.

Josh, his head still full of might-have-been, looked across the room to see a figure slumped in contemplation on the opposite bench. It was Ben. As was their usual custom these days – after the fiasco of the inquiry at Uttoxeter – they'd exchanged no words after the race. Not that they'd had the opportunity in the back-slapping scrum of well-wishers who'd descended on them.

This is stupid, Josh thought. We've just fought each other to the line in a race that will go down in history.

He walked across the room.

Ben looked up, his face registering nothing. The mask, as ever, firmly in place.

Josh held out his hand. 'Bloody brilliant ride,' he said.

For a moment, he thought Ben was going to continue to

blank him but slowly a grin crept across the Irishman's features and he took Josh's hand. Suddenly he looked like the inexperienced youth he was, overwhelmed by the moment.

'You too,' Ben said. He let go of Josh's hand and added, 'But I'm still going to beat you to champion jockey.'

Chapter Eleven

Leo made the call he'd sworn not to make. He never liked to go cap in hand to his half-brother, especially not in matters like this. But the older man was an expert in the affairs of the mind, had degrees as long as your arm and had devoted himself to the barking mad – or the mentally challenged, as modern medical speak doubtless had it – for all his distinguished professional career. So who better to advise his younger sibling who was facing a personal crisis.

He'd lost it completely in the yard that morning, had reduced his secretary to tears with an outburst that had sent her scurrying off, probably never to return. Well, maybe she would after some heavy grovelling and a bunch of flowers. And it had come about not because she was five minutes late but because he'd overheard her discussing the Grand National with one of the girls and saying what a shame it was that Josh Swallow and Wet Spring hadn't hung on to win.

He couldn't go on like this, abusing valuable staff just because they mentioned Swallow's name. He had to find a way of living with his hatred. Part of his strategy was offensive – he'd put his head together with Clive to see what further bricks could be thrown at Swallow's reputation. But he also needed to lance the boil of his obsession. To relieve the day-to-day pressure so he could avoid the temptation to say to poor Sheila that just because she had an arse like a horse it didn't mean she was any judge of one.

That comforting voice came down the line. 'Leo, I'm so pleased to hear from you. You've been on my mind.'

Why didn't he have a smooth-as-silk put-the-other-fellow-at-his-ease voice like that? Leo wondered. Instead of the parade-ground bark that blew people's hats off at ten yards. It was having different fathers, he supposed. The son of a colonel and the son of a biology professor were bound to have their genetic differences. It was in the blood.

'So you'd like to take up my offer, after all? What's made you change your mind?'

'Nothing much.' Just the fact that I'm wandering around like a volcano about to go off, shouting at people who don't deserve it and getting drunk every night. And I've been fantasising about killing people. 'I just got to thinking about what you said.'

'When would you like to come and see me? I've a jam-packed appointment book but I'm sure we can work something out.'

Oh. What had happened to 'I'll drop everything'?

'Of course I can always get you an appointment with someone else. My colleague Elizabeth Longman is greatly admired.'

Good God, a woman! Talking to a male shrink was bad enough.

'Maybe this isn't such a good idea,' Leo muttered. 'I haven't got the time anyway now I think about it.'

A familiar chuckle poured down the line. 'Leo, I'm teasing you. It's unprofessional, I know, so forgive me. I will come and see you. We will stroll in your delightful grounds and admire the burgeoning spring flowers with the scent of horse manure in the air. And we'll have a quiet talk. How does that sound?'

Leo was humbled with gratitude.

Susie forced herself to concentrate on the canvas in front of her. She had to force herself to do lots of things these days, especially going to the local shops. Her neighbours would all have read the papers. They knew that she'd been held under suspicion of murder. Worse, they now knew she'd been an indirect victim of murder herself. How could she cope, knowing what they must be thinking?

She just bloody had to, that's all, otherwise those evil people like Leo Lovall and the sly letter-writer would have won. She couldn't let that happen, for several people's sakes, some alive and some dead. So she compelled herself to go out and hold her head high. And at home she no longer burrowed under the bedclothes but made herself do useful things, like complete the painting she'd promised Carmen Cook.

She had been labouring over a study of Carmen's ranch near Cape Town ever since she had returned from South Africa. At the ranch she'd filled a notebook with sketches and taken a ton of photos, all with the aim of working up this picture. She'd enjoyed planning the composition, with

Normandy, Carmen's star sprinter, in the foreground and the mountains in the distance rising above the terracotta roofs of the horseboxes. Now all the fun had gone out of it, there was nothing new to discover in the scene, just the slog to the end.

It was hard to concentrate and her mind kept wandering to the small object sitting on a table next to an ancient sewing machine and other old, interestingly shaped domestic items: Annabelle's hideous pink phone.

Before Josh left for Kelso that morning she'd raised the matter with him. She'd told him about the phone before but somehow, amidst the excitement of the Aintree meeting and in the aftermath of the National, it had never fully commanded his attention.

'What shall I do about Annabelle's mobile?' she'd said in the dim dawn light as he was dressing for the slog up north to the Borders.

'Chuck it,' came the reply.

'I can't do that. Shouldn't I give it to the police? Or Leo?'

He'd sat down on the bed next to her. 'Look, Susie, if you're right about this phone and Annabelle was using it to conduct a secret affair, then it'll do no good giving it to anyone. Especially not Leo, poor sod. If I were you I'd get rid of it and forget all about it.'

But Susie hadn't chucked it. It wasn't noble of her, she was well aware, but the desire to know the identity of Annabelle's lover was overwhelming. Especially since whoever it was ought to be the real target of Leo's anger and not Josh.

She turned the phone over in her hand. The cover was the height of cheap tack. The scarlet hearts were decorated with words in white, scrolling script: 'Luvya!', 'Kisses!', 'Mmm – bliss!' It was a phone intended for a thirteen-year-old on her first crush, not a married woman who'd just turned thirty-five. But maybe that was why Annabelle had bought it, so she could feel like a teenager again, gripped in a whirlwind of adolescent excitement.

The first thing Susie had done when she had returned from the dress shop last week had been to try and turn the mobile on but the battery had been flat and her charger didn't fit. This morning she'd bought one that did and she'd had the phone plugged in all morning.

She picked it up and turned it on.

The man in the phone shop had told her the manufacturer's default setting for the security code; she'd also found out Annabelle's birthday and her lucky number from Josh ('What do you want to know that for?'), so she had some ideas if the device were to ask her for a PIN number. She always used a PIN whereas Josh never bothered and nor, according to him, did any of his racing mates.

What was it with horse people? Didn't they realise there was a world of mean-minded light-fingered people out there? All her life Susie had done sensible things like keeping chequebooks separate from guarantee cards and noting down serial numbers of electrical appliances, just like Aunt Brenda had taught her. Josh didn't bother with any of it.

The little window in the phone lit up and a graphic swirled across the scene. 'Welcome to Orbbis' it read. And that was it, the phone had no security at all.

On reflection, she might have known. Annabelle was a horse person too.

Maureen was getting on Mouse's nerves and so was everyone in the garage but Mouse forced herself to keep her temper. It was one of those days. She knew it was mad but the frustration of Josh not winning on Saturday – and the way he'd lost! – just wouldn't go away.

'At the end of the day, Foxy, it's only a horse race.' That's what Terry had said. Thanks for the cliché, dummy. At the end of the day, Terry was as stupid as anyone else.

To make her feel better, on Saturday night she'd put another bug in Josh's house. Just breezed in there after she'd shrugged off Terry, who'd virtually pleaded with her to stay the night at his place (well, what would be the point of that?). She was sure Josh and Blondie would be up in Liverpool so there was no risk. But she still felt a thrill as she entered his house, and she liked that. And she wouldn't have minded that much if the Mistake had been there on her own anyway. She could have had another crack at her.

She'd bugged the kitchen this time, inserting the fake adapter into the power point behind the microwave – no one would look there.

When she'd finished she'd turned and come face to face with yet another of the Mistake's objectionable artworks. This one particularly annoyed her. Shades of red and orange and yellow that cast a puke-making light over the whole room. You couldn't avoid it.

Mouse hadn't been able to resist. She'd seized a squeezy

plastic bottle of tomato ketchup from a shelf and flipped up the lid.

It was a delicious feeling to flick and squirt. A trail of red sauce spewed across the picture from top to bottom. Just the one squirt – you'd hardly notice the result, it blended in so well. Actually Mouse thought it had improved the painting.

But now, on Monday morning, back in her little work uniform with a Fordyce Motors smile stitched to her lips, the excitement of the break-in had gone. If one more person said what a great race it had been on Saturday she might just smack them in the mouth.

Looking through the call history stored on the phone, it was plain to Susie that her theory had been correct. Annabelle had been using it to phone just one person. The last call was logged at 12:05 on 22 January, the day of her death. Maybe she'd called her lover on the way to the dress shop.

The call history only went back to the beginning of the year. So Annabelle hadn't had the phone long. The first calls were made on New Year's Eve: one at 17:30, another at 23:17. Susie could imagine the circumstances, Annabelle sneaking off from whatever family celebrations were taking place to call her lover on her secret new phone. Maybe he had given it to her for that purpose.

It was a poignant scenario. Perhaps Josh had been right – she should have minded her own business.

What was worse, however, was that she had no idea who the other person was. Annabelle hadn't entered a name into the address book. Not even an initial. All Susie had was a number and it meant nothing to her at all. And it was a mobile phone code so she couldn't even get a geographical fix on it.

That left only one option, the obvious one – call the number. But what would she say? 'Excuse me, were you having an affair with Annabelle Lovall just before she died?' Hardly.

She pressed the numbers into the little device. If she touched the green telephone symbol the connection would go through. She hesitated. Was she about to make a big mistake?

Yes, if she called on this phone. She had a sudden flash of a mobile ringing at the other end and the recipient, whoever he may be, looking at the incoming number on the screen. Surely he'd recognise his caller – a woman who'd been dead since January.

She cancelled the call and thought for a moment. She'd almost ruined her stealthy detection – and caused a heart attack as well. Imagine if your dead lover called you from beyond the grave? She shivered.

That didn't mean she couldn't ring the number, however, but she mustn't make it on this phone. Nor, on reflection, would it be a good idea to call on any other phone that could be connected to her.

She picked up her purse and made for the door. She'd ring from the pay phone at the bottom of the hill.

What made Ben O'Brien's victory worse for Mouse was that it was treated as a local triumph. Moondance had been trained just a few miles away and all sorts of impromptu celebrations were in the offing. One of the mechanics, passing through reception, had told her about a parade in town and showed her a flyer for a banquet in honour of horse and rider. If Josh could just have hung on for a few more yards, the banquet would have been in honour of him.

She picked up the flyer. The tickets were quite pricey but Terry would take her if she asked him – he could afford it. Terry, it turned out, was T. J. Jones, Landscape and Garden Design Consultant, working on commissions across the Midlands. She should have guessed from his home, a detached cottage with a half-acre garden containing a stream, a waterfall and a secret gazebo.

Terry sounded surprised to hear from her – she had turned him down pretty emphatically on Saturday – but pleased all the same. Her request took him back a bit, however.

'Why do you want to go to a dinner in aid of Ben O'Brien? The way you were going on the other night you wouldn't spit on his grave.'

'All those top racing types off the telly will be there and it might be a laugh. Anyway, I want to make it up to you for being such a cow on Saturday. You did say the Grand National was our race, didn't you?'

He fell for it.

Susie took a deep breath as she thumbed coins into the call box. She couldn't remember when she'd last used a pay phone. These days, with everyone on their mobiles, she'd bet it was only the criminal fraternity who made regular use of them, people who didn't want their calls traced – like her.

She'd worked out a script in her head. On the basis that Annabelle's mystery lover would probably have a connection with horses, she'd say she was doing market research for a horse-feed company. That way she could ask for personal details and get him talking. Who knew what information she might obtain? And if it all went pear-shaped she could just hang up.

What have I got to lose?

She dialled the number. The connection went through and the phone rang at the other end. Susie found she was gripping the receiver so tightly her knuckles were white. She made herself breathe deeply, preparing to speak.

The phone connected. A robotic voice said, 'Leave a message.' Then silence.

She called again.

'Leave a message.'

A fat load of use that was. She'd try later.

He came just as he had promised, striding into the yard with nonchalant confidence and turning the heads of the girls mucking out. Leo rushed to welcome him, relishing the firm clasp of his handshake and the warmth that radiated from the intimacy of his smile.

Leo thought, not for the first time, that his brother should have been a politician. He had a gift for pressing the flesh.

It was ironic that, in the presence of his saviour, Leo didn't feel the same boiling frustration in his veins that he struggled daily to control. And the corresponding black times, when he was so fatigued with self-pity that he could scarcely drag himself into the yard, also seemed remote.

As they strolled along the paths of the old farm and up on to the gallops, he described his symptoms.

Everything kept returning to Josh Swallow. 'It would help,' Leo said, 'if I didn't have to see him every day. But he's there at almost every meeting I go to. The man who screwed my wife and my marriage. Every bugger there knows what a fool he's made out of me and I can't lay a finger on him. Though I'd like to. I'd start with a horsewhip.'

His brother let him lay it out in detail. Gave him permission to vent his anger. That helped.

And after he'd let the bile out, he did feel calmer, more at peace with himself.

'I'm going to write you a prescription for some pills, Leo. Just to even out your moods.'

'I'll stick to whisky, thanks.'

'No, you won't. You'll put the Scotch away and take these instead. It's a difficult period, grief for the loss of a loved one. In a strange way, your obsession with Josh is helpful. It focuses your feelings externally. Just as long as you don't act on them, of course.'

'Of course.'

'It's a good thing he's retiring soon. Then you won't have to bump into him so often.'

After his brother had gone, Clive Cooper rang up. He'd just heard that Josh Swallow was setting up as a trainer for next season.

Leo cursed. So he'd be seeing the bastard at racecourses just as often.

It had taken some time for Susie to find the courage to go back to the health centre. It was inevitable the staff would be talking about her and she hated the thought of them sniggering behind her back. 'You can't hide for ever,' Josh had said, and more importantly, 'You've got nothing to hide about.' So she'd resumed her regular visits.

Today she made straight for the cafe pay phone in the corner to try the number again. It rang as before then the recorded voice cut in. 'Yeah, I know,' Susie muttered to herself. 'Leave a message.'

As she turned away she almost fell over a tall man with wet sandy hair: Mel the resident swimming coach.

'I'm sorry, I was miles away.'

He waved away her apology. 'How's the swimming going?' Some months ago, he'd given her a lesson to improve her breathing technique.

She pulled a face.

'We can run through it again, if you like,' he said. 'After the National I figure I owe you something.'

'You might owe my boyfriend, but you certainly don't owe me.'

'I mean it. Come on Thursday. I've got some lads at four but we could have a session before they show up.'

He seemed sincere but had he been reading all about her in the paper? Was he offering her free lessons so he could boast that he was helping that poor girl whose father had killed her mother and sister?

He was saying something about a friend of hers called Tina.

'Tina?'

'Tina Carter. Her son is in my Thursday group.'

'I don't know any Tina Carter.'

Mel's face registered surprise. 'I thought you did. She

used to ask after you all the time. Well, you and your feller.'

Alarm bells went off in Susie's head. Why did this woman have an interest in her and Josh? What did she know? Enough to write the Susie Sausage letters?

'Tell me about her, Mel. I'm curious.'

Mel didn't look displeased at the request. For all his hunky masculinity, he was a bit of a gossip.

'She's a non-swimmer so she booked lessons with me to get over her fear of water. Suddenly she stopped coming and turned up a month later to explain that she'd had a bad experience and couldn't face getting back into the pool. Her husband's a psychiatrist and one of his patients got a fixation for him and used to sneak into their home. One day Tina came back and found her there. She called the police but it was all a bit nasty.'

Susie could see that. The woman didn't sound like a vindictive letter-writer, however. She was a victim.

But her husband was a psychiatrist. Maybe he'd worked elsewhere in the country, like Cumbria, and had access to medical records that were relevant to her past as Susan Merrivale? Or perhaps he'd seen trial documents – all sorts of psychiatrists had been involved in her father's trial.

She put a brake on that train of thought. She'd end up needing a psychiatrist herself soon.

Mel was staring at her, concerned.

'OK,' she said. 'I'll take you up on that lesson.'

'Didn't you like it, dear?' The square-faced woman peered at the half-eaten bowl of prawns and lettuce in front of Mouse.

'It was all right,' Mouse replied.

'I understand.' The woman nodded, a co-conspirator. 'You're saving yourself for later. I don't have the willpower, I'm afraid.'

'What she means,' chipped in the woman's husband, a man with three chins, 'is that she's a greedy cow.'

'Gordon!' Square Face remonstrated. 'That's not nice.' But Gordon had turned back to the man on the other side of him and was taking no notice. The woman chuckled indulgently and smeared butter on her bread roll. 'He's so naughty. Twenty-seven years married and never a cross word. Do you want to know our secret?'

That was about the last thing Mouse had any interest in, but she was trapped. The room must have held two hundred people, maybe more, but seated on one of twenty or so round tables she was wedged between Square Face – Mrs Doreen Millington, she had learned – and Terry, with no one else within talking distance. And, for the moment, Terry was nattering away to the sharp-suited type on the other side of him and she didn't want to interrupt. They were only at the hors d'oeuvre stage of the celebratory banquet for Moondance and her frustrations were increasing by the minute.

She'd invested in a new dress for the occasion and put her hair up. She looked different, more sophisticated. 'Foxy, you look sensational,' Terry had murmured into her ear as he handed her into his car, a silver Audi she'd not seen before. He explained he kept it for impressing clients, and for special occasions 'like this'.

Of course, there was a reason she'd made an effort. She'd

thought, when she'd bullied Terry into taking her, it might be possible to get close to some of the top people in racing. If she looked her best she could get their attention and tell them about Ben O'Brien at Uttoxeter. How he'd been knocked out for over a minute and should have been laid off riding. Or, maybe, she could have a word with the jockey himself, get him in front of his friends and tell them what he'd been up to. At least she could embarrass him. She'd even had the idea of grabbing a microphone when it came to the speeches and telling everyone what a cheat he was.

Only, now that she was actually here, it all seemed a bit feeble. She needed to make a real mark.

She knew how to do that – if she got the right opportunity.

She'd already had a go at the Millingtons, telling them she knew for a fact O'Brien had been knocked unconscious at Uttoxeter and should have been prevented from riding. And he'd lied about it to the medics!

Gordon had laughed. 'So what are you saying, girlie? They ought to ride the National all over again?'

And Doreen had added her tuppence-worth. 'It just goes to show what a wonderful rider he is, if he wasn't even fit and he still won.'

It made her blood boil.

Susie didn't like spending the night at home alone but sometimes she had no choice. Josh had wanted to come back after the afternoon's meeting at Exeter but she'd forbidden it. He'd driven up to Kelso the day before and was due at Chepstow the next day; what was the point of putting in more hours behind the wheel?

They spoke on the phone throughout the day, though they'd not actually *talked* since the newspaper exposé. Josh had not asked any more about her father and the things that had happened in her childhood and she hadn't volunteered. He didn't know about Susie Sausage. He didn't know about the letters. It was unspoken between them but all of this was on hold until the season was over. So when she'd started telling him about Mel and the woman with a strange interest in their lives, he hadn't cottoned on. After all, if he didn't know she'd been receiving threatening letters he wouldn't share her suspicion that Tina Carter might have written them.

With less than three weeks to go, Josh was chasing every ride he could find in a final effort to catch Ben. But no matter how hard he went after his rival, it seemed he could never close the gap. Ben was twelve winners ahead, much as he had been for months. Susie didn't blame Josh for trying; she just hoped the effort wouldn't be in vain.

She'd been painting. It kept her hands busy while her mind probed and nagged in other directions. If she carried on like this, maybe she could get the picture finished by the end of the week. At least Carmen would be happy.

Mouse knew she shouldn't drink but she didn't care. Last time she'd had a drink she'd nearly snuffed the Mistake. She wouldn't mind snuffing half of these cretins around her. The Millingtons, for a start. When she'd mentioned how much she admired Josh, they'd started telling her all sorts of stupid crap. About how he'd schemed to destroy Leo Lovall and had hired a contract killer to push Annabelle off the balcony when she'd turned up at his door carrying his child.

She wondered what they'd say if they knew how close they were right now to the real killer.

And Terry hadn't proved much of a diversion. He'd spent the evening discussing bets with the man on the other side of him, who turned out to be a bookmaker.

By now they had reached the post-dinner triumphalist speeches. First, the owners of Moondance got up on their hind legs, all four of them, some sort of syndicate of farmers. They sang the praises of the trainer long and loud, and the horse and the jockey. It seemed to Mouse that they made a particular point of bigging up Ben O'Brien. Were they doing it on purpose to piss her off?

Gordon Millington announced loudly that Ben would be champion jockey for the next ten years.

'He hasn't won it this year yet,' said Mouse hotly. 'Josh Swallow could still beat him.'

'Don't be daft, young lady. The bookies are paying out on the lad already. Swallow hasn't got a prayer.'

Terry leaned over to say he'd just been quoted 5/1 against Josh being champion and he was going to have a piece on her behalf.

Good idea. It was an act of faith.

As Ben rose to his feet to speak amid a tumult of applause, Mouse felt in her bag for the knife.

Turning from the fridge, Susie noticed something that arrested her movement.

There was a stain across her red and orange painting. Now she looked closely, it was glaring. Like a scar slashed across a face. How had she not noticed it before?

And how had it happened?

Carefully, with a piece of kitchen towel soaked in water, she removed the mark. What on earth could it be? It looked like – and tasted like – tomato ketchup. Only one person ate tomato ketchup in this house.

What on earth had Josh been playing at?

'You all right, babe?' Terry was leaning closer, his arm along the back of her chair. From that angle she reckoned he could see right into the neck of her dress.

'The smoke's getting in my eyes.'

Glen the bookie had produced cigars and now he and Gordon were puffing away like garden bonfires.

'Let's just have a look at Moondance, then I'll take you to the bar for a nightcap.'

Moondance?

Then Mouse noticed that the waiters had carried the serving table away from the far wall and pulled open some drapes to reveal large french windows. A roll of brown matting now led from the double doors to the centre of the room which, she assumed, was normally used for dancing. Tonight, though, it was to serve as a parade ring.

A roar went up from the drunken diners as the french doors opened to reveal the sturdy chestnut gelding, flanked by two stable girls. The Grand National winner didn't seem entirely thrilled by the smoky bedlam suddenly revealed to him, but as the girls tugged on his bridle he condescended to step inside.

Applause, hearty and sustained, filled the room as Moondance allowed himself to be paraded. Some of the more boisterous in the audience whooped and drummed their heels on the wooden floor. When the horse halted in the centre of the room, men and women rushed forward to pat his flanks and pose by his side in a hail of camera flashes.

'Aaah, isn't he lovely?' said Mrs Millington in Mouse's ear but Mouse ignored her.

By now some of the younger lads had lifted Ben O'Brien up on to their shoulders and were heading through the crush towards Moondance. A path opened for them and Ben, protesting ineffectually, was hoisted on to the blanket that covered the animal's back. Everyone still seated at the tables stood and applauded.

Moondance, seemingly not displeased to be reunited with the jockey who had ridden him to glory, pricked up his ears and stared disdainfully over the heads of the spectators. Ben raised both arms high and, his long white face stretching into an unfamiliar grin, accepted the applause which washed over the pair of them like a cloudburst.

Mouse did not join in the applause. She felt sick. The acclaim should have been for Josh. He had been robbed in the last few strides of the race by a man who shouldn't even have been riding. And here Josh's name was unjustly reviled, while Ben O'Brien was treated like a Messiah. The champion jockey elect. Destined to be champion for the next ten years.

It wasn't fair.

Terry, like everyone else, was standing up to watch the goings-on in the middle of the room. It seemed they were all desperate to have their photo taken with the victorious horse and rider.

She gripped his arm. 'I've got to take my lenses out. It's the smoke.'

For a moment, she thought he was going to follow her but she waved him back imperiously then, as a brilliant second thought, blew him a kiss. She was getting smarter in her old age.

She headed round the side of the room towards the exit to the bar and the hallway where the toilets were situated. But she kept going past the door, almost to the far wall, before cutting back through the throng, choosing a path that took her behind the tallest men. Everyone's eyes were on the centre of the room, focused on the horse and the scrum of activity around him. The stable girls and other workers from the trainer's yard were trying to impose some kind of order on the chaos but without much success. As Mouse got closer to Moondance, wriggling between bodies, taking care to remain inconspicuous, she prayed that a halt would not be called to the proceedings. Not just yet.

She was close now to the centre of the action, approaching from the horse's rear. A pair of burly fellows were preventing the crowd from standing immediately behind the horse; another was struggling with a broom and a long-handled dustpan. The smell of horse dung filled her nostrils and the air was thick with farmyard remarks.

As Mouse insinuated herself into the ring around the horse she watched with dismay as helping hands lifted Ben from the animal's back. Damn. She was going to be too late. But Moondance remained in position, good-naturedly putting up with the liberties that were being taken as one of the owning connections was boosted up on to his back.

She couldn't see Ben O'Brien in the crush. All around was a sea of back-slapping jollity, with enthusiastic hugs being exchanged and cameras flashing.

Suddenly there he was in front of her, being mauled by a couple of matrons and their beery spouses. They faced away from her, posing for more celebratory snaps.

Mouse slipped her hand into her bag and grasped the knife. She knew she had only one strike. And she'd never stabbed anyone before. She'd imagined it though. Read about it and seen it in the movies. How difficult could it be? She'd butchered plenty of pieces of meat in kitchens in her time.

If you wanted to damage someone you had to strike deep, where there were vital tendons and nerves that would take time to heal. And if you only had one strike you had to make the biggest hole possible.

She took a deep breath and dropped to her knee. Down at waist level, she felt invisible, as if she had removed herself from the company all around her. Good, that was just what was required.

Immediately in front of her was the flannel of the jockey's navy blue suit. Beneath it was his left leg. She plunged the point of the knife into the flesh behind his knee. She felt it hit home, lodging amongst hard gristly things, and she twisted it back and forth, not just to cause damage but to get it free. Then it was out and she was turning, ducking back the way she had come.

There was a cry behind her, as much of surprise as pain, but she knew it was Ben and she looked up, she couldn't help it. He was staring over her head, his smile still in place

but now glassy and fixed there by reflex, suspended somewhere between surprise and pain. Then he was falling to the
ground and she was gone, slipping away through a crowd
that surged forward in ignorance and hysteria, aware that
some new excitement had taken place.

She put the knife back in her bag as she scurried through
the exit door and along the corridor to the Ladies. As she
went, she passed the open door to the kitchen where, just
inside, stood a metal trolley piled high with dirty plates and
glasses. And cutlery. It was easy to place the incriminating
weapon in the pile.

Ten minutes later, Mouse emerged from the Ladies toilet.
Her hands had shaken as she removed her contact lenses but
she had recovered her nerves now. There had been blood on
her spectacle case and on the lining of her handbag but
she'd washed it off surreptitiously at the sink, jostled by
other women oblivious of everything but titivation.

Terry was waiting for her in the corridor outside, his face
grim. He carried her cardigan and whisked it over her
shoulders as he grabbed her.

'Come on, we've got to go,' he hissed, propelling her
away from the crush.

'What's the matter?' Mouse asked innocently – as you
would.

'There's been an accident.' He hustled her out of the
door. As they reached his car, he turned and hugged her
close. 'Thank God you're all right. I'd never have forgiven
myself if you'd got caught up in it.'

'I still don't understand, Terry.'

'I'll tell you on the way home.'

As they accelerated away down the drive and on to the main road, an ambulance and a police car passed them on the opposite side of the carriageway.

They'd made a clean getaway.

Mouse put her hand on Terry's thigh and squeezed gently. 'Can I stay at your place tonight?' she said softly.

He shot her a look of astonishment that softened into his familiar, knowing grin.

'I thought you'd never ask, Foxy.'

She smiled back and left her hand where it was.

There was nothing like a bit of insurance.

Chapter Twelve

Susie woke late and turned on the radio.

Ben O'Brien was in hospital, the victim of a stabbing at a post-Grand National celebration that had turned sour. He was due to face surgery on a wounded leg and it was unlikely he would race again this season.

Within seconds, she was dialling Josh.

'Have you heard about Ben?' she demanded without preamble. From the crackle on the line, she guessed Josh was on the road.

'Only what's been on the news,' he said. 'I can't get hold of Tony and I've been trying since early. This business with Ben must be serious.'

'What on earth happened?'

'Too much boozing, from the sound of it. Let's hope Ben's not too bad.'

From anyone else with so much to gain, Susie might have doubted his sincerity. She didn't doubt Josh, however, though she wondered whether he'd thought through all the angles.

'You realise some people are going to blame you, don't you?'

'That's crazy, why should they?'

Sometimes he was too naive for his own good. 'You know what people are like, Josh. I've just heard someone on the radio comparing this to a tennis player being stabbed back in the nineties.'

'Monica Seles. Some nutter did it because he wanted Steffi Graf to be number one. I don't see what that's got to do with me.'

'You don't?'

'Oh, Jesus.'

The penny had dropped.

'Hey, Mouse, you don't do things by halves, do you?'

Baz was grinning fit to bust as he stood in his office doorway, holding the newspaper. Mouse gave him her frostiest glare but there was no shutting him up. He turned to Maureen as he sauntered over. 'She goes out once in a blue moon and starts a riot. Bloody typical, don't you reckon?'

'I didn't see any riot,' Mouse said.

'What did you see then?' Maureen was staring at her, bursting with curiosity, analysing Mouse's every twitch – and there were plenty of those; she wasn't feeling so hot in the aftermath of last night's drinking. 'Go on,' Maureen persisted. 'What happened?'

'Nothing much. I went to the loo to take my contacts out. Next thing Terry came to find me and whisked me away. He said there'd been an accident.'

'So you didn't see it kick off?' Baz sounded disappointed.

'All I saw was a load of pissed people crowding round the horse. It must have happened after I left the room.'

'It says here,' Baz rustled the paper, 'that a hit squad of Ben O'Brien's racing rivals tried to cut his leg off. And you ruddy well missed it.'

'Don't believe everything you read in the paper, Baz. He probably just fell over.'

'Oh yeah? It says he won't be riding again this season. Bloody convenient for your mate Josh Swallow, wouldn't you say?'

Mouse shrugged. Baz didn't mean anything by it but it wasn't a road she wanted to go down. Fortunately, Maureen provided a diversion.

'All the same, it's nice that Terry was looking out for you.'

'He was great. At the first hint of trouble he rushed me home.'

'And which home would that be?'

Mouse could see that this was the question that really interested Maureen. For once, in the interests of the greater scheme of things, Mouse decided to drop her guard.

'That would be telling, wouldn't it?'

Maureen's eyes swelled to gobstopper proportions and Baz's face emerged from behind the paper with a smirk.

That should give them something else to chew on.

Josh called back after ten minutes. This time there was no noise of traffic in the background.

'Where are you?' Susie asked.

'I stopped in a lay-by. I might come home. I don't think I should be riding today.'

'Because of Ben?'

'If people are going to think he's been hurt because of me, I'm not sure it's right.'

She'd been afraid of something like this. 'Before you do anything rash, Josh, just listen to me for a moment.'

'OK.' He sounded distant.

'Did you have anything to do with what happened to Ben last night?'

'What?' He didn't sound so distant now. 'Of course I didn't. I might not be Ben's best friend but the last thing I'd do is harm another rider. You know that.'

'I'm only asking to make a point. The thing is, Josh, you've got a job to do and responsibilities to carry out. You're a top professional and people are depending on you. You can't just walk out.'

'Maybe just for today, Susie. Out of respect.'

She gritted her teeth. He was infuriating. 'Look at it this way. If Ben hadn't jocked you off Moondance, it might have been you there last night instead of him and you might be lying in hospital now. And if that had happened, do you think Ben would consider laying off for a day?'

There was silence on the other end of the line, followed by a familiar chuckle.

'You sound just like my dad.'

Susie breathed a sigh of relief. 'I know you don't want to be seen taking an unfair advantage, Josh, but you've got to realise this is your opportunity to get back on terms with Ben. He might not be out for long – no one knows. You've been off plenty of times this season and he hasn't. Now it's his turn to miss out.'

'OK. You've made your point. I hope he's not badly hurt though.'

That went without saying.

After he'd rung off Susie remembered she had a bone to pick with him on another subject. On reflection, it could wait. Now was not the time to complain about him squirting ketchup over her painting.

There was only one topic of conversation in the weighing room at Chepstow. Some of the lads had been at the celebration the previous evening and their stories were getting a good airing.

'One moment we're all having a laugh, with a whole bunch of people wanting to get their pictures with Moondance. The next there's screaming and shouting and Ben's rolling about on the floor,' said Charlie Coyle. 'I thought he was having us on until I saw the blood. Jesus, it was all over the place. The people up next to him started freaking out but no one else knew what was going on. They're still drinking and laughing while some vet's trying to stop the bleeding.' He paused dramatically. It was the third time he had told the story and he was getting quite good at it. 'If you ask me the calmest person there was the horse.'

'But what actually happened to Ben?' someone asked. 'Didn't anybody see?'

Charlie shook his head. 'Not me. It was a complete scrum.'

'What about the people right up next to him? Someone must have seen something.'

Charlie shrugged. 'You'd think, wouldn't you? I don't envy the coppers. They wouldn't let us go till they'd got all our names and addresses. Now they're going to have to talk to a couple of hundred people.'

'And one of them,' a lad added in a stage whisper, 'could be the killer.'

'For God's sake,' said Josh, 'it's no joke.'

The rest of them laughed nevertheless. It was inevitable, Josh supposed, that the gallows humour of the changing room would surface sooner or later.

'You wouldn't like to account for your movements last night, would you, Josh?' said one of the other riders who'd been at the dinner. 'I swear I saw someone just like you with an ice pick down his trousers.'

Josh forced himself to laugh along with the rest of them but it was an effort.

He left the weighing room in search of Tim Daniels and found Leo's assistant in the stables, looking grim and flustered as he squatted on his haunches next to a novice hurdler with a bandaged rear leg. The sight of Josh did not improve his mood. Nevertheless he responded to Josh's inquiry about Ben.

'He's got a wound in the back of his knee. Some kind of blade was shoved right up into the joint, cutting through one of the cruciate ligaments.'

'Bloody hell.' That was the kind of injury that could keep a jockey out of the saddle for months.

'So you won't be riding against him any more this season, Josh, if that's what's concerning you.'

Josh kept his temper. He might have wished minor misfortune on his rival – a few days off with concussion or a ban for misuse of the whip, say – but nothing like this.

'You know me better than that, Tim.'

Tim stood up. 'Yeah, I guess.' The pair had worked together well in days gone by. 'I'd rather you buggered off, Josh. Leo's at the hospital with Ben and I've got a ton of stuff to do.'

And though he could hardly say so, Josh knew it also wasn't politic for Tim to be seen talking to him – word would get back to Leo. But he had one more request.

'Do you think Ben would mind if I got in touch?'

Tim shrugged. 'I don't see why not. Give it a few days though. His family are coming over from Ireland and everything.'

'I don't have his phone number.' It was one of the reasons Josh had been trying to get hold of Tony. Now he thought about it, the agent was probably helping Ben and his family sort his life out.

'Leave it to me,' Tim said and turned back to the horse.

Josh didn't ask whether the animal had been down to be ridden by Ben, though he guessed as much when later he saw a young apprentice sitting nervously on board as the horses ambled round the parade ring. In the race itself the lad didn't do badly but, in the long back straight, he went to the front too early and Josh caught him just before the last hurdle. He didn't think it would have been such a comfortable win if Ben had been riding.

After he'd weighed in, his valet handed him an envelope with his name scrawled on it in neat blue ink. Inside was a slip of paper with the name of a hospital, the Dryfield Orthopedic, Swindon, and a mobile phone number. Tim had been as good as his word.

'I had Glen on the phone today.' Terry chased a strand of bean sprout round the bowl with his chopsticks and popped it into his mouth.

'Glen?' Mouse couldn't think who he was talking about. She was concentrating on eating. The chopsticks had been his idea and she wasn't much good at it. She kept dropping bits of food.

'Come on, Foxy. The bookie bloke on our table last night. He's very suspicious of you. He thinks you done that jockey.'

Terry was grinning as if it was hugely funny. He sat across from Mouse on the sofa, his bare torso surprisingly muscular for a slim man – but then, he did do a lot of heavy gardening work. She hadn't wanted to spend the evening with him but it had seemed like a good idea to keep an eye on him after last night. So she'd accepted his offer of a Chinese which, after he'd had his wicked way with her on the sofa, had turned out to be a takeaway. With chopsticks. And she'd got black bean sauce all down his shirt, which happened to be the only garment she was wearing.

Anyhow, it was obviously just as well she'd put up with it all.

'What was he getting at?' she said, trying to keep the sudden swoop of panic that gripped her out of her voice.

'It was just a joke. Don't worry about it.' He speared a lump of water chestnut from one of the foil containers on the low table between them. 'He was having a bit of a moan, actually. 'Cos no sooner had we put money on O'Brien losing than he gets injured and can't ride.' Terry shook his head in wonder. 'I ask you, a bookmaker complaining of bad luck.'

'Yes, but what did he say about me?' She put her bowl down on the table, still half full. All of a sudden, she'd lost her appetite.

'I said, "Don't tell me you think I did it, I was sitting next to you the whole time." And he said, "You might have been but your girlfriend wasn't."'

Mouse concentrated on the thin chain round his neck, the gold cross nestling in the black tuft of hair on his chest. 'Really?' she said. Keep it light. 'What did you say to that?'

'I laughed. I told him you'd gone to the Ladies and he said he was only kidding.'

OK, that was better.

'Then he said we were smart making a quick getaway. Apparently, he got held up for ages waiting to give his details to the police. They'll want to talk to us, too, babe.'

What?

'But we left before they arrived,' she said hastily. 'They don't know about us.'

'Yeah, but they'll need our statements, won't they? It's what happens in an investigation. The cops plod around talking to everyone who was there, even if they didn't see anything. So they can eliminate them from their inquiries.'

Mouse didn't like the sound of this. She got out of the armchair and sat next to him on the sofa. He grinned at her and put down his food.

'Terry, I really don't want to talk to the police.'

'I shouldn't think it'll take long. I'll give them a bell and see if they'll do us together. Maybe they'll come round here.'

She wiped a grain of rice from the corner of his mouth and somehow her arms ended up round his neck.

'But there's no point, we don't know anything. It's just a waste of everybody's time.'

'I know, Foxy, but we don't have any choice. That's why Glen rang. He said he'd passed on my number to them because they asked who else was on his table.'

Oh.

She tilted her lips towards his mouth and he jumped at the invitation. He tasted of soy sauce and beer but she accepted it, her thoughts racing ahead.

When they came up for air, she said, 'Terry, I'm worried the police aren't going to believe me.'

He smiled at her fondly. 'Aren't going to believe what?'

'That I was in the Ladies. It was just when I went to change my lenses that it happened and I wasn't with you.' The anguish in her voice sounded real – she thought so, at any rate.

'Oh, sweetheart!' He stared into her eyes, concern furrowed on his brow. 'They're not going to suspect you.'

More bloody fool them if they didn't.

'How do you know, Terry? There'll be lots of pressure to find who did it because Ben O'Brien's a famous sportsman and it's all over the papers. The police don't care who they catch as long as they get someone. There's all those miscarriages of justice, aren't there? The Guildford Four and things. I've read about it. And I was there and it's my word against theirs and it's all because I should have stayed with you. I wish I'd stayed with you, Terry. Honestly.'

And she burst into tears, sobbing in his arms, wetting his broad bare chest.

She'd never been in plays at school when she was a kid – why ever not?

'Foxy, Foxy, listen!' He was getting quite agitated, his face a horrified mask as she wept all over him. 'It's OK. Honestly, it'll be fine. None of that is going to happen.'

'How do you know?'

'Because I'll say I was with you. I'll say I watched you go out of the room and then I followed you and waited outside the Ladies. You were in there all the time. I mean, it's the truth, isn't it?'

She nodded, her hysteria subsiding.

He hugged her to him. 'You poor baby. Beneath that hard shell you've got a real soft centre.'

She didn't contradict him.

'I can't see anything,' Josh said. He was peering closely at the painting in the kitchen, looking for evidence of assault by tomato ketchup.

'Of course you can't. I spent half an hour cleaning it off. I even retouched the yellow, there in the centre. I can tell.'

'Right.' To Josh, the picture looked exactly as it had always done, but Susie would know.

In any case, all this was beside the point. If Susie said the painting had been damaged then it must have been. But he hadn't done it.

'You really think I squirted tomato sauce all over your picture?' he said, not for the first time.

'Not deliberately, no. I assumed it was an accident.'

'You mean, like I just missed my plate and accidentally chucked ketchup over the wall six feet away.'

The accusing look in her grey eyes softened and her mouth twitched into a smile. 'You are a bit of a messy eater,' she said.

He smiled too. It was good to have a laugh about something.

'I blame the cleaner,' he said.

They didn't have a cleaner. Some day, maybe, but they never seemed to get around to organising it.

'Seriously, Josh. How do you think it happened?'

'I don't know. Things have a mind of their own, I reckon. Like you complain I've moved all your make-up and I haven't. I ask what you've done with my sweater and you swear you've never touched it. It's just what happens in houses.'

It was typical of Josh to bring up the matter of his lost sweater, thought Susie as she cleared away the dinner things. It had disappeared months ago but its loss still rankled, as he never let her forget. She knew he thought she'd borrowed and lost it – where, exactly? – just because he'd once caught her wearing it when she was cleaning up the studio. It was old and shapeless and nowhere near as stylish as any of his newer ones – which was why he was so fond of it, of course. She also had clothes that had become part of her and which she'd throw out only when they fell to bits. So she was sorry it had disappeared but it had nothing to do with her. One day, God willing, he'd stop going on about it.

She made her way upstairs, turning out the lights as she went. Josh had gone up already to have a bath before bed, on her orders. He'd travelled many miles in the past three days, racing in Scotland, England and Wales, and an early night made sense – apart from the selfish reason that she hadn't seen him since the early hours of the previous day and she wanted his full attention.

As she passed the bathroom she heard him singing softly – that was a good sign. The crisis over Ben O'Brien appeared to have passed. He'd had a couple of winners at Chepstow, too, and that was always balm to a jockey's troubled spirit. That put him just ten behind Ben. *And Ben isn't going to be riding any more winners this season*. She guiltily put the thought aside. Josh might be too squeamish to face up to it but there was no denying that he had a great chance now of becoming champion.

There was another reason why the mood was lighter in the house. Colin Smart had called her to say that DI Picard had more or less admitted that she had no case to answer in the matter of Annabelle's death.

'I don't think they found Mrs Glazier a very satisfactory witness. At any rate, they don't want to risk building a case on her evidence.'

Colin said he was pressing them to make a public statement but had had no luck so far. That was a pity, because the damaging coverage of her arrest lingered on. She knew Josh was still losing rides because of it.

His clothes were strewn across the bed and the contents of his trouser pockets – coins, car keys, wallet – scattered on the dressing table. As she tidied his things away she picked up a slip of paper. On it was written the name of a hospital and a phone number.

'Josh.' She stuck her head round the bathroom door.

He leered at her cheerfully through a mist of steam. 'This is bliss,' he said. 'Get your kit off and jump in.'

She ignored the suggestion. 'What's this?' She held up the slip of paper.

'That's the place where Ben's getting patched up. I got it off Tim Daniels.'

'So this is Ben's mobile?'

'I thought I'd give him a call. You know, to wish him luck and say no hard feelings.'

That would be typical of Josh, she thought as she climbed the stairs to the next landing and stepped into her studio.

The pink phone was where she'd left it and she switched it on. She was sure, damn sure, but she had to be certain.

The number was familiar from having tried it on the pay phone at the bottom of the hill and at the health club. She'd had a couple of goes since then but she'd never got through.

The digits illuminated on the small screen of the pink phone were the same as those written on Josh's piece of paper. The man who'd been having an affair with Annabelle

Lovall, the man she'd left her husband for and whose child she was carrying, was Ben O'Brien.

A ringing noise woke Mouse and for a moment she couldn't work out where she was. It came to her soon enough. She'd woken up in Terry's house again but this time she'd overslept. She was on her own in the luxurious big bed and she stretched out languorously.

From downstairs came the sound of the front door shutting – was it the doorbell that she'd heard? – the murmur of music and the smell of toast. This was nice. She'd better not get used to it.

A moment later Terry stepped into the room carrying a breakfast tray. On it, next to the tea and toast, stood a small cream-coloured bag and a card with her name on it.

'What's this?' she said suspiciously. She mustn't let him think she'd gone too soft after last night's performance.

'Take a look,' he said, plonking the tray on the bed between them and opening the curtains. Spring sunlight flooded the room.

The card said, 'Foxy, you're first past my post every day of the week', which was not the most sophisticated of greetings but the card itself was satisfyingly thick and expensive in feel. Inside the bag was a box in matching cream, tied in black ribbon. Despite herself, Mouse felt excited as she lifted the lid to find a square glass bottle with a sleek metallic cap.

'Perfume!' she said, unable to hide her pleasure. No one had ever given her perfume before.

'Actually, it's eau de cologne,' he said. 'I hope you like it.'

She removed the cap and gave her wrist a little squirt. A woody aroma overrode the smell of toasted bread. It wasn't sweet; a subtle, complicated smell unlike other scents she'd ever used. 'Wild fig and cassis cologne' it said on the side of the bottle.

'I wanted you to have it for the other night,' he said, 'but I had to order it over the phone and they've only just delivered.'

The doorbell, she supposed.

'What do you think?' he asked.

She sniffed her wrist again. It smelt expensive. The Maureens of this world would never wear anything like it. But the Annabelle Lovalls might. It was the sort of perfume that had clung to those filmy bits of underwear on the bed in London that day.

It was just the kind of trendy, upmarket scent a man like Josh would appreciate.

Terry's eyes were on her, anxiously searching for approval. It wouldn't be a good idea to deny it to him.

'I love it,' she said.

His face lit up like Piccadilly Circus.

Susie had no plans to tell Josh about Ben, not yet anyway. He'd made it plain he disapproved of her snooping into Annabelle's phone. 'Nothing good's going to come of it,' he'd said. 'It's only going to stir up more trouble. Just leave things be.'

He had a point. But that didn't mean he was right.

Susie found it hard to credit that Annabelle would fall for someone like Ben. He must be a dozen years younger –

more. In Susie's opinion he was a strange choice for a toyboy. She'd come across him at a couple of racing dinners and found him reserved to the point of being gormless. But then, she'd been by Josh's side at the time. This recent discovery put Ben's antipathy towards Josh in a new light. It was obviously more than professional rivalry. Ben could hardly be expected to be friends with Annabelle's previous lover.

Susie picked the newspaper from the mat and at once noticed the strapline above the masthead. 'Top trainer speaks out on jump-racing's season of crisis – see sports pages.' This was accompanied by a small head shot she instantly recognised: the crumpled spaniel face of Leo Lovall.

Quickly she turned to the inside back page and began to read.

Unusually for one of the nation's best-known National Hunt trainers, today Leo Lovall is not spending the afternoon at a racecourse, instead he is sitting anxiously in the Dryfield Orthopedic Hospital in Swindon. His concern is for the young Irishman who has become as integral a part of the Hoar Frost success as any Gold Cup winner: Ben O'Brien.

'That boy's a magician with animals,' Leo says. 'He has a way of communicating with them that's not human. I've no doubt that he'll be a legend by the time he's through. Not that he's the finished article yet because he hasn't got the experience. That's why I let him transfer to Moondance for the National, even though he was supposed to be on Trumpet Major for me. Major's owner was very gracious about the switch and thank God he was. To get brought down at Canal Turn, then catch your horse and remount *and* win the race takes some doing – an epic achievement. It would have been a complete travesty if a no-hoper like Wet Spring had got home by default. At least it saved everyone an embarrassment on the day.'

Susie frowned. The insult was gratuitous.

What happened the other night was a disgrace. Someone deliberately tried to maim the best jump-jockey in the land. But the lad lives like a priest, dedicated to his profession. He's got no enemies so why would anyone want to put him out of action? The way he was attacked has to be a professional assault, in my opinion. Sadly, there are dark forces at work in our business and certain people are willing to collude with them for purposes of their own. Whether it's money or revenge or simply a lust for glory, I don't know, but something's got to be done about it. The decent people in racing should turn their backs on the rotten apples in the barrel and I'm delighted to say that's already beginning to happen.

I try to press Leo on the identity of these rotten apples but he is reluctant to name names. 'I can't say what I know to be true unless I have the evidence to back it up in court and, so far, I don't. What I will say, however, is that if anyone else emerges as champion jockey as a result of Ben's incapacity, then their achievement will be as a consequence of criminal activity and should be regarded as worthless.'

Susie was fuming. Leo had stopped short of naming Josh as a crook and blaming him for Ben's injury, but only just. To those in the know the implication was clear. He'd also attempted to undermine the race for champion jockey now that Ben was out of action. Even if Josh managed to overhaul Ben's total, Leo was saying, it wouldn't count for anything.

She wondered what the trainer would have said had he known the truth about Ben, the boy who 'lives like a priest'. Thanks to her discovery of the phone she was in a position to tell him. She pondered how best to use the knowledge to Josh's advantage.

It was time to fight back.

Mouse had been decidedly edgy since Terry had called to say the police had asked them to drop into Barwick Close station to make a statement.

'I thought you said they'd come to see us,' Mouse protested.

'Yeah, but I think they're a bit pushed. It makes sense if we help them out, doesn't it?'

So he picked her up – in his silver Audi, she noted – and took her down in her lunch hour. To her dismay, they were separated but the female detective constable who spoke to her seemed appreciative of her voluntary appearance.

'We'd have got round to you eventually,' the policewoman said, 'but it's a great help you turning up off your own bat. There were over two hundred at that dinner, plus the hotel staff – that's a heck of a lot of interview time, considering.'

'So this'll be quick? Only, this is my lunch hour.'

'Don't worry. You'll be out of here in twenty minutes.'

And so she was. She stuck to the story she'd spun Terry, that the cigar smoke had hurt her eyes and she'd left the dining room for the Ladies to remove her lenses, where she'd spent a good ten minutes, maybe more, it being very crowded.

The DC asked her if she knew any of the other women who'd been in there with her and she described a couple in vague terms. She was able to duck questions about the precise time of her visit, saying she wasn't wearing a watch. This was true enough, her shabby timepiece had not matched her smart new outfit and she'd left it off.

After she was finished, the policewoman asked her to wait and left her on her own. Mouse assumed a look of boredom, on the assumption that she might be being observed. Inside, anxiety gripped her. Maybe Terry wasn't going to back her up, as he had promised. Perhaps they had a statement from another witness who had seen her with the knife. Or, and this could be just as bad, maybe there was some copper out there who knew her from before and even now was peering at her through some spyhole. Though previously she'd not been in this nick – the business with Gavin's wife had taken place on another patch – policemen moved around a lot, didn't they? Also, there might be some computer record on her, even though she'd never actually gone to trial.

Just as she felt she couldn't hold her panic down any

longer, the DC returned with a smile on her face and Terry at her shoulder. She'd never thought she'd be so pleased to see his gold-toothed grin.

'Is that Clive Cooper?'

Susie had spent five minutes at the mercy of the newspaper switchboard and it had given an edge to her belligerence which she relished. She was conscious she had to make the most of it.

'Who wants him?' The voice was all business.

'Susie Brown.'

The voice changed. 'How can I help you, Susie Brown?'

Susie had only just put two and two together about the reporter who'd visited her Aunt Brenda and had conducted today's interview with Leo. She'd noted the byline and rung her aunt. Brenda had dug out the card the man had left and confirmed his identity. 'He's a bit smarmy,' she'd added.

Susie had already formed the impression that that was an understatement.

'I want to know who tipped you off about me,' she said.

'Sorry, Susie, even if I could answer that question, I wouldn't. A journalist never reveals his sources, as I'm sure you know.'

'Surely you can tell me how you heard. Did you get a letter?'

'Possibly.'

'What did it say?'

'I really couldn't tell you that. Unless, of course, you reconsider the chance to talk to me about your situation.'

Reconsider? Of course, after her arrest, there had been

offers for her story from the papers. Josh had got Tony to turn them all down.

Cooper was still talking, putting in a sales pitch. 'You've got a unique and valuable story to tell, Susie. This newspaper would love to help you put your point of view to the public.'

'No.' It was unthinkable.

'I can assure you we would be most generous.'

She put the phone down on him. She felt soiled.

As he drove home from Shropshire, Josh tried hard not to let the Leo Lovall article in the paper spoil his day – the last in which he would ever ride at Ludlow racecourse. Since the Grand National he'd become conscious that on each of the remaining days of the season he'd be saying goodbye as a jockey to the venues where he had plied his trade for nearly twenty years.

Some of these courses he was quite happy to consign to riding history but Ludlow, perversely according to many jockeys, was not one of them. He'd never minded the sharp bends, the firm going or, even, the four road crossings which, he felt, just added to the character of the course. The reason, naturally, was that Ludlow had always been one of his lucky tracks. He'd learned early on that to be successful here it helped always to be up with the leaders and to ride the bends as tightly as possible. The very first ride he'd had at Ludlow had been a winner and he didn't think he'd ever spent an afternoon at the course without coming first at least once.

He'd thought his sequence was about to be broken this afternoon. With just one race left, he'd managed two close seconds and a third – so he'd been thereabouts without actually doing the real business. Fortunately Agincourt, a lively six-year-old, saved his bacon in the final hurdle race and the pair of them had bolted up in triumph, ten lengths clear.

Now, as he flogged through the heavy Midlands traffic on the M42, Josh savoured the moment again. There was a remarkable symmetry in winning on his first and last rides on the same course – maybe he should have mentioned it to the press boys. But he feared that, these days, this was not the kind of detail they were interested in printing about him.

His thoughts had found their way back to Leo's extraordinary interview. With Annabelle's death and Ben's injury, Leo was bound to feel that fate was conspiring against him. On the other hand, that didn't justify turning fate into some plot instigated by 'dark forces' and 'bad apples'. Josh had no doubt Leo had been aiming the remarks in the paper at him. It always came back to the same thing: Leo had never forgiven him for falling in love with Annabelle all those years ago.

But the affair with Annabelle hardly made him a criminal, as Leo appeared to be suggesting. And to link him with the assault on Ben was daft. Though he might benefit from Ben's indisposition, how on earth could the attack have anything to do with him? Was he supposed to have paid some professional assassin? It was ridiculous.

All Josh could think of was that Leo was trying to put extra pressure on him by mounting some psychological attack. Well, that wouldn't work. Susie's words yesterday morning had hit home. Now it was Ben's turn to sit on his hands and watch.

Josh had fourteen days left in his career as a jockey, fourteen days to land the one prize that had eluded him. Whatever the circumstances, he didn't intend to blow his last chance of becoming champion jockey.

'Leo?'

Clive's voice was distant, but most things seemed distant at the moment, let alone a voice over a mobile phone connection.

'Hello, Clive.' It seemed to take an age to get the words out. The new pills certainly worked. They slowed him down no end.

'What did you think of the article? It did the business, didn't it? I've had people calling me all day about it.'

Really? That was good.

'You did a sound job, Clive.' He was obviously expected to say something.

'It's put the cat among the pigeons and no mistake. I've even had Susie Brown on the phone.'

'I hope you gave her a flea in her ear.'

'You bet.'

That was good. If the article had got up the nose of Josh's little girl it must have been on the money. It showed he'd been right to take Clive's advice.

In the light of his brother's words of wisdom, he'd gone along with the idea. He'd also locked the whisky bottle away, and the gun, and he'd started on the medication. It had got him through the week without him losing his temper or shedding a tear. Even Ben's terrible injury seemed to have occurred in a place removed from reality, as if it were an episode in some medical drama on the box. And he'd allowed Clive to put sober words into his mouth for the newspaper article. He was delighted to hear they'd hit home.

But frankly, even in his current state, he couldn't see what good mere words could do.

Chapter Thirteen

The girl who opened the door to Susie bore a striking resemblance to Ben O'Brien. Even if Susie hadn't had her card marked she would have realised she was talking to his sister. But whereas the jockey's long pale face seemed dour, the sister was strikingly attractive. Maybe it was the black ringlets and the sparkle in her amethyst-blue eyes. The warm smile did no harm either.

'Hi, I'm Brenna. Tony told me you were coming.'

Tony Wylie had fixed things for Susie, not that he'd had much choice. After Susie had extracted Ben's address on the basis that she wanted to send a goodwill message, she'd come clean.

'I'm going to see him, Tony, whether he likes it or not. I'd prefer not to turn up at a bad time though.'

Tony had assumed – and she'd not contradicted him – that her visit was intended as a bridge-building exercise between Josh and Ben and he'd been keen to help. He explained to Susie that Ben's mother and sisters were tending to his needs and he'd promised to sound out the position for her.

So here she was, being ushered through the jockey's spanking new house in Lambourn out into the back garden.

'We stick him out here as much as we can,' said Brenna. 'He needs all the fresh air he can get.'

Susie was apprehensive. Politeness and a smile would only get her so far. When it came down to it, she was here to force Ben to do the last thing he would want to do. Some might call it blackmail.

At least, Susie thought, as Brenna led her to a figure sitting in a reclining chair with his left leg stretched out in front of him encased in plaster, he couldn't run away.

'I'll bring you some tea in a few minutes,' said Brenna and headed back up the path to the house.

Ben held out his hand and Susie grasped it. 'Sorry,' he said, 'but I can't get up.' It was probably the first time he'd ever voluntarily addressed her. Maybe, she thought as she took in his shy grin, he was just socially inept.

'Thanks for letting me come,' she said. 'You probably think it's a bit odd.'

He shrugged. 'To be honest, I'm so bored sitting on my arse I'm happy to see anybody.' His face registered dismay as he realised what he'd said. 'Oh God, I'm sorry. I didn't mean it like that.'

Susie squeezed his arm. 'It's OK.' So he *was* socially inept.

The rattle of teacups covered the awkward silence that followed, as Brenna unloaded a generous tray of refreshments that included biscuits and a chocolate cake.

'Would you stop this, Bren?' the jockey said. 'If I eat that stuff I'll never get up on a horse again without breaking its back.'

'Huh.' Brenna looked unimpressed. 'My orders are to feed you up. You've got more whinges about food than some teenage girl on a diet.'

Susie took charge of the teapot as Brenna retreated. The pair of them left the food untouched.

'Josh rang me,' Ben said, 'to wish me luck and say he was sorry about – you know.' He indicated his leg. 'It was good of him.'

Susie knew about the call, Josh had mentioned it though he'd not elaborated on what had been said. Susie could imagine – the usual macho platitudes.

'He was shocked by what happened. Me too. I hope you won't be out long.'

'Who knows? I'm a quick healer, mind.' He shot Susie a brief grin.

There was another awkward pause. It was her cue. She'd set this whole thing up and she'd got the opportunity she wanted. But now she wasn't sure exactly how to proceed. She found he wasn't as easy to dislike as she'd imagined.

'Ben.' She pushed aside her tea cup. 'Josh doesn't know I'm here.'

Surprise registered on his face.

She continued. 'If he'd known the reason why I've come he would have forbidden it.'

Surprise turned to bewilderment.

Susie plunged on. 'I want to talk to you about Annabelle Lovall.'

His face froze into a mask and she could no longer read it.

'You were having an affair with Annabelle, weren't you?'

He looked towards the house, hopeful maybe of rescue, but there was no sign of Brenna.

'That's ridiculous,' he said.

'Some might think so, Ben, but it's true all the same. Isn't it?'

'No.' A bare-faced denial. 'It was kind of you to come but if you've finished your tea, I'm feeling a little tired.'

She ignored the remark. 'I've got proof, Ben.'

'I want you to go now.'

'I've got Annabelle's mobile phone. The pink one she used to call you on. It's pointless to deny it.'

'Oh God,' he said and the mask crumpled.

Mouse had the urge to go for a spin, so she upped and went. 'Be back later,' she said to Maureen as she marched to the door.

She was in a very good mood.

Baz had been lunching a client whose brother was a detective on the Ben O'Brien case. He'd called her into his office to give her the gen.

'You'll never guess what he told me about the knife that was used on Ben.'

'The knife?' Her heart had lurched. They hadn't got hold of it, had they? It would have her fingerprints all over it.

'They've found it. But the thing is, and they're not giving the information out because it's a bit embarrassing, it's been through a dishwasher. So they've got no fingerprints, no

DNA, nothing. Just a very clean knife. You've got to laugh, haven't you?'

And she had. She was untouchable.

'Are you saying Josh didn't put you up to this?' There was an edge to Ben's voice and two matching shillings of pink flushed his cheeks. Shock was swiftly turning to anger.

'I told you, Josh doesn't know I'm here. And he has no idea what's on Annabelle's phone.'

'So you've just turned up on your own account?'

Susie didn't bother to reply to that.

'This is none of your business,' said Ben. 'Sure, Annabelle and I may have been having a bit of a fling but that's a private matter. It would all have been sorted out if . . . well, if she hadn't died.'

'Do you think she killed herself?' She couldn't resist asking.

'No!' He was adamant. 'She was on top of the world because she was doing a runner from Leo.'

'What do you think happened?'

'It must have been some fluky accident. Something to do with that thick-headed dog.'

She took a deliberate sip of tea. 'Everyone's got to have someone to blame, I suppose.'

His blue eyes were studying her. 'What do you mean by that?'

'You blame the dog. Lots of other people – Leo, the press, people who don't know any better – blame Josh.'

There was a short silence.

'So that's why you're here, is it?'

'Everyone's got it in for Josh. He's being made to pay for once having a fling, like you, with Annabelle, and for lending her his flat. It's not been a private matter for him.'

'That's hardly down to me,' Ben said. 'There's nothing I can do about it, is there?'

This was her moment.

'Oh yes, there is,' she said hotly. 'You can tell Leo Lovall the truth, for a start.'

He glared at her and said nothing.

'Leo's the one who's really got it in for Josh. He's running a campaign against him. There are lies being told over the internet, Leo's friends in the press are spreading poison about Josh and owners are stopping him riding their horses. And all because Leo thinks Josh renewed his affair with Annabelle. You can put the record straight.'

'No, I can't.' Ben looked stricken. 'He'd kill me.'

Susie leaned forward, staring deeply into his eyes so he couldn't doubt the seriousness of her intentions. 'He'll kill you twice over if he hears it first from someone else.'

From his mournful gaze she had no doubt he understood who that someone else would be, but just in case he didn't, she added, 'Technically that phone belongs to him. I believe I'm duty bound to return it.'

Mouse's jaunt took her to the lane above Ridge Hill. The urge was upon her, so why not?

The Mistake's car wasn't there and Josh was at Plumpton so she breezed straight in. She was beyond skulking around.

She went straight to the bedroom and threw herself face

down on its cream lace cover, burying her face in his crisp plump pillows and breathing in the scent of him.

Bliss.

Imagine if Josh turned up now. Just appeared in the doorway to find her lying on his bed. Would he shout at her? Call the police?

Or lie down beside her?

'Don't speak,' he'd say, hushing her explanations. 'I know everything.'

And there'd be no need for words. Just the two of them in this room lying together, shutting out the rest of the world for ever.

'You don't know what you're asking me to do,' Ben muttered.

Susie did not reply, just sipped her tea – Brenna had supplied them with fresh when Ben had urged Susie to stay, although a few minutes earlier he'd been keen to see the back of her. He needed time to wiggle out of the hot spot she'd placed him in.

She nibbled at a slice of cake; it was as delicious as it looked, and as sinful, no doubt, but for the moment she didn't care. A burden had lifted from her shoulders now that she'd laid her intentions bare. Ben hadn't eaten or drunk a thing. It was plain where that burden now lay.

'It's not really going to make any odds,' he said. 'Josh is retiring at the end of the season, isn't he?'

'He wants to set up as a trainer. These kinds of slurs are the last thing he needs when he's setting out to build a business.'

Ben considered for a moment then leaned forward, his

eyes insistent, his tone imploring. 'Believe me, Susie, whatever I say to Leo is not going to make any difference to what he thinks of Josh.'

Susie replaced her cup carefully on the tray. She didn't want to hurt Ben – she was warming to him – but there was no getting round some things.

'You don't think that Leo finding out that you were responsible for Annabelle's pregnancy would make any difference?'

Ben blinked, as if she'd slapped him in the face. But said nothing.

'I bet,' said Susie, 'that one of the reasons Leo is so bitter towards Josh is that he thinks it was Josh's baby.'

'But it wasn't mine either.'

Susie stared at him hard, disappointed he was resorting to lies.

He read her expression. 'Honestly, it wasn't. It didn't start between us till after Christmas and we never slept together till the New Year. At the inquest it said she was four weeks pregnant so it couldn't have been me.'

She thought about the phone log. It was true that the calls hadn't begun till New Year's Eve.

'Look, Susie, I've thought about this over and over. You can imagine. But I swear that baby wasn't mine.'

'So you're saying it was Leo's?'

'You're joking. They had separate bedrooms and anyway they couldn't have children – she told me.'

'Whose was it then? Do you know?'

He didn't say anything for a bit, just sat there with his leg up, looking miserable. He deserved a girl his own age, she thought. Unattached and uncomplicated. What on earth was so attractive about a devious woman like Annabelle?

'I do know who it was,' he said at length. 'She told me about it. He was a Christmas present to herself, she said. He wasn't important to her.'

Was he telling the truth? She couldn't tell. Either way, she wasn't letting him off the hook.

Susie caught sight of Brenna coming out of the house. She only had a moment more.

'Well, I'm sorry about it, Ben, but as far as I'm concerned you're the one in the frame. I'm giving you a week. And if you haven't talked to Leo by then, I'm going to him with that phone.'

Over the sound of the radio, Josh thought he heard an unfamiliar note in the car engine as he drove back from Plumpton. He wasn't surprised, the vehicle had taken a mighty hammering of late, as had he.

This afternoon he'd said his farewells to one of the tightest and toughest tracks in the country. Like most jockeys he was not overfond of Plumpton's steep hill and frequently boggy ground. Today, however, it had been dry and the ground hard – as he had cause to rue, having come adrift from his mount in a Class F novice chase. No serious damage had been done, apart from a general shake-up to his already much-shaken system, but it had been a close call. His horse, the inappropriately named Head of the Class, had pulled strongly down the hill and come a predictable cropper at the second fence while three lengths in the lead. Josh had been left at the mercy of the chasing pack, unable to do more than curl up into a ball and pray that a misplaced hoof wouldn't kick him into retirement earlier than planned. That would have given the conspiracy theorists something to chew on.

He'd also left empty-handed. Now he had to ride a winner a day to catch Ben, which was easier said than done. Peter would stand by him, of course, but he was aware Tony was having a hard time finding him spare rides. It could only be due to the rumours and bad press as he hadn't become a poor rider overnight.

'What about Ben's rides?' he'd said to Tony. 'He must have had others lined up apart from those for Leo.'

'I'll do what I can,' the agent said. So far, however, it had not borne much fruit.

Josh stopped at a service station on the M1 and washed down a couple of ibuprofen tablets with some mineral water. He was eating them like sweets these days. The car was definitely sounding notes of pain as he joined the petrol queue. That made two of them.

Newcastle tomorrow – he hoped the pair of them would make it.

The smell hit Susie the moment she entered the house – an insidious aroma that reminded her of wood and leaves, and an exotic sweetness she couldn't place. It wasn't a natural fragrance but a perfume, and an expensive one at that.

It lingered in the air as she climbed the stairs. It seemed even stronger as she approached the bedroom. It made her feel jumpy, as if someone was lurking behind her. She jerked her head round but there was no one there. The orderliness of the well-lit landing mocked her.

She stood stock still in the bedroom doorway, her hand on the light switch though she did not press it. In comparison with the hall behind her the air was murky, dusk thickening in the confines of the room. The perfume clung to her and she shivered. Spooky. She snapped on the light.

The reassuring brightness did not banish the smell. She looked around with suspicion. Had anything been moved in her absence? Were Josh's things on the mantelpiece – some pens, a packet of chewing gum, a racecard from Ludlow – exactly as he had left them? And her make-up on the dressing table, the bottle of moisturiser and the hair-tie she should have put in a drawer – were they in the same position as when she left the house?

Something was wrong with this room, she knew it. Apart from the alien smell.

It was the bed. The bedspread was tidy and smooth but wasn't there a flattening of the covers on the door side of the bed? She considered it from another angle. Josh was going to laugh at her when she told him about this. She put on the bedside light and turned out the central one. This gave her a new angle on the minute variations in the humps and hollows of the bed.

She bent down to view the contours from a new perspective, like a golfer reading a green before a tricky putt. Watching them on the television she'd sometimes wondered why they bothered. Surely they couldn't see much.

But now she could see the point of it. The side lighting caught a tiny ridge in the material, throwing a faint shadow down the length of the bed. A body-shaped shadow. And there, on the cover over the pillow, was a distinct depression.

Susie leaned close to the cover and pulled it gently back from the pillow.

A whiff of perfume – that perfume – kissed her face like a breath of air.

Then realisation hit her with the thud of certainty.

A strange woman had been lying on her bed.

'What do you mean, you can't smell anything?'

Josh had known something was up the moment he walked in the door. He'd been alarmed for a moment, thinking there'd been further damaging articles in the press, or that Colin had rung with bad news – 'Mrs Glazier's changed her mind. The police are on their way.'

But it was nothing like that. 'Smell there,' she said, pointing to the pillow.

He sniffed and told her he couldn't detect anything. Mild hay fever numbered among his ailments, though that wasn't something he could blame on racing.

'Look then,' she said, pointing to the bed. 'Can't you see? Someone's been in here while I was out.'

But he honestly couldn't see anything, which was worrying. He'd thought Susie was over the worst because she'd seemed much more spirited these past few days. But this was a setback.

He looked on helplessly as she set about stripping the bed.

Luckily Josh had long disappeared before the post arrived. As Susie came downstairs, the sight of the letter on the mat drained the strength from her legs. She sat down heavily on the carpet, clutching the brown envelope in her hand. She'd foolishly believed this torture was over.

You thought I'd forgotten about Susie Sausage, hadn't you?
Impossible – not while you're still here.
Why don't you bog off somewhere your sort are welcome? Like Blackpool pleasure beach.

Oh God, how did this person know about Blackpool? Susie stumbled to the toilet and threw up.

It had been the best day of her life to date. Bar none. Better even than if Sharon had been there because she'd have been too little to go on the big rollercoaster and she'd have cried when Susie wanted to go and said it wasn't fair. And if Mummy had been there she'd have said it was too dangerous and not let her go anyway. Of course if Mummy had been there she'd only have allowed Susie one ice cream and no candyfloss, let alone a big bag of Pick'n'Mix. Anyway she'd bet Mummy wouldn't have let them go in the first place because it was a proper schoolday and she'd missed Miss Eliot's maths test.

Dad hadn't cared about that. He'd said, 'I'm a doctor and I say a day at the seaside's the medicine you need', and off they'd gone in the car with Rita who was lovely to her, not having a go at her for being clumsy when she knocked over her Coke in the cafe, and buying her a little charm bracelet with the Tower on it as a souvenir. But the best bit was on the rollercoaster with Dad because he was more scared than she was and gripped her hand ever so tight all the way round and said, 'Thank God you're with me, Susie Sausage. You're much braver than me.'

Later, at home, she'd felt sad because Dad said she couldn't ring Mummy and Sharon because the phone still wasn't working at Uncle Simon's in Scotland and why didn't she write it all down in a letter and he'd post it on the way to the surgery the next day. So that's what she did, covering three and a half sides and filling up the space left over with lots of hearts and kisses because she really did miss Mummy and Sharon ever such a lot and hoped they'd be back soon.

Susie had found out later, when she'd learned the whole grisly truth, that her letter had been submitted in evidence at the trial. Dad had never posted it. What would be the point? Mum and Sharon had been in the lake for ten days before she even set pen to paper.

The swimming lesson didn't go well but Susie hadn't come for that. After twenty minutes, Mel called a halt.

'I'm sorry,' she said.

He smiled, good-natured fellow that he was, as two boys of about seven emerged from the changing room, followed by a woman in blue plastic overshoes.

'Is that the psychiatrist's wife?' asked Susie. She had already reminded Mel of his offer to introduce them.

Mel shook his head. 'Mrs Carter usually cuts it fine.'

'So I've got time to get dressed?'

'Sure. I'll tell her you're here.'

Susie was towelling her hair in front of the changing-room mirror when she saw a slender woman approaching over her shoulder, a hesitant smile on her lips.

Five minutes later, they were sitting in the cafe. Mrs Carter – Tina – had picked out a table in the far corner and begun chattering about Mel and her son's swimming, the words tumbling out breathlessly. Her mouth was energetic, seeming to work of its own accord. The rest of her large thin face was still, her sad eyes searching Susie's.

Was this the woman who had written those vindictive little notes?

Susie pulled the latest from her bag and placed it on the table top.

'Did you send me this?'

The chatter shut off like a tap. Bewilderment filmed the woman's face. 'Why would I do that?'

'Read it. Tell me if you recognise it.' Susie was aware she must sound strange, barking out orders like this. She didn't care.

Tina examined the envelope and the note. 'No, I don't. Should I?'

Only if you sent it.

'I've read about you in the papers,' Tina said. 'So I know your father was called Merrivale.' She pointed to the name on the envelope. 'But a lot of people must be aware of that now.'

Susie nodded and put the letter back into the envelope. As she did so Tina took her hand. 'I'm sorry.' Her big amber eyes burned into Susie's. 'I'd never write a letter like that to anybody. Honestly.'

Susie really wanted to believe her and only one thing held her back. She extricated her hand.

'Mel says you used to ask him about me and Josh, my partner. Why did you do that?'

Tina sighed heavily and leaned back in her chair. 'So that's why you think I might have written that shitty little note.'

'I'm grasping at straws as you can imagine. Tell me why.'

'It's a bit of a story.' Tina pulled a packet of cigarettes from her handbag and Susie realised they were sitting in the smoker's corner. Tina shrugged apologetically and lit up. 'I just started again,' she said, 'after seven years. Pathetic, isn't it?'

Susie smiled weakly. *Just get on with it. Please.*

'Right.' Tina dragged on her cigarette, hollowing her cheeks. 'My husband, Gavin, is a psychiatrist – that's relevant – and I'm a solicitor, though not full time these days. Last May I came home from dropping the children at my mother's. It was half-term week and she was looking after them while I got on with some work.'

Susie nodded, straining to hear Tina's voice, which had dropped to a whisper.

'I'd intended to go straight to the office but I'd forgotten a file so I came back for it. I shut the front door behind me and went into our study, just a box room really, next to the living room. But the file wasn't there and I remembered I'd taken it upstairs to read in bed the night before. I dashed back out into the hall and came face to face with someone coming out of the kitchen. A young woman. I didn't recognise her – I assumed she was a burglar. I froze and so did she, then she just turned round and went back into the kitchen.

'I was shouting at her by now – what on earth do you think you're doing? I'm going to call the police – things like that. I can't remember exactly. And I followed her, which was stupid of me. If it had been a man I would have just run out of the house. But she didn't look dangerous – I was much taller than her, for a start. And I was angry. What right did she have to come into my house? A bit of me was thinking, thank God Luke and Amy aren't here. If they had been, I hope I'd have just bundled them both outside.'

She lit another cigarette from the butt of the first. Susie waited impatiently for her to resume.

'I went after her into the kitchen, still shouting. She had her back to me, standing at the sink. Then she turned round and she was holding a carving knife in her hand – she'd taken it from the knife block on the counter. I knew it was sharp because Gavin had put a new edge on it that weekend. I remember thinking, if she stabs me with that at least it'll make a clean cut. I suppose I could still have run but I'd gone a long way into the room and she was as close to the door as I was. And I thought, suppose she comes after me down the hall and sticks me in the back as I'm trying to open the front door? Anyway, they say if you come up against a wild beast the worst thing you can do is run – something about smelling your fear. So I just stood there and she started talking.

'She said, "Time's up, Tina. He doesn't want you any more." She didn't shout or anything, she was completely matter-of-fact, but it was about the most terrifying thing I've ever heard. Because she called me Tina. How did she know my name? I couldn't work it out. Once she'd started talking, she didn't stop. She said things like, "Gavin's too soft to tell you but you and him are washed up. You're just a skinny old bitch and he can't bear to look at you. Why don't you get out now? Get lost and don't come back, you and your whiny brats. He's got me now. This is my house so you can sod off, you ugly old bag." '

'My God,' said Susie. 'What did you do?'

'I was completely freaked but I knew I had to stay cool. She'd mentioned Gavin so I realised she must be a patient or connected to his work at the hospital. And the way she was going on, it was clear she wasn't entirely straight in the head. Her voice was getting louder and she was swearing a lot, working herself up – and, of course, she was still holding the knife, pointing it at me. But what was worse was some of what she was saying. About how Gavin had never loved me or our children, that he'd hidden how he really felt about me on our honeymoon – she even knew where we'd been! And how much he despised family celebrations, like Luke and Amy's birthdays. How tedious it was for him to sing baby songs and change nappies and film children's parties. I was telling myself this was rubbish, that she was sick, but another bit of me was wondering, had he said any of these things to her? God knows what psychiatrists tell their patients but it must be tempting sometimes to let your guard slip and give out personal stuff. But when she talked about filming birthday parties something clicked and I thought, she's been watching our videos. I realised then how she knew about me and our family life. She'd been in our house going through our things. I was devastated.'

Susie could understand that. It had taken her a while to empathise with this odd woman but she was fully engaged now. She watched as Tina reached once more for the cigarette packet, then pushed it hastily back into her bag.

She sat up straighter and said firmly. 'Frankly, if I'd been the one holding the knife I'd have cut her throat without a qualm. Fortunately, I wasn't.'

'What did you do?'

'I worked out that the best thing was to agree with her, just to calm her down enough so she wouldn't hurt me. So I told her I never realised Gavin felt that way and if he really didn't love me any more then we would have to consider our future together. I tried to sound low-key and reasonable about it all – you know, not give her back any emotion to get her worked up more than she was already.'

Susie nodded, her admiration for Tina growing.

'I told her that I'd have to discuss it with Gavin when he got home and if he wanted me to leave then I would. I suggested she called round later after he and I had had a chance to talk about it.'

'How did she react?'

'She looked a bit surprised. Then she told me she wasn't effing going anywhere and I should get out right now. So I said OK, if that was what she wanted, and walked out of the room. As I went down the corridor, I had to force myself not to run. I was waiting for her to follow me and in my mind was a picture of her thrusting the knife so hard into my back that I'd be pinned against the door. But she didn't come after me, thank God. The moment I was outside I locked myself in the car and called the police.'

This time Tina couldn't resist the lure of her cigarette packet. She lit up in a slow ritual of concentration. To keep the memory at arm's length, Susie imagined. Even so, Tina's hand trembled as she lifted the white tube to her lips and dragged.

'Anyway, the police came and arrested her. Gavin turned up. I spent ages being interviewed by a series of detectives over the next few days, then I got ill and flaked out for a bit and our lives basically turned crap for a few months.'

'What happened to the woman? Was there a trial?'

'Oh no. For one thing, when the police arrived she opened the door to them with a smile on her face. She told them I'd invited her indoors and had suddenly rushed outside leaving her on her own. She'd put the knife back where it belonged and she'd washed it so there were no fingerprints or anything on it. They found a set of our house keys on her and she said Gavin had given them to her which, of course, he hadn't. He said he'd mislaid them one day and they turned up later at the hospital reception. I imagine she nicked them off his desk during one of their sessions and copied them before handing them in.

'Anyway, what with me being ill and Gavin not wanting me to press charges – which he didn't because he said she was his responsibility and it would be an admission of failure on his part as her doctor – nothing bloody well happened to the little bitch.'

Tina stubbed out her cigarette viciously and glanced at her watch. 'I've got to go and get Luke in a moment.' She began to gather up her things.

'Why did you think this had anything to do with me?' Susie asked urgently, grabbing Tina's hand as she began to rise from her chair.

Tina stopped. 'Oh, sorry. I haven't told you about the phone call, have I?' She sat down again. 'A month or so after it happened – I'd just started back at work – there was a message on the answerphone. From her. It was the day after I'd heard they'd dropped the charges against her so I was feeling especially raw about the whole thing. To hear her nasty voice in my house again was just horrible. But I had to listen. Basically, she said I was bloody lucky she'd decided not to sue me for telling lies about her and getting her arrested and she was never really interested in Gavin anyway. He might call himself a doctor but he was just a useless wanker who sat on his arse and used big words. She'd found someone a million times better, a real hero who rode horses for a living and risked his life every day. Compared to a real man like Josh Swallow, Gavin was a pathetic wimp and I was welcome to him.'

'Oh, Jesus,' murmured Susie. 'Did she really say Josh's name?'

'Yes. I played that tape over and over so I know just what she said. Gavin wiped it clean and told me to forget about it, but how could I? I know nothing about horse racing but I didn't have to look very hard to find Josh Swallow's name in the paper.'

'Why didn't you warn him?'

'Because . . .' Tina looked sheepish. 'Well, Gavin was insistent that I didn't speak about any of it. He said it would be in breach of his patient confidentiality, though I pointed out that she wasn't my patient. He said she'd only become obsessed with him because she saw him every week and she wouldn't have that kind of access to a jockey. He honestly thought it would turn out to be a harmless infatuation, like a lot of people in the public eye get. It goes with the territory, he said.'

'Did you agree with him?' Susie heard the note of anger in her voice. Too bad. 'Obviously not, otherwise you wouldn't have asked about me.'

'When I found out that Mel coached Josh's girlfriend, naturally I was curious. That's why I used to ask him about you. Just to check that everything was all right.'

Susie was thinking rapidly, had been ever since the mention of Josh's name. If someone infatuated with Josh had somehow got hold of the keys to the house it would account for a lot.

'Some of our things have gone missing,' Susie said. 'Josh lost an old sweater from his wardrobe.'

Tina nodded. 'She took some of Gavin's clothes. Trophies, Gavin called them.'

'And a painting was damaged. Josh swears he didn't do it and I know I didn't. And when I came home yesterday, the house smelt of perfume – not mine. It was really strong in the bedroom.'

Tina wrinkled her nose. 'She could have been up there, lying on your bed. That's the kind of thing she'd do, Gavin told me. I don't remember perfume though.'

'You didn't smell anything when you were in the kitchen with her.'

Tina gave a short mirthless laugh. 'Apart from my own fear? No. I didn't.'

'It could still be her though, couldn't it?'

Tina nodded. 'Yes. It could.'

'Do you know where I could find her? Have you got an address or a phone number?'

'I'm sorry.'

'But you can tell me her name, can't you?'

'Mavis Morgan.'

Susie thought hard. 'I've never heard of her.'

Tina smiled thinly. 'Neither had I.'

While she was waiting for the locksmith to arrive, Susie looked for the shoebox at the back of the wardrobe. She knew she shouldn't have kept the letters but somehow, when you'd once had a father you adored and then you didn't have him any more, it didn't seem right to throw away his letters. So she'd put them with her luggage when she moved in and tried to forget she had them. She'd buried them really, like a lot of things. Maybe that wasn't such a good idea after all. You hid your secrets and some evil sneak still dragged them into the light of day.

She tipped the letters on to the bed. They'd started to arrive once she'd turned eighteen – perhaps there had been some restriction about him writing to her as a minor. Or maybe it had just been his own sensitivity, if you could call it that. In some ways they were excellent letters, full of well-turned phrases and shrewd observations of prison life, written in a confident and legible hand. It was one of her father's jokes that he was a doctor in a million because he had legible handwriting.

Reading his letters brought back his voice. And the half-proud, half-embarrassed expression on his face when he made a bad pun and she'd groan and say, 'Oh, Daad.' She could still hear herself say that. As she looked at the letters again, sitting on the bed, she recalled the first sensation she'd felt when she'd read them. How much she missed him. And no matter how hard and often she declared to herself that he was dead to her, a stranger, no longer part of her life, his words proved the contrary.

There was no remorse in these letters. No mention of her mother or sister or even poor Rita who, like herself, had been so completely taken in by his lies. There was, however, nostalgia. At some point in every letter he would invoke a shared memory. 'Do you remember when we . . .?' 'You can't have forgotten that . . .' Some things she had indeed forgotten and others were dim recollections that his words brought to life. It was funny how often these memories fell in that short period before his arrest, when it was just the three of them playing happy families.

She'd written back hesitantly at first then found herself looking forward to his next. After a bit she'd realised what was happening to her. He wasn't just giving her back some childhood memories, he was reclaiming her as an accomplice. She couldn't face that. She still couldn't.

So she'd forbidden him to write. If he'd persisted she would have asked the prison authorities to prevent him. She'd discovered she could do that. And for four years, despite

Brenda's regular entreaties, she'd left him to rot. My daddy the monster. Who I still love. It was a terrible secret to keep.

And somebody – this Mavis Morgan – had found it out.

How many letters had there been? Seven or eight, she thought. There were only seven on the bed. And one of them – how could she forget? – had talked about their day at Blackpool pleasure beach.

She quickly flicked through the pile.

It wasn't there.

Nearly home, Josh thought as he left the M1 on the last stretch of his long journey back from Newcastle. Nearly finished with riding. Nearly champion jockey – though he was beginning to doubt he ever would be. After last week's triumphs the winners had dried up; this was the second blank day in a row. It was hardly time for panic and, in the normal course of events, barely worth worrying about. But these weren't normal times. There were eight days left in the season and Ben was still seven ahead. A few more meetings like this and Ben would be celebrating his first champion-ship without having sat on a horse in weeks. For a fleeting moment, Josh felt a pang of envy. Then he dismissed it. No one in his right mind would be envious of the misfortune that had befallen Ben.

All the same, it had been a pig of a day. Leaving aside the journey and his aches and pains and the horses that hadn't lived up to their promise – all that was regular fare – it wasn't every day you saw someone almost killed in front of you. What had happened to young Andy Mister had cast a long shadow.

The pile-up took place in the fourth race, a three-mile steeplechase. Josh was on only his second ride of the afternoon; apart from Peter and a few other stalwarts, his options were increasingly limited. He would have thought that people would be more generous in the last few days of his riding career, especially with his last chance at the championship so obviously on the line. In his situation, you certainly found out who your friends were and he was discovering that he didn't have as many as he thought.

Diamond Sky, his mount in the chase, came courtesy of Rob Styles, a local jockey he'd shared digs with when they were apprentices. Rob had rung Josh the week before and offered him any of his rides if it would help his cause. Now there was a pal. After a bit of arm-twisting, Josh had asked for Diamond Sky and Rob had squared it with the horse's connections. When he took up training, Josh vowed to himself, he'd be on the phone to Rob whenever he needed a jockey in the north-east.

He'd done his homework on Diamond Sky, a headstrong but talented six-year-old and the youngest horse in the field. If left to his inclinations, the horse would run his race on the first circuit and blow up before he even turned for home. Josh's strategy, therefore, was to hold the horse up from the start and drop him in at the back of the field for the first half of the race.

As a consequence, Josh was perfectly positioned to see disaster unfold in front of him as the second-placed horse crashed straight into the last fence on the downhill leg heading away from the stands. The runners were tightly bunched and the fall split the pack as effectively as a well-aimed cue ball smacking into a pack of reds on a snooker table. The horse just to the rear of the faller was also brought down, landing in an ugly tangle of furiously pumping limbs as he rolled over trying to regain his feet.

Josh yanked on the reins, jerking Diamond Sky out to the right and taking a long way round the chaos. The horse seemed spooked by the accident, clattering the top of the first fence in the back straight and nearly dumping his rider into the open ditch that followed. By the time Josh had coaxed him back into his rhythm, all hope of winning the race had gone. The leader, unaffected by events to his rear, had serenely galloped round the course on his own and passed the post five lengths clear with Diamond Sky galloping on strongly in a lost cause.

Later, news reached them that Andy Mister had suffered a smashed pelvis and a punctured lung, sustained when a horse had landed on top of him. The short-term prognosis was not good and Josh could imagine the headlines on the racing pages already: CURSE OF HOAR FROST STRIKES AGAIN – or something like it. Andy was the second jockey at Leo Lovall's yard and had been filling in for Ben. Josh thanked God he'd not been directly involved in the incident – Leo couldn't blame him this time.

He parked in front of the house and lifted his key to the lock. It didn't fit.

Josh tried the key again. Was he so knackered he couldn't even open his own front door? But he wasn't even able to slide it into the breech.

With a click, the door was opened from the inside to reveal Susie in paint-streaked overalls with her golden hair tied haphazardly off her face. She threw herself into his arms.

'I changed the locks.'

Josh looked at the letters on the table and then at Susie. 'Why didn't you tell me?'

It was what he'd said to her last time, when the papers exposed her father's crimes. Dragging this stuff out of her was like getting water from an empty well.

He'd been pretty much unmoved by stories of missing sweaters and psychiatrist's wives but if Susie wanted to change the locks that was fine by him. This was different, however. Poison-pen letters and the unhappy secrets of her terrible childhood. His heart went out to her.

'Shall I call the police?' he said.

She shook her head.

'They should be able to find this woman. She's been in trouble with them recently, even if there wasn't a conviction.'

'But if they couldn't even get her to trial when she threatened Tina with a knife, what are they going to do here? Our only evidence is an answer-machine call which has been erased.'

Josh thought. 'If she's been in this house she'll have left traces. Fingerprints and DNA. I'll get them to sweep it. And I'll pay for it myself if they kick up a fuss.'

She smiled at him. Her first smile since he'd stepped in the door.

'And,' Josh continued, 'I'll talk to Colin. If we can't get her prosecuted maybe we can go for a restraining order. That's what they do in stalking cases.'

'Stop, Josh. That's all great and I love you for it, but no. I don't want to talk to the police or a lawyer or a court about . . .' she hesitated then placed her hand on the pile of her father's letters, 'this.'

It seemed he always ran into the high wall of her past. He knew about the case now – not from Susie but from his own research – so he was familiar with the train wreck of her family life. But he was no nearer to understanding the experience that had forged her. Though he had no doubt she loved him, even he was not allowed to look over the wall.

'Whatever you say, Susie.'

Chapter Fourteen

Gavin Carter tactfully allowed Mrs Wright to finish mopping her tears before telling her their session was over. Guiltily she began to gather up the piles of crumpled tissues that had accumulated around her chair but Gavin told her to leave them. For the amount she – or, rather, her insurance company – was paying she was entitled to make a little mess. Not that he said that. Instead he ushered her to the door and murmured, 'Well done, you've made real progress today,' and placed a reassuring hand on her arm.

Regrettably, it was the only physical contact he permitted himself with a patient. Mrs Wright, he observed as she walked unsteadily along the carpeted corridor in the direction of the Ladies' Room, had very well-turned calves. In his experience, no matter how unappetising a female might look on first acquaintance, there were invariably some points to admire.

Anna, his secretary, was at his elbow, regarding him with a jaundiced eye. 'There's a gentleman in reception to see you. He says he's got an appointment but it's not in the book.'

'That's right. Ben O'Brien. It's a personal matter.'

Her expression softened. 'He's the Grand National jockey, isn't he? The one who got stabbed.' Anna was always impressed by Gavin's connections with the turf.

Gavin had been surprised when Ben called. He'd met him once or twice at the races with his brother Leo, though the jockey had not had much to say for himself. But, as Leo had pointed out, the lad did all his talking in the saddle. Gavin headed for the stairs, curious to discover what Ben wanted.

Maybe it was Susie's presence in the stands that changed Josh's luck – he thought so anyway. He'd insisted she accompany him for the next few days, here at Taunton and tomorrow at Sandown – not that she'd raised any objections. Whatever the reason, things went his way. Wave Goodbye showed the rest of the field a clean pair of heels in the first race of the afternoon; and Josh edged home on another of Peter Stone's horses in the steeplechase that followed.

Suddenly, after not knowing where his next winner was coming from, he had two in the bag with the afternoon not half over. He felt on top of his game and firmly at home on the tight bends of the right-handed track. More to the point, his luck was in. The only problem was he had just one remaining booking for the afternoon.

He sat out the next race and watched with some dismay as a jockey was stretchered off after a nasty fall. Word soon came back that he was suffering from mild concussion and Josh pushed his way through the crowd outside the weighing room looking for a beaky-face woman in tweeds. He'd never liked the ambulance-chasing aspect of being a jockey but he did it when he had to and, if he wanted a ride in the next, he had to right now.

He spotted his quarry bustling towards the weighing room.

'Mrs Russell,' he called, cutting off her progress.

Catherine Russell was something of a legend in jump-racing circles, having started out with six horses, three children and no husband, and landing the Gold Cup twice, together with a string of other eye-catching wins. In a traditionally male-dominated sport she had not achieved her success by fluttering her eyelashes and could be counted on to be more aggressive than any of her male competitors. Like many jockeys, Josh would rather tackle a six-foot fence on an iffy jumper than ask Cathy Russell for a favour, but needs must.

'Do you need a rider for the next?' he asked.

'You know damn well I do,' she barked. 'I was about to ask Charlie.'

Charlie Coyle rode a lot for La Russell, he was always bitching about the indignities she heaped on her jockeys. Right now, however, Josh was prepared to put up with her jibes.

'Come on, Cathy, this could be my last chance to get my leg over one of yours. Let me retire a happy man.'

She snorted cheerfully but didn't look entirely convinced. It had been some years since Josh had last ridden for her and they'd fallen out over a point of technique.

'You still ride too short,' she objected. 'On the other hand,' she added after a long pause, 'you're a better jock than Charlie Coyle with one hand tied behind your back. So I suppose I'd better take you up on it.'

She was a bit of an eccentric, Josh thought as, a few minutes later, she legged him up into the saddle of Misfit, an awkward-looking chestnut chaser. Her parting words were hardly calculated to inspire confidence. 'Don't let him take all day at the ditches. He's not keen on them.'

But Josh took that as a positive sign. Horses almost never fell when they were having a good look at what they were about to jump. As a jockey, you didn't want to be on the animals who saw a fence and immediately quickened up. They were the ones who had you picking yourself up from the turf. If Misfit needed driving into his fences, Josh would be quite happy.

Instinctively he tuned in to the animal beneath him, whom he'd never clapped eyes on before encountering him in the ring. Josh was absolutely in the dark about his mount's capabilities, yet he was trusting this strange horse to carry him over three miles and seventeen fences and, if luck was on their side, to finish ahead of the ten other runners in the race. It was a challenge he loved, a real test of his riding skill. This was one more thing he would miss.

Misfit didn't seem a nervous sort, taking the first few fences briskly though clearing them with nothing to spare. Josh picked up the horse's mood and rhythm. Go on, son, show me what you can do, he thought as they cleared the last fence first time around and headed out into the country.

After they'd jumped the first fence in the back straight, Josh nudged the horse out wide to give him a clear view of the first open ditch. At once he felt the animal falter. The steady long-striding gallop tightened and Misfit lifted his head. He knew what was coming and he didn't like it.

Josh raised his whip and gave the horse as hard a crack as he could, right across its quarters. It had no effect whatsoever so he pulled his whip into his other hand and repeated the treatment on the other side. All the time the animal was slowing down and the pair eventually crawled over the obstacle, but they had given away at least a dozen lengths. At this stage that wasn't a complete disaster, there was still a mile and a half to go. If Misfit did the same next time around, however, when the race was on in earnest, he doubted very much if they would be good enough to get back.

Josh pushed the horse back towards the inner, where the other runners were strung out along the racing rail. The animal was fine at the plain fences and Josh had a circuit to decide what to do – not that he had a lot of choice. His only option was to bury the horse behind a wall of horses so that he didn't see the ditch until the last possible moment. Then he'd have no choice but to react quickly. Or else fall on his ugly head.

As they approached the ditch for the second time, Josh almost stuck Misfit's head between the back legs of the runner in front. He had to be careful that the horses didn't clip heels, and his timing had to be perfect. The knack was to pull Misfit's head away just half a stride from the guard rail.

The trick worked. With no time to slam on the brakes, Misfit put in a huge leap as he suddenly saw the ditch in front of him. He lost barely any ground and the shock of what he'd just done seemed to fill him with fresh impetus. As they rounded the sharp bend into the straight, he came right back on the bridle and jumped the last two like a champion. Josh didn't even have to ride him out hard to win by four lengths.

'You're learning,' said Cathy as she welcomed him in the winner's enclosure. 'You don't ride as short as you used to.'

Josh laughed and gave her a kiss. He'd remember that race for a long time – he'd really enjoyed it. And it gave him his third winner of the afternoon. The target set by Ben O'Brien was getting closer.

Gavin kept his cool. He always kept his cool, no matter what provocation he faced in his smart consulting rooms here at the Grange or in the shabbier surroundings of the NHS hospital where he did a two-day conscience stint. But despite the aggression of many of his patients he'd rarely been so personally provoked.

They were sitting in a private lounge on the ground floor. Gavin would have preferred the one-upmanship setting of his walnut-shelved office with its discreet wall of framed certificates and school-of-Canaletto riverscape hanging over the fireplace. But it would have been cruel to make Ben O'Brien struggle upstairs on crutches. Not that the lad's helper, a simply gorgeous colleen with ravishing black curls, would have stood for it. She'd fussed around for ages making sure her wounded charge was comfortable before leaving them to their tête-à-tête.

Gavin had been itching with curiosity about this unexpected visit. He suspected it concerned his brother and he wasn't wrong. But what Ben had to say took the wind from his sails.

'I'm in a bit of a spot,' Ben opened, 'and only you can help me out.'

'Tell me.' He went into listening mode almost by reflex, studying the lad's fidgeting fingers and other signs of nervous stress.

'Back in January I got involved with the guv'nor's missus. Annabelle.'

Really? So the lovely Annabelle had been cradle-snatching. Gavin wasn't surprised.

'We got pretty close. Really close.'

Gavin observed that the lad's voice choked as he talked about Annabelle. He must have fallen hard for her. How interesting.

'She bought this little mobile phone just for us,' Ben went on. 'So we could talk without our calls being traced or anything. She was worried about Leo finding out.'

'I see.' He did indeed. Anyone would be worried about Leo finding out.

'After she died, the phone disappeared and I thought it was lost. But someone's found it and they're threatening to show it to Leo as proof that me and Annabelle were having an affair.'

How awkward. He wouldn't want to be in Ben's shoes when that happened. But, of course, he wasn't.

'And you want me to intercede on your behalf?' He supposed he could do that. Play the elder statesman, plead youthful indiscretion, soften the blow. On the other hand, why should he?

'Not exactly,' Ben said. 'He'll think I got her pregnant, you see, and I didn't.'

'Didn't you?'

'No, I ruddy well didn't. You did. You were knocking her off over Christmas and she told me all about it.'

Oh. He felt a sudden surge of anger, a rare moment of raw emotion in the controlled sterility of his inner life. The stupid, stupid bitch. Why on earth had she confided in this young fool?

'I wouldn't go around repeating that, if I were you,' he said. 'No one, least of all Leo, is going to believe it.'

'He will if he does a DNA test on her body.'

'What do you mean?'

'There'll be an embryo, won't there? Or maybe they took some tissue when they did the autopsy. Anyhow, I bet they could do tests to find out who the real father is. If Leo put his mind to it, he'd get it done.'

Gavin did not doubt it. Leo was capable of digging up his wife's body himself to pursue some misguided vendetta.

'What is it you want me to do?' he said.

The jockey looked relieved, as if the worst part of his task was over.

'I want you to tell him you got Annabelle pregnant. He thinks it was Josh Swallow but it wasn't, and I'm not prepared to take the blame for it either.'

'And if I don't agree?'

Ben shrugged and fixed Gavin with an unblinking stare. 'Then I'll tell him it was you and demand he does the tests. If I have to I'll put my hand up to what I've done but I'm not going to be blamed for something I didn't do.'

Gavin had no reason to doubt him.

*

Susie was not enjoying herself. Though she was out at the races on a sunny day and her man was riding like a champion, she felt at one remove from her surroundings. She also felt physically ill. The taste of vomit in her mouth seemed a constant hangover of yesterday. Of picking that last vile letter off the mat and rushing to the toilet to be sick.

Josh had been great when he came home last night. By rights he should have been mad at her for not telling him about the anonymous letters she'd been receiving, but all he'd said was, 'Is there anything else I should know?'

She'd shaken her head and stuffed her father's letters back into the shoebox. He'd looked at the pile curiously but he'd made no move to read them. She should have let him. Maybe she would, when she told him the whole truth.

Gavin Carter didn't often find fault with himself. In any event it was good mental practice to guard against being judgemental. But with Annabelle Lovall he admitted that he had slipped from his usual high standards.

How could he have slept with his brother's wife?

How could he not, when presented with an opportunity he'd dreamt of for years?

It was Christmas Eve. Tina was in the kitchen and Leo was playing with the children. He'd succeeded in fitting up their new PlayStation and the three of them were having a hilarious time with some puerile shoot-'em-up game.

Annabelle had appeared in a high-necked woollen over-coat, holding a half-full bottle of champagne by the neck. 'Let's go and check on the horses,' she'd said. He could hardly refuse.

It wasn't flattering, on reflection, to think that she had been desperate. They hadn't talked much as they strolled along the row of stalls, admiring the magnificent racehorses within, taking it in turns to swig from the bottle.

After they finished the champagne in Leo's office, she said, 'Isn't marriage bloody?' and unbuttoned her coat.

He remembered the anger and greed she'd put into the act – the need of an unhappy woman. No wonder she'd fastened on to the young Irishman a week later.

But at the time he, the great doctor of the mind, had simply accepted the gift of her body as his due. Not as a cry for help.

On paper, Josh wouldn't have rated his chances of making further inroads into Ben's lead of four at Sandown the next afternoon but after three winners at Taunton, there was no doubt he was on a roll.

In Circus Sands, a six-year-old hurdler of Peter Stone's, he was teamed with an animal on a similarly hot streak. They won the second race in a canter.

Ben's lead was now down to three. Josh didn't even mind sitting out the next two races before taking on his long-overdue commitment to ride Carmen Cook's Vendange.

Today Carmen wore peacock blue and her flame-red hair, as ever, blew wildly in the wind. She dwarfed both Susie and Billy Christie, Vendange's trainer, and seemed more interested in dinner arrangements than her horse's chances.

'What are you doing tonight?' she demanded of Susie and Josh. 'Why don't you stop over in town and we can talk business?'

Josh looked at Susie. The exchange of contracts on Arlington Mansions was imminent and there were some things he had to remove. But he knew how much Susie hated staying there.

She read his look and summoned a brave grin. 'We can stay at the flat,' she said.

At least he wasn't completely in the dark about Vendange. He knew of the horse's impressive French pedigree and he'd watched his ride at Cheltenham, where his jockey that day had made his bid too early and the horse had been caught on the run-in. Like Cheltenham, Sandown also had an uphill final climb to the line, which was where many contenders fell short. And this race was more than half a mile longer. It was imperative, Josh thought, to preserve the young horse's stamina.

Fortunately, the contenders in this race were not as daunting as at Cheltenham. He also cheered himself with the reflection that this time out, Vendange had a better pilot aboard – at least, that's how others rated him and he was determined to prove them right.

The field for the two-and-a-half-mile bumper was not large, just six runners, and Josh considered only one of them, Secret Policeman, to be a serious contender. Accordingly, he dropped Vendange in a couple of lengths behind the big black horse with the aim of tracking him throughout the contest. Naturally he'd also aim to cover any moves made by the other runners but, throughout the first circuit, Secret Policeman seemed happy to make the running.

Josh had been on the Policeman himself in the past and he knew that the horse did not have a turn of foot. Possessed of almost bottomless reserves of stamina, he wore opponents down by sheer strength, plugging on at his one pace and never giving in. However, if Vendange could stay with him and attack with the winning post in sight, Josh was sure the black horse would not be able to respond.

They turned for home, with Vendange just a couple of lengths down and the killing uphill run to the line ahead of them. This was the test.

Josh began pushing in earnest. He could feel Vendange slowly begin to respond beneath him, stretching every sinew to try and get to the horse in front. It took almost a furlong and a half but, with the post in sight, they did it. 'We've got him!'

Then he became aware of movement on the outside. They might have disposed of the big black horse but another runner was arriving out of the blue. Josh worked hard with whip and thighs, urging Vendange to keep up his momentum but he could feel the horse tiring rapidly as the gradient took its toll. The outside runner was level with them now and Vendange, it seemed, had shot his bolt. *Damn*.

Only now did the animal beneath him seem to notice his rival as the other horse edged past them into the lead. To Josh's amazement, Vendange found something extra from deep within himself. The last fifty yards were a strength-sapping mountain of endurance but Vendange was up to the task. They got up in the shadow of the post.

Two more victories and Josh would pull level.

*

There was nothing for it but to talk to Leo.

Gavin had tried to think of a way out but Ben had made it clear that he would tell Leo if Gavin didn't.

Maybe it was for the best. If the business had to come to light – and it appeared it did – then there was no better time to break it to his brother than the present. The medication he'd given Leo had taken the sting out of his temper for the moment.

It was just a question of how he went about it. Damage limitation, in effect.

Gavin knew one thing, however – that jockey wasn't getting off scot-free.

Susie was trying hard to hold it together as the taxi dropped them off at Arlington Mansions. She'd only nibbled at the food throughout dinner and, out of politeness, sipped a glass of wine – which had been a mistake. But her real concern had been not to spoil things for Josh.

'If you're going to be a trainer,' Carmen had said to Josh, 'I'm going to give you some horses. I like old Billy fine but I can see it's not mutual and, anyway, I reckon you'll be better than him.'

Josh wasn't able to agree with that. 'Thanks, Carmen, but I've not trained a seaside donkey yet. I'll be learning on the job.'

Carmen shrugged and demolished a bread roll in two bites. 'I reckon you know what you're on about. You were the one who spotted Mountain Range had a bad tooth at Uttoxeter, not Billy or his stable staff. Besides, you've just given me my first winner here in England. That's a good omen, if you ask me.'

Josh opened his mouth to say more – probably – about how unworthy he was when Susie kicked him under the table. He was going to have to sharpen up if he was setting out as a businessman.

In the end, though, Carmen had commanded Josh to take Susie home and put her to bed. Susie leaned against him as he opened the door to the flat, almost dead on her feet.

'Sure you don't want to change this lock too?' he said as he extricated the key.

Was he making fun of her? She didn't care.

'Are you all right, darling?' he said, peering into her face. She said nothing.

He put his arm round her. 'What is it, Susie?'

But she wasn't going to tell him yet. Not till she was certain.

Leo pulled the tea bag from his mug and dumped it in the sink. Then he slopped milk messily into his tea. He wasn't the most domestic of creatures and no one was around to take care of him on Sundays.

Ten past eleven and he was still in his dressing gown, his face unshaven. It wasn't like him. Even on a Sunday he'd be in the yard by seven. There was always plenty to do. Horses didn't put their feet up on the day of rest and neither did he. Till now anyway.

He glanced idly at the many sections of the paper lying on the kitchen table. He could scarcely be bothered to look at any of it. He paged laboriously through the sports section out of duty and read: SWALLOW CLOSES IN ON CHAMPIONSHIP.

'Swine,' he said aloud, but he could hear that the word didn't pack its usual venom.

Poor Ben. Cheated of his title. 'We'll win it for you next year, lad,' he muttered.

A bell sounded from a long way off. The front door. He didn't want to answer it when he looked such a wreck. It rang again, loud and insistent.

He got to his feet and shuffled down the hall.

Susie left Josh in the flat packing away his few remaining belongings and went downstairs. She crossed the road to the block opposite, which was nowhere as salubrious as Arlington Mansions. The downstairs door was wedged open, a mess of junk mail scattered across the cracked linoleum. On Mrs Glazier's landing, however, all was as neat as a new pin.

Recognition dawned immediately on Mrs Glazier's sharp features. 'I thought you'd gone for good.'

'This might be our last visit. I wanted to say goodbye.'

Susie followed her into the small dark hallway and allowed herself to be seated in the front room, the one she had looked at so often from across the street. It was cosy and well-ordered, with every polished mahogany surface covered with ornaments and framed photographs. Susie had the sense that a lot of history was contained in this small space.

Mrs Glazier poured coffee from a tall cafetiere and pushed a Chinese-patterned biscuit tin in Susie's direction.

'I was wondering,' Susie said, 'whether you'd like that old roll-top desk that used to belong to Mrs Swallow.'

'Well.' The elder woman considered the matter. 'That would be delightful. I'm most grateful.'

'Good.' Susie squeezed the old lady's hand. 'I'll arrange for someone to bring it over to you.' If she slipped Archie the caretaker a few pounds she was sure he'd fix it for her.

'I had the police here, you know. A young woman called Potts.'

Susie nodded. DI Picard's mirthless sidekick who stared a lot.

'We didn't get on very well because I wouldn't tell her the thing I saw on your balcony was you.' Mrs Glazier beamed at her. 'What do you think of that?'

'Did she mention me by name?'

'Of course not. But she showed me lots of pictures and some were of you. Just like that reporter showed me pictures of you. But I wasn't having any of it. You'll be interested to know that I've now had my eyes tested and they're in tip-top shape for a woman of my age. I can't make out features at that distance but you can tell a person by the way they stand. That thing was broader than you, bigger all round.'

'Why do you keep saying "thing"?'

'Because, on reflection, and after talking to my friend Helena, who is a distinguished local historian, I think it might have been a ghost.'

'Did you tell that to the policewoman, Mrs Glazier?'

'Certainly.'

No wonder the police had dropped their case, Susie thought.

*

Leo offered his brother refreshment but left it to Gavin to make the coffee while he dragged himself off to get dressed. He was obviously being checked up on and he ought to try to make a decent impression.

The coffee wasn't as strong as he liked it but he didn't complain.

'How are you feeling, Leo?' Gavin asked.

'As serene as the vicar's mother.' This was true. In the last few days he'd lost another jockey to injury and half his owners had phoned up to discuss the 'curse' on the yard. He hadn't turned a hair.

'And the anger? Are you keeping it under control?'

'My staff in the yard hardly recognise me. I haven't thumped any of them all week.'

'It's good to see you are maintaining your sense of humour, Leo.'

'Can I stop taking these pills then? I feel only half alive.'

'I'm going to do a test on you first to see how you react. I'm going to say something that will make you very angry.'

Impossible. Since they'd been grown-ups, Gavin was the last person to ever get on his tits.

'Listen to me, Leo. Last Christmas, when we were staying in this house, I slept with Annabelle.'

'When you get to my age,' said Mrs Glazier, 'you'll realise there are many things in this life beyond a rational explanation.'

Susie offered no criticism. She'd often wondered, when she was growing up, whether the spirits of the dead observed the living. It had been hard to come to terms with the sudden disappearance of her mother and sister. For as long as she could, she'd hung on to the belief that they were watching over her, still part of her life.

'According to Helena,' Mrs Glazier continued, 'a girl killed herself by jumping from one of those balconies opposite in the nineteen eighties.'

Susie shivered. Thank God she'd never have to go back to that building again after today.

'I've got as far as finding the precise date of her death, the twentieth of August nineteen eighty-four. And this week my historian friend and I are taking a trip to the newspaper library in Colindale so we can looked up the reports of how she died.'

'You're going to a lot of trouble,' Susie said.

Mrs Glazier looked gratified. 'You probably think I'm a bit potty but I'm determined to get to the bottom of this little mystery. It's not nice being shown up in public as a silly old fool, you know.'

'That's the last thing you are,' Susie said, and she meant it.

So he could still laugh, that was something. Those pills hadn't knocked all the life out of him.

Gavin was watching him intently, as if he wanted to climb inside Leo's head. His professor look.

'I'm serious, Leo. We were both a bit drunk and I suppose, because it was holiday time, it seemed permissible. I'm ashamed, Leo. I can't tell you how much I regret it. But Annabelle offered herself to me and I . . .' Gavin paused and it dawned on Leo that the professor look was riddled with embarrassment. 'I accepted the offer.'

Leo was confused. 'Wait a minute. You're telling me this to test my reactions?'

'No, Leo, this is the truth. I'm sorry.'

'You shagged Annabelle?'

'We went down to the stables on Christmas Eve when the rest of you were up here in the house.'

Leo remembered. He'd been playing with Luke and Amy, and Tina had been cooking in the kitchen.

'That was the only time we did it. It was wrong, I admit, but these things happen. I know it wasn't fair to you or Tina but I didn't think either of you would ever find out.'

'So why are you telling me?'

'Because, now I think about it, I realise I might have been responsible for her pregnancy. I wanted you to hear it from me.'

'Who else might I have heard it from?'

'Ben O'Brien. He was sleeping with her too.'

Leo felt numb. The medication certainly worked, no doubt about it. A part of him was still not convinced – this admission could be some kind of smart psychiatric trick.

'Go back a bit, Gavin. On Christmas Eve, where exactly did you and Annabelle . . . do it?'

'In your office.' The professor look had vanished. Gavin was grey-faced and his thick black hair was dishevelled. 'She took off her coat and we put it on the office floor.'

And they left an empty champagne bottle standing upright in the basket of his in-tray, thought Leo. He'd assumed one of the lads had put it there on purpose. Now he knew better.

Leo didn't say anything, just sat there, waiting for the

blood of his anger to flow. Here was cold proof of Annabelle's infidelity – a confession, by the last person in the world he would ever have expected. He would be justified in blowing up. But he didn't. He was in a mist, anaesthetised from his feelings, thanks to Dr Gavin.

He looked up to see his brother still sitting across the table, peering at him anxiously and talking. Leo blocked the words out. Did the hypocritical bastard think he could just slip back into his big brother role? More likely, he wanted to make sure Leo wasn't about to lose the plot. Well, he was in no condition to do that – yet.

In the end Leo had to ask his brother to leave. Gavin seized his hand in his trademark grip and stared deep into Leo's eyes to express the depths of his remorse. And assured Leo that what really mattered in the long run was the bond between the two of them. Whenever Leo needed him, Gavin promised, he would answer the call. As he had always done.

When he'd finally gone, Leo had slowly set about clearing up the mess in the kitchen – just to keep his hands busy while he tried to see through the clouds in his head. He tidied away the coffee cups, cleaned the tea bags from the sink and threw all the pills Gavin had given him in the rubbish.

Then he opened a fresh bottle of whisky.

Maureen pursed her lips as Mouse made a delayed entrance on Monday morning. 'It's all right for some,' she muttered, at the same time tagging a customer's car key and hanging it on the row of hooks behind her. It was always chaos on reception first thing and being late was a sin.

Mouse smiled without warmth at her co-worker. Beneath what she hoped was a calm exterior, Mouse was far from all right. Yesterday she'd been up at Ridge Hill, just to get inside – to get her regular Josh fix. What a shock she'd got.

She'd stood there in the porch for what seemed like hours, trying over and over to fit the key into the lock. But it wouldn't go.

Why had they changed the locks?

That wasn't the only question. Were they on to her? Had they found the listening device?

Jesus. It had thrown her completely.

Things didn't improve when Maureen said, 'One of your jockey fellers has got his car in today. Josh Swallow. You like him, don't you?'

What? Josh had been in and she'd missed him?

'Actually,' Maureen told her, 'it was his girlfriend who dropped it off. Susie. She's ever so pretty.'

Mouse was conscious she was staring open-mouthed. She shut her trap and let Maureen blabber on.

'And she's really nice too. When I said I knew Ridge House because my granddad used to do the garden up there, she said I could pop in and have a look. I'm going to ask if I can take his car back tomorrow, so I can have a look round. I bet it's changed from when I used to ride on the lawn-mower with my granddad. What do you think?'

Mouse thought plenty but none of it was for Maureen's consumption.

Susie worked feverishly at Carmen's painting. She wanted it finished and out of the way – like a lot of other things.

Thank God she'd said goodbye to Arlington Mansions; now she couldn't wait to get rid of this place. Someone had been in here, picking through the bones of their lives. Changing the locks didn't make her feel any better about that.

Besides, it was time for a new start in more ways than one. She had confirmation.

She waited for Josh to return so she could break the news.

Leo didn't go to Chepstow, he had other fish to fry. In any case Tim and the other lads were quite capable of keeping the show on the road.

First he made a phone call to Tony Wylie, then another to Clive Cooper. Both had been astonished at his decision to fire Ben O'Brien with instant effect.

'Let's not be hasty,' Tony had said. 'Let me talk to Ben. I'm sure we can patch it up, whatever it is.'

Leo had told him if he wanted to waste his time that was his business.

Like Tony, Clive had pressed him for a reason to put it in the paper.

'I don't have to give a reason,' Leo told the journalist. 'I'm not renewing O'Brien's contract for next season, end of story.' Not that it would be, but Leo wasn't bothered.

That made him feel better, taking action to get one two-faced little shit out of his life. He was a man of action after all. Sitting around moping and jawing didn't get you anywhere.

Effective action required a plan, however.

By the end of the day he had lots of names on a list.

It was obvious to him now that at some point Annabelle had lost control of her morals. Her most recent lover had been Ben O'Brien – he was on the list. And before that had been his brother. Gavin was down there too. But how many others had there been?

The list of possibles was long. If she was capable of a quick hump in the yard with Gavin, then almost any of the stable lads who'd passed through the yard might be candidates. He put their names down – there were a lot of them. Some, frankly, seemed ludicrous choices but there were others who he knew Annabelle had taken a shine to. That strapping lad Richard who'd broken a wrist in a fall, she'd spent a lot of time driving him around to doctor's appointments, hadn't she? Then there were the vet and the blacksmith – not to mention the owners. She'd socialised with a fair few of those, drumming up business for the yard, as she put it. He put their names down too. He could imagine how she'd gone about the drumming.

But the name at the top of his piece of paper, the one who'd corrupted Annabelle and turned her from a loving, faithful wife into a cold-hearted whore, was the man who had been his worst enemy all along.

Josh Swallow.

Susie was on the brink of telling him something when his phone went off. 'Sorry,' Josh mouthed as he answered. It was Tim Daniels.

'Are you at Market Rasen tomorrow?'

'Sure am.'

'Don't go.'

'Why not?'

'Leo's going to be there and he says he's going to kill you.'

Josh laughed. 'So what's new?'

'I'm serious, Josh. He's behaving very oddly. He asked me if I'd ever slept with Annabelle and then said he wasn't angry with me because you were the one who'd corrupted her.'

'He's going off his rocker.'

'You know he's got a gun, don't you? He says he's going to shoot you. I wouldn't show up tomorrow if I were you.'

Josh ended the call. That was all he needed. After his winner this afternoon he was only one victory behind Ben. Nothing would stop him riding tomorrow, not even a death threat.

Maybe it was just a trick to keep him from riding so Ben could win the championship.

Susie waited impatiently until Josh finished the call.

'I bought a pregnancy kit this morning,' she said.

He looked startled. 'Oh yes?'

She didn't like the tone of those two words. Exactly what emotions were hidden there? Suspicion? Apprehension? Not joy or excitement, at any rate.

'I was due ten days ago but I didn't think much of it. Not till the weekend.' It had hit her out of the blue at Sandown, when Carmen had grabbed her in the excitement of Vendange's victory. She'd thought, be gentle with me, I might be pregnant. But she'd not got around to finding out for sure till today.

He studied her face. 'What's the result?'

'Positive.' She'd used two kits, just to make sure. 'We're going to have a baby.'

He was slow to react, just stood there, his face a mask of nothing. Then he pulled her to him gently and held her close. She could feel her heart beating as the silence stretched on.

'Well,' she said in exasperation. 'Aren't you pleased?'

'To be honest, Susie, I don't know what I feel. I mean, it's not what we planned, is it?'

Jesus! If that's the best he could do . . .

'Hey, Susie, where are you going? Come back!'

His voice followed her as she blundered down the hall, tears blinding her progress.

Mouse, too, was in shock. She'd heard every word of the conversation that had just finished – Josh coming into the kitchen and the phone going off. Then the bombshell: the stupid cow was pregnant!

But, as Mouse sat frozen with horror at the news, there came the most telling moment of all. Silence, long and profound. No words from Josh at all until Susie had forced him to speak: '*To be honest, Susie, I don't know what I feel.*'

Mouse knew what he felt, though. He felt as she did, that Susie had no business getting herself pregnant without warning. '*I mean, it's not what we planned, is it?*' He'd said it himself. She'd deliberately got herself in the club against his wishes. It was obvious, he didn't see his relationship with her as long-term and he didn't want her child.

He was in trouble now, though, wasn't he? Susie would

be much more difficult to dump if she was carrying his baby. He wouldn't have the courage to dump her, Mouse could tell. He was too nice a man – a warrior on a horse but a pussycat at home.

Her thoughts crystallised. He'd needed her help in the past and she'd come through. That bloodsucker Annabelle – gone. Ben O'Brien, the man who stood in the way of the jockeys' championship – out of the picture.

She'd have to think fast. Then act.

It looked like the Mistake had just made her biggest mistake of all.

Chapter Fifteen

Mouse made sure she got to the garage early on Tuesday morning, even before Baz. There was no need to piss people off unnecessarily. Besides, she had work to do – she had to put Maureen out of action.

Mouse locked herself in the women's toilet and rummaged in the cupboard beneath the sink. She soon found what she was looking for: a pair of rubber gloves and a bottle of bleach.

Since she and Maureen were the only female staff, they'd got in the habit of leaving their things by the sink. Maureen had a collection of lotions and make-up. Mouse pulled on the gloves and selected a screw-top silver bottle – Maureen's hand cream. Not just any old cream but *Lait corps a l'huile essentielle de lavande*, fancy French stuff that she bought at the upmarket chemist round the corner and slapped on twice a day.

The lotion was thick white gunk, much like the bleach. Mouse added a substantial quantity of bleach and mixed it with a pencil. It blended pretty well. Maureen would never notice.

The morning proceeded without incident until, on cue at eleven, Maureen downed the last of her coffee and wiggled off to the loo to repair the ravages of the day. Mouse picked up the phone – she knew Terry wasn't working today because he'd been on a crisis job all weekend. It rang for a while before he answered sleepily.

'Did I wake you up?' she said.

'No sweat, Foxy. The pump failed on the water fountain, I was there half the night fixing it.'

'Poor you. I hope you're taking the day off.'

'I said I might pop round later, just to see what it looks like in daylight.'

Uh-oh, that wasn't in the script.

'That's a pity. I was planning to skive off early this afternoon and minister to your needs.'

'Really?' He sounded surprised, but pleased too.

'Why don't you just catch up on your beauty sleep and I'll be round later to join you. In bed,' she added, just so the hook was well baited.

So that was that. Now she had to get the rest of the timing right.

Maureen was returning to her work station and, thank God, rubbing cream into her hands as usual. She didn't seem to be in any discomfort as she picked up her phone.

Mouse seized the opportunity, holding up five fingers and pointing to the door. 'Hello, Mum,' Maureen said into the receiver, acknowledging Mouse's mime with a nod of her head.

Mouse had a panic in the chemist when she couldn't see the hand lotion but she located the last bottle tucked behind the own-brand containers. She also bought an aerosol spray of fly-killer and a handy washing line for travellers. Outside the shop, she transferred the goods into a Tesco carrier so it wouldn't be obvious where she had been.

In the event, Maureen was still on the phone when she returned and scarcely glanced at her as she walked straight to the loo. As she passed, Mouse was able to observe a pink blush suffusing the back of the hand that held the phone.

It took a couple of minutes to swap the containers and pour half of the new lotion down the sink. Mouse carefully positioned it in place of the doctored one which she wrapped in the chemist's paper bag and slipped into her carrier. To cover herself further she flushed the loo and noisily ran the handbasin taps. Even ruddy Sherlock Holmes couldn't pin anything on her.

Josh cursed himself all the way to Market Rasen in Susie's little car. He knew he'd cocked things up. There was only one way he should have reacted to Susie's bombshell last night and that was to uncork the ecstasy bottle – instantly. But she'd sprung it on him just as he'd been digesting Tim O'Brien's call about Leo's death threat. It had utterly blindsided him, coming from nowhere and completely turning his thoughts upside down.

Early in his racing career he'd been approaching the finish on a sure thing, confident there were no runners about to overtake him, when an animal had squeezed through on the inside and beaten him on the line. He'd not seen the winner and only believed it when he watched the replay on a TV monitor. This baby news was similar, except that at least he'd known the other runner had been entered in the race.

So he was going to be a father. He'd never even realised it was on the cards.

How he wished he had not made that remark about it not being what they'd planned. That had hurt Susie, as if he'd accused her of betraying some master strategy for their lives. But they'd never had any real strategy, just the assumption that they'd stick together while he had a go at being a trainer. Sure, there'd been practical discussions about selling properties and where to set up business, but nothing about them as a couple. About the reason why they were doing these things together.

Some things needed to be said, he could see that now. He could only kick himself for not understanding that sooner but it was not too late. When he got home, he'd make everything right.

That's if he got home, of course. On reflection, he'd decided Tim wouldn't have rung him if he hadn't been convinced Leo posed some sort of threat. And given the morning's surprising news that Ben had been fired from Hoar Frost, something was obviously up with Leo.

Did Leo really have a gun?

For a moment Josh considered turning round and going home. He could put things straight with Susie and avoid Leo.

But what would he do tomorrow? He couldn't duck all race meetings till the end of the season, not if he wanted to be champion jockey.

He put his foot down and pressed on. He'd take his chances.

On reception Mouse curbed her impatience. She heard Baz check with Maureen that she was OK to take Josh's car back around half two and they'd embarked on a conversation about Ridge House and the bloody woman's grandfather. It was enough to make you want to scream.

All the time, though, she'd been sneaking looks at Maureen's hands. The backs were more than pink now, they were glowing a fiery red, made worse by the way she kept scratching and rubbing.

Eventually Mouse affected to notice, crying, 'Oh my God, Maureen, what's the matter with your hands?'

Maureen shook her head. 'I don't know, they've gone all tingly.' She held them out, appearing to examine them closely for the first time. 'They look a bit funny, don't they?'

'They're in a dreadful state,' said Mouse. 'They must hurt.'

'Yeah, they do rather.' Maureen lifted her fingers to her face and sniffed. 'I think I must have got bleach on them. It did pong a bit bleachy when I was in the loo. Ow,' she said, realisation dawning, 'they really do hurt.'

'I'm going to get Baz. It's his responsibility, he's got to get you to a doctor.'

Maureen's protests were feeble and within ten minutes she'd been packed off to her doctor's surgery with orders not to return that day. Fantastic.

'You can cover, can't you?' Baz said as Maureen's taxi

pulled off the forecourt. 'I'll get Gerry to take Swallow's car back.'

'No, Baz, please can I take it? Get Gerry to sit on reception, he won't mind.'

For a moment, Mouse thought she'd miscalculated. If he said no she'd have to come up with some other plan. Then he broke into a grin. 'You and your jockeys,' he said. 'You just want to drive his car, don't you?'

Mouse didn't contradict him. 'Would it be OK if I hold the fort through my lunch hour then pop in on Terry on the way up to Swallow's place? I promise I'll be back by five.'

He nodded grudgingly. 'That ruddy Terry. At least some people are getting it regular,' he muttered as he returned to his office.

Thank God for that.

After Josh had left for Market Rasen, Susie climbed the stairs to her studio. Now she'd finished Carmen's painting she was eager to start on something new. She stood a new canvas on her easel and flung open all the windows and the door to the balcony. She craved as much of the brilliant spring sunlight as possible, both for the painting she had in mind and to chase yesterday's blues from her head.

She knew she had overreacted to the way Josh had taken the news of the baby. After all, she had been stunned herself when she had seen the red line appear in the window of the white plastic pregnancy detector. And by the evening, when she was able to tell him face to face, she'd had time to get used to the idea, to look at it from all angles, and embrace it. Suddenly she was a mother-to-be, and she and Josh were a family in the making. For the first time as an adult she imagined she could see into the future and conjure up a picture of how life would be – with three of them.

Naturally she couldn't expect Josh to take all that on board in a blink. After she'd fled the kitchen he'd come running after her to tell her how fantastic it was and how much he loved her and what a wonderful mother she'd make.

But was he just saying that to keep her happy? What did he really feel?

She couldn't get the moment when she'd told him out of her mind. The long silence when he'd held her, as if commiserating with her, and then, 'It's not what we planned.'

She began to mix paint, determined to banish negative thoughts. She was carrying the beginnings of another person within her and negative thoughts were infectious. From now on, no more neurotic self-doubt.

That's why she was painting, creating the soft greens of new growth on her palette. She didn't know exactly what she was going to paint, only that she had a feeling that she had to get it on to her canvas. A feeling of celebration.

The phone rang, shattering the mood. Damn.

Of all people, it was Mrs Glazier.

'I hope you don't mind me calling you, my dear, but I did promise to keep you informed.'

About what? Her last conversation with the old lady seemed distant now.

'I've just got back from the newspaper library and I've seen the reports of that girl's death.'

Of course, the ghost on the balcony. Susie tried to inject interest into her voice as she said, 'What did you find out?'

'That the girl who died was not the one I saw.'

There was no real surprise there.

'I mean,' Mrs Glazier continued, 'that if I saw a ghost it could not have been the spirit of this particular girl because she was an African. It said in the paper her father was a Nigerian diplomat. The woman I saw on the balcony was white. They looked quite different. And then there were the leaves.'

'The leaves?' It could be bewildering having a conversation with Mrs Glazier, she hopped all over the place.

'On the trees. I don't know why I didn't think of it before but one of the reports had a picture of Arlington Mansions and that reminded me. You see, the Nigerian girl died in August when the trees were in full bloom. The woman I saw was standing on the balcony in winter, there were no leaves on the trees at all. The picture in my mind is quite clear.'

'So,' Susie was confused, and eager to get on with her work, 'what exactly are you saying, Mrs Glazier?'

'I'm saying what I've always said. I saw a woman on your balcony that day and it wasn't the lady who died. I'm only telling you because you were kind enough to express an interest, though I don't suppose you believe me either.'

It seemed like the longest ten minutes of Josh's life. Or, to be precise, the longest nine minutes and forty-three seconds, the length of time it took to decide the result of the 2:15 at

Market Rasen. In the great scheme of things, the outcome of a Class G two-mile hurdle on a Tuesday afternoon at a rural track probably didn't count for much. But for the punters with money on the line and for the connections of the two horses in contention, it seemed that nothing else in the world mattered.

Josh had been on No Worries, a fast but green four-year-old trained by Peter Stone. The horse had been reluctant to race and the rest of the field had been twenty lengths ahead by the time Josh had cajoled the animal into action. Then, his temperament being what it was, No Worries had been hellbent on joining his fellows in the distance. It had taken an entire circuit of the track to get within shouting range. By then, No Worries was travelling like a dream and Josh was bitterly regretting their poor start. He'd been banking on this race to get the one win he needed to equal Ben's total. In this company, No Worries was clearly a superior animal.

Rounding the bend into the home straight Josh was up with the other runners and beyond most of them as No Worries hopped over the penultimate hurdle. The leader, Dark Stranger, was ten lengths to the good, a heck of a distance to make up. Josh went for it, however, knifing through the field on the inside rail and taking the last hurdle just four lengths down.

Dark Stranger was on the far side over by the stands and clearly his jockey, Neil, thought he'd won, for Josh noticed him lowering his hands and sitting up straighter. At the last moment he glanced to his right to see No Worries arriving like a runaway train and went for his whip. But it was too late to make any difference. The winning post had come and gone and neither man knew for certain who was the winner.

Josh had trotted over. 'What do you reckon?'

Neil pulled a face. 'The sooner you retire the better, mate. My gaffer will slaughter me if we've not held on.'

Josh understood his anguish. If Neil had not eased up before the line, the race would have been his.

They returned to the unsaddling enclosure without further conversation, waiting like everyone else for the result of the photo finish.

Nearly ten minutes later they were still waiting.

Susie was struggling. The conversation with Mrs Glazier had broken her urge to paint.

So who had the old girl really seen? Not a ghost, obviously. It was plain she really had spotted someone on one of the Arlington Mansions balconies shortly before Annabelle died.

But which balcony? Since the verdict of the inquest, and in particular Mrs Glazier's treatment at the hands of Leo's barrister, Miss Duncan, Susie had assumed this mystery person had simply been a neighbour. Either that or, as Colin Smart had thought, Annabelle in a different coloured sweater trying to get up the nerve to throw herself off, some forty-five minutes before she actually did so.

But Susie now knew Annabelle had been having an affair with Ben and that the relationship was serious. According to the jockey, Annabelle had been 'on top of the world' on the day she died. Ben certainly hadn't thought her capable of killing herself. Her sister Jenny, too, had said Annabelle sounded in great spirits over the phone shortly before she died.

Then there was the ritzy dress Annabelle had bought that lunchtime; surely she couldn't have had suicide in mind when she'd flashed out on that?

Anyway, apart from the sweater, Mrs Glazier's woman hadn't looked like Annabelle. The height and general build had been different. And according to Mrs Glazier's optician, the old woman's eyesight was 'tip-top'. Surely she would not have mistaken which balcony the mystery woman was standing on.

Susie put down her brush. She couldn't paint with these thoughts distracting her.

She wandered out onto the little balcony, far less spacious than the one in London, and surveyed the garden below. Fancy that girl Maureen at the garage saying her grandfather used to look after it. She didn't mind showing Maureen round when she came up with the car.

She returned to her easel. The bleached wheat of the empty canvas dared her to make her first marks.

She couldn't. There was another strand of thought spoiling her vision, like a stray hair on a camera lens.

Saturday night, returning tipsily from dinner with Carmen, Josh had turned to her as he opened the door to the flat, saying, 'Sure you don't want to change this lock too?'

That was it. If someone had obtained the keys to Ridge House, why couldn't they have got them to Arlington Mansions as well? If they'd been in here snooping around, they could easily have found the address. So why not?

She knew what Josh would say: 'We've not lost any keys so they must have been copied. You can't copy the key to the London flat without proper authorisation.'

But she knew this wasn't true. The man at Logan Bros. in Hammersmith had told her the key was no longer exclusive – 'out of copyright', he'd said – and that it could be copied anywhere.

So, if someone had had access to Josh's keys for a few minutes they could have copied the lot at any corner cobbler's shop.

Susie shivered, despite the warmth of the spring day. She didn't like the cold road these thoughts were leading her down. But she had to follow.

Suppose then that this someone had gone to Arlington Mansions on a day when Josh was racing and she herself was travelling down to Heathrow, and then Annabelle had turned up out of the blue. Suppose this person couldn't leave without being spotted and so she'd hidden on the balcony, pressing herself against the wall in her blue sweater so she wouldn't be seen.

But she was seen. By Mrs Glazier across the road who had obstinately stuck to her guns in saying so, because she knew she was right.

Susie knew she was right too. Now that she had heard Tina Carter's story of the intruder threatening her with a knife in her own home, she had a fair idea what had really happened to Annabelle Lovall. For some reason Annabelle had gone out on to the balcony and encountered the woman in the sweater – and she'd ended up smashed to bits forty feet below.

So Annabelle hadn't taken her own life and she hadn't had a drunken accident either. Mrs Glazier's woman in blue had killed her. And, what's more, Susie knew her name: Mavis Morgan.

She ran downstairs, all thought of painting gone. She had to talk to Tina Carter at once.

The delayed result at Market Rasen caused a flurry of activity amongst the bookies.

'Dark Stranger's 11/10 on, we're evens and the dead heat's favourite at 2/1 on,' Peter Stone murmured into Josh's ear. 'Of course, the longer we have to wait, the shorter the price on a dead heat. Perhaps I ought to get some money down quick.'

Peter was looking remarkably unruffled about the whole thing. It was all Josh could do to raise a grin in response and Dark Stranger's connections were standing around like mourners at a funeral. They'd all settle for the dead heat, that was plain. That way, the race counted as a win for both parties. Punters lost out, in that they were only paid out on half their stake, but on the other hand no one was left holding a losing ticket.

The finish was played over and over again on the course monitors but, to Josh's eye, it was impossible to call. Obviously the race officials, even though equipped with superior technical aids, were having the same difficulty.

Josh told himself it didn't matter. There were plenty of forthcoming races when he could draw level with Ben. It didn't have to be this one. But if it was . . .

He turned to the trainer by his side. He'd made his decision. 'If I get this win, Pete, I'm retiring right now.'

Peter looked puzzled. 'I thought you needed two more to beat Ben.'

'One puts me level.'

'Yeah, but –' Peter looked at him in disbelief – 'don't you want to win it outright?'

'Sure, but I've been thinking about Ben. What happened to him the other night wasn't right and that's the only reason I've got this close. I reckon he's entitled to his share of the championship too.'

'Blimey.' The trainer looked shocked. 'Do you think he'd feel the same way if the boot was on the other foot?'

Josh shrugged. What Ben might do was not relevant, it was how he felt that mattered. He would have said as much to Peter but just then the public address system burst into life to announce that the race had been adjudged a dead heat. Peter crushed him to his chest in a bear hug and pandemonium broke out all around as everybody celebrated.

It was a good moment to end his career.

In her haste Susie misdialled the number Tina Carter had given her. She forced herself to take a deep breath and dialled again. *Please be in*. It was answered on the third ring. Thank God.

'Tina?'

'Hello.' It was a man's voice. Rich and reassuring. 'I'm afraid Tina's not at home at present. May I take a message?'

'Can she call me please? As soon as possible?' Susie left

her details and the man took them down. He sounded warm and sympathetic, though he didn't give any indication that he'd heard of her.

'Are you Tina's husband? The psychiatrist?'

'That's correct.'

This was stupid, Susie thought, leaving a message for the monkey when she was already talking to the organ-grinder.

'Look, Mr Carter,' she blurted, 'this is really all about one of your former patients. Mavis Morgan. I've got to find out where she is and what she's doing now. Someone's been breaking into my house—'

'I can't discuss patients.'

'But there's other things, really serious—'

'I'm sorry but I can't help you. And neither can my wife.' He didn't sound so sympathetic now.

'Won't you just tell me how to get in touch with her?'

'If any offences have been committed against you, I suggest you report them to the police. Goodbye.' He put the phone down on her.

Damn.

She supposed he was right. Her first port of call should be the police but she had no intention of picking up the phone to DI Picard. She would wait till Josh got home and tell him her new theory. He could talk to Colin and work out who best to approach.

One thing was certain, she couldn't speak to Tina about it any more.

She'd probably landed the poor woman right in it.

*

Leo wasn't drunk or doped up or out of control. He was icy calm with the coolness of certainty in his veins. He'd made a point of smiling at everyone that morning and giving the impression that, once more, the leader of Hoar Frost Yard knew what he was doing.

He'd been particularly reasonable with Tim Daniels because he suspected Tim was on to him. But what was Tim going to do? Search him and take away his revolver? He'd like to see him try.

His task was simple: to get Josh Swallow on his own. All he needed was a minute. Time enough to look into the jockey's petrified face and say, 'You destroyed the woman I loved and now I'm destroying you.' He'd put one between his eyes and one in his heart, just to make sure.

Then he'd put the barrel in his own mouth.

A minute would be more than enough.

As Josh changed out of his silks for the last time, his fellows came over one by one. They'd heard the rumour and were amazed he was rushing off, like a man dodging his own leaving party.

They said some fine things, about how they'd miss him and the changing room wouldn't be the same and when was he having a celebration piss-up? But they had the next race to think of and suddenly he didn't.

It was strange, he thought as he packed his bag, how the significance of an occasion was rarely felt at the time. He'd just become champion jockey and pulled the plug on twenty years as a professional rider, all in the same moment. Later, he guessed, at some unspecified moment in the future, he would have time to take stock.

Right now, however, he had no inclination to celebrate his achievement. Peter met him at the weighing-room door, shoved a bottle of champagne in his hand – he must have blagged it from the restaurant – and embraced him.

'Well done, mate,' he said.

Josh hugged him back. He wouldn't have stood a cat in hell's chance of landing the championship without the trainer's support.

Then he headed for the car park and home to Susie.

A figure blocked his way. Leo.

Was there any likelihood he might be waylaying him to offer an olive branch?

Then he saw the gun. So Tim had been right.

'Josh Swallow.'

Leo was pointing the weapon at his head.

Josh's stomach flipped. It was the moment everyone dreads. The thought of a bullet smashing into his face, exploding his head like a ripe melon, stopping his life in an instant. The championship, Susie, his baby – all blown away by this deluded fool.

His mind was paralysed but his legs were still working. The gap between them had closed as if he were programmed. 'You destroyed the woman I loved . . .' he heard a voice say.

But he took no notice. He pushed past Leo and kept walking. Whatever happened, he was heading home.

*

When the doorbell rang, Susie had abandoned all thought of work for the day. Her urge to celebrate the seed growing within her had been displaced by images of psychotic madwomen lurking in the hidden corners of her home, waiting to spring.

The woman at the door wasn't who Susie was expecting, but she wore a Fordyce Motors name tag over her left breast and Josh's car stood in the driveway behind her.

'Mrs Swallow?'

'Er, no, actually.'

The woman was about her age, with a pointed nose and unblinking blue eyes.

'I thought Maureen was going to be bringing the car back,' Susie continued. 'I promised to show her round.'

'Poor Maureen was taken ill.' The woman's thin lips curled downwards in exaggerated distress. 'But I'd love to have a look around.'

This wasn't exactly what Susie had in mind but she didn't object. The woman had produced a clipboard and was checking the exterior of the Fordyce Motors courtesy car for damage.

'That all looks in order,' she said. 'I'm afraid there's a spot of paperwork to go through.'

'You'd better come in then.' Susie stood to one side to let the woman into the house. 'I hope there's nothing seriously wrong with Maureen.'

The other woman laughed, a squeaky high-pitched giggle. 'Oh no, nothing serious.'

The woman walked ahead of her down the hall and somehow found her way into the kitchen. She put her clipboard on the table and turned to face Susie. The faint aroma of her perfume was discernible in the small room. It was disturbingly familiar.

There was another thing, the woman was wearing gloves. The kind that doctors put on just before they do something intimate and painful to you. Creepy.

Susie read the name tag on the woman's breast. The first word had been written in black pen on a neat square of tape: Mouse. The second word was as printed: Morgan.

Susie wasn't thinking fast. The facts would only assemble themselves in slow motion.

What did it say under the tape?

'Is your name Mouse?' she asked.

'It's a nickname. Like a computer mouse. Click click.'

'What's your real name?'

But there was no need to ask. She'd recognised that perfume now. Knew from the way the woman had walked confidently down the hall that she'd been here before.

Knew that the name printed on the tag read *Mavis Morgan*.

Knew that she must run.

Mouse was taken by surprise when the Mistake made a bolt for it. She'd seen suspicion taking root in those wide grey eyes and noted the little furrows tugging the baby-pink lips at the corners. It was all those questions about her name – the Mistake must know something.

But she'd not expected her to turn and rush for the door.

She'd had a plan in coming here, which was based on Susie – sweet, trusting, naive Susie – welcoming her inside and allowing herself to be distracted. If Susie was bending over the garage paperwork she wouldn't notice her taking the can of fly spray from her bag. A long squirt in Blondie's eyes should knock any fight out of her. Then tie her up with the washing line and she could take her time – she'd calculated she had a good half-hour. There'd be knives in the kitchen, like there'd been in that Carter woman's house.

It wasn't in the plot for her prey to get spooked and run. Mouse went after her – she had to.

Susie was fumbling with the front door when Mouse reached her, charging into her slim back with her shoulder like a rugby player. There was an 'Oof' of pain as the breath was slammed out of Susie and then Mouse had her pinned up against the painted wooden surface.

Susie found her voice. 'Get off me! Let go, you maniac!'

Mouse grabbed the blonde shock of hair in her fist and banged the Mistake's head against the door. How fantastic! As she did it again, she found herself muttering through clenched teeth, 'Take that, you stupid little cow!'

But Susie twisted sideways to avoid the worst of the blow and Mouse's foot inexplicably shot from beneath her, plunging the pair of them to the floor. The bitch had kicked her!

She still had hold of Susie's hair and she pulled and twisted, relishing the squeal of pain it caused, trying to roll on top of her. She had a stone or two on the little fool and was going to make it tell.

But a hand came out of nowhere, groping for her face, nails scratching her cheek – No! She couldn't allow herself to be marked! – and as she turned her head a finger brushed her eye.

Ow! The pain was familiar but no less devastating as the hard edge of the dislodged contact lens bit into her cornea. Instinct made her loosen her grip and suddenly the Mistake was wriggling free. Through blurred vision Mouse saw her running back into the house and up the stairs.

She couldn't let her get away.

Susie didn't know where she was going – anywhere to escape from the awful female who'd appeared in her life like a monster from a horror movie. She must lock herself in a room and call the police.

She was on the first floor landing – which way? There was a phone in the bedroom but no lock on the door. A lock on the bathroom door but no phone.

Over her shoulder she could see the madwoman coming, one eye closed, blood on her cheek.

She ran for the first door on the landing.

Bang! A blow landed in the middle of her back, pitching her forward. Her head smacked into the doorframe. She tottered dizzily. It was as if a shutter had been brought down in her head, cutting her off from everything but the all-consuming pain.

Hands gripped her shoulders, lifting her to slam her down again. She raised her arm to take the force. She had to fight!

She jabbed back with her elbow and spun round, pulling her assailant off balance for a second. Then was free.

She ran for the end of the corridor and the attic stairs. She didn't look back, just pumped her legs as she blundered up the steep narrow staircase, all the while hearing the monster woman behind her. She mustn't let her catch up.

There was only one refuge left to her now, the studio in the attic. There must be a weapon there – like the big scissors she used for cutting old material for paint rags.

She stumbled across the scarred wooden floor, her eyes desperately scanning the messy table surfaces, the trolley where she stored pastels and paints, the stained draining board next to the sink. Where were the scissors?

Thank God!

She snatched the dull silver implement from the seat of her old cane chair and turned—

Everything stopped.

After she'd finished trussing up the Mistake with the silk scarves she'd found in a cardboard box, Mouse allowed herself a breather.

Only now, looking blurrily into the mirror above the sink, could she appreciate what a mess she was in. Her hair was sweaty and bedraggled, a trail of blood was crawling down her cheek and her left eyelid was growing before her eyes. First she repositioned the contact lens and things swam back into focus. She grabbed a handful of tissues from a box and wiped away the blood, carefully blotting the neck of her blouse. She had to think ahead. She couldn't reappear looking as if she'd been in a prize fight.

Still, she looked a damn sight better than the Mistake. Mouse smirked at her reflection as she dabbed her eye with water. But then she hadn't been smacked over the head with an old-fashioned smoothing iron. It was extraordinary what sort of funny old junk cluttered up this room.

She returned to the pathetic bundle lying in the middle of the floor. Blondie wasn't dead, she'd checked that out at once, but she couldn't tell when the lights would come back on. It wouldn't be a disaster if they didn't, but it would be preferable – and less of a physical effort for her – if they did.

Mouse was back on track now. Plan A – knife the bitch in the kitchen – was out of the window. But now she had Plan B and that was better.

She must have noticed the balcony when she'd sneaked around the house before, but she'd not thought anything of it. Certainly she'd never been out there and looked down. It was not as high as the one in London but it was still a long way to fall. And the stone slabs of the garden patio would provide the kind of landing that would account for the Mistake just as efficiently as the railings had for that Annabelle woman.

There was a neatness in this. The kind that Terry, as a film buff, might appreciate. She could imagine him going on about 'dramatic symmetry', the sort of arty remark he made when he forced her to sit through his dopey movies. It was a pity he wouldn't get the chance to appreciate the beauty of her scheme. But he had a different role to play.

Blondie moaned, a pitiful whine that Mouse found quite appealing in the circumstances. At least the silly cow hadn't checked out totally. The moan stretched into a howl of pain. That was no good. The last thing required was hysteria.

Mouse knelt down next to her. 'Pull yourself together, Susie,' she said briskly. 'You're going to be all right.'

The blonde head turned towards her, nastily matted in blood. The grey eyes sought hers, swirling with some kind of deeply felt emotion. Was the Mistake about to beg for her life? She'd enjoy that.

'Get out of here, you crazy bitch!'

So Susie was angry. Got to give her credit.

'You're going to jail, Mavis. You'll rot there for the rest of your sick life!'

With a sigh of resignation, Mouse picked up the scissors Blondie had been holding and jabbed them into the girl's thigh. *Nobody* called her by her real name.

Josh put his foot down as he drove back. The police wouldn't stop him today – he was living a charmed life.

Why hadn't Leo shot him? With every step he had taken across the car park he had expected a bullet between the shoulder blades. But it hadn't come.

Now the scene with Leo seemed like something out of a bad dream. An irrelevance. He'd bet the gun wasn't even loaded. The fool was probably drunk.

He forced his mind to other things – there was a lot to be done. He'd called Tony. The agent didn't sound surprised when Josh told him he'd packed in riding. All he said was, 'Are you certain this is what you want? You've still got four days to find another winner.'

'I'm not going to change my mind, Tony. Would you put out a press release? Say I'm stopping now I've matched Ben's total because, in the circumstances, I believe it's the fairest way to settle the championship. And say I'm finishing as a jockey forthwith.'

'Tell them yourself. I'll line up a proper press conference for you tomorrow with a bit of razzamatazz. After a career like yours, you can hardly sneak out of the back door.'

'OK.' Josh wasn't wild about the idea but Tony was usually right about these things.

He hadn't called Susie. What he had to say to her could only be said face to face. And if it went as he planned, by tomorrow he might have an extra announcement to make. If Susie agreed to marry him.

Leo didn't know how long he'd been sitting in the car. It seemed an age since Josh Swallow had strode past him.

He'd had his chance and he'd muffed it. He could have shot the fellow. He would have done if Josh had behaved as any sane man should, instead of charging past him as if the gun didn't count. Whatever the reason, it had been a smart move. Leo couldn't shoot a man in the back, whatever he'd done.

He'd been sitting here ever since, contemplating his failure. There was only one end to this pathetic adventure but he hadn't yet summoned up the courage to do it. Put the barrel of the gun in your mouth. Aim upwards towards the brain. Pull the trigger.

Go on.

A hand rapped on the window. Tim was standing by the car. Leo hadn't seen his assistant arrive.

He slipped the gun beneath the seat. 'What is it?'

'Decameron's playing up and we can't calm him down. You're the only one who can sort him out.'

'Ah.'

'I wouldn't have disturbed you but it's a bit of an emergency. We've only got ten minutes.'

Leo was already out of the car. 'We'd better get a move on then,' he said, surprised at the eagerness in his voice. At least he knew how to deal with horses.

Susie hurt but that wasn't important. There was pain in her head and in her thigh from where the monster had stabbed her but she couldn't let that stop her functioning. Wounds could heal later – if there was to be a later. She'd been stupid to shout at Mavis, it had only invited the woman to stick the scissors in her leg, She could see from the wicked glint in the creature's crazy eyes that she was itching to do it again.

Mavis yanked her to her feet. Scarves – her lovely, multi-coloured silk scarves – had been wound round her ankles but Susie found she could stand and shuffle forward. Her left arm was secured behind her somehow – tied to her belt? – but her right arm was free. That had to give her a chance to do something – grab the woman by the throat, put out her eyes – something surely!

But first she had to show willing. Do what the nutter told her to do. Then talk to her, try and gain her confidence. *Make it harder for her to kill you.*

Susie didn't think Mavis would find it hard to do that at all.

She was being pushed towards her easel standing next to the balcony door where she had placed it that morning to catch the light. The sun had moved round the room now, flooding in from the opposite window and bathing the big friendly space with afternoon sunshine. Fancy dying on such a beautiful day.

'Here.' The woman had picked up one of her brushes and was jabbing it into the whirls of oil paint Susie had carefully arranged on her paint tray. Susie had got as far as starting to mix colours, groping towards a range of hues that would express her half-imagined vision. As ever, she had worked intuitively but with precision. Her method did not include mess. Watching Mavis stab insensitively at her colours, scouring the brush around the tray like an amateur house-painter, was as big a violation of herself as anything else that had taken place over the last half-hour.

'Here,' the woman repeated, pressing the loaded brush into Susie's free hand. She pointed to the virgin canvas. 'Paint the word "sorry" on that.'

Susie gazed at her in bewilderment. 'Why?'

Mavis was still holding the scissors. She held them up, close to Susie's face. 'Just do it. Or I'll cut your pretty ickle nose off your pretty ickle face.'

Susie shuffled to the canvas and made a mark with the brush. A buttery smear of charcoal-grey bloomed on the white of the primed surface. She opened her mouth to speak.

I've got to talk to her. Gain her confidence. What did she like to be called?

'Mouse—'

'Shut your face and paint.'

'But—'

Susie felt the point of the scissors pricking her side, just beneath her ribs.

'Just get on with it. "Sorry". Nice and big. In capitals.'

The clock on the studio wall opposite read 3:26. Josh would just have finished the third race of the afternoon. He wouldn't be home for another four hours.

The scissors dug into her insistently.

Susie began to fashion a big letter S.

Mouse wanted to cut the Mistake some more. The knowledge that she was completely in her power was exhilarating. But there were larger concerns at stake. Wounds on the corpse inconsistent with a fall might be noticed. And she'd have to clear up a bit after the cow took her dive. Check for bloodstains in the hall, for example, and collect her things from the kitchen. Most important of all, she must remove the scarves from the body and dispose of them.

Susie was only on the second letter, spinning it out probably.

'Hurry up,' Mouse barked.

She couldn't afford to spend long, not if the rest of her scheme was to work. She had to be at Terry's within thirty minutes and stay long enough to keep him sweet. That would take a bit of acting but she'd done that before – and it would be worth it. He'd alibi her for whenever she liked, if she played her cards right. Then she'd go straight back to the garage in Josh's car and report that no one had been at home to take delivery. Later, when they discovered Susie's body, she could go into shock. 'To think I was ringing on the doorbell when the poor girl was lying dead at the back of the house!'

She might even be able to use it as a means of building a bridge to Josh. The two of them united in grief. 'If only I'd arrived earlier,' she'd say to him, 'I might have saved her!'

Of course, there'd be a lot of people suspicious of Josh. How many pregnant girlfriends could a man lose and maintain his reputation? But she'd stand by him and steer his life into calmer waters. 'Tragic ex-jockey saved by the love of a good woman' – it would make a good headline next to pictures of their wedding.

And he'd never suspect a thing.

Ow!

She'd not seen it coming, the Mistake turning to jab the brush into her face, aiming for her eyes.

She grabbed Susie's arm and twisted it, sending her to her knees and the brush skittering across the floor. She yanked the arm hard up Blondie's back. How satisfying it would be to lean on it with all her weight until it snapped.

Instead she hauled her to her feet. The message on the easel was now complete. 'SORRY' it read, big and bold.

A one-word suicide note painted on canvas. How fitting.

An unexpected pregnancy can play such terrible tricks on the artistic temperament.

Mouse shoved Susie towards the balcony door.

As Josh turned Susie's Golf into the drive, he was pleased to see that his car had been returned. Why was the garage car still here though? He must have arrived in the middle of the handover, which was a pity. He wanted to get Susie on her own as soon as possible.

His hand shook as he opened the front door. Why on earth should he be nervous? Susie had been nothing but steadfast and loving since the bad days of the inquest. And she was carrying his child. Surely she'd want to be his wife.

On the other hand, he had a poor track record with women and there were plenty of people happy to cast doubt on his character. A lot of them had already done so in print. Not to mention that her aunt loathed him. Pregnant or not, a talented beauty ten years his junior could do far better in the husband stakes.

Shut up, you fool. Susie loves you.

At least, I think she does.

Josh strode down the hall but all the rooms were empty. He noticed an unfamiliar bag and a clipboard with Fordyce Motors forms attached to it lying on the kitchen table. So someone from the garage was here. Perhaps they were in the garden. But the back door was locked and he could see no sign of anybody through the window.

There was nobody upstairs, either. Maybe Susie was showing the Fordyce person her studio. Now he thought about it, she'd said she was expecting a woman who used to visit the house as a child.

He took the stairs to the attic.

As Mavis pushed her on to the balcony Susie realised what was going to happen to her. This monster was going to throw her over the parapet.

She could feel the hot breath of the woman who was about to kill her in her ear. And smell her hideous perfume.

Do something!

Susie flailed behind with her free hand, hitting and grabbing, trying to inflict damage. But she could get no power in her wild swipes and her blows had no effect.

'No, no, no!' she heard herself crying but the woman took no notice, just shoved her to the balcony edge.

Susie dropped to the floor, gripping one of the metal railings.

The woman yanked upwards on her arm, bending it almost to breaking point, and grasped her round the thighs. Mavis was strong, much stronger than Susie, who tried to hang on to the railing but couldn't get a firm grasp on the metal with her slippery palm.

Up. She was being lifted up.

She was going to die like Annabelle. And her unborn child with her.

Josh reached the top of the stairs. 'Susie?'

He could hear strange sounds, like someone panting hard with effort. And moans of pain or fear.

But there was no one in the studio. The big sunlit room was empty. A new canvas stood on the easel. 'SORRY.'

What did that mean?

Then his eye caught movement on the balcony. Two figures were locked in a weird embrace, dangerously close to the parapet. A broad-shouldered woman in a blouse and skirt was lifting a familiar and beloved form, whose tangle of blonde hair was clotted with blood.

'Susie!' he cried.

And charged.

The sight of him in the flesh transfixed Mouse, even as she lifted Susie on to the parapet. He was so film-star handsome as he ran towards her, his jade-green eyes brimming with passion.

This was good. Now he could see how she swept all the dead wood from his life. Goodbye, Blondie.

'No!' he shouted.

Then they were struggling, all three of them locked together.

Mouse felt his arms go round her and prise her away from the Mistake.

At last.

Now it was just the two of them and she was lost in his embrace, holding him tight as they toppled over. Sailing out over the parapet. The pair of them tumbling through the air.

Together. Like it was always meant to be.

Epilogue

Susie had a lot of time to contemplate what she would say to Josh when he regained consciousness. Twenty-four hours. Plenty of time to get used to the idea that her child might be born without a father.

And when he did show signs of life she still had to wait and let him get used to his broken body. The hospital staff were amazed at his resilience but she wasn't. She knew jockeys were tough.

Apart from his head injury, he had a broken leg, three cracked ribs and an all-over bruise the colour of a ripe aubergine. 'Don't worry, I've had worse than this from some novice chasers,' he said with a grin – a stubbly, lop-sided grimace that was the best he could manage.

While the medics fussed over him and he slept the sleep of the heavily sedated, Susie gave interviews to the police. They were very nice to her now. They told her about visiting Mouse Morgan's flat and finding it crammed with bags of rubbish, and old newspapers piled knee deep in the hall. They'd asked her to identify Josh's sweater and some old photographs of a boy on a pony. And also a letter addressed to Susan Merrivale on notepaper headed HM Prison, Wakely Moor. It was proof enough of Mouse's guilt.

Not that it mattered much, because they'd turned off Mouse's life-support machine after three days. So there wouldn't be a trial and Susie was grateful for that. And, mean though it might be, she was very happy that Mouse was dead.

Some had wept for Mouse, however. She'd seen a couple of men, red-eyed and sombre, in the canteen because, bizarrely, Mouse had been in the same hospital as Josh. Sally, the nice DC she'd got close to, told her they were Mouse's cousin and a boyfriend. It had been a surprise to hear about the boyfriend but Sally said she thought Mouse had just been using him. She'd persuaded him to take her to the dinner where Ben O'Brien was stabbed and to make an inaccurate statement about her whereabouts when the assault took place. So Mouse had been responsible for Ben's injury too.

Susie had fed all this information to Josh in small bites as he became more like his old self. She told him she'd talked to Ben and how he had trainers falling over themselves to use his services once he got fit. And she admitted to her detective work with the pink phone – it was good to get that minor confession out of the way.

Finally, on the fifth morning, with sun flooding into the room and bathing the banks of well-wishers' flowers in a golden light, she knew she couldn't put it off any longer.

'There's something I've got to say,' she told him.

'I've got something to say too,' he replied. 'That's why I got back from Market Rasen so fast.'

'Let me go first, Josh. There are things I should have told you ages ago and I want you to hear them now. You might not want to talk to me at all after that.'

She paused and he kept quiet, as requested. She took a deep breath.

'I loved my father. Doctor Death, the papers called him. Not very original. He wasn't Doctor Death to me or any of his patients, everyone said he was a marvellous doctor. And he was a lovely dad to me and my sister. I suppose he was a bit soft where we were concerned, we could always get round him. Unlike my mum, who had a cruel temper. When she lost it she'd really go for us, slapping us and giving us the edge of her tongue. If Dad was around he'd take our side and she'd have a go at him instead. I loved him for that and I used to think he liked me best, because I was older than Sharon and was more useful to him. He had two names for me, Susie Sausage, which had stuck since I was a baby but I didn't mind. And DLH, Daddy's Little Helper, because I was always helping him out.'

Susie looked across at Josh to see if he was OK and still alert. He nodded at her.

'Mum used to go out on Wednesday nights. She wanted to keep up her French, so she went to an evening class. When she went out, of course Dad had to put us to bed and babysit. Sharon was three years younger than me so Mum's orders were that she was in bed first. The year it all happened, Dad would get Sharon settled and then go next door to see our new neighbour, Rita. He knew her through the surgery because she was a district nurse. Mum didn't like her, of course, and there'd been one or two rows, which I knew about. But naturally I was on his side. Rita was a warm smiley lady who was always very nice to me and I couldn't see why Dad shouldn't be friends with her. So Dad and I had an arrangement about Wednesday nights. If Mum came home unexpectedly then I had to go up to my bedroom and tap on the wall. He said that he and Rita would be in her sitting room having a chat and he'd rush back quickly and say he'd been out to post a letter. I'd never been upstairs in Rita's house. It never occurred to me that she didn't have a sitting room on the first floor.

'One night Mum came home early. She just suddenly appeared in the house and I could tell she was in a very bad mood. "Where's your father?" she said to me and I told her Dad had gone to post a letter. Then I went to go upstairs and tap on the wall, as Dad and I had agreed but she stopped me. She pushed me into the front room. "We'll just sit here and wait for him, shall we?" she said. "If he's gone to the post box he won't be a moment." Well, of course he didn't come back and I was sitting there squirming, knowing I had to warn him somehow but I couldn't. Mum sat there glaring at me and saying mean things about how I was Daddy's little poodle and did we think she was stupid. In the end I pleaded that I had to go to the toilet. I ran upstairs into my room and tapped on the wall but she followed me up and caught me. "I thought so," she said and stormed next door.

'There was a big scene, of course. I could hear shouting through the wall. Then Mum and Dad came back and carried on downstairs while I was up in my room. In the end, I just pulled the blankets over my head and cried myself to sleep. I thought it was all my fault, you see. Because I'd not given Daddy the signal. Some little helper I turned out to be.'

'But it wasn't your fault.' Josh's voice was firm. He reached over and gripped her hand. 'You were only ten, for God's sake.'

'I know all that. Everyone said so afterwards. And Daddy told me not to worry about it the next day. He brought me breakfast in bed – a boiled egg and soldiers – and said Mummy and Sharon had gone to stay with her relatives in Scotland. He said they'd had to catch an early train and didn't want to wake me up. I did wonder why Mum hadn't taken me too but I thought she was still angry with me and it was sort of a punishment. Anyhow, I preferred staying with Dad, and Rita starting coming round a lot and she was nice. They took me out of school on trips and spoiled me. We had a really lovely time though I missed Sharon, even though she was such a pest sometimes, and after a few days I missed Mum too because I thought she couldn't still be angry with me. Then one day I came home from school and the police were there.'

'I suppose you've been blaming yourself all this time.'

'If I'd let Daddy know, none of it would have happened. I'd still have a mother and a sister. And I'd have a proper father, not a monster locked up in prison. You're going to tell me that's not rational and I know that. But it's the way I feel.'

Josh said nothing for a bit. He still held her hand.

Finally he spoke. 'Will you let me get a word in now?'

She nodded. She'd done speaking.

'There's nothing you can do about the past, Susie. Let's think about the future. Are you going to marry me or not?'

It was an inconvenient moment for the phone to ring. She answered it and passed the receiver to Josh. It was Tony Wylie. After a few seconds he ended the call.

'What was that all about?' she asked.

'You haven't answered my question.'

'Tell me about Tony first.'

Josh gave her a lop-sided grin. 'One of Ben's winners last month failed a dope test. The result's only just been announced.'

'You mean Ben was doping horses?'

'It just means the animal had been eating something it shouldn't. You can easily contaminate horse feed if you're not careful. It's really bad luck on Ben.'

'Why?'

'Because it means he loses a winner for the season.'

Now it was her turn to smile. The sudden glow of happiness burst from deep within. She had unburdened herself at last and he still loved her.

He looked at her, his eyes dancing. 'So?' he said. 'I'm still waiting.'

'OK, Josh, I'll marry you now.'

'Now?'

'Now you're the champion jockey in your own right.'
It was the cherry on the cake.

Inside Track

John Francome

'Thrills to the final furlong . . . Francome knows how to write a good racing thriller' *Daily Express*

When champion jockey Jamie Hutchison is released from prison, all he wants is to escape the past. He can't remember what happened the night his car went out of control – but he'll never forgive himself for causing a boy's death.

Jamie's sister Pippa, a top trainer, has troubles of her own. Owners are moving their horses to rival Toby Priest, and she can't understand how he's turning slowcoaches into express trains.

Meanwhile DI Jane Culpepper is investigating the murder of a girl who used to work at Toby Priest's yard. The word is that it was a drug-related execution, but Jane's not convinced. She won't rest till she's made sense of the loose ends, wherever that might lead her.

Ex-National Hunt Champion Jockey John Francome is a broadcaster on racing for Channel 4, and his electrifying racing thrillers have won him legions of fans. Don't miss the previous bestsellers from Headline.

'Francome brings authenticity to tales of the horse-racing circuit and, like Dick Francis, goes beyond the thunder of the turf to the skulduggery of the trading ring' *Mail on Sunday*

'Francome provides a vivid panorama of the racing world . . . and handles the story's twist deftly' *The Times*

'The racing feel is authentic and it's a pacy, entertaining read' *Evening Standard*

0 7553 0062 9

headline

Dead Weight

John Francome

'Thrills to the final furlong . . . Francome knows how to write a good racing thriller' *Daily Express*

There's no hiding place for a jump jockey when his courage deserts him. After a crashing fall, champion rider Phil Nicholas returns to racing, but though his body has healed his mind has not. Flashbacks of his accident invade his dreams, rob him of his sleep and freeze him in the saddle. The tough guy of jump racing has lost his bottle.

But when one of Phil's colleagues is viciously attacked after losing a race he should have won, the jockey can't sit on the sidelines any longer. If he wants to save the sport – and the woman he loves – it's time for Phil to recover his nerve . . .

Ex-National Hunt Champion Jockey John Francome has been voted TV's most popular racing commentator for his broadcasting for Channel 4, and he has established himself as one of the front runners in the racing thriller stakes. Don't miss his previous bestsellers from Headline:

'Francome provides a vivid panorama of the racing world . . . and handles the story's twist deftly' *The Times*

'Francome brings authenticity to tales of the horse-racing circuit and, like Dick Francis, goes beyond the thunder of the turf to the skulduggery of the trading ring' *Mail on Sunday*

'The racing feel is authentic and it's a pacy, entertaining read' *Evening Standard*

'An action-packed storyline that gallops to a thrilling end' *Racing Post*

0 7472 6608 5

headline

Now you can buy any of these other bestselling books by **John Francome** from your bookshop or *direct from his publisher*.

FREE P&P AND UK DELIVERY
(Overseas and Ireland £3.50 per book)

Inside Track	£5.99
Dead Weight	£6.99
Lifeline	£6.99
Tip Off	£6.99
Safe Bet	£6.99
High Flyer	£6.99
False Start	£6.99
Dead Ringer	£6.99
Break Neck	£6.99
Outsider	£6.99
Rough Ride	£6.99
Stud Poker	£6.99
Stone Cold	£6.99
Riding High (with James MacGregor)	£6.99
Eavesdropper (with James MacGregor)	£6.99
Blood Stock (with James MacGregor)	£6.99
Declared Dead (with James MacGregor)	£6.99

TO ORDER SIMPLY CALL THIS NUMBER

01235 400 414

or visit our website: www.madaboutbooks.com

Prices and availability subject to change without notice.